COURTHOUSE

John Nicholas Iannuzzi

COURTHOUSE

1975

DOUBLEDAY & COMPANY, INC. GARDEN CITY, NEW YORK

Library of Congress Cataloging in Publication Data

Iannuzzi, John Nicholas, 1935–
  Courthouse.

  I. Title.
PZ4.I125Co   [PS3559.A55]   813'.5'4
ISBN 0-385-01148-2
Library of Congress Catalog Card Number 74-9454

to my Mother,
GRACE M. IANNUZZI
with love;
and to Poppa and Uncle Binny
whom I never cease missing.

COURTHOUSE

I

Marc Conte walked slowly beneath the heavy overhang of shade
trees that lined the Broadway side of City Hall Park. It was
a scorching day; not a single leaf overhead fluttered. Waves of
heat seemed to radiate from the sidewalk. If it weren't that his
law school chum, Vinnie Bauer was being sworn in as a Judge of
the Criminal Court this afternoon, Marc would already be far
out on the cool, deep blue waters of the Atlantic, the sails of his
forty-foot motor sailer, *Pescadorito*, furled, searching for the
breezes. Today, there were probably few breezes to be found
even there, Marc thought.

Marc's full name was Marc Antony Conte, J.D. He never used
his middle name or initial however; he thought Marc Antony a
little too dramatic. The J.D. was for Juris Doctor; he didn't insist
on being called Doctor either.

Marc was thirty-two, a born and bred New Yorker, with dark,
penetrating eyes and features that were at once rugged and mysterious. A thin, white-lined scar across his left cheekbone from a
childhood accident, added to a wiry, graceful body, gave him the
classic appearance of a *matador*. Which appearance was appropriate, since Marc was a trial lawyer, specializing in criminal cases,
and he was often pitted in the public arena in a life and death
struggle (the police are sometimes called bulls), the ritual
bounded and orchestrated by strict, classical ceremony.

The newspaper vendor at the kiosk on the corner of City Hall
Plaza saw Marc and a smile creased his broken face. He was an
ex-pug and a little light in the head.

"Hiya, Marc, pal," said the newsy. "Hot as a bitch again, hanh?"

"Sure is, Champ," said Marc, stopping a moment. The newsy
liked being called Champ.

"You look like a million," Champ said. He felt Marc's lapel. "Nice suit, nice," he smiled. "How much'd you go for?"

Marc was wearing an elegant beige, almost white, suit that had been custom made. "A few bucks, I don't remember," Marc said.

"You want your paper now, pal?"

"Not now, Champ," Marc smiled. "I'll get the late one on the way out."

"Oh? You going to see His Honor?" Champ asked, jutting his chin at City Hall.

"A friend of mine's being made a judge," Marc replied.

"Better get in there quick, before His Honor changes his mind and gives it to somebody else." Champ bent over to clip the wire from a bundle of papers. "He's a bum, this one. Couldn't last two minutes with me." Champ rose with some papers in his hands. He began to dance and feint with his shoulders. "Not even a round."

"See you later." Marc smiled, thinking that Champ, who was white, was one of the last of a vanishing era. His contemporaries and compatriots had now emerged from the ghetto, leaving the tenements and the broken noses to Blacks and Puerto Ricans.

The clock in the cupola over City Hall indicated 2:55. The swearing-in was set for three o'clock. Marc paused a moment to admire City Hall, standing amid its tall trees and wide lawns, with its pink granite base, its veined, white limestone structure, topped by the cupola presided over by a statue of Dame Justice.

At the top of the wide stairway leading to the columned portico of the main entrance, a plainclothes policeman gave Marc a careful look, then nodded for him to enter.

"Where's the swearing in?" Marc asked the officer.

"Up in the Board of Estimate chamber."

"Thanks." Marc started across the marble lobby toward the double stairway rising in graceful spirals on each side of a center rotunda which separated the main floor. One side of the building was occupied by Mayor Scott U. Davies and his chief aides. The other side housed the City Council and Marty Dworkin, president of the Council. Recently, Dworkin had started making mayoral-candidate sounds, and the factions at each end of the building suddenly became enemy hosts within the same camp. After all, it was election year. And, although Mayor Davies kept telling the press that he was not a candidate for re-election, the odds makers were taking bets that he was going to make the run.

"Hey, Marc," called George Tishler, Counsel to Mayor Davies. Marc, Vinnie Bauer, and George Tishler had all been classmates in law school.

"Hello, George, old pal," smiled Marc, shaking George's hand. George, who had gained a few pounds since law school, looked hot and rumpled, his dark blue, pin-stripe suit seeming a heavy choice for such a hot day.

"Come over to see Vinnie Baby get sworn?" asked George, as the two of them walked up the stairs together.

"Sure did. I wouldn't believe it unless I saw it with my own eyes."

"Vinnie's really been doing a great job as Deputy Administrator of the Criminal Court," said George seriously. "Judge Goldman, Vinnie's boss, thought he was really functioning magnificently over there. That's how come he's getting a judgeship; figured he'd really be able to move things if he was on the bench."

At the top of the stairs, Marc and George made a right turn to the Board of Estimate's chamber—a long, rectangular room with vast, high ceilings and intricate, gingerbread-scrolled woodwork. The scrollwork was traced around the top of the walls and six large windows. The entire room was white, very elegant in a colonial style, with several large crystal chandeliers hanging from the ceiling. At one end of the room were several carved desks in a semicircle. A high, carved canopy overhung these desks. The rest of the room was filled with oak benches and carpeted with a thick-pile red rug. Television cables had been stretched down the aisles, secured by an adhesive tape to the rug.

The chamber was crowded with judges, politicians, important commissioners and aides of the Mayor, city officials, and relatives and friends of Vinnie Bauer. Marc saw Vinnie sitting on a folding chair in front of the permanent desks, facing the audience. He was sitting right in the center of the action, near the microphones. Judge Goldman was seated on a similar chair next to him. Many other chairs were still unoccupied.

"Looks like Vinnie wants to be sure he doesn't get left out," said Marc.

"Yeah." George laughed. "See Gloria, Vinnie's wife, and kids right in the first row?"

Marc nodded.

"Say, how's Maria, that beautiful wife of yours?"

"Great, just great," Marc replied.

"Still teaching the kids remedial English up in East Harlem?"

Marc nodded.

"She's some girl," George said. "I don't know what the hell she sees in you though."

"She says the same thing to me about you," Marc kidded.

"Oh, that's very cute," said George. He put his arm around Marc's shoulder. "It's good to see you, Marc. We really ought to get together for lunch one of these days."

"Okay, when?"

"When the hell can I make it, is right," George said. "If I ever get time to eat lunch around here, the Mayor'll have me investigated for gold-bricking."

Marc laughed.

George raised himself up on his toes, and waved toward the front of the chamber. Vinnie Bauer saw him and smiled, waving back. George pointed at Marc. Bauer smiled again, waving to Marc.

"He's nervous as hell," said George.

"You would be too, getting a ten-year guaranteed job at thirty something thousand per year," said Marc.

"Oh, Vinnie's not getting a ten-year appointment." George lowered his voice.

"I thought Criminal Court judgeships were ten-year appointments."

"They are. But Vinnie's not being given a full ten-year term. There are seven of those open, and the Mayor intends to fill all of them before the end of the administration. But he's giving Judge Walsh's spot to Vinnie."

"Is Judge Walsh up for reappointment?" asked Marc.

"No. He's got three years to go. But the Mayor decided to roll Walsh over to one of the ten-year spots and give Walsh's remaining three years to Vinnie."

"Ah, this way if he's a lousy judge they can get rid of him in three years," said Marc.

"Smart boy," replied George, smiling, shaking the political hands of the people coming into the chamber. "Besides, Walsh is a cousin of Jimmy Bainbridge."

"You mean the district leader from uptown on the West Side?"

"The very same," George grinned. He waved at someone across the room. "It's election year, you know."

Mayor Davies entered the chamber from a door behind the permanent desks at the front. There was a back stairway leading to this chamber from his offices below. Some people in the audience began to applaud when they saw him. A pleased murmur filled the room. More people turned around, and in staggered waves, began to stand. The Mayor smiled, then waved. He was tall, trim, balding, with dark eyes and hair. He had a kind of All-American, Anglo-Saxon look which was one of his major assets with the voters, particularly the women.

"I've got to go up front," George said to Marc. "I'll see you just as soon as it's over. Don't go away."

The Mayor stood at the center of the row of folding chairs in front of the room. He shook hands with Judge Goldman, seated two chairs away, who then introduced him to Vinnie Bauer, who now stood in place, three chairs away. The Mayor had never before met Bauer. His Committee on the Judiciary, as well as several Bar Association committees, screened and evaluated judicial candidates. Ordinarily, the Mayor left the approval of the judicial candidates to the committees and George Tishler, who was the Mayor's liaison man in charge of matters dealing with the courts, judges, criminal justice, and the like.

A couple of newspaper photographers asked the Mayor to pose with Vinnie Bauer so they could take some pictures. The two struck a smiling, nonchalant pose as the cameramen flashed away.

An engineer from WNYC, the city radio station, approached the microphone which had been placed near where the Mayor was standing. He tapped on the head of the microphone. A light rapping noise carried over the loudspeakers into the room. He nodded to the Mayor.

"Ladies and gentlemen," the Mayor began. The people who had been standing about the room chatting, began to file into the rows of seats in the audience. The main guests sat on the folding chairs. These included Justice Lawrence McLouglin, the Presiding Justice of the Appellate Division, First Department; Justice Matthew Silver, Presiding Justice of the Appellate Division, Second Department, several Justices of the Supreme Court, the Mayor, the Deputy Mayor, George Tishler, Judge Goldman, and Judge-designate Vincent M. Bauer.

As the Mayor began to speak, Vinnie's little son, Timothy, wanted to sit with his father in front of the room. Vinnie's wife was embarrassed as she tried to restrain the child discreetly. Vinnie squirmed. The Mayor stopped speaking, walked over to the boy, lifting him high in the air, smiling, then placed the child on Vinnie's lap. The audience loved it. They cheered. They clapped. Most of them were connected with Mayor Davies' administration, either in the capacity of department officials, or as political advance men, publicity men for the Mayor, who had been given city jobs to cover their salary.

"Unaccustomed as I am to public speaking," the Mayor said, pausing and smiling. They loved that too. They smiled back and laughed. "And in order to keep the proceedings today short, I'm going to turn the microphone directly over to Judge Goldman, Administrator of our Criminal Court."

The audience applauded as Judge Goldman rose and took the Mayor's place at the microphone.

"I, too, am going to keep today's ceremony very brief," said the Judge. "Especially the speeches. I know how hot it is outside, and I know that many of our friends and guests want to get away before one of our famous weekend traffic jams begin." He paused, but his remark wasn't as effective with the audience. "So, I'll just say a few words in tribute to Vincent," he smiled at Vinnie, "a man who has been of tremendous help to me and service to the city by his unstinting effort and talent in helping to get the Criminal Court to move more quickly and efficiently."

The audience applauded lightly.

Marc, who was seated on the center aisle, almost in the last row of the audience, caught Vinnie Bauer's eye. Marc flashed him a disbelieving face. Bauer began to smile, then suppressed it, looking down to the floor.

"Since Judge Bauer—I can call him Judge Bauer now, can't I, Mister Mayor?" Judge Goldman turned to the Mayor.

The Mayor laughed, nodding.

The audience began to laugh.

"Since Judge Bauer became the Deputy Administrator of the Criminal Court," Judge Goldman continued, "the backlog of cases pending in the Court has been drastically reduced. Our statistics show that there has been an increase by twenty per cent in the number of cases disposed of in the courts. And, at the same time, a decrease by twenty-eight per cent of the number of people awaiting trial in our jails. In short, the criminal justice system is moving, and moving well now."

More light applause.

Marc wondered if any of the people sitting in the audience really had any idea what the jails, even what the courts looked like. This elegant setting of government, this attractive gathering of important and powerful officials and citizens, seemed to bode well for the court system into which Judge Bauer was about to step. But the courtrooms, the jails, the actual justice system, were a different story all together.

Marc wished Judge Goldman would cut his speech shorter still so the Mayor could swear Vinnie in. Maria was waiting at the Twenty-third Street marina on *Pescadorito*, and Marc wanted to get there, wanted to get under sail, wanted—for a little while, at least—to forget about courts, defendants, and judges—even Judge Vincent Bauer.

II

MONDAY, AUGUST 7, 9:15 A.M.

The Manhattan House of Detention for Men, known as The Tombs, is probably the busiest prison in the world. Built originally to detain fewer than 1,000 men waiting to answer criminal charges in New York County, it was now crammed with more than 1,900 men; the weakest of the 3 men in a 2-man cell slept on the floor, between the gate and the cell toilet. Each day, The Tombs has a turnover of close to 500 prisoners, 250 new men to await trial, 250 others leaving on bail, parole, for state penitentiaries, or acquitted of the charges.

Outside cell D-3 on the eighth floor, Captain Bill Casey, of the City Department of Correction, was peering through the bars, talking quietly to a prisoner.

"Come on out of your cell, Ray," said Casey. "We're not going to hurt you. You have to go to court. The Judge is waiting. Your lawyer's waiting."

Inside the cell, naked and hairy, his muscular body slicked with sweat, inmate #483267, Raul DeJesus stared out through the bars, his eyes wide. DeJesus, who had spent seven years in Matteawan, the state institution for the criminally insane, was now certified as competent to be tried on a charge of raping a housewife.

"You want to trick me. You want to trick me, I know," DeJesus said. "Don't try to trick me, Captain, sir. I am too smart to be tricked." He was silent for a few moments. The cell stank of urine. A three-day growth of beard covered DeJesus' powerful jaw. There was a tattoo on his right forearm. "What's your name, Captain, sir?" he asked.

"Casey." The Captain frowned and pushed his uniform cap to the back of his head. He was in his work uniform—dark trousers, white shirt open at the neck, dark military cap with a gold braid. The shirt was darkening with perspiration, showing slightly pink where it was stuck to Casey's back.

There is no air conditioning in The Tombs, and the August heat and humidity had fired the stone walls and thick glass-bricked windows to kiln intensity. No air came through those sealed windows, no one could see out of them.

"You Christian, Captain?" DeJesus demanded.

Casey nodded.

"The Judge, what's his name, sir? What's the name of the Judge?"

"Binder. Judge Binder," Casey replied.

"He's a Jew, isn't he? Binder's a Jew name, isn't it, sir? Isn't Binder a Jew's name?"

Casey shrugged. "I don't know if the Judge is Jewish," he said wearily. "Maybe he is. What's the difference?"

It seemed to make quite a difference to DeJesus. "Don't try to come into this cell," he howled suddenly, bringing both his fore-arms down violently onto the metal spring of the iron double-decker bed. There were no mattresses. He twisted full around to study Correction Officer Davis, who was standing in a corridor on the other side of the cell, then lashed around again suddenly, as if to catch Casey off guard. He began gesturing, jabbering incoherently.

The Tombs is only one section of the Criminal Courts Building complex, located at 100 Centre Street, Manhattan. There are four parallel wings to the complex, the first three of which contain courts, judge's chambers, and offices connected by corridors. The last wing is The Tombs connected to the courts by two bridges— the Bridge of Sighs, named after the Florentine bridge of the same use—over which prisoners are brought to face their accusers and their fate. On each floor of The Tombs, there are two identical cellblocks, one at each end, separated by a center core of elevators and common messrooms. Each cellblock contains a long double line of cells which have outside corridors on each of the far sides of the cells and a wide interior corridor in the center. During certain hours of the day, on most floors, the inmates are allowed into the wide corridor between the cells, to talk and socialize. Tables, bolted to the floor, are there for that purpose. On the eighth floor, however, where DeJesus was held, some of the men were judged too dangerous to be left out with the others. Near the center elevators, the guards have a desk and telephone. Above the elevator and desk area, reached by a stairway inside the bars, is a large cage for washing and shaving as a guard watches the single safety razor passed from inmate to inmate.

Captain Casey looked at Davis, a young Black, thin, with a pencil-line mustache. His work uniform was dark trousers, dark military cap, and light blue shirt. Davis shrugged.

"The Jews and the super-rich, the important people," DeJesus growled out. "They wish to destroy me." He looked over to Casey, then stealing a look at Davis, moved closer to Casey. "They know who I am. They know! And they wish to destroy me. They are sending out radio magnetic waves to influence your brain chemistry, Captain, to make people do things, to make me do things. They want me to plead guilty so I'll stay in jail. Are you Christian, Captain, sir?"

Casey nodded.

"Then believe me, Captain, believe me, and I will reward you greatly. They want to destroy me. They influence the Judge. The Judge is a Jew, don't you see?" He looked hopefully at Casey. "They influence the D.A., even my lawyer, with their machines. But I won't plead guilty to anything, anything," his voice rose. He shook his fists.

"Ray, I don't want you to plead guilty," Casey said softly. "You don't have to plead guilty to anything. I just want you to come out of the cell for a while. I'm your friend. I won't let them hurt you. I mean that. I don't want them to hurt you."

Casey turned his head toward the center core of the building. There stood three additional correction guards sent up by the Deputy Warden. Earlier, DeJesus had assaulted the regular floor guard who had opened the cell to take him to court for a sanity hearing. The "Dep" then ordered his men to get DeJesus out of the cell, even if they had to tear-gas him. Casey had stationed the three guards where DeJesus couldn't see them. He wanted one last shot at talking DeJesus out of the cell.

"What are you looking at? What's there?" DeJesus demanded, moving to the barred cell door, pressing his face brutally into the bars. His eyes twisted wildly to the side. "See, see, they've sent them to come and get me. But I won't come out, I won't," he screamed, moving violently away from the bars, bringing his arms down on the metal spring again. He began mumbling and cursing in Spanish. DeJesus was strong, and he knew his best defense was to stay in the cell, letting the guards come at him one at a time through the small cell gate.

"Come on, man," said Davis now, "don't be no fool. I'm a brother. I won't let them do things to you."

DeJesus grumbled and growled to himself, moving back to the middle of the cell. His eyes roved from Casey to Davis in mad terror. He was motioning with his hands wildly as he muttered. He raised both arms over his head, gazing heavenward.

"They're trying to kill me, kill me, again," he screamed at the top of his lungs. "The lousy Jews, the capitalists, the super-rich. They're trying to destroy the son of god. I am the son of god, and they want to destroy me."

Davis stared across at Casey. Casey took out his handkerchief and dabbed at the back of his neck. He didn't want to order the tear gas if he could avoid it. It wasn't only DeJesus he was worried about. It was the other prisoners. In this humid, stifling heat, the potency of the tear gas would be intensified, and it would affect every prisoner and guard for two floors above and below. Everyone's eyes would burn for hours.

And it was not just the discomfort. Casey knew the inmates were restless. Not that they weren't always restless, because of the crowding, the food, just being caged, because they were facing trial. But now they were exceptionally edgy because of the heat. Over 95 degrees four days in a row. In the last two days, Casey knew of three serious altercations between guards and inmates.

Casey glanced over to the center core again.

Lou Adler, one of the three waiting guards, caught Casey's eye.

Casey shook his head. He knew it was hopeless. DeJesus wasn't coming out of the cell, not today, not peacefully anyway, not without being gassed. The prisoners from all the adjacent cells had already been evacuated. They were standing in the common messroom in the center of the building behind the three waiting guards, talking quietly among themselves, listening to every sound, watching every move with suspicion and hostility.

"Ray, come on out, just stand out here with me," said Casey. "I'll go with you to the courtroom. I'll go with you myself. Don't make trouble, Ray. It's too hot."

"They are influencing you too, with their electro-magnetic radio waves, Captain, sir," DeJesus shouted. "They are trying to kill me." His voice echoed in the high ceilings of the cellblock. "Don't let them kill me again," he called to the other inmates. "They are trying to kill me. Save me, you oppressed and untrodden, and I shall reward all of you greatly, I promise you this, all who save me."

Casey saw the other prisoners shifting uneasily, the echoing voice spooking them.

"Put everyone in their cells," Casey ordered suddenly, walking to the center of the building. He wasn't going to risk any more trouble than he already had. He decided to forego gassing DeJesus for the moment, wanting to talk to the Judge, to see if one day's appearance in court was worth this much stirring up. Besides, Casey thought, it would be easier to get DeJesus out of the cell

19

during the movies, when all the other inmates were off the floor anyway.

Adler, Scott, and Lockwood, the three waiting guards, opened the interior gate and started moving the inmates back into the cellblock.

One of the prisoners, Oscar Johnson, also known as Ali Al-Kobar, a dark Black man with a shaved head, wearing a black, red, and green skullcap, was staring at Casey. He nudged another Black prisoner next to him as they came abreast of the Captain. The second prisoner looked at Al-Kobar, then pushed back against him. Al-Kobar seemed to fall off balance, then, suddenly, he violently shouldered into Casey. Casey, wiping the sweat band in his cap with his handkerchief, fell backward, twirled, landing hard against the cells. Al-Kobar was upon him in a flash. A second, then a third prisoner was on the pile in a moment. Suddenly, there was screaming and thrashing. And running. And curses.

Lou Adler, seeing Casey go down, spun toward the gate leading to the elevators and the regular floor officers. An inmate still in the messroom jumped on a table and leaped onto Adler's back. Adler staggered, and he and the inmate sprawled onto the floor. Lockwood and Scott were surrounded simultaneously by a host of screaming inmates. The three guards were hauled bodily into the corridor where Casey was jammed against the cells by three of the excited inmates.

Now screaming and howling echoed through the cellblock on the opposite end of the building. They wanted out too. Casey and the others were relieved of their keys, cigarettes, money, and whatever else was in their pockets.

Davis, who had still been in the narrow outer corridor when the screaming started, was snapped up in a pincer move as prisoners moved in from each end. He just lifted his hands in surrender.

The two regular guards at the desk near the elevator had already pushed an emergency button. Bells were sounding through the building, their claxon intensifying the yells of the inmates. One of the guards at the desk was on the phone. He pressed a finger into his free ear to try and keep out the pandemonium of violence erupting around him.

"You tell those motherfuckers downstairs we're going to kill these motherfuckers up here," one prisoner shouted at the guard on the phone.

"We're going to cut their balls off, and then their cocks . . ."

"And their heads too," added another.

"And their assholes," yet another.

They were all bold now, and elated, slapping palms in jubilation, saluting each other with the rebel's clenched fist, running around the cellblock, screaming, pounding each other on the back.

Ali Al-Kobar was the hero of the shouting. He stood tall in the midst of a milling herd, a great toothy smile playing on his face.

The shouts for freedom from the inmates at the other end of the floor were getting louder. They wanted to share this moment.

"Open the other side of the floor," someone yelled.

"Let's free our brothers," exhorted Al-Kobar, raising his fists in defiance and joy.

Realizing they could use the keys removed from Casey and the officers, the inmates began to open all the cells on the floor.

"What the hell is going on up there?" Deputy Warden Margolis demanded into the phone as he stood in his office on the ground floor. He was tall and bald. Bells and lights were sounding and flashing all around him.

"They got the whole floor opened up, Dep," shouted the floor guard on the phone at the eighth floor desk. "They got Casey and four others inside. Got the keys. They're just opening the cells on the other end of the floor. All the prisoners are getting out now. They're starting to break the legs off the tables."

"You two get on the elevators now before you're hostages too," Margolis directed. He quickly motioned one of the captains standing in his office toward the elevators. The Captain nodded and ran from the office toward the barred door leading to the interior of the prison. "What happened to the guards and Casey?" asked Margolis. "Are they hurt?"

"Don't know, Dep." The guard on the phone was stuttering now. "They took them inside. I can't see them." He could see, however, that the prisoners were coming toward the barred doors that led to the elevators. "They're coming this way now, Dep. They're coming this way now." Panic edged his voice clearly.

"Just hold on," Margolis urged. "The elevator's coming. It's on its way. Try and put your key in the lock to the main gate. Break it or jam it in the lock!"

"Too late for that now." The two floor guards were both on their feet at the elevator doors, wanting to go, wanting to run, shifting nervously on the balls of their feet like relay runners awaiting the baton.

The prisoners were gleefully swinging open the last gate. They began to sprint toward the desk.

The elevator door opened. The two guards threw themselves inside, leaving Dep. Margolis with a banging sound in his ear as the phone hit the floor. The Captain on the elevator punched the CLOSE button. Prisoners grabbed at the sliding door. An arm reached inside the elevator, groping. But the door closed. Immediately, pounding and kicking and cursing began to assault the door.

"Get this mother going," one of the guards screamed. He was sprawled on the elevator floor, his face a mask of terror.

"We're gone," said the Captain as he repeatedly banged the control panel. His eyes were transfixed on the buckling door.

The sound of the shouting and pounding and stomping carried to other floors. The guards on those floors had quickly herded all their prisoners into their cells before the contagion spread. Bells and alarms intensified the panic, as guard and inmate alike awaited whatever was coming.

"We got you, you blue-eyed devil," shouted Ali Al-Kobar, "and we got you good." He was addressing Casey, who was now surrounded by half a dozen inmates. "We're going to bust out of here. We're going out, man, and you're going to get us out."

Screams of delight engulfed them all.

Al-Kobar looked at the joyous faces around him. He was a leader of rebellion at last. The thrill was electrifying.

One of the inmates began beating and pounding a window with the leg of a broken table, chipping away steadily at the thick glass bricks. The inmates watched. A big chunk of glass gave way, falling out into the street. The bright, clear blue of the sky could be seen.

"Free, we're going to be free," shouted one prisoner soulfully. "Look out there, that's where we going. Look, ain't that beautiful."

They began dancing. One of the prisoners ran into his open

cell and gleefully put a lit match to his mattress. Black smoke spiraled up. He put a match to another mattress.

Other prisoners started smashing at the glass bricks, wanting more of that sky, more of that heady feeling of freedom.

"Use your head, brother," urged Officer Davis as he looked around. "How can you win this way?"

"Don't call us brother," shouted Al-Kobar. "You're the brother to a pig. You're a white man."

"Let's give them a trial."

"Give them a trial like they tried me," shouted Raul DeJesus, still inside his cell. The inmates wanted everyone to be free, but they weren't about to let DeJesus out of his cell. "Hurry before the machines are turned on again. They must have shut the machines off, thinking we were beaten. Hurry."

The inmates from the cells on the other end of the eighth floor had now converged to the side where Casey and the officers were being held captive. There were about 230 inmates crowding, shouting, dancing, smashing.

Al-Kobar stood on the only table in the cellblock that hadn't been destroyed.

By now, many glass bricks had been knocked out of place. Some prisoners were hacking at the remaining windows. Others sat on the shoulders of fellow inmates and could see down into the street. The police had already cordoned off the building. Riot police in helmets surrounded it.

"The pigs are all over the place down there," one of the inmates shouted from his perch on someone's shoulders.

"Fuck them, they're not getting in here," shouted another.

Some inmates tried to get the elevators to stop on the eighth floor, but Deputy Warden Margolis had ordered the floor sealed off. The eighth floor was being monitored from the main control board in the Warden's office on the ground floor.

Restive and anxious, aroused for action, prisoners began using the weapons they fashioned from the broken tables to break everything in sight—the toilets, the sinks, the beds. Several mattresses were on fire. The entire floor was filling with black smoke.

"Smash open all of those windows."

"We're going to break every fucking thing in the place."

Water started to gush out from the broken toilets, flooding the floor. The inmates began slipping as they swung at the windows. Some fell to the floor, laughing hysterically as they tried to get up.

Margolis ordered the water mains shut off for the entire building. Everyone was under siege now.

"Burn the place down, burn it down."

"Let's kill these bastards."

"Kill them, kill them," the chant began.

"No, we have to give them a trial," shouted James Phelan, a thin white man with cold, beady eyes. A tooth was missing in the front of his mouth. "Give them a trial, and *then* we'll kill them."

Casey and the guards were tied and gagged by now. They stared at the inmates around them, then looked at each other. Their eyes were glazed. Sweat was soaking their uniforms.

"Before we kill them, I got a better penalty," said a Black inmate. "We'll give them a little ass-fucking." He took out his penis and shook it at the guards.

Other inmates began a general shouting and shoving and laughing with that suggestion. Several of them took out their penises, shaking them at the prisoners, then at each other, laughing.

"Hold it. Wait a minute." A thin Black man with glasses stepped onto the table next to Al-Kobar. "We have us some hostages and we all been bitchin' 'cause they been treatin' us like shit, right?" His voice was hardly heard over the din.

"Right on!" from the crowd surrounding the table.

"What the fuck you doin' up here, man?" asked Al-Kobar, not wanting to share the limelight. "Mind your fuckin' business."

"Leave him talk," said a burly Black man, standing amid a group of prisoners from the other side of the building. "Let him have his say."

"We want out," Al-Kobar urged the crowd.

He was cheered lustily.

"Well," said the thin Black man on the table, whose name was Moody. "They ain't about to let us out of here. Kill these pigs or not."

Boos and curses.

"But we got these guys alive now," Moody continued. "Maybe we make a stink, give them our grievances, we can get faster trials, better food . . ."

24

"More dessert . . ." shouted another.

"Yeah," chorused some of the inmates.

"And air conditioning . . ."

"And better food."

"And bail. Let's get the fuck out of here and I'll eat my momma's cooking at home."

"Yeah," said Al-Kobar. "We want out, not some shit-ass jive. If you got no balls, step down, man." He was glaring at Moody.

The inmates stood quietly now, looking at each other, perplexed as to the next move.

"We want blood," shouted Al-Kobar.

"Right on," returned some.

Others were not so sure.

"Well, if we ain't got these pigs alive," said Moody, still standing on the table, "we ain't gonna get nothin' but life in the fuckin' can. With them alive, we got bargaining power."

Some agreed and nodded; others grumbled, looking at each other.

"We want freedom . . . freedom . . . blood . . ." Al-Kobar urged his lagging followers.

The crowd murmured restlessly.

"Man, they not about to let us out of here, kill those pigs or not," said Moody. "And if they don't let you out, and you burn them pigs, then what you gonna do?"

"Kill all the pigs. Kill all the whiteys. Kill them," Al-Kobar exhorted.

"How many of you cats want to have a murder rap over your heads too?" asked Moody.

"Not me, Moody."

"Me neither. I only got a junk bust here, man. I don't need no murder even it be a pig."

"If we hold them alive," shouted Moody, "we can get a break, maybe get some newspapers to put it in the paper. You know man, protest."

"Yeah, I'll get my picture in the paper," said a Puerto Rican with a mustache and beard. He ran his hand over his hair and smiled.

One of the officers, Lockwood, had been forced to his knees and his gag removed. James Phelan had taken out his penis and was

25

now menacing the officer, coming ever closer to him. There was a satanic smile on his thin lips. Other prisoners in the crowd were watching with excitement, some held the officer down on his knees.

"Hey, you cats, cool that," said Moody, still on the table.

Ralph Santiago, the Puerto Rican who wanted to pose for the pictures, jerked Lockwood out of the hands of the other prisoners. He stood him up.

James Phelan gave Santiago a hard look. He saw other inmates backing up Santiago—shrugged, tucked his penis back in his pants, and shuffled off to where the windows were being shattered.

"We want a break here, we want them to do something for us," Moody continued. "They ain't gonna do it if we fuck up these pigs here."

"You afraid, man?" demanded Al-Kobar, turning to Moody. "You're just a shit-ass nigger."

Moody turned angrily. The crowd watched. Al-Kobar grabbed Moody by his shirt front.

"Leave the little man alone," said the burly Black man who had been standing at the table backing Moody. He reached up and grabbed Al-Kobar's arm.

"What the fuck you buttin' in for?" said Al-Kobar.

" 'Cause I want to hear what the little man has to say," said the burly one starting to haul Al-Kobar off the table.

Al-Kobar released Moody. "Okay, okay, listen if you cats want to just sit around here bitchin' and bull-shittin' . . ." Al-Kobar waved his hand at Moody in disgust.

More sirens were wailing in the streets below. Inmates at the windows relayed the message that the fire department had arrived. The streets were swarming with police and firemen. Bull horns were blaring.

"Hey, you guys from the newspaper?" Santiago shouted down to the street. He was now sitting on another inmate's shoulders. Something must have been shouted back. "Hey, guys from the *Daily News* are down there, man," Santiago announced.

"Yeah, yeah, put it in the papers how they give you shit to eat around here. How they keep you like an animal."

"Let's get some demands together," shouted Moody, over the

din. "Put the hostages away in cells. Let's get something out of this besides more jail time."

"Moody's right," shouted a white prisoner standing at the table. "The first thing they'll want to know is how these hacks are. Let's put them on ice while we get some demands."

"Who's got paper?"

"Get Lacey. He's the law man. He's got all kinds of paper."

Lacey was a jailhouse lawyer, an inmate who spent his time reading law and drafting legal papers for himself and other prisoners.

Paper and pencils were assembled, and seven men sat at the table, each with paper, each with pencil, surrounded by fellow inmates.

Captain Casey and Lou Adler were put in one cell. Scott and Lockwood in another. Davis in a third by himself. The three cells were quite far apart from each other. The hostages were untied and their gags removed. Each had been given cigarettes, and even Casey, who didn't smoke, was smoking.

"What the hell's going on up there now," demanded Margolis, as he stood at his desk.

The officers around him shrugged.

"Dep, ABC television is on the phone," said an officer.

Margolis made a face. "Christ, man, tell them if they want to know anything come down here and join the party. Everybody else is already here."

"They wanted to talk to their news team."

"Pritchett," Margolis said impatiently. "I got other things than to be running a messenger service. Tell them we're a little busy."

Captain Walker, a Black captain, came into the office quickly. "Dep, the hot line is all lit up. It's the Commissioner."

"Come on, what's going on up there?" demanded Margolis. "The Commish is calling every five minutes. They must be on his ass from City Hall. What the hell is going on up there?"

"Here's the Chaplain."

"Father, Father," said Margolis, walking over to the priest. "Maybe they'll listen to you."

"Here," said Father McGuinis, handing Margolis a paperback book with a piece of paper sticking out from its pages. Father McGuinis was short and bald. "One of the police just gave this to me on the way in. Someone threw it out from the eighth floor. They want to be heard, want the newspapers to know what a rotten, overcrowded place this is. They're right, you know—it's a disgrace to cage men up like this."

"Sure, sure, Father," said Margolis. "But right now, they have five of my men hostages. We have to establish some communication."

"I'll go up," said the Chaplain.

"Take Father to the elevator," said Margolis.

"I'll go with you, Father," said a Black officer.

"Okay, Johnny," said Father McGuinis.

Margolis went to the hot line to tell the Commissioner, who in turn could tell City Hall, that something was being done.

III

MONDAY, AUGUST 7, 9:25 A.M.

Marc pushed through the revolving doors into the large, marble main lobby of the Criminal Courts Building. He moved quickly away from the doorway, out of the stream of people being churned into the lobby. In that flow were policemen in uniform, and lawyers carrying briefcases, and court personnel, and young kids being pulled along by their mothers, and old couples, and worried-looking young women, and some men with bandaged arms or heads—who might have been victims of crimes or apprehended criminals; and there were many Black people, and mostly poor people, dressed in cheap imitations of the styles of the day. All these were to take a role in the meting out of justice this day; the accusers, the accused, the families, the friends, the prosecutors, the defenders, the judges, the bondsmen, and the court buffs who come to court to take in the spectacle.

Some of the young Black men coming into the building were loudly dressed, with large floppy hats pulled to one side of their heads, and bright-colored suits, and high-heeled clunky shoes, and flashy rings on their fingers. They were pimps come to wait while some of their girls—both Black and white—were processed and released with a fine.

As it was every morning, the terrazzo floor of the lobby was coated with gray, grimy streaks, the result of the cleaning crew's mopping dirty water around the night before. A pile of cigarette butts and orange peels, and half frankfurter rolls, and soiled tissues, and candy wrappers, had been swept to the side of the entrance. The sweeper, a young Black man, was leaning against the wall, his broom resting against his shoulder as he watched the people entering the building. He looked sleepy but was more likely a methadone patient the city was helping to rehabilitate.

In the center of the lobby, there was a large circular information desk under a round, four-faced clock. No attendant was ever posted at this information desk. And the clock above hadn't been cleaned in so long the numerals were barely visible. A lanky young Black lay full length atop the desk counter, leaning back on one elbow, one foot on the counter, one dangling over the edge, eating a frankfurter oozing fried onions, drinking orange soda from a bottle. These had been purchased from the umbrellaed pushcart stationed between the parked cars directly outside the building. A variety of other people were lounging around the outer perimeter of the desk, some drinking coffee from paper cups, some reading the morning paper, some just smoking, staring into space, others waiting for their lawyers or friends, talking loudly or whistling or silent. On the floor, at the base of the desk, sat several long-haired, unkempt hippie types. They enjoyed the stares and consternation of the cops moving toward the courts. There was an open antagonism between these young people and the conservative, young cops.

Marc walked along a corridor toward Part AR-1—one of the approximately fifty courts in the Criminal Courts Building. Some of these were under the jurisdiction of the New York City Criminal Court, and handled misdemeanors, crimes which bore a maximum penalty of one year; the other courts were part of the New York State Supreme Court, which had jurisdiction over felonies, major crimes which bore penalties from one year to life and even death.

In Part AR-1, people arrested for crimes in New York County (Manhattan) are first arraigned, that is, formally advised of the charges against them. As Marc walked toward the courtroom, he wondered how respect for the dignity and majesty of the law could survive in the filthy mess of this courthouse, with eaters, loafers, and loungers permitted to do whatever they liked, wherever they liked. He stopped outside the AR-1 courtroom, studying the faces in the crowd, looking for Mrs. Maricyk. She had called him earlier to tell him that her husband, Joey Maricyk, had been arrested last night and was to be arraigned this morning. Maricyk was a former cop who resigned from the force under pressure after some disciplinary action relating to an affair with a married woman during a time Maricyk was separated from his wife. Marc had represented Maricyk at his departmental hearing.

A young woman in a pair of tight slacks, sandals, and a sleeveless, cotton shirt which seemed a shade too tight walked toward Marc.

"Mister Conte?" she wondered.

"Mrs. Maricyk?"

"Yeah," she smiled somewhat shyly. Her smile was marred by a couple of teeth in front which were rotted at the edges. "I thought it was you."

Mrs. Maricyk wore pierced earrings, long ones, and her hair was bleached blond. The roots were quite dark.

"Has Joey been brought into court yet?" Marc asked.

"Not yet. The cop said it'd be a while yet."

"Where is the cop now?" asked Marc.

"I don't know. He was here a couple of minutes ago," she replied, looking about the corridor.

"You said on the phone that Joey was arrested for trying to bribe a policeman?" said Marc. "Is that what the charges are?"

"That's what Joey said," she replied.

"You spoke to your husband?"

"Yeah, they let me see him down at the station house. You shoulda' seen what a mess he looked like," she said, raising one hand to her mouth. "He wasn't even able to stand up. His ribs was all sore; his back was all scarred up. He said one of the cops worked him over with a ax handle he keeps in the back of the cop car."

"The cop kept an ax handle?"

"That's what Joey said. I guess they got it in for him 'cause he's a ex-cop, you think?"

"They might," replied Marc. He had heard of policemen doing all sorts of strange violent things to people they arrested. Marc knew that some—perhaps only a few—policemen joined the force merely to give vent to their sadistic natures.

"How did all of this start?" Marc asked.

"Joey said he was stopped for speeding or an illegal turn, or something like that," she said. "And you know Joey, he sort of mouthed off, I guess. And they took him down to the station house. And then he's supposed to have tried to give the cops some money to leave him go. That's what the cop said. But I don't believe him anyway." She hesitated for a moment. "Say, Mister Conte. This cop's got funny ideas, you know," she said, looking at Marc, hoping he understood.

"What kind of funny ideas?"

"Well, I was down at the station house till about three or four this morning, you know? And the cops said that Joey'd be in court this morning some time. So I go home, you know, just to change. I didn't even bother to change or put make-up on when I first got called. I just went right down to the station house. So when they said that Joey wouldn't be arranged . . ."

"Arraigned," Marc corrected.

"Yeah." She smiled. "Well, I go home, you know? And about seven-thirty this here cop from the case shows up at my house."

"The same cop who arrested Joey?" Marc asked, surprised.

"Yeah, the same cop. And he comes on, like, you know. He says he knows it's rough, and he wants to help me out and all that crap. And he says he'll wait for me while I change and then he'll take me down to the court. Now I know this guy ain't just lookin' to help me out. I mean, you know? He's a cop that just arrested my husband. So I told him he better take Joey to the court and not worry about me. But he says to me his partner is going to take care of Joey. I told him he already took care of Joey real good, the rat. He thought that was funny, you know. The dumb kraut."

Marc studied Mrs. Maricyk. She was poorly spoken, poorly educated, seeming now small, lost, pathetically defenseless in the grips of the vast, impersonal, intricate machinery of justice. That face, that voice, that defenseless floundering which Marc had seen so often before, heard so often before in other people, was one of the driving forces in Marc's defense of people accused of crime, whether they could afford his services or not.

"What's the arresting officer's name?" asked Marc.

"Schmidt," she replied. "He's a typical kraut, mean, like a gestapo. He even started to brag about being the weight-lifting champ of his precinct or his division, whatever that is. And he starts telling me about having plenty of money. He's got another job as a bouncer somewhere. And he's giving me all this crap, you know? So I told him the baby was sleeping, wait downstairs for me, you know? I don't have no baby, Mister Conte. I just said that. Can you get this guy off my back, I mean, without making it worse for Joey on his case?"

Marc frowned, looking around the hallway. "Do you see this cop yet?"

Mrs. Maricyk looked around. "Nah, I don't see him."

"I'll try and straighten it out," Marc assured her. "Just point him out to me when you see him. I have to go inside for a moment to see if I can get the case called quickly."

"Okay, Mister Conte. Listen, I only got a couple of hundred with me," she said, taking some bills from a pocketbook containing nothing more than a lipstick, keys, and a used tissue. "That's all I could get this morning. I had to borrow from my mother. But I'll get some more, whatever it is. Don't worry about that. Can I give you the money here?"

"Why don't you hold onto it and we'll talk about it later," Marc smiled, trying to reassure her. "Let me get the case called first."

Marc pushed open the first of a double set of brass-studded, leather-padded doors at the rear of the large courtroom. An oval window was set in the center of each door. Hand-printed paper signs, indicating POSITIVELY NO EATING OR DRINKING IN THE COURT-ROOM were pasted over most of the glass ovals. Marc stopped to peer under a paper sign into the courtroom. The high-ceilinged courtroom was painted beige, with wood paneling on the lower half of the walls. The paint was peeling in great patches from the walls and ceiling, and the paneling was stained where the maintenance personnel carelessly wiped it with wet rags, causing the paneling to lose its finish in streaks and to warp.

At the front end of the room, inside a heavy wooden railing, under the somewhat askew motto "IN GO WE TRU T" sat Judge Arnold Rathmore. Seated next to Judge Rathmore was Judge Vincent Bauer, in his brand-new black robes. He was being phased in before assignment to his own court.

Marc smiled. Good old Vinnie looked a little hesitant up there behind the bench. He was watching and listening intently.

Judge Rathmore was Black, moon-faced, with dark-rimmed glasses. He was wrapped in his black robe as he sat in a high-backed chair on the judge's dais. Judge Rathmore had spent twenty-four years in the District Attorney's office, and after all those years of faithful service, was elevated to the bench by mayoral appointment.

The front rows of the courtroom were reserved; on the right, sat policemen, some in uniform, some in civilian clothes, their silver badges pinned to their shirt fronts with large safety pins. On the left, were attorneys.

Standing in front of the judge's dais, his shoulder almost as high as its front ledge, was a court officer known as the bridge man. He was the officer who called the cases on the calendar, read the charges to the defendants, advised them of their rights, and stamped the papers with the appropriate rubber stamp so the Judge could thereon place his initials and notations of what action had been undertaken on this date. The bridge man stood between the judge's dais and the counsel table at which the defendants, their lawyers, and the District Attorney stood to address the court.

Also within the well of the courtroom, at tables and desks against the side walls (none of the tables or desks in the courtroom matched—they were a hodgepodge collection, missing drawers and scarred tops) were the Legal Aid lawyers whom the Judge assigned to represent defendants who could not afford their own attorneys, and the court personnel necessary to process the calendar.

On one side of the courtroom, through the streaked wall paneling, was a door leading to the prisoner's detention cells, the bull pen, as it was called. Along the wall of the court near the entrance to the bull pen was a long bench. Here, a sorry collection of female prisoners, mostly prostitutes, awaited the call of their cases.

Marc walked to the front of the courtroom. Judge Bauer saw

him and could hardly suppress a smile. A young uniformed officer saw Marc walking toward the opening in the railing, and interposed himself between Marc and the well of the courtroom.

"What can I do for you?" the officer said abruptly.

"I'm counsel. I have a case on this morning," Marc replied.

"You can't come in, Counselor," he said, not overly impressed with Marc's announcement. "Have a seat and wait. Your case will be called soon."

"He's okay, Smitty," said Charlie Brady, the bridge man as he stood to the side of the judge's bench, awaiting the conclusion of a whispered conference between the Judge, a Legal Aid lawyer and the assistant District Attorney. The lawyers were standing at the front edge of the judge's dais, and Judge Rathmore was leaning forward in his chair. Judge Bauer listened to everything carefully. A defendant stood at the counsel table, silently watching the proceedings.

The court officer at the railing moved aside, letting Marc approach the bridge man at the side of the counsel table.

"Hiya, Couns," said Brady the bridge man. He was an old-timer. He was holding the papers for the next case to be called. "What can I do for you?"

"I've got a fellow on the calendar named Maricyk," Marc replied.

Brady began to leaf through court papers which were folded into a narrow file drawer on the counsel table. The papers were numbered according to their position on the morning's calendar.

"Okay, I got a long calendar today, Couns. A hundred and five cases," Charlie said unhappily as he continued to leaf through. "You're number eighty-nine. I'm only on forty-eight now." Charlie was heavy-set, with curly reddish hair and thick glasses. His uniform was a bit too tight around a developing beer belly.

"Charlie," replied Marc quietly, "if I were to buy you a cigar or two, good ones, do you think you could pull my case and put it on the top of the calendar?" Marc smiled, knowing that Charlie was awaiting just such a cue.

"That's possible, Counselor." Charlie smiled innocently, taking Marc's court papers out of the file drawer, placing them on the desk before him. "I got a couple of cops I got to get out of here before you, Couns. I'll get to you in a couple of minutes. Okay?"

"Fine. I'm going back outside to find the cop. I'll be right back."

"That's a good idea, Couns," said Charlie. "Get the cop and everybody in here. This way when I give you a call, I can get you out of here right away." He winked and returned to his post. The bench conference was still in session.

Marc walked toward the rear of the courtroom. Mrs. Maricyk was standing in the corridor, leaning against a wall, smoking a cigarette.

"Did you see Joey?" she asked.

"No. They only allow Legal Aid lawyers to see defendants in the bull pen in this court," Marc replied.

"You mean you can't even talk to him?" she asked. "How can he tell you what happened?"

"I'll have to ask him when he comes out and we're standing at the counsel table."

Mrs. Maricyk looked at Marc skeptically. "But you said Legal Aid can talk to the prisoners? Is that the ones who don't pay for their own lawyers?"

Marc nodded.

"How come?" she asked. "I mean don't you have to talk to a prisoner whether he's able to pay or not?"

"Yes, but those are the rules."

Mrs. Maricyk shrugged, shaking her head. "That's the cop over there," she said, pointing to a young man in police uniform standing at the side of the corridor smoking. He was crew-cut and rangy, talking to another cop with a mustache. "The one in the mustache is his partner," Mrs. Maricyk added.

"Which is the one who has the ax handle?" Marc asked, studying the two policemen.

"The one with the crew cut."

Marc walked toward the two policemen. The hallway was still crowded by milling people. A veritable carpet of cigarette butts covered the floor.

"Officer," said Marc, addressing the policeman with the crew cut. "I represent Joey Maricyk. Can I speak with you a moment?"

The two policemen looked at Marc warily, then at each other.

"Sure," replied the crew cut, shrugging.

"I just wanted to find out about the case," Marc said. "Just wanted to know if you've a good arrest; more or less, what I'm up against."

"You don't really think we can talk to you about the case without the District Attorney, do you, Counselor?" said the policeman with the mustache.

"Why not?" replied Marc. "I'm not trying to change anything, or bribe you, or wheedle information out of you that's against the law or police rules." He was still talking directly at the crew cut. "Especially since I know that you two do things exactly by the book. Tell me, are ax handles authorized equipment these days?"

The crew cut's eyes narrowed ever so slightly. "What's that supposed to mean?"

"That means that working my client over with an ax handle isn't in the book," Marc replied.

"Who told you that, his cute wife?" said the crew cut sarcastically.

"She told me something even better," Marc said curtly. "Going to the defendant's house and driving his wife to court is one that I'm sure the Commissioner would love to hear."

The crew cut shifted from one foot to the other.

"Listen, Counselor, if you want to talk about the case, you better talk to the District Attorney, not us," said the mustache.

"Oh, I'll talk to him all right. And the Judge, too," replied Marc. "I'm not bashful. Right now I'm talking to lover boy. Just as a lawyer for a client, of course. But if my client's wife tells me that she sees either of you hanging around her house again, you can bet your shields that the Commissioner will be listening to a long, sad story from a weeping wife."

"I didn't do nothing," said the crew cut annoyedly, getting red in the face now. "The guy fell down in the station house. That's how he got hurt. He was starting to get wise, resisting arrest in the station house. Her, I only tried to be friendly."

"Don't even talk to him," said the mustache. "Let him do his talking in court."

The crew cut jutted out his bottom lip as he listened to his partner. He nodded, just watching Marc.

"Okay, see you inside," said Marc. He turned and walked back to Mrs. Maricyk. "Come on, let's go into court."

"Wait a minute, Mister Conte," she hesitated. "What's going to happen in court now?"

"Joey'll be arraigned. They'll tell him what crime he's charged with. Then he'll plead not guilty. We'll ask for a preliminary hearing, that's where the cops will testify about what Joey was supposed to have done. If there's not enough evidence, the Judge can dismiss the case."

"Oh, that's good," she said. "You think the Judge'll throw the case out?"

"I don't even think we'll get the hearing," Marc replied flatly.

"How come?"

"Because Joey supposedly tried to bribe a cop," said Marc. "That's a felony, a large crime. And, besides, there may be some question of the police roughing Joey up. So rather than letting the case go to a hearing in this court where we can hear part of their evidence and do a lot of questioning, the D.A. will probably want to present the case to the grand jury."

"What does that mean?"

"That means that the grand jury is like a regular jury you see in the movies," Marc replied, "only bigger. Perhaps twenty, twenty-three people. And their job is to listen to the evidence the D.A. presents, and if they think there's been a felony crime committed, they vote for an indictment. That's a fancy word for a formal charge. That's how a felony gets to court. After that you have a trial and all. Now, the grand jury proceedings are supposed to take the place of any hearing we might be entitled to in this court. The only difference is, the D.A. prefers the grand jury hearing because we can't be present to listen to the witnesses or cross-examine them. It's a secret proceeding."

"A secret proceeding?" Mrs. Maricyk's face went blank. She stopped in her tracks. "You're kidding! That's got to be against the law or something?"

"Not yet, unfortunately," Marc replied.

"Well, let's get the hearing in this court today, where we can be present and you can ask questions and everything. Don't let the D.A. give Joey no secret hearing."

"I'd like to do just that, believe me," said Marc. "But the D.A. will explain to the court that he's going to present the case to the grand jury and the Judge will delay this proceeding here until he does."

"Don't let him do it," Mrs. Maricyk insisted.

"I can't force the Judge to do anything," said Marc. "I can only give him what I think the law is. He doesn't have to agree. The reason the Judge will use for the delay today is that a Supreme Court indictment would take precedence—is more important—than a case in this court, so if the D.A. were to get an indictment, the case would go to the Supreme Court and this court would be wasting its time having a hearing."

"They're going to railroad my husband, in other words," Mrs. Maricyk said angrily, her head nodding. "Ain't you gonna do something? What am I paying you for?"

"I'm going to argue and object as hard as I can, Mrs. Maricyk. But the Judge can do whatever he wants, and if he goes along with the D.A., we can only appeal to another court after the case is over."

"What happens to Joey meanwhile?"

"I'll have bail set. Can you afford to bail him out?"

Mrs. Maricyk's eyes welled up with tears. "This stinks, Mister Conte. Can't we do something. Go to another judge? I haven't any money to put up for bail. Will the bondsman take my engagement ring?" She fingered a small diamond on her left hand.

"No, unfortunately, only a bank book or the deed to a house," Marc replied resignedly. "I don't make all these difficulties," he tried to say consolingly. "This is just the way it is. I'll try and get Joey paroled without bail."

"Can't we do something, get a hearing to have the case thrown out today? Go to another judge?"

"I've already mentioned, the only time we can appeal is after the whole case is all over. But, by that time, not having a hearing today is just a technical little violation nobody cares about."

"You know, Mister Conte, I know you're a good lawyer, so I trust you, but this system really stinks, you know." Mrs. Maricyk now turned and walked into the courtroom angrily. Marc followed. They found seats in the spectator section of the courtroom. The two cops on the case came into the courtroom shortly and sat in the rows reserved for the police. Mrs. Maricyk watched the activity about her in bewilderment.

A short Puerto Rican prisoner, dressed in jeans, a dirty T-shirt, and sneakers, was brought into the courtroom from the bull pen. The court officer who accompanied the prisoner directed him to stand at the counsel table in front of the Judge.

"Docket Number A29257, Gugliermo Del Gato," Charlie the bridge man announced loudly. "On charges of a violation of one thirty point thirty-five and one twenty point five of the penal law. On the complaint of Nereida San Fermin. Officer O'Callaghan." Charlie looked toward the police section of the audience.

A short, blond man in a light windbreaker and blue slacks rose from his seat and looked around. His badge was pinned to the collar of his jacket. The policeman motioned to a thin, dark girl sitting in the back of the courtroom. She walked toward the front of the courtroom carrying a baby in her arms. Another child followed behind, clutching the hem of her dress. One of the Legal Aid lawyers who had been sitting at a desk on the side of the courtroom, walked to the counsel table, and stood next to the prisoner.

"The defendant is represented by Legal Aid," Charlie the bridge man continued. "Do you waive the formal reading of the charges, Counselor?"

"Yes," replied the Legal Aid lawyer.

"What's going on?" Mrs. Maricyk whispered to Marc.

"The Puerto Rican in the sneakers is being arraigned on a rape charge," Marc replied softly.

"Rape? He raped the one with the two kids?" Mrs. Maricyk was shocked.

Marc shook his head. "I'm sure the woman is what is known as the defendant's common-law wife," he explained. "And I'm also sure that those are his children, and they all live together. The man and the woman were probably having an argument, and he beat her up, so she ran out of the house, got a cop and charged him with rape. Somebody must have told her she could charge him with statutory rape because she's under age and not legally his wife."

Mrs. Maricyk's face rippled with a smile as she looked forward again.

The assistant District Attorney huddled at the counsel table with the woman complainant and the arresting officer. The woman was crying. The defendant was alternately talking to his

Legal Aid lawyer and leaning over to speak in Spanish to the woman.

"Don't do that," Charlie the bridge man harshly reprimanded the defendant. The defendant glared at Charlie and continued talking to the lawyer.

"Your Honor," said the District Attorney, turning to the Judge, "because of a lack of evidence, and after a conversation with the complainant and the arresting officer in this case, the People have determined that there would not be sufficient evidence here to sustain the burden of proof or to make out a *prima facie* case. Therefore, the People will move to dismiss these charges."

"Why's that?" Mrs. Maricyk turned to Marc.

"I guess she's sorry she had her husband arrested and now she doesn't want him to go to jail. So she's refusing to press charges," Marc explained. "On a case like this, the People have no objection."

"Why'd they bother to bring the case to court in the first place then?"

"Because the woman made a complaint," said Marc. "The policeman in the street is not a judge to decide if a crime was really committed. He received a complaint and made an arrest. Besides, the cop got paid a hundred dollars overtime to come to court, so he doesn't mind a bit."

Mrs. Maricyk frowned.

"The defendant will waive any suit for false arrest or for anything else against the City and against this officer," the Legal Aid lawyer announced to the Judge for the court reporter to include in the record.

"Very well," said the Judge impatiently. "Have him sign the affidavits to that effect. Case dismissed. Call the next case. Let's go." Judge Rathmore looked to neophyte Judge Bauer to be sure he took in the entire lesson. Judge Bauer nodded, and watched Charlie put three different rubber stamps on the court papers, then toss them in a basket next to the bench.

The defendant in the sneakers turned, put his arm around his wife, and walked toward the rear of the courtroom. One of the small children held his hand. The other tailed along behind. The wife was crying, nuzzling her tears against her husband's chest.

"Docket number A29630," intoned Charlie. "William Turner,

charged with violations of one forty point thirty, one fifty-five point forty, and one forty point thirty-five. On the complaint of Arthur Stark."

A man with a bandaged head rose from the audience and went forward to swear to the truth of his complaint as another police officer got a Black prisoner out of the bull pen and stood him in front of the Judge. The District Attorney spoke to the cop as Legal Aid spoke to the defendant.

"This place is wild," said Mrs. Maricyk. "This always go on?" Marc nodded.

"When's Joey's case get called?" she asked.

"In a few minutes," Marc replied.

"Why are all the women sitting inside the rail?"

"They're mostly prostitutes," said Marc. "Our male chauvinist past makes us regard women—even prostitutes—as too delicate to be kept in those animal cages in the back. Maybe women's lib should complain so they can all get tossed in the cells equally."

Mrs. Maricyk grimaced, then turned to watch the court proceedings. After a few minutes, Mrs. Maricyk tapped Marc's arm. "She really likes you," Mrs. Maricyk said, motioning toward one of the women sitting inside the rail. "She's been staring at you for ten minutes now."

The woman staring at Marc was Black, exotic-looking, tall with a solid, taut figure. Her dress had a deep décolletage.

"She's beautiful," said Mrs. Maricyk. "Is she a prostitute?"

"First of all," Marc replied, "*she* happens to be a *he*."

Mrs. Maricyk stared at Marc and then turned to stare at the person in front of the courtroom. "You're kidding!"

"No, I'm not."

"She's got breasts," Mrs. Maricyk countered.

"Silicone," said Marc.

"How do you know about all these people without even knowing who they are?" she asked.

"You get a sense about cases when you've handled enough of them."

"That good-lookin' thing is a *man*?" repeated Mrs. Maricyk incredulously, looking forward again.

"Sure is. A strange man, but definitely not a woman."

"But how, I mean, after all, if he's a prostitute, I mean, the

41

customer finds out and . . . does she, he, make money doin' this?"

"I imagine so," replied Marc. "He must pick up a customer and after they get through the preliminaries, he tells the customer that it's one of those times of the month. But just so the customer's not disappointed, he says he's sure he can do something for him. And he does. And the customer pays him, and then the customer goes home to East Cupcake, Nebraska, and tells all his buddies about the really hot time he had in New York. Never knowing he was really out with a man."

Mrs. Maricyk studied Marc dubiously. She looked back to the figure in the front.

"Next case," said Judge Rathmore, finishing with the case before him. The Black man, originally charged with a burglary, pled guilty to a petit larceny misdemeanor. His sentence was set four weeks ahead.

The bridge man called another case. The he-she prostitute stood and strutted exaggeratedly to the counsel table.

"Back again, hanh, Ruthie?" Charlie the bridge man said softly, smiling.

"A girl's got to work," Ruthie replied effeminately. His-her skin was very dark, smoothed with very carefully applied make-up. He-she glanced over his shoulder at Marc and smiled.

Ruthie had a private lawyer who made an application for an adjournment of two weeks. The Judge granted the adjournment and paroled Ruthie until the return date. Ruthie swayed saucily out of the courtroom, probably straight to put together enough money to pay the fine to be imposed and the lawyer's fee.

"Docket number A46753 Joseph Maricyk," announced Charlie, looking over and winking at Marc. The policeman with the crew cut rose and walked into the bull pen. He returned with his prisoner. Joey Maricyk was short, wide, with blond straight hair. He had an angry bruise under his half-closed right eye. Maricyk walked slowly with discomfort, winked at Marc and mumbled a hello. He stood next to Marc at the counsel table, facing the bench.

"This defendant is arraigned under two hundred point forty-five and two twenty point five of the Penal Code," continued Charlie. "Do you waive the formal reading of the information, Counselor?"

"Yes," replied Marc.

Judge Bauer sat slightly back of Judge Rathmore, and he smiled down at Marc.

"Will you give your appearance to the stenographer, Counselor."

"Marc Conte, two thirty-seven Broadway, New York City." The stenographer, a thin Black man, was slouched in his chair, looking across the room. Only his fingers moved, and they quickly, on the stenotype machine.

The District Attorney began speaking to the crew-cut cop. He was being informed for the first time about the charges against Maricyk, and based on this information, he would decide how to handle the case and the amount of bail, if any, he would allow. Although bail was exclusively the province of the judge, when the D.A. recommended an amount of bail, very often, particularly with a judge like Rathmore, that recommendation carried a great deal of weight.

"This prick worked me over with an ax handle," Maricyk whispered to Marc.

"I know. Your wife told me," replied Marc.

"A real tough punk," said Maricyk, standing with his head lowered so the Judge couldn't see him speaking. He held his hands behind his back. "I'd love to see him try something like that out in the street, where he didn't have all the cops in that station house to back him up. I'd rip the top of his skull off. The bastard."

"Not so loud," Marc cautioned softly, as the D.A.'s conference continued. The Judge on the dais sat back silently, waiting. He turned and chatted with Judge Bauer. "One of the sections of the penal code the bridge man just read has to do with narcotics, Joey," said Marc. "Did you have narcotics with you?"

"What the hell would I do with that," said Maricyk. "Nah. These punks planted a marijuana cigarette on me, just to be sure I got hung with something so they'd have an excuse for the beating they gave me."

"Counselor, here's your copy of the papers," said Charlie, handing Marc a copy of the complaint sheet.

The District Attorney broke his huddle with the crew cut and turned to the Judge. "The People are going to request an adjournment of two weeks in this matter, Your Honor," he said.

The Judge glanced at Marc. "Counselor, do you want to be heard on this?"

"I certainly do, sir," replied Marc. "The defendant is ready for a hearing right now, and moves that a preliminary hearing be held forthwith."

"Counselor," said the Judge thinly, "the District Attorney had made an application for an adjournment. I'm sure there's a good reason for that request. Is there, Mister D.A.?" He glanced at the D.A.

"Certainly, Your Honor. This matter is very likely to be presented to the grand jury this afternoon. All the witnesses, the policemen, are here already."

The Judge looked back to Marc, a satisfied look on his face.

"Your Honor," said Marc, "most respectfully, I suggest that this is the first time the D.A. ever heard about this case. It has not been scheduled for grand jury hearing. The D.A. merely says it very likely will be presented today. However, I'm sure the schedule for the grand jury is already filled for the day with other cases. Since all the witnesses in this case are *here* right now, right in front of you in this courtroom, this court should hold a hearing. Until an indictment is actually handed down by the grand jury, this court has jurisdiction over this case, and the defendant demands an immediate hearing."

Judge Bauer sat silently now, watching Judge Rathmore.

"Counselor, I know the law, thank you," the Judge said coldly. "I just want to know what you want to do about an adjournment. Is two weeks acceptable?"

"Can we have a representation from the D.A. that this case is, in fact, going to be presented to the grand jury today?" asked Marc.

"I don't know of any statute or rule which allows me to require the D.A. to make such a representation. Unless he wants to . . ." The Judge looked to the D.A.

"I do not want to make such a representation," said the D.A., picking up the Judge's cue.

The Judge looked back to Marc with a shrug, a thin smile on his lips. "Two weeks, Counselor?"

"Your Honor," said Marc, "most respectfully, section one eighty point sixty of the Criminal Procedure Law requires that if a hearing is postponed, it can only be postponed for twenty-four hours. I'll consent to an adjournment only until tomorrow."

"I guess counsel hasn't read the law correctly," the young District Attorney said haughtily. In the District Attorney's office, the younger men had to work their way through each of the bureaus or departments, and the youngest of the court men handled the Parts in the Criminal Court. The more experienced men handled the pre-trial proceedings in the Supreme Court, and then, finally, trials in the Supreme Court. "The statute speaks of a seventy-two-hour limit only if the defendant hasn't made bail," continued the D.A. "The People have no objection to reasonable bail being set in this case, Your Honor. I'd recommend five thousand dollars. And I press for a two-week adjournment. Counsel can't have objection now."

The Judge looked to Marc patiently.

"While I appreciate my learned colleague's dissertation on the law," Marc said softly, "his reference, if Your Honor pleases, is to a section requiring parole for a defendant in jail if his hearing is not held within seventy-two hours. I refer to a completely different section, Your Honor, section one eighty point sixty, which indicates that any hearing, whether there be bail, parole, or not, can only be adjourned for twenty-four hours at a time. I realize the District Attorney prefers to curtail the defendant's right to a preliminary hearing . . ."

"The People can present a case to the grand jury at any time they wish," interrupted the District Attorney. "If counsel doesn't like the law . . ."

"May I finish, Your Honor, without interruption." Marc addressed the Court firmly. "I gave the District Attorney a chance to speak without interruption, and I'd appreciate the same courtesy."

The Judge nodded patiently, looking at the D.A., assuring him in a glance that all was not lost.

The stenographer, still slouched, still glancing at a side wall, said: "Don't speak both at the same time. I can't get it."

"The District Attorney is right, you know, Counselor," said the Judge indulgently. "But go ahead and make the record if you wish."

"While it is true," said Marc, "that the People can present a

45

case to the grand jury at any time it wishes, this case isn't even scheduled for a grand jury yet—as we stand here now. The law doesn't eliminate this court's jurisdiction based on what the D.A. is likely to do in the future. Nor can this court eschew its jurisdiction by adjourning cases for inordinate lengths of time so as to give the District Attorney the opportunity of obtaining an indictment."

"Are you saying that I'm eschewing jurisdiction to accommodate the D.A.?" asked the Judge indignantly.

"I am merely repeating the words of the Court of Appeals in the case of People versus Markovitch," said Marc. "That Court used the very words I just quoted to Your Honor."

The Judge looked down to the bridge man. "Give me a copy of the Criminal Procedure Law," he said. "What section did you say, Counselor?"

"Section one eighty point sixty," repeated Marc. "And, Your Honor, while I am on the subject, and before it slips my mind, I wish to indicate to this Court, that the defendant was physically manhandled in the precinct house by the police. I wish Your Honor to note the defendant's physical appearance for the record."

The Judge looked down at Marc, then to Maricyk. "I'm not going to get into medical descriptions for the record, Counselor. I'm the Judge, not the doctor. If you want to note anything for the record, you do so. I'll mark the defendant's papers for medical attention if you wish, but I certainly am not going to be used by defendants to further any schemes or purposes they may have to escape justice."

"Your Honor refuses to note the defendant's condition for the record?" asked Marc.

"I do." The Judge began to thumb through a book the bridge man handed him.

Judge Bauer looked at Marc, then looked over to Judge Rathmore.

"May I note the defendant's condition for the record, Your Honor?" asked Marc.

"You may do as you wish," said the Judge, without looking up.

"Is your back really bruised?" Marc whispered to Maricyk.

"It's all cut up like a son of a bitch," Maricyk replied.

"Take off your shirt," said Marc.

Maricyk looked at Marc, shrugged, then opened the cuff buttons on his shirt. He slid the shirt over his head without unbuttoning the front. His back bore several large, long welts that were very red and sore-looking.

A murmur and stir went through the courtroom.

"What are you doing, Counselor?" the Judge demanded with surprise. Judge Bauer watched Marc with fascination.

"Turn around," Marc said to Maricyk. "Look at this man's back, Your Honor. I want to note for the record, in compliance with Your Honor's direction, several large, parallel bruises or welts starting at the defendant's left shoulder and sloping downward to the right about eighteen inches."

The courtroom was silent. Judge Rathmore looked annoyed.

"The highest one," Marc continued, "starts about three inches down from the top of the defendant's left shoulder, and the second is approximately three inches below that. The third three inches farther down, and the fourth near the waist. They seem to run in parallel lines at about thirty-degree angles from the horizontal. Am I correct in that, Your Honor, so that this record is exactly accurate?"

Judge Rathmore looked at Marc, then looked back to Maricyk resignedly. "There do appear to be some marks on the defendant's back. I don't know if they're bruises or what they are . . ."

"Or how they got there," added the District Attorney.

"Or how they got there," repeated the Judge. "However, you have indicated them accurately for the record, Counselor. Put your shirt back on, young man." Judge Rathmore went back to the book, looking up over the edge of the book at Marc as Maricyk put his shirt back on.

"I wish further to note that the defendant's face bears a bruise beneath the left eye, on the cheekbone. It appears to be black and blue."

"Your comments are on the record, Counselor," Judge Rathmore said impatiently. "Now here is the section you referred to. It states that the hearing shall not be adjourned more than twenty-four hours without good cause shown by the District Attorney. Repeat the reason for this delay for the record, Mister District Attorney?"

"This is a serious case where the defendant is accused of attempted bribery of the policeman who is the arresting officer, Your Honor. And the defendant additionally faces a narcotics charge, miscellaneous traffic violations, and resisting arrest. This is a matter that rightly should be presented to a grand jury for indictment and the People are going to present this matter, if time permits, to the grand jury this afternoon," said the District Attorney. He looked to the cop to be sure he knew enough to go directly upstairs to the indictment bureau. The cop nodded.

"I think that's sufficient cause for an adjournment," announced Judge Rathmore. "I'm setting this down for August 16. That should give the People enough time to present this case to the grand jury. You know, Counselor, the People still have rights in courts these days. I think that too often the bleeding hearts and the newspapers forget that. It would be a total waste of time to conduct a hearing here when this matter may be presented to the grand jury today, at which time the defendant will have a hearing before that body."

"The defendant will not be there nor will he be afforded the right to cross-examination or be faced with the witnesses against him," Marc said.

"That's the law, Counselor. You're well versed in the law. You know that," said Judge Rathmore. "I don't make them. I just enforce them. What's that?" the Judge said, turning toward the loud sound of sirens outside the courtroom.

During the last several minutes Marc had heard sirens. But these did not seem unusual in the court area. Now, the sirens seemed to surround the building, growing louder and more demanding.

"Officer," said Judge Rathmore to one of his court officers. "Go out and see what that's all about." The Judge turned back to Marc. "Now do you wish to be heard on bail, Counselor? The District Attorney has indicated that he has no objection to five thousand dollars bail being set."

"Your Honor," Marc said, undeterred by the stone wall this Judge had set up. "The defendant is a man who has never had any conflict with the law in the past. He has roots in the community. He resides with his wife in Manhattan, and has so resided for five years at the same address. There's no reason to believe that the defendant will not show up for the next court appearance. As a matter of fact the defendant is an ex-policeman . . ."

"He surely is an *ex*-policeman," said the District Attorney acidly, "dismissed from the force."

"Your Honor, whatever his difficulties with the Police Department, they were not criminal in nature, and since bail is only required to insure the defendant's appearance, rather than punish or cause preventive detention, I suggest that a more reasonable bail would be five hundred dollars bond or a hundred dollars cash bail."

"These are serious charges," said the Judge, "and the defendant has had disciplinary problems in the past. The fact that he was a policeman speaks poorly for the defendant. He should know better. However, I think that thirty-five hundred dollars bail will be sufficient to protect the people." He smiled at Maricyk.

"Your Honor, may I respectfully suggest that the bail you just set is out of the financial reach of this defendant, he being merely a laborer—temporarily unemployed—without sufficient collateral to post with a bondsman. Even thirty-five hundred dollars is tantamount to no bail at all for this defendant."

"Counselor, you're an eminent counsel in this court. You're high-priced. He's got enough to afford you. And to allegedly bribe policemen. Defendants who go around passing out money so liberally ought to be able to post bond. Remand him. Call the next case." He turned away from Marc, shuffling some papers on his desk.

The crew cut led Maricyk back to the bull pen.

The court officer who had gone out to find out about the sirens came back into court. He had heard that a full-scale riot in The Tombs was in progress. He whispered the news to Charlie the bridge man. Charlie informed the Judges.

"There'll be a five-minute recess," announced Judge Rathmore abruptly. He walked quickly off the bench. Judge Bauer followed. The audience moaned and started to shuffle out of the courtroom.

Marc saw Charlie giving him a covert sign, motioning Marc to the side of the counsel table. Everyone else had already left the well of the courtroom. As Marc walked toward Charlie, he reached into his pocket and put his hand over the two single dollar bills he had folded into a small square. Charlie feigned looking for something. He searched the top of the counsel table, then pulled out one of the drawers. He left the drawer open as he turned and began to look on the judge's dais. Marc, now standing next to the counsel table, dropped the bills into the drawer. Charlie turned, saw the bills, and nudged the drawer shut with his leg. He smiled.

"Thanks, Counselor," said Charlie. "You sure broke old Rathy's balls."

"Didn't do much good," replied Marc.

Charlie shrugged. "Hey, you hear, there's a riot in The Tombs. The place is on fire and everything."

"Is that what all the sirens are for?" asked Marc.

"Yeah, do you believe it? These guys complaining about the room service in The Tombs. What did they think they were going to get, the Waldorf?"

Marc turned and walked out of the courtroom. The noise and the hustle and all the varied people were still filling the corridor outside. A girl with long blond hair and wearing jeans came out of the courtroom. She stood in the corridor close to Marc, talking to several other young people. They had all been in the courtroom. The blonde looked at Marc and smiled. Her smile was wide and bright. She lit a cigarette, then walked toward him.

"You really laid it on that old man," she said, reaching out to shake Marc's hand. Her hand was firm and vigorous.

"Thanks," Marc said absently.

"I'm Andy Roberts," the girl said. "You're one of the few lawyers who really gives it to those decadent judges."

"You know a lot about lawyers?" Marc asked.

"My father's a lawyer. And with all the demonstrating we do and with the hassle that the pigs give us constantly, we get to court quite a lot. You're really tough."

"Thanks."

"Can I have your card?" she asked. "If I get in trouble, I'll call you."

Marc took a card out of his wallet and handed it to the girl. She smiled her pleasant smile again. Marc smiled back. He and Mrs. Maricyk then made their way out to the main corridor.

IV

WEDNESDAY, AUGUST 9, 10:15 A.M.

George Tishler moved at a jog out of his small, partitioned office
on the Mayor's side of City Hall. He was hustling on his suit jacket
as he sped past the battery of secretaries. When he reached the
main corridor, George turned so quickly that he slipped on the
marble floor, almost losing his balance. He regained his footing
halfway to his knees, then continued on rapidly. The plainclothes
policeman on duty at the reception desk nearby was startled from
his crossword puzzle.

"You okay, Mister Tishler?"

Tishler said nothing, other than uttering a mild epithet directed
at the cobbler and the cow that supplied the new leather heels
on his shoes. He slowed down as he reached the door of the Blue
Room.

Ordinarily, George would have been inside the Blue Room right
now, sitting beside Mayor Davies at the press conference called
concerning Monday's Tombs riot. But just as the press conference began, George had to take a telephone call from one of the
money men who were backing the Mayor's re-election campaign.
The Mayor was starting to put together his major campaign
strategies—although to the news media, he continued voicing in-
decision about running—and he wanted to be sure he had enough
money in his war chest. Thus, the Mayor directed the call to
George, thinking that it was more important for George to stoke
the warm fire of good will for a possible fifty-thousand-dollar
pledge than to be in the Blue Room for the start of the conference.

It was just that whim of fate which kept George at his desk to
receive the emergency call from Corrections Commissioner Stein
announcing the grand news that a new and bigger riot had just
broken out in The Tombs.

51

George stopped just outside the door of the Blue Room, buttoned his jacket, straightened his tie, then walked in. Television camera crews filled a small elevated platform across the back of the large room called Blue because of the color of the draperies and rug. Camera lights had the room ablaze in stark blue-whiteness. Filling the chairs from the cameras to the front of the room were a mass of reporters and photographers. Facing all these news hounds from behind a desk, the Mayor was answering a question. A flash of a photographer's camera streaked across the Mayor's face.

"I have appointed a committee of top advisers in the corrections field, the criminal courts field, and all related fields having any bearing on our justice system," the Mayor was saying as George walked toward the desk. "And I have given this committee *carte blanche* to investigate and report to me within the shortest possible time ways to improve even further this city's detention facilities, to speed trial waiting time, and to obtain more reasonable bail for indigent defendants . . ."

George moved quickly behind the long, carved desk. He slid into the empty seat directly next to the Mayor.

". . . I expect to have answers and solutions to this problem almost immediately," the Mayor continued. "So that we can avoid further unfortunate disorders as we experienced Monday at Manhattan House of Detention for Men."

The Mayor glanced about the room to choose the next reporter to bat out a question.

George discreetly touched the Mayor's arm to gain his attention. "Mayor. Hold it up for a minute," he whispered.

The Mayor half-turned toward George. If you were close up and looked carefully, you could see a look of condescending annoyance harden in the Mayor's eyes. The rest of his face, however, remained calm, relaxed.

"Mayor," George Tishler whispered, leaning closer, "we've got another riot in The Tombs."

Now the Mayor turned to Tishler, his eyes widening, searching George's.

George nodded affirmatively.

The Mayor leaned closer to George, wanting to screen out the reporters. "Another riot? How bad?" the Mayor whispered.

"Worse than Monday."

The Mayor turned to the reporters and rose. "Gentlemen. Please excuse me for a moment. Something important has come up. I'll be right back." The Mayor strode toward the door. George was right behind him. They left a room filled with murmuring.

"Who told you?" the Mayor demanded as they moved rapidly across the corridor and into the complex of offices used by the Mayor, the Deputy Mayor, and their covey of secretaries.

"Commissioner Stein just called," George replied.

The Mayor shoved open the door to the Deputy Mayor's office. Deputy Mayor Anthony Lanza, seated at his desk, in shirt sleeves, his tie loose at his neck, was startled by the Mayor's abrupt entrance. He had been reading a letter, dictating notes to a secretary who sat in a chair opposite Lanza's desk.

"Excuse us, Marcy," the Mayor commanded the secretary.

The secretary said nothing. She rose and left the room quickly.

"What the hell's the matter, Scott?" Lanza asked.

"Tell him," the Mayor directed George.

"We've got another riot over in The Tombs," George repeated. "Worse than Monday's."

Lanza stared at George for a moment, letting it sink in. His mouth soured.

The Mayor was angry; he started to pace. "Jesus H. Christ!" His right fist came down into the palm of his left hand. "Is it the eighth floor again?"

"No. The third, fourth, seventh, and ninth," George replied reluctantly. "Stein said they're wrecking the whole place."

Lanza almost pushed his finger through the top of his desk as he pressed the button next to his phone. His secretary's voice answered over an intercom speaker.

"Get Commissioner Stein on the wire right away," Lanza directed. "And hold everything else."

"Four floors now," the Mayor repeated, reeling from the blow. He absently reverted to a nervous habit usually repressed—he began repeatedly to rub the skin under his eyes and across the bridge of his nose.

The intercom buzzed, Lanza pushed the button on his desk and listened.

"Commissioner Stein isn't in his office," the secretary's voice announced to the room. "He's gone to The Tombs personally."

"Well, tell them to find him and have him call me immediately," Lanza directed. "Immediately! He told you four floors, George?"

"That's what he said. They're wrecking four floors. I have no idea if they have hostages or what the hell's going on."

"George, go into the goddamn Blue Room and tell the reporters what the hell's going on," the Mayor directed painfully. "They'll know in a few minutes anyway. Tell them, under the circumstances, we'll have to check this out before we continue the conference."

"Right, Mayor." George turned and left hurriedly.

The Mayor slumped into the chair on which the secretary had been seated. He and Lanza looked at each other blankly for a moment.

"Goddamn it," the Mayor shouted. He stood up so quickly that he knocked over the chair on which he had been seated.

"Take it easy, Scott," said Lanza.

"Take it easy? Take it easy? The place is coming down around our ears, more each day, and you tell me to take it easy." The Mayor paced two yards and turned back. "And it couldn't happen at a worse time. Westom, Wesson . . . just called about his campaign contribution."

"Wescomb," Lanza corrected.

"Wescomb, Wesson, whatever the hell it is. He just called. George spoke to him. Christ, we can't afford to have any more of this shit. Not now. Not with the campaign looming up. We have to keep Wesson on the bandwagon."

George returned, closing the door behind him.

"What happened?" the Mayor asked.

"Half of them were gone already," replied George. "The other half didn't even wait for me to finish speaking."

"That's what I mean," the Mayor turned to Lanza. "They'll have a field day on this. Especially people like that bastard Dworkin across the hall. With his law-and-order pitch, he'll have plenty of new ammunition to start throwing at the conservative homeowners in Queens and Brooklyn."

"You want me to go over to The Tombs, Mayor?" asked George.

The Mayor thought, then nodded. "Since you worked out the

settlement with the inmates on the eighth floor the other day, these bastards'll probably be looking for you to give you their goddamn demands too."

"They'll probably have a few more by now," added Lanza.

"Maybe they'll want two desserts," George added lightly.

The Mayor was only half listening; he was apparently absorbed in something else. His face was stern, tinged with a look of hurt. "And after we gave them more contact and dialogue than inmates have received anywhere else in the country. I simply don't understand what the hell is wrong now."

"Maybe the other floors just want to vent their spleen, have their say," suggested Lanza. "From the information George got, the eighth floor hasn't even taken part in this one. They must be satisfied from Monday."

"The rest of the inmates didn't imagine we were just going to take care of the eighth floor and not bother about the other floors, did they?" wondered the Mayor.

George shrugged. "That doesn't make any sense."

"Not to me either," agreed the Mayor. "But then neither does the whole blasted riot. But I tell you this, George, I want the whole damn problem cleared up, and I want it cleared up quick." The Mayor speared the air with his index finger. "We can't afford this kind of image smeared all over the headlines. Not at this time."

"It may not be as bad as all that," consoled Lanza. The Mayor turned to him. "Remember the polls; there's a law-and-order wave that's sweeping the City," Lanza continued. "The people in Queens, Brooklyn, and Staten Island won't hold it against you that prisoners aren't getting filet mignon and two desserts in the jails."

"But chaos and inefficiency . . ." George started to add.

"Chaos and inefficiency?" demanded the Mayor, whirling. "Where the hell did that come from? Chaos? Inefficiency?"

"That's what the prisoners were griping about the other day, Mayor," George explained hastily. "No bail, no trials, just rotting in The Tombs for months on end before they get to court. And the courts are backlogged and log jammed, they say. That's what they emphasized most in their demands the other day. Speedier trials."

"Is what they say true, George?" the Mayor asked. "Are the courts inefficient? Are those judges I appoint just sitting on their asses, doing nothing?" The Mayor walked across the room and turned Lanza's air conditioner higher. He gazed out at the trees hanging limp in the heat. "The other day when we swore in Broder, Brauder . . ."

"Bauer," George suggested.

"What the hell's the difference?" the Mayor said impatiently. "You know who the hell I mean. When we swore him in everybody was making grand speeches about how well the courts are doing, how many cases they're moving. Are they all playing with themselves? And with me?"

"Not from the reports I get each week, Mayor," George replied. "It's all been fine up to now."

"Are you on top of this, George?" the Mayor asked pointedly. "I mean do you really keep on top of it? Do you really know what's going on?"

"Yes, Mayor, I am," George said firmly. "There is a great backlog of cases, Mayor. But there are lots of, thousands more, arrests each year than the year before. We . . . the whole country," he added quickly, "is in the midst of a crime wave. We just don't have enough courts, enough judges . . ."

"Enough money," the Mayor added flatly. "If the Federal Government would only give us the additional money we need. That bastard in the White House. He's orchestrating the whole thing to make himself appear like Saint George coming to the rescue. We're the ones who have to cope with the riots. To the Government in Washington, this is merely an exercise in theory, in sociology. But to the people in the city, it's a crisis; it's a wave of terror sweeping down from the rooftops." The Mayor obviously liked the tone of what he had just said. He searched for the next phrase, as if listening for a new sound. Tishler and Lanza just waited.

The buzzer on Lanza's desk sounded.

"I told you to hold everything," Lanza said firmly as he touched the intercom button.

"The Tombs is on fire now," the secretary's voice blurted out.

The Mayor's speech stuck in his throat as he was gesturing broadly. "On fire?" He turned, his arm still out in the air. "On

56

fire? George, get your ass over there right now, and get the god-damn thing settled before we're on the front page of every news-paper and magazine in the country. Jesus H. Christ," he said, pounding his palm again. "George, get the damn thing settled fast."

"Yes, Mayor." George started for the door.

"Wait a minute, George," the Mayor called.

"Yes, Mayor?"

"When you get back here, George, I want you to start an investi-gation of those judges, The Tombs, the whole goddamn court-house. I want you to shake our whole justice system by the neck until it cries uncle. Get the damn thing working properly, effi-ciently. I want records kept of everything. And I want it done quickly."

"We already have records on every detail of operation, Mayor," replied George.

"Well, then the record keepers are covering up for the judges, and the clerks, and the court officers. Something's got to be wrong, George. The records we get say everything is peachy, and mean-while, obviously, the jails are busting at the seams and the cases aren't moving."

"If I can make a suggestion, Mayor," said Lanza.

The Mayor nodded.

"What we need is somebody over there that nobody would even suspect is working with us. Someone who could give us the real lowdown, the true picture."

George nodded. "That's a possibility."

"It's a good suggestion, Tony," said the Mayor. "We need a spy. Somebody in the courthouse that no one will suspect. Some-body who can pass."

"A court officer?" suggested George. "A clerk?"

"No," said Lanza, shaking his head. "Their movements would be too confined. Officers and clerks have to stay in one place, one courtroom."

They were each silent as they thought of possible spies.

"How about a lawyer," suggested Lanza. "Someone who handles criminal cases, who's there every day, who can be all over the place and look normal, natural."

"A criminal lawyer. Excellent," agreed the Mayor, pointing an index finger at Lanza. "A criminal lawyer can go everywhere . . . into the courts, into the jails, into every phase of the criminal justice system. Who do we know?"

They each thought again silently.

"I know a tremendous criminal lawyer, Mayor," said George. "A guy I went to law school with. I don't know if he'd be interested in the job."

"Who is it?" asked the Mayor.

"A fellow named Marc Conte," George replied. "He represents all kinds of criminals, rich ones, poor ones. And he must know his stuff. He represents some of the biggest organized-crime figures: Gianni Aquilino, Action Townes."

"Christ, I tell you I want a lawyer that knows the criminal law, and you suggest one who represents notorious gangsters. For Christ's sake, he sounds like he's almost part of organized crime himself."

"Not at all, Mayor," replied George defensively. "He represents plenty of indigent defendants on court assignment. He represents the very sort of people who are involved in the riots. He knows the courts, the defendants, the whole thing."

"But his connection with organized crime," the Mayor said skeptically.

"Mayor, this guy's got the highest integrity. We've already had him checked out," said George. "He came out clean."

"When was that?" The Mayor sat again, crossing one leg over the other.

"When you wanted to appoint an Italian commissioner to replace Allan Weinberg in Markets," said Tishler.

The Mayor looked up sharply, his legs uncrossing. "Don't even mention that bastard's name. Did he get sentenced yet?"

"Next week, Mayor," replied George.

"All of them?" the Mayor inquired further, referring to Francis X. McCarthy, a former Democratic congressman, and Eugene Scally, a reputed racketeer, both of whom, together with former Commissioner Weinberg, went on trial for bribery and conspiracy. All were convicted.

George nodded. "All of them."

The Mayor's grave look began to ease.

"George is right," agreed Lanza. "When you wanted an Italian commissioner, I remember interviewing him. Nice guy."

"Who did the checking on this lawyer Marco Polo, or whatever the hell the name is you just mentioned, George?" asked the Mayor.

"Marc Conte, Mayor," George corrected. "Our police department checked him out. And so did the FBI."

"And you remember this fellow?" the Mayor asked, turning to Lanza.

"Yes, Mayor. He came up clean, as I remember. He's apparently just a defense lawyer who does a good job, and some big-time people use him."

"Why the hell didn't we appoint him then? We still need an Italian commissioner, an Italian judge, an Italian something. George Tucci's on my back about a goddamned Italian every time I see him at one of the political dinners. We have to appoint an Italian to something soon, Tony," the Mayor urged. "Otherwise, we're going to blow the whole Italian community."

"I know," replied Lanza. "And Tucci is the man we need to carry Brooklyn."

"So why the hell didn't we appoint this guy a commissioner, if he's so good then? We need Brooklyn to carry the city."

"Remember, Matty Slavin in the Bronx recommended one of his men, Frank Deely, and we made a deal with Slavin in exchange for him going with us on the two Supreme Court judgeships at the Judicial Convention."

"Right, right," agreed the Mayor, remembering. "You think this lawyer of George's can help us out, Tony?"

"I think so, Mayor. From what we know, he's a good criminal lawyer. He really knows his way around the criminal courts."

"Representing the people he does, I can imagine," replied the Mayor. "Okay, George, let's bring this fellow in. And if he turns out okay, maybe we can appoint him a judge. He's Italian isn't . . . On fire!! Jesus H. Christ. We're standing here talking and The Tombs is on fire. George, what the hell is holding you?"

"I'm gone, Mayor," George said, moving quickly out of the office.

"Tony," the Mayor said, turning to Lanza. "Will you get me an Italian so I can make him something?"

"I'm looking, Mayor. I'm looking."

The Mayor nodded. "Well, get one soon. Election is coming up and I don't want your *paisanos* saying I appointed an Italian just to get their vote."

V

THURSDAY, AUGUST 10, 11:05 A.M.

Marc stood quietly at the counsel table, watching Judge Anthony T. Jennings of the Federal District Court for the Eastern District of New York (which includes and is located in Brooklyn), intermittently read from a report before him on the bench and extemporize as he addressed Pasquale Pellegrino, the defendant who stood next to Marc. Pellegrino was also known as Patsy the Crusher.

The Crusher was tall and broad, with large, sinewy arms and hands which, as a youth, had earned him his *nom de guerre*. His hair was styled forward to cover impending baldness. When The Crusher spoke, his voice rasped out the New York accent. He was modishly dressed in a patterned knit suit and ankle-high, laced boots.

"Oh, I remember your client well, Counselor," said the Judge, a smile creasing his face momentarily. "The trial before me that ended in his conviction lasted, mmm, was it three weeks, Mister Malone?" The Judge looked toward the assistant United States Attorney, who stood at the prosecutor's table.

"Exactly," replied Michael Malone, formerly of the FBI, who wore a dark blue, two-button suit and short-cropped hair. He looked toward Pellegrino contemptuously.

"I thought that's what it was." The Judge nodded, smiling. "I remember it very well. And I remember your client very well, too," the Judge said, now returning to Marc. "Four years, I thought at the time of sentence was very lenient. Very minimal, under the circumstances. And I permitted you to have bail pending an appeal too." The Judge spoke directly to Pellegrino now. "Very liberal, if I do say so. But, instead of behaving yourself while that appeal is pending, instead of staying out of trouble, you have to start throwing your weight around." The Judge was grave now.

A man in a brown suit entered the courtroom through a door cut into the paneled wall to the left of the judge's bench. He tiptoed up the steps to the dais. The Judge turned, and the man whispered something.

"Gentlemen, will you excuse me for a few short moments," said the Judge, rising, gathering his robes about himself.

"All rise. The court will take a brief recess," intoned the clerk, who sat at a lower desk directly in front of the judge's bench.

The Judge disappeared through the paneled door.

"His bookie must want him on the phone," rasped The Crusher loudly, smiling as he turned to Marc.

"Just take it easy, Patsy," Marc cautioned. "He's right now making his decision whether to revoke your bail and put you in jail or not. I think he may rule in your favor, so don't antagonize him. You seem to have antagonized Malone already. He glares at you as if you two have a personal vendetta going."

"Ahh, that's his tough shit," dismissed The Crusher with a shrug. "He's still pissed off because of that interview he gave me when I first got arrested, before I went to trial on this case."

"What interview was that?" Marc asked. "Remember, I didn't handle your trial. I only came into your case on the appeal."

"That's right. You weren't handling my case then, Counselor," recalled The Crusher. "I wish you had. Anyway, this Malone has the FBI bring me to his office when I first got arrested. And he starts the regular United States Attorney bullshit routine on me, you know? All the U.S. Attorneys got their directions from Washington to ask guys they think are connected with organized crime about co-operation. Co-operate against the mob and get a break for yourself," The Crusher explained.

"Now you know there's no way I'm going to rat out *anybody*, I don't care who it is. Even I don't know the guy," The Crusher continued proudly. "But this Malone gives it a shot anyway. And me, I make like John the Gom, like I don't even know what he's talking about, you know? And he tells me, *you know Patsy, this is a serious charge, but you don't have to take all the weight here, you can make it easy on yourself.*

"And I say, *oh, really, Mister Malone, how's that?* Like I don't know what he's going to tell me. And then he says to me, *well, if you co-operate with the Government, maybe give us information concerning organized crime, I can help you with the charges pending against you, maybe get you a good plea, and talk to the sentencing judge, help you get a light sentence.* So I say, *yeah, really, Mister Malone?*" The Crusher started to laugh. "Counselor, you should have been there, you would have pissed in your pants."

"What happened then?" Marc asked.

"So I say, *really Mister Malone,*" The Crusher continued, "and he says, *that's right, Patsy.* So, I say, *in that case, sure I'll co-operate, Mister Malone.* And he gets all excited, you know. He figures he's about to make a good score. And I say, *sure I'll co-operate. I'll tell you all about it. I remember it was a Tuesday, Mister Malone. And I went to your mother's house and threw her a mean fuck. Not bad either. And then I bagged your sister, but she was on her monthlies, so she only gave me a blow job . . .*"

The Crusher started to bend double with laughter at this point of his remembrance. He began to stamp his foot with glee. "This Malone went crazy, Counselor," The Crusher sputtered through his laughter. "You know how they never get angry; they try to get *you* angry, so maybe you'll say something by mistake. Well, this guy went crazy. He jumped up behind his desk, his face went purple, and he screamed for the marshals. *Get this guy out of here,* he screamed. *Get him out of here!*" The Crusher clapped his hands together in delight. "*Monaga madon,* he went crazy."

Marc shook his head in wonder, captivated by the sheer boldness of The Crusher to do or say something like that after just being arrested. It was no wonder that Malone hated him, that the FBI agents hated him. He wasn't playing the good guy-bad guy game properly. He had no proper respect for the authorities or the righteousness of their cause.

Judge Jennings returned to the courtroom and took the bench. The Crusher calmed himself, letting the smile fade from his face.

"All rise," intoned the clerk.

"Sorry, gentlemen," said the Judge, "now where were we? Oh,

yes, Mister Pellegrino, we were just extolling your many virtues. And trying to decide whether the United States Government and the people of New York would be in less danger if you were behind bars. Now let me see." The Judge swiveled on his chair and began again to read from the papers before him. "Ah, yes, you started throwing your weight around on the picket-line demonstrations with the Italian-American Freedom Council. Isn't that the group controlled by the notorious Phil Compagna's crime family?" The Judge looked to Marc.

"I do not represent the Italian-American Freedom Council, Your Honor," replied Marc. "I can't answer for it, nor, therefore, am I in a position to give the Court any information concerning its internal make-up."

"Oh, come, come, Counselor," scoffed the Judge. "Everyone knows that Boss Compagna is behind the Council. It's splashed on every front page in the city."

"May I respectfully suggest to Your Honor that I would not rely on information printed in newspapers in order to answer Your Honor's questions."

"I appreciate that, Counselor," said the Judge. He smiled. "However, the Italian community would be better served if they chose a representative other than someone of the notorious organized crime reputation of Boss Compagna. And I know of what I speak, Mister Conte, about the Italian community. *Sono mezzo Italiano, mezzo Irlandese.* My mother was Irish."

The Crusher bent slightly toward Marc, whispering softly, "The rat son of a bitch. He changed his good Italian name. The Italian blood oughta curdle in his veins."

Marc stilled The Crusher with a stern glance.

"I feel however," the Judge continued from the bench, "that it is unfortunate that the Government was not able to produce more compelling evidence showing the defendant's terrorizing of the workers at the *Brooklyn Home News* while he picketed for the Italian Freedom Council. If they had, I assure you, Mister Pellegrino, I'd have you hauled off to jail so fast your head would spin. But I haven't been shown enough here, unfortunately, I say again," the Judge looked at Malone now, "to revoke Mister Pellegrino's bail and remand him to jail."

The Crusher nudged Marc softly with his elbow.

"If the Judge sees you screwing around he'll change his mind," Marc admonished The Crusher in a whisper.

"But I do want to comment on one thing," Judge Jennings continued. "And that is the fact that your client is an indigent before this Court, Counselor. That is, he allegedly doesn't have sufficient money to pay a lawyer; thus the United States Government is going to pay you. Is that correct, Counselor?"

"As I understand it, yes, Your Honor."

"Did not this defendant sign a pauper's oath, and the United States Government agree to assign and compensate you for his defense?" the Judge repeated in wonder.

"Yes, Your Honor."

The Judge shook his head. "You know, Counselor, I remember your client very well when he was on trial. He was the best-dressed defendant ever in my courtroom." The Judge looked at The Crusher appraisingly. "He still is. Dresses very sharply. A little loud and too mod for my taste, perhaps. And expensive, I might add. And he lives in a marvelous house in Long Beach, or someplace like that." The Judge leafed through the papers before him. "I have that probation report here somewhere. Ahh, here it is. Yes, Long Beach, an eighty-five-thousand-dollar house. And he has a caretaker come in twice a week. Oh, I know, he says his brother-in-law owns the house and he only pays his brother-in-law rent."

"And I owe him two months' back rent," The Crusher whispered from the side of his mouth.

Marc ignored him.

"He lives in all this affluence and he doesn't even have a job. Does your client have a job, Counselor?" The Judge looked up. "No, I don't imagine that he does," said the Judge, without waiting for a reply. "You know, Counselor, and by the way, I'm not blaming you for anything, or in any way implying any wrongdoing on your part by my remarks."

"I appreciate that, Your Honor."

"But it's a crime, I mean literally, a crime, that someone like this defendant of yours has to be supported by the United States Government, his attorney paid for, when he's a bum, a bum! I mean that. A man whose money is made illegitimately, who supports himself with a life of crime. Look at this record. Just look at it," the Judge said, lifting several teletyped pages. "In 1944—that would make this man twenty years old at the time—rape."

"I was in the Army," The Crusher whispered to Marc. "This dame and me went out on a weekend and had some kicks. Then her mother got angry 'cause we stayed out all night and she called the cops. That wasn't no rape."

"And then Assault and Robbery, 1946," continued the Judge. "And another Assault and Robbery, 1948." The Judge flung the papers to his desk angrily. "Mister Pellegrino, you're a bum. It's an absolute disgrace that you are permitted the farcical position of being a pauper before this Court. Who knows why? And it's a further outrage that you're permitted to be one of the leading members of the Italian-American Freedom Council and picket in the name of justice and liberty. I imagine you're participating in the Italian-American Freedom Council rally at Columbus Circle next Monday?"

The Crusher looked to Marc.

"You can answer."

"I sure am, Your Honor. And being now that you're Italian, half Italian anyway, you ought to be there too." He smiled boldly. "I'll get you on the stage for a speech."

The Judge chuckled. "I'm not sure a lot of the people in the Freedom Council would want to see me there. I probably put many of them in jail."

"There'll be a lot of big stars there, Your Honor, important people like yourself," Pellegrino added. Marc recognized the jocular tone rising in The Crusher's voice.

"Can it, Patsy," Marc said softly but sharply.

The Crusher stifled a grin.

"Your Honor," said Malone, "may I suggest, that it's exactly because of the defendant's long record, as well as the proof adduced at this hearing, that the Government contends that the defendant is a danger to the community, and should therefore have his bail forfeited."

"Look at that Irish punk," said The Crusher, glaring at Malone. "I'd like to step on his face." The Crusher saw Marc's face. "Okay, Counselor, okay. I'll take it easy. I gotta admit, you're a tough guy, Counselor."

"I'm well aware of the defendant's record, Mister Malone," said the Judge. "I was aware of that selfsame record when I let him out on bail after I sentenced him. After all, even Mister Pellegrino is entitled to the protections of the Constitution, and a chance to pursue his legal remedies."

"Thank you, Your Honor," said The Crusher.

"Oh, I'm not doing it for you, Mister Pellegrino, believe me," the Judge emphasized. "It's the law, and it applies equally to all men before this bar. Wait," said the Judge suddenly. "I'm just thinking of another mysterious aspect of this defendant's status before this Court. How can an indigent post ten thousand dollars bail? There are plenty of indigents in our jails who can't post a thousand dollars. And here's a defendant, supposedly indigent, and he posts ten thousand. Have you spent the time, Mister Malone, to check out the validity of Mister Pellegrino's indigence?"

Marc thought of Joey Maricyk back in The Tombs, who wasn't indigent, who hovered in that category of being employed and earning a living, but not sufficiently propertied to post a bond.

"We did, Your Honor," replied Malone. "It seems his brother-in-law and another person, a friend, signed as sureties on Mister Pellegrino's bond. They vouched to forfeit ten thousand dollars if the defendant did not appear in court. It isn't the defendant's money or credit that has been posted on bail, Your Honor. At least not that we can prove."

"This is an outrage," said the Court. "But I don't imagine we can force a person to pay a lawyer's fee for someone else. People can still spend their assets any way they see fit. It's too bad they don't see fit to pay the fee rather than the bail. One of these days, Mister Pellegrino, this merry-go-round will stop."

Pellegrino stood with his hands clasped behind his back, a blank look on his face.

"However, the question before me now is simply, did Mister Pellegrino forfeit the right to that bail as a result of his subsequent picketing activities? Unfortunately, and, at the risk of repetition, I repeat that, unfortunately, the record is totally insufficient as it stands to show he is a danger to the community." The Judge looked at Malone. "That's how I see it, Mister Malone. That's my ruling. Petition denied."

Malone glanced at The Crusher fiercely, then silently gathered the papers on the table before him.

"There being no further business before this court, this court stands in recess. All rise," said the clerk as the Judge left the bench.

"Holy shit," exclaimed The Crusher. He was elated, smiling as he turned to friends sitting in the courtroom. There were several men and a couple of women all smiling, waiting for The Crusher. "You were beautiful, Counselor," said The Crusher, wrapping his arms around Marc and squeezing him tightly.

Marc let out a half-feigned moan as The Crusher's arms enclosed him.

"You were fabulous. You're the greatest," The Crusher persisted as he put his arm around Marc's shoulder. They started to walk out of the well of the court.

One of the men waiting at the railing for The Crusher, a swarthy, chunky, dark-haired man with a bulbous nose and a heavy five o'clock shadow, handed The Crusher a diamond watch and a platinum star sapphire ring. The Crusher had taken them off before the proceedings, not wanting to flaunt his jewelry before the Court, and also in preparation for being remanded to jail.

Marc glanced toward the back of the courtroom and noticed George Tishler sitting in one of the audience benches. George smiled as Marc saw him. Marc moved toward George.

"Still batting them out, eh, Marc?" George smiled broadly, reaching out to shake Marc's hand.

"What the hell are you doing here?" Marc asked, grasping George's hand.

"Just came to see the great Conte at work."

"Counselor," interrupted The Crusher as he and his retinue moved toward the rear of the courtroom. "We're going downstairs. You want us to wait for you?" The Crusher held the door open as he spoke to Marc.

"No, that's okay, Patsy," said Marc. "I'll talk to you later."

"Okay. Hey, listen, don't forget to come up to the rally at Columbus Circle Monday. We'll all be there. Philly'll be there. Come on up, we'll have some laughs."

"I doubt that I can make it," said Marc. "I'm going sailing this weekend. I won't be back until Monday some time, so I may not be able to make the rally at all."

George stood silently next to Marc.

"Not make the rally?" exclaimed The Crusher. "What a time

you're gonna miss. You can go sailing any time, Counselor. But this rally is going to be fabulous. A real show of strength. There's gonna be a hundred thousand people there to show those FBI bastards they can't walk all over innocent people, women, kids. They want to arrest us, if we do something, fine. But following our kids into school; following our wives into church. That's rat-bastard bullshit, if you pardon my French," The Crusher said to George.

George smiled and nodded.

"I'll try and make it if I get back in time," Marc deferred, knowing he wouldn't.

"Yeah, make one of your courtroom speeches on the deck of your boat." The Crusher began to laugh. "You'll breeze all the way in on the hot air. I'm only kidding, Counselor. Hey, listen, you oughta invite me on your boat. I'll bring some 'sangwiches'—provolone, salami, capacullo, wine, the works. Just tell me when. And listen"—he mugged for George's benefit now—"if you ever need your boat sunk for the insurance, I got just the guy for you." He laughed boisterously and left the courtroom.

"Your client, sir, is a complete madman," said George, watching the large doors to the courtroom close behind The Crusher. "That's going to be quite a rally," he added.

"Compagna is doing a job," said Marc. "He's going to build a hospital; he's already raised the money. He's even opening a camp for kids—all kids, all races and religions, and all that."

"He is doing good work," admitted George. "It's too bad Compagna has such a bad reputation. And people like your client here definitely do not help their cause."

"He's just a big kid," said Marc.

"I wouldn't want to meet that kid in an alley, day or night," said George.

"Neither would I," agreed Marc. "Come on, now, tell me why the hell you're here and not in City Hall running the city."

"I came to see you, of course," George replied. "I need your help on something."

"You name it, you got it," said Marc. "Come on, I'm going to meet Maria for lunch. We'll go to Ponte's. Join us."

"That sounds great. I haven't seen that lovely and groovy wife-

68

lady in ages," said George. "And besides life is beautiful, the food at Ponte's is great." George was now reciting a motto from the top of Ponte's blackboard menu.

They both laughed as they left the courthouse.

VI

THURSDAY, AUGUST 10, 1:05 P.M.

Marc and George Tishler stood alone at the long, dark, quiet bar in Ponte's Restaurant. Each held a tall vodka and tonic filled to the brim with ice. Maria had just excused herself to go to the powder room. At the far end of the bar, the bartender was talking softly with three customers. Somehow, the dimness of the bar, bathed in the cool of the air conditioner, and the chilled glasses of vodka and tonic helped Marc and George forget the humid dog days pitilessly lying in wait just beyond the front entrance.

"You really going sailing for the weekend?" George asked. He lifted his drink toward Marc, then sipped.

"As soon as I finish a couple of little things in the office after lunch," Marc replied, lifting his glass to return George's *salute*. He too sipped. "Franco's already on the boat getting it rigged out."

"Who's Franco?"

"He's our man Friday," Marc replied. "He was a client I got out of trouble. He had no family of his own, no relatives, so Maria and I sort of adopted him into our family. He drives the car, sails the boat, keeps the house in order."

"He live with you?"

Marc nodded as he took a long drink from his glass.

George drank again. "That's the life. All weekend sailing. You won't be back before Monday?"

"No."

The maître d' walked over to them. "We're ready any time you are, Mister Conte."

"In a few minutes, Ruggierio," said Marc.

"Now that you two decadent people have induced a public servant who usually grabs a ham on rye at his desk to this den of luxury, I'm dying to order something fantastic," said George.

"You won't be disappointed," said Marc. "Here's Maria now."

Maria was tall, dark-haired, and beautiful in an exotic way. Her body was lithe, with firm breasts and taut buttocks and legs. She wore a beige pants suit and her hair was back and off her neck. She had small gold hoops through the lobes of her pierced ears. Maria smiled widely as she reached the two of them.

"With a smile like that, I don't even mind waiting," said George.

"You want to go in?" said Marc. "I'll have them send the drinks to the table."

"Don't bother about mine," said George, draining his glass.

Marc did the same.

"That solves that problem," said Maria. She reached out and held Marc's hand as they walked through the passage to the dining room.

The maître d' showed them to a banquette against the wall in the first room. About three quarters of the tables were filled. It was still a little early for the Friday lunch crowd. The room was dim, decorated in reds, with paintings hung every few feet on the walls.

"Hello, boss," said one of the captains, smiling as he approached. "Hello, Mrs. Boss."

"Hello, Romano," said Maria.

"A bottle of red wine okay with you, George?" Marc asked. "Sure."

"The usual?" the captain asked. Marc nodded. "Thank you, sir."

"You look great," George said to Maria.

"Thanks."

"And that outfit looks fantastic on you," he added.

"Thanks again, George."

"Are you trying to turn Maria's head?" chided Marc.

"I wish I could. I told you I don't know what she sees in you, anyway."

"I do," she said, her hand touching the back of Marc's head.

"There, that ought to put you in your place," said Marc.

"I'm put in my place."

The wine arrived, and the captain poured a small amount into Marc's glass. He tasted it and nodded. The captain poured wine for all of them.

"How's your teaching job going?" George asked.

"Great, just great," replied Maria.

"She's doing an amazing job," said Marc, "even if she won't say so herself. She takes these kids from deprived backgrounds, mostly Puerto Rican and some Black—her school is in East Harlem— they can hardly communicate when she gets them. They can't even speak in sentences."

"Their parents probably can't either," said George.

"That's exactly right," said Maria. "A couple of years ago, these kids would have been considered retarded or stunted. Now, we take them at pre-school age and prepare them to go to school, teach them a little, make them comfortable by bringing them into our world a little."

Marc smiled as he watched Maria talk.

"It sounds good," said George.

They sipped their wine silently for a moment.

"Where did you get it?" George asked Maria. "The great outfit, I mean."

"Marc and I found it in Saks."

"You two still buy all your clothes together?" asked George.

"The only way to do it," said Marc.

"I can just see me telling Phyllis that we should go shopping for her clothes together. My clothes, she doesn't mind helping me buy. But her clothes. She'd tell me to take the air."

"She's missing out on a lot of fun, George. So are you," said Maria sipping her wine.

"I am?"

"Sure. I love Marc and the most fun I get out of life is making him happy," she said. "The happier I make him, the happier I am. And since he feels the same way I do, he wants to make me happy. You see, we get twice as much happiness this way. Remember, loving is giving, George, never taking."

"That's a nice theory, Maria," said George. "But it doesn't seem to be too popular among the adult population. Do you think people are really able to do that—just give? I mean, it's like opening yourself up to get kicked in the teeth."

"Being in love does mean opening up and being very vulnerable," Maria agreed. "But the person who loves you in turn doesn't want to take advantage or take anything. They go out of their way not to hurt. And you do the same. So you end up neither hurting or being hurt."

George looked to Marc, then back to Maria skeptically.

"It's really easy, George," assured Maria. "There are so many things in the world—so many everything, that I can easily find something that both Marc and I like or enjoy. Why choose anything that doesn't make both of us happy? Take clothes, or shoes, for instance. There are so many pairs of shoes in a shoe store. Suppose we're looking for shoes, and I see a pair I like. And Marc tells me he doesn't like them. I don't buy them. We keep looking, and then he sees a pair of shoes he likes. And I don't like them. We still keep looking. Eventually, we'll find a pair of shoes that we're both happy with and buy them. That's giving to each other, George."

"But then your theory requires taking," said George. "You take your partner's love, don't you?"

"No, you're making them happy by being gracious enough to accept the love they extend to you. That's still giving to them."

"I'll tell my wife," said George. "I can also tell you what she'll tell me to do."

"That's enough psychology," Marc said. "How about lunch?" He signaled the captain, who rolled the blackboard menu to their table.

"What should I order?" George asked.

"Try the calamari and shrimp casserole," Marc suggested.

"What is it?"

"Trust us on this, George," Maria smiled.

"Oh, it's one of those things I shouldn't ask about until after I've tasted it?"

"That's it," Maria smiled. "I'm having the same."

"Me too," said Marc.

"That's good enough for me," said George.

The captain noted their order and left.

George looked around the room. Maria and Marc sipped their wine, table watching for a moment. The room was full by now. Marc noticed Judge Feld from the Supreme Court standing at

72

the maître d's desk, waiting for a table. To those who didn't know he was a judge, he looked just like any other person waiting for a table. All those accouterments of the bench, the court officers, the robe, the official importance which create a world of pomp were gone. The Judge had to leave them behind when he ventured into the rest of the world. Marc thought Feld looked uncomfortable being treated like a mere mortal.

"Captain," Marc said softly.

"Yes, sir?"

"That man over there at the desk—gray hair, dark suit."

The captain looked. "Yes, sir."

"He's a judge and a friend of mine. Tell Ruggierio to make a fuss over him. Get him a table."

The captain nodded and walked to the desk. He whispered to Ruggierio, the maître d'. Ruggierio walked to Judge Feld and extended a gracious greeting, apologizing for keeping the Judge waiting. The Judge beamed and felt more comfortable now. The maître d' began to lead them to a table near Marc and the others.

"Hello, Judge," said George rising. Marc rose too. They all shook hands.

"Gentlemen," he said. He nodded to Maria. He was vital again. "Didn't know you fellows came here too. Business must be good at City Hall."

"Always busy, Judge," said George.

They all smiled pleasantly again. Ruggierio showed the Judge to a table.

Marc, George, and Maria settled back waiting for their lunch. "As long as I'm going to spend the city's money and pick up the tab, we might as well talk a little business," George said.

"Who says you're going to pick up the check?" asked Marc.

"That wouldn't be fair otherwise," said George.

"Who said anything about being fair?"

"A fine thing. I ask you to lunch, and you pick up the tab."

"One good turn deserves another, George," said Maria.

George smiled. "Well, how about it?" he asked Marc. "Do you think you'll have time to do some discreet snooping in the courts for the Mayor?"

Maria looked to Marc.

"I'll do it for you, if you want, George," Marc replied.

"I do."

"Only don't expect me to do any in-depth statistical analysis or anything. I'll just be able to tell you about individual cases and situations, point you in the right direction perhaps."

"That's exactly what we want, Marc," said George. "You give the Mayor the leads, and he'll follow them up."

Marc looked at George skeptically.

"He will, Marc, he will. You don't know this Mayor," George assured him. "He's really a very progressive guy."

Marc poured some wine, then leaned forward, his elbows on the table.

"George, the Mayor's a politician, and politicians are only interested in what the voters are interested in. And the voters, the general public, hardly cares about defendants' rights. That is, until one of their kids or someone they know is arrested."

"The public isn't as cold as that," George said.

"They're not cold," said Marc. "They're afraid. They read all the sensational stories in the papers, and get so scared they want to destroy every hint, every mention of crime, including the defendants."

"I really don't think that's true, Marc," said George.

"No? Go into court as a defendant—even if you're innocent—and see how you'll be treated. Look at the laws, and how the courts apply them; see if even the Legislature permits a defendant the means to protect himself."

"You're not saying what all these hippie demonstrators say, that the system is evil, fascistic, are you?" George asked.

"Not at all," Marc replied. "But it's an uphill struggle just to defend yourself from the moment you're arrested. It shouldn't be stacked against the defendant that way."

"How is it stacked, as you say?" pressed George.

"Take the start of a case, the preliminary hearing to determine if a crime has been committed," said Marc. "The Legislature gives a defendant the right to a hearing within a certain number of hours or days. That's only theoretical, however. Practically speaking, when a judge refuses to give a defendant his hearing, which happens twenty times a day in 100 Centre Street alone, what can the defendant do about it? The Legislature hasn't provided a way of enforcing the law until an appeal after the trial, after the whole

74

case is over. But, it's too late then. So why does the Legislature go through the motions of making laws that have no teeth?"

George was silent.

"How about the way we send people to jail, George," Marc continued. "Why do we send a person to jail who's committed a non-violent crime for the first time? No question about it, he committed a crime without violence, say embezzlement, a stock fraud, income tax evasion. And he has no previous criminal history whatsoever. Why do we send him to jail?"

"The classic answer is to rehabilitate him," said George, with a shrug.

Maria sipped her wine, quietly listening.

"Penologists have been saying for years that in the first place, jails are not rehabilitating," Marc countered. "Second, it's a known fact that more than sixty-five per cent of the people who commit a crime for the first time will never commit another crime whether you give them one day, one year, or ten years in jail. They learn their lesson right off the bat. And the other thirty-five per cent if you give them one year, or ten years, or twenty years in jail, they'll commit a crime the first chance they get when they get out, no matter what. So how does a judge know to which side, which percentage group, a defendant who's never been in trouble before is going to fall? Why not put all non-violent first offenders on probation? If they step across the line and violate probation, even once, they can always be sent away for the full time they should have gotten in the first place."

"Sounds reasonable," said George. "But it takes time to change traditions and old principles." George thought for a moment. "The Mayor's the right guy to do it, though, Marc."

"Why then are there so many mayorally appointed judges who act like D.A.s with black robes on?" asked Marc.

"This guy never stops, does he?" George said to Maria lightly. She smiled. "You ought to know that by this time, George."

"Okay, put this in your pipe and smoke it," George said to Marc. "How would *you* like to be screened for a judgeship?"

Maria stared at George, then Marc.

"Come on, George, let's not talk nonsense," said Marc.

"I'm very serious."

"I haven't even been a lawyer long enough, have I?" he asked.

75

"Sure you have. It'll be eleven years next June," said George. "You only need ten."

"But I have no political affiliations, George. Your Mayor isn't interested in a guy like me. Besides, I don't want to be a judge. I like what I'm doing."

"But if you say we're not appointing the right men," said George, "and then the Mayor says to you, okay, we'll appoint you, don't you have some kind of obligation, at least to your own principles, to consider the offer? I mean, if all good men say, I like what I'm doing, I don't want to be bothered, then the only ones left for the Mayor to appoint are hacks."

"I agree with George," said Maria.

The waiter came with trays of steaming food. He set a plate in front of each of them and refilled their glasses with wine. George rubbed his hands together, picked up his fork and began eating.

"Man, this dish is fantastic!"

"It's extra good today," agreed Maria.

"What the hell happened to eleven years?" mused Marc. "I mean that's a long time, George. What the hell did we do with all that time?"

"I was just thinking the same thing," replied George. "You know, when you're younger, you think, gee, guys who have been out of law school eleven years, they're old. But suddenly, you turn around yourself, and here we are, ten years later."

"I don't feel old," said Marc.

"Me neither," said George. He laughed and then continued eating. "You remember Professor Stone? Did we ever tell you about Professor Stone, Maria?" George asked, turning to Maria.

"Many times," she smiled. "But tell me again. I love to hear about him. I would have liked to have known him."

"He was a great man," said Marc. "Even if he started all this aggravation."

"What aggravation is that?" asked George.

"The criminal law," replied Marc. "Stone is the one who got me started in it."

George nodded, then continued eating. He thought about the Professor, a bright, interesting teacher, a hard taskmaster, who brought about results. Professor Stone taught them to think, to stick to the point, not to assume anything, to deal only with facts. You had to know the difference between the chaff and the wheat, the incidental from the real for Stone.

George remembered Professor Stone standing on his teacher's platform, looking around the room, that almost-smile ever present on his full face. Stone was a big man, tall, full-chested, with dark hair.

"Okay, let's see what they taught you in those colleges you went to," the Professor said to his first-year law students. "The first problem I want you to solve is as follows. If we call a cow's tail a leg, how many legs does it have?" Stone looked over the faces of his skeptical students. "I'm serious now." He pointed to a student.

"Four."

"Oh, come on." He pointed to another.

"Five."

Another said four. Another said five.

Stone stopped pointing, a mocking smile spreading on his face. "They didn't teach some of you too much, I see," he taunted. "You can call a cow's tail anything you want, but it's still a tail, and the cow still only has four legs. Boy, that's really dumb." The Professor was smiling, his criticism never reaching down to viciousness or embarrassment. "You let me fake you right out. Listen, you people, you want to be lawyers or accountants?"

His eyes ranged over the class. No one answered.

"Well, accountants are important. But they deal with facts and figures, two and two, five and five, black and white. But lawyers deal with concepts, things that aren't always even, always odd, or always easy to add up. As a lawyer, you have to deal with things that you won't always be able to look up, won't always be solved by the application of formula."

George remembered that Marc, who sat next to him, was right from the start, rapt with attention when Stone spoke.

"The law is the essence of our civilization," continued the Professor. "It's what separates us from the animals in the jungle. Or at least some of us," he said sardonically. "And as long as there is the discipline of the law, civilization lasts. When people run berserk, stampeding their desires any old which way, that's chaos.

"But remember," the Professor cautioned, "the law doesn't stand still. As life changes, so too must the law. When the ghosts of old laws that once applied—the laws regulating the speed of horse carriages, for instance—stand clanking their ancient chains across the way of progress, they must be struck down like some useless cobweb in the barn at springtime."

George remembered studying the Professor when he made that remark about barns and springtime. He looked like a big, raw-boned farm kid, who somehow grew and got himself involved in the law. Stone looked as though he'd be more at home behind a plow, or driving a truck, something rugged, outdoorsy. But his mind was a well-honed cutlass.

"And if some of you are unwilling to reach out and grasp at the unknown, the new, then maybe you ought to go to Poughkeepsie to hang up your shingle. You could handle a few real estate closings, a few contracts between the farmers and the Grange. New York City, well, that's something else."

"You remember that summer intern program the Professor started between our second and third year?" Marc asked, turning to George.

"Sure," said George. "Weren't we in that together?"

"So we were."

The Professor, when he wasn't teaching, handled cases for defendants who couldn't pay a lawyer's fee. He wouldn't handle a case for a paying client. There were enough lawyers to do that, the Professor had always said. Not that he'd take just any case, but money wasn't an issue with him.

To help with the cases, the Professor always picked two or three top students and let them intern with him, that is, when they were not in class, they could go to court with him and assist him, and help in the preparation of briefs.

"The Professor taught me never to get angry or emotional in a courtroom," Marc said, smiling at the remembrance.

"I can't imagine you getting angry in a courtroom," George said. "How'd that come about?"

"Well, once the Professor was representing a poor Black guy who had spent about ten years in jail. He'd been trying to find someone to handle his case, because he said he got a raw deal."

"And naturally, he found Professor Stone."

"Naturally," agreed Marc. "During the investigation, we discovered that originally our defendant was indicted with another

78

man. At the beginning of the original trial, the D.A. said to the Judge that because of some new circumstances concerning only the other defendant, circumstances which required investigation, the D.A. wanted to separate the cases and just put the Professor's client on trial."

"What did the Judge do?"

"He permitted it. It turned out there were two main witnesses in the case," Marc continued. "One was a former girl friend and the second a friend of the other defendant. They both testified that the two men planned the robbery together, right in the girl's apartment, showed pistols, and went out to pull the job. They also testified that the two men returned later on and admitted they had robbed a Greek man and shot him."

"Sounds like a fairly strong case, to say the least," said George.

"True. All through the trial, although only one defendant was on trial, the D.A. told the jury that the two men acted in concert and committed the crime together. The D.A. told the jury that they were equally guilty."

"Did the jury convict the first defendant?"

"They did," replied Marc. "And then, a couple of months later, the D.A. made a motion to dismiss the case against the second defendant."

"How come?" asked George.

"The D.A. actually said in an affidavit that the two main witnesses—that is, the girl friend and the other friend—were unsavory, unreliable characters, whose credibility was highly doubtful."

"*The two same witnesses* the D.A. used to convict the Black guy?"

"Right," said Marc. "In addition, the D.A. said that the second defendant had an alibi; he was at work, and it was very unlikely that he could have left his job, committed the crime with the Black guy, and then gone back without being noticed."

"Are you kidding?" asked George. "I thought you said that the D.A. said they pulled the job together."

"That's what the D.A. told the jury that convicted the Professor's client. Can you imagine what the defense counsel for the Black guy could have done with that alibi information at the trial?"

"He would have destroyed the D.A.'s whole case."

"So there we were in court, the Professor, me, and the Black guy, ten years after he went to prison. The D.A. who originally tried the case was now a judge; a big Irishman from the old school, you know, they owned New York and what's a nigger anyway. Well, the former D.A. took the stand, as calm and bold as can be, and testified he didn't know about the alibi until after the conviction of the Black guy."

"Did it make any difference?" asked George. "I mean, if it was discovered afterward, you'd be entitled to a new trial on newly discovered evidence. And if it was known before, you'd get a new trial because the D.A. suppressed the evidence."

Marc laughed. "I didn't know that at the time. While the Professor was cross-examining the former D.A. on some point or other, I got a little angry. I don't know what got into me. I just started to stand and say, *Your Honor* . . . Needless to say, the Professor was next to me in a flash. He sat me back in my chair, then apologized to the Court for my actions. The presiding judge threatened to remove me from the counsel table if I said another word."

"What did the Professor say afterward?" George asked, smiling at the thought.

Marc ordered another half bottle of wine. "After he got the guy his new trial," Marc continued, "he asked if I heard the expression about a lawyer who defended himself having a fool for a client? I told him I had."

"Well," the Professor said, "the saying should be changed to *he who represents himself has a fool for a lawyer.*"

"How come?" Marc had asked.

"Well, all clients are nervous," the Professor continued. "That's natural. They can't make objective decisions about what should be done because their rear end is hanging on the outcome. It's hard to be objective about your own rear end."

"What does that have to do with the old saying?" Marc had asked.

"As a client," the Professor answered, "the lawyer is acting normally—nervous. But a nervous attorney isn't normal. He can't make the right, the incisive decisions for his client. The lawyer's the fool, not the client. And, that's what you do for your clients when you get emotional about their cases. They have a fool for a lawyer."

"I just got steamed tonight, Professor," Marc had said, "listening to that witness lie about what he did when he was a D.A."

"How would it be for a doctor at the operating table to get upset about the cancer he's trying to cut out of his patient?" the Professor asked.

"He'd probably perform a poor operation."

"Exactly," said the Professor. "Your function is to be a lawyer, not a pal, not a sob sister. Don't you think that lying witness was getting me steamed too?"

"I don't know, it didn't show."

"Well, let me tell you something. I defend people who can't afford a lawyer, because I see them getting chewed up in a vast machine. And it burns my ass to see it. It tears my heart up too, to see people ground into powder by uncaring, unfeeling prosecutors and judges who aren't doing anything purposely but have become callous and impersonal. Who somehow forget they're not dealing with just indictment numbers but people. Well, someone has to come along and show them that the defendant is human, his case has merit, the facts different, that this defendant shouldn't be convicted. Not with emotions, not with anger, not by fist-fighting them. With the facts, Marc. Remember that, and you'll have learned more than most law students."

"I'll never get angry in a courtroom again, Professor," Marc had said. And he had meant it.

"Fine," said the Professor. "You're a good student, Marc. You're going to be a helluva lawyer."

"Quite a guy," admitted George as he sipped his wine. He looked at his watch. "He was right about you, Marc. You are a helluva lawyer. And you'll make a great judge. I'm going to talk to the Mayor about it. Okay?"

"Okay. You talk. I'll think."

"Fantastic," said Maria. "I can't wait to see you in your black robe."

VII

"Good night, darling," said Toni Wainwright, as she walked Courtnay "Sissy" Miller to the front door. Toni was petite, with short blond hair. She was dressed in a flowing caftan of crimson and pink woven with swirls of gold. Sissy was tall, dark-haired, in a long, black dress, slit rather high on one side, trimmed in rhinestones.

"Thank you, darling. The evening was sensational. As usual," said Sissy, turning to touch cheeks with Toni, as they both made kissing noises. The butler opened the door and rang for the elevator. Toni's apartment, a co-operative on Fifth Avenue and Sixtysixth Street, was the only apartment on the eleventh floor of the building. The elevator stopped in a small foyer.

"See you tomorrow?" Sissy asked as she stepped into the elevator.

"At '21' for lunch," agreed Toni. "But not too early."

"Heaven forbid," said Sissy, raising her eyes to the top of the elevator.

The elevator operator stood at the controls, staring straight ahead at the inside wall of the elevator, hearing everything, but pretending not to hear at all.

"I'm sorry Zack had to leave so early," said Sissy.

Toni was separated from her husband, Lafayette Wainwright. And pending their divorce, she was seeing a great deal of Zack Lord, a wealthy industrialist impressed by the importance of his own enterprises. Wherever Zack Lord went, there was always at least one telephone handy. Lord had left this evening's dinner party early in order to fly in his private jet to Chicago for a morning conference on the acquisition of Chicago Roller Bearings, Inc.

"Give the dear boy my love," Sissy continued. "And don't be

upset about that damned fool husband of yours. His arrival just gave the party the right touch of drama. It was marvelous!"

Toni smiled, blowing a kiss to Sissy as the elevator door slid shut. Her smile quickly evaporated as she turned back into her apartment. The butler shut the door behind her and silently moved toward the kitchen.

Toni walked into the library and over to the small bar set into the wall. She filled one of the oversized, crystal cocktail glasses with ice, then suddenly twirled and flung the glass against the far wall. It smashed, sending a shower of glass splinters and ice across the room. Her face was streaked with violent anger. The butler appeared at the door quickly, looking around. He saw Toni's face, then the shattered glass. He moved forward to begin picking up the wreckage.

"Leave the fucking thing alone," commanded Toni. The butler stopped abruptly. He was familiar with Toni's temper. "And fix me a martini. A very dry, very large, martini." She sat on the couch.

The butler nodded, moving toward the bar. He put ice into a fresh glass and mixed the drink.

Toni was in a fury because Lafayette Wainwright had shown up at her apartment, uninvited and unannounced. He was, as usual, drunk, and as usual when he was drunk, loud and abusive. Everyone was uncomfortable, and, although Lowell Borden, who was also at the dinner party, was able to persuade Wainwright to leave, the dinner party never really regained its balance. Toni did not agree with Sissy. As far as she was concerned, her husband had ruined the evening. She had switched from wine to martinis at dinner just to settle her nerves.

The butler handed Toni a fresh drink. He moved toward the broken glass again.

"You'd better fix me another one," Toni said harshly, not looking at the butler. He returned to the bar and began to mix another.

"I could break that lousy bastard's skull." Toni addressed the air. She brought her glass down hard on top of the cocktail table. The liquid slopped over the rim of the glass. Small fragments chipped away from the bottom of the heavy glass.

The butler put the second glass on the table before Toni, then

83

moved toward the broken glass on the floor and began to pick up the pieces.

Toni downed the first drink quickly and picked up the second. The butler moved as rapidly as he could, wanting to get back into the kitchen, out of the line of fire. He knew from past experience that Mrs. Wainwright and martinis were a volatile mixture.

Toni spent about an hour sipping her drink, and muttering to herself. She was chewing the ice as she moved to her bedroom, a large room with much chrome and mirrors. She flung her clothes against every wall and into every corner, and crawled into the huge bed, naked. She was almost unconscious as she hit the pillow.

Suddenly, there was a resounding booming noise echoing through the darkness of the bedroom. First, Toni just opened her eyes, as if to do that would silence the pounding. It didn't. The noise became worse now, and louder and closer. Toni lifted her head. The lighted clock face indicated 1:05 A.M. She was groggy. She shook her head, but it didn't clear. The pounding was incessant, booming, resounding through the room as if she were inside some giant, black, bass drum; it filled the entire room with its sound and vibration. Toni rose, quickly dashing to the doorway. At the end of a short hallway was another door leading from her bedroom suite to the rest of the apartment. Someone, something, on the other side was pounding, beating, battering that door, with fists, and kicks, and sometimes with a shoulder. The door was straining. The lamps on the tables in Toni's room were vibrating.

"Who is it? Who is it?" Toni demanded. She was becoming sober very fast.

There was no reply. Just the constant boom, booming in the dark, echoing hollowly like the portals of Hades pounded by the devil.

Toni lifted a shaking hand to her head. She felt queasy.

BOOM! BOOM!

Toni could hear the crunch of the wood straining. Any moment that horror on the other side of the door was going to break through and pour into the darkness of her bedroom.

BOOM! BOOM!

The wood was beginning to splinter now, as were Toni's nerves. She put both her hands to her head, trying to think clearly.

BOOM! BOOM!

A panel of the door shattered. Toni could hear someone panting and grunting, tearing at the wood fragments.

BOOM! BOOM!

Toni ran to the night table and grabbed for the phone. The extension button on the phone lit up, casting an eerie yellow glow to the blackness. Toni's trembling finger dialed 911, the police emergency number; she screamed for help even before the number began to ring.

BOOM! BOOM!

The pounding was unbearable now. Toni was shaking. She felt unbearable nausea. She held her stomach with her free hand, screaming into the phone.

The policeman on the other end was trying to calm her to get the address from her. She couldn't stop screaming. It was an echoing, disembodied voice, reverberating through the room, adding to the cacophony.

BOOM! BOOM!

Her screams were now splintered by the breaking of wood as more of the panels collapsed and came flying into the hallway. She heard someone fumbling with the key on the inside of the door. It would only be a moment now.

Toni dropped the phone, fumbling with the drawer in her night table. She felt the metal coldness of the carved-silver, pearl-handled .25 caliber automatic. She clenched the pistol in her hand and stumbled around the bed. In the jet darkness, in the dizziness of her head, she stood shakily facing the door.

Now she heard the sound of the door giving way, and a body hurtling, charging in, falling to the floor, struggling to get up. She saw a mass, a dark, bulky shadow, as her head still pounded with the noises of the door being splintered.

The shadow rose and started to move toward her. It came closer. Toni retreated. And still it came closer, panting horribly in the darkness. Toni retreated farther. The bed was now behind her legs and she could retreat no farther. The dark figure stalked the blackness, reached toward the bed, trying to find her, moving closer. There was a tremendous explosion, a flashing of light, a scream.

"Toni, you rotten bitch," rasped an alcoholic, pain-seared voice from the blackness. "Toni, you whore. Zack, you too."

It was Lafayette Wainwright. Her husband. He was shot and bleeding profusely.

"Toni, you rotten bitch whore," Wainwright coughed, gasping for breath. "Zack, you rotten bastard."

Toni felt herself fainting, falling into a chasm of deeper, softer black. And then all was totally black, quiet, silent, tomblike.

VIII

MONDAY, AUGUST 14, 4:53 A.M.

"I realize that you pay us a substantial retainer as your lawyers, Zack." James Cahill looked sleepily at the clock atop the night table on his wife's side of the bed. It was almost 5 A.M. Cahill's wife, sleep wrinkles lining her left cheek, was sitting up in the bed, staring wide-eyed at Cahill. He shrugged at her. "But this is a homicide charge you say Mrs. Wainwright is facing. It's just not the kind of thing we're used to handling," Cahill explained. "We'll have to retain a lawyer who specializes in criminal law."

Zack Lord said something on the other end of the phone.

"We will get the best one there is. Of course, Zack, but it's only 5 A.M. I can't get anyone now."

Cahill shook his head, then listened.

"I do realize the police are at Mrs. Wainwright's home right now," Cahill protested, "but . . ."

Cahill's eyes moved nervously.

"All right, all right, Zack, calm down. We'll get someone from our staff over there immediately. We'll protect her rights, and meanwhile, we'll get a top man for her."

He listened again.

"It's not a question of extra money, Zack. What?" He paused. "It's a question of the hour, the time. It's an odd hour to call an attorney to ask him to step into a case."

Cahill scratched the arm holding the phone.

"I realize Mrs. Wainwright didn't pick an odd hour purposely." He was cut off by Zack's harsh, terse words on the other end. "All right, Zack. Don't get upset. I'll get on it right now. I guess you're right, criminal lawyers are more used to being awakened like this than we are. Meanwhile, I'm sending one of our men." He hesitated. "Yes, of course he'll know how to handle himself."

Cahill's wife was lying down on the pillow again, her eyes wide open, watching and listening.

"Right away, Zack. That's right, right now. And then I'll phone you back. That's right. All right. I'll meet you at the airport at eleven. Right, eleven this morning." Cahill listened again, then hung the phone back on its cradle.

"Tell me what happened." Molly Cahill was excited. "Zack's girl? That Toni whatever her name is? What happened? Who did she kill?"

"Not now, Molly, not now," said Cahill picking up the phone and dialing. "Her husband," he muttered aloud, as he listened to the phone. Molly Cahill's eyes grew wide with curiosity. He waved for her to quiet as a sleepy voice on the other end rasped a hello.

"John, this is Jim. Jim Cahill, for God's sake. Listen . . . I know it's five o'clock. Zack Lord just called me from Chicago and woke *me* up. Yes, Zack Lord. His girl friend, Toni Wainwright is being held on a goddamned homicide charge and Zack wants us to get one of our men to her right away and help out until we get a criminal lawyer to handle the case."

Cahill listened. "She's at her home right now. The police are there." He listened further. "They're from the nineteenth precinct." A pause. "I don't know where it is either." Another pause. "I know we don't. That's just what I told Zack. But for Christ's sake, someone on our staff, of sixty-three lawyers, should be able to go over there and protect the woman's interests until we get someone to take over." He listened again. "Okay, get someone down there. Fast! And then start making calls to locate a criminal lawyer. Of course I will too. What, oh, she allegedly shot her husband, Bob Wainwright. That's right. Wainwright is dead."

IX

The wide-beamed motor sailer *Pescadorito* coursed swiftly down-stream on the rushing ebb of the East River. The engine throttle was half open. Marc manned the wheel, guiding the boat through the raging swirls of Hell Gate from a small jump seat just behind the windshield on the starboard side.

Maria sat on a similar seat on the port side. Franco was on the forward deck, securing the sails. The sun was high and bright, the heat cut only somewhat by the coolness of the water.

Franco's full name was Franco Poveromo. He was fifty-two years old, medium in height, stocky, with thinning blond hair. His smile, as he, was ingenuous and shy. Franco was a former client of Marc's. Two years ago, he had been charged with attempted murder. And, Marc had taken such concerned interest in Franco's case, almost as if it was his own life and liberty at stake, that Franco was, thereafter, totally devoted to Marc, and, therefore, Maria. This loyalty resulted, in addition to gratitude, partly also as a result of the feeling of security and stability that Franco found with Marc and Maria. Franco's early existence had been sad and very unstable—his father went to prison when Franco was two; his mother spent the waiting years on bar stools. Almost as soon as he could walk, Franco began shining shoes in bars late at night and in the early hours of the morning; he was most careful never to frequent one of his mother's haunts. He became expert at hustling quarters and dollars, trading wisecracks with the drunks and semi-drunks who animate that seamy, smoky world.

When Marc took charge of Franco's case, Franco assured him that he had not attempted to kill anyone. He did know, in fact, the person who had attempted that crime. This knowledge, how-ever, rather than a key to freedom, was even more of a jail to Franco. For Franco was a man of the street who, as a matter of honor, could not put anyone else into jeopardy with the authorities even if that meant taking the misdirected blame. Marc's defense had won Franco his freedom without having to betray another, and Franco's gratitude was unbounded. Additionally, he delighted in Marc's way of life. He liked to hear Marc and Maria talk; he liked the way they lived, their life style, their *joie de vivre*. And this pleasure led to the legitimate bent Franco's life had now taken. He became man Friday for Marc and Maria: chauffeur, valet, bodyguard. Whatever it was that Marc or Maria needed, whether mean or menial, Franco was there to get it or do it. And that meant anything. With years of street education behind him, Franco was crafty and tough. He didn't look like much, but he had legs like a mule. And his fists could feel as if one were kicked by the same animal.

"Careful, Franco," Marc called forward. "We're going to get some heavy waves now."

Franco looked aft, then followed Marc's pointing arm to see a huge oil tanker, its belly full of fuel, plowing heavily upstream toward them on the port side. Franco nodded, and held one of the guy wires as he worked. The boat began to buck through the tanker's wake.

Pescadorito was forty feet of highly varnished, natural-wood-finished boat, with an aft cabin that slept two, a forward cabin beneath Franco's feet which also slept two, and a main salon which was fitted out with more than the usual comforts: a soft, thick carpet, a couch, a bar, a television set, a Spanish tile dining table along one wall. The galley was to the rear of the main cabin.

They were now at about Eighty-fifth Street. The tide was really running, and *Pescadorito* was lifting a great cockade of water on its prow as it bettered twelve knots. Sunlight glinting from the windows of luxury apartment buildings lining the Manhattan shoreline sparkled from the water. The slow movement of heavy traffic on the triple-leveled East River Drive beneath Carl Schurz Park, made Manhattan seem a fantasy land. Too often, the City is lost to the viewer because each outstanding edifice or feature is obscured or crowded by some other feature of equal importance. In Manhattan, there are buildings, which, in other locations, would be important attractions, drawing people from miles. In Manhattan, there are so many buildings, and each so close, one upon the other, that the architect's dream, his vision, is lost in a dazzling forest. So too, Marc thought as he watched the traffic ashore, was the East River Drive itself at the point past which *Pescadorito* was now moving; northbound traffic flowed on an open, three-lane highway built along the water's edge. And directly above that, on a second level, also open, except for the retaining wall, the southbound traffic moved in the opposite direction. And over that, on a third level, a promenade was built with benches, and children running in the summer sun and people talking, sunning—there were always New Yorkers with sun reflectors near their faces—leaning on the railing, watching the river. Behind the promenade was a park and Gracie Square, and in the midst of the park, the Mayor's official residence, Gracie Mansion.

Franco held fast now, as the largest waves cut by the tanker sent *Pescadorito*'s prow high into the air then plunging down into the trough. Maria held on as the boat bucked. Marc cut the wheel sharply to port, guiding the boat more directly across the waves. Franco edged his way along the side of the boat, toward the cockpit.

"Had enough?" Maria smiled.

"I'll do the rest when we get into the slip," replied Franco. He stood in the center of the cockpit between the two jump seats, in front of the stairs leading down to the galley. "Want some hot *cafe con leche*, boss?"

Marc looked over to Franco impatiently. "You calling me boss again?"

Franco shrugged. "To me, you're always the boss." He smiled. "You want some hot *cafe*, Mrs. Conte?" Franco refused to call Maria anything but Mrs. Conte.

"I'll get it," Maria said.

"No, I'll get it." Franco moved down the steps. "You want to get me fired," he added as he leaned back through the passageway. A pot of coffee was still warm on the small stove.

"It ain't hot. It's warm though," called Franco.

"It's not hot," corrected Marc.

"That's what I meant. It's not hot," Franco said with a tinge of self-annoyance. He was trying as hard as he knew how, as he described it, to speak good.

"That's okay," called Maria. "It'll be fine just the way it is."

Franco came on deck and handed each of them a mug. He sat on a bench at the rear of the cockpit, sipping from a mug of his own.

They were now passing beneath the filigreed Queensboro Bridge, which, as the boat passed directly beneath, seemed to sizzle from the tires of passing cars. Ahead was the UN, and farther inland the Chrysler Building, its silver point glinting sunlight brightly. Farther downtown, the Empire State Building pierced the cloudless azure sky. All the way down at the foot of the island, the financial district could be seen. The twin towers of the World Trade Center soared into the sky.

"I wonder how that rally is going?" said Franco as he looked shoreward at Fifty-ninth Street, directing his gaze as if the buildings of Sutton Place and those farther inland did not obscure Columbus Circle, many blocks across town.

"The Italian-American Freedom Council rally?" Maria asked.

"The very one," agreed Marc. "I'm sure The Crusher is there with all splendor and splash." He smiled at the thought.

"That guy Compagna's really doing some job, don't you think?" Franco asked.

"He's got a lot of people united together," Marc said. "That's a feat in itself."

"At least he's not one of them lousy politicians. They tell you they're going to do something, and do nothing. Compagna said he was going to build a hospital for all kinds of people—not only Italians—and he already got the money raised with a couple of benefit performances. Frankie came to sing at one. He said he's going to put up a summer camp, and I bet he's going to do that too."

"The way it's going, I'm sure he will," replied Marc. He sipped the cafe.

"How can he be so bad—supposed to be the head of a Mafia family—if he's doing such good?" asked Maria. "Does he have a criminal record?"

"I read he only got arrested once for playing craps in the street," said Franco from the rear bench.

"That doesn't sound too terrifying," said Maria.

"Compagna keeps proposing," said Marc, looking ahead as he guided the boat, "that if he's committed a crime—or anyone he knows committed a crime—the FBI or police ought to arrest them. If not, get off their back. That's what brought the Council into existence in the first place. People complaining that the FBI was harassing Italians for the sake of keeping congressional appropriations high in the fight against some fictitious syndicate. Compagna complained the authorities were even following his grandchildren to school, and telling the teachers those were a gangster's grandchildren."

"Did they?"

"You bet your life they did," said Franco. "And I bet the FBI is going bananas about all that picketing the Council's been doing against them."

"I imagine," said Marc, "that the FBI might really be boiled about the Council publicly flouting the FBI's shining-knight image. All the agents must have very strict orders to nail Compagna—and soon."

"He's going to get fifty years for putting together this rally," Franco said flatly. "They'll charge him with something, frame him up, do something to him, if the rally comes off the way they said in the papers. They expect a hundred thousand people there."

"Turn on the radio," said Marc. "Let's hear what's going on at Columbus Circle." The boat was passing the UN Building now. The East River Drive traffic could be seen speeding beneath overhead gardens which surrounded the building.

Franco disappeared into the salon. A radio sounded and music could be heard momentarily, then different music, as Franco searched from station to station for a news program.

"IT IS NOT KNOWN AT THIS TIME," a radio announcer's voice said urgently, "IF COMPAGNA IS ALIVE OR DEAD. ALL THAT IS KNOWN FOR SURE IS THAT HE WAS SHOT, MOST PROBABLY IN THE HEAD . . ."

"My God," Maria exclaimed.

"Louder," Marc shouted.

". . . THE EXACT NUMBER OF TIMES HE WAS STRUCK BY BULLETS IS NOT KNOWN AT THIS TIME. COMPAGNA'S ASSAILANT, A PRESENTLY UNIDENTIFIED BLACK MAN ABOUT 25 YEARS OLD, LEAPED OUT OF A CROWD AT THE VERY BEGINNING OF THE RALLY, AND

BEGAN BLAZING AWAY. THE ASSAILANT IS DEAD. THAT IS KNOWN FOR SURE, ALTHOUGH WHO KILLED HIM IS AS YET UNCLEAR. COMPAGNA IS PRESENTLY UNDERGOING EMERGENCY SURGERY AT ROOSEVELT HOSPITAL WHERE . . ."

"God, that is just shocking," said Maria. They were back in their apartment now. Marc was standing at the glass wall of the living room, high over the City, staring across the Hudson River at the panorama of buildings and streets in New Jersey. Franco was in the kitchen making sandwiches.

The apartment was high in a tower of a building at the edge of Greenwich Village. It was a penthouse which took up the entire thirty-seventh floor. A planted terrace complete with willow trees surrounded the apartment. The walls of the living room were almost entirely glass, giving a spectacular view of the City.

"I told you they'd give him something for making that rally and that Council so popular," said Franco, entering the living room. "I didn't figure they'd try to knock him off. Not in front of a hundred thousand people."

"What do you think happened, Marc?" Maria asked. She was seated on one of two white, matching couches. The sun's rays streamed into the room and across the floor. "I mean, do you think the radio reports are right, about some organized crime family possibly being responsible?"

"I don't think so," Marc said tersely.

"You don't agree with Franco about the FBI being responsible, do you?" she asked.

"It's possible." Marc was studying a single building very far off on the Jersey horizon. It could only be seen on a very clear, bright day, and Marc was always intending to find out where it was and how far away it was.

Franco was silent in the kitchen again.

"But, I don't think so," Marc added. "It would be a perfect opportunity for the FBI to get rid of a festering thorn in their side and discredit the Council at the same time as being what they said it was all along—a haven of organized crime maniacs. But I don't think anyone, not the FBI, a gang, or anyone else, could have planned with such precision the shooting of Compagna, and the killing of this Washington, or whatever his Black assailant's name

93

was, with police surrounding the place, and no one saw the assailant's killer, and the weapon mysteriously disappeared. It's just so perfect that I don't think it could have been planned."

"You don't put it past the FBI to do something like this in the name of national security or some crap like that, do you?" Franco asked, coming to the door of the kitchen.

"No, I don't put it past them," said Marc. "We know and complained, long before Watergate, that agents or police were breaking into the homes of alleged organized crime people when the authorities didn't have any grounds to obtain a legal search warrant. They'd go in allegedly as burglars but really to collect and photograph papers. If they were caught, the authorities denied they ever heard of the burglars. But this shooting today was too bizarre, too difficult to control to be planned."

"Then who was this Black guy, Washington? And why did he shoot Compagna?" asked Maria.

"Probably only a madman, that's all," replied Marc. "If you can allow yourself to say *only* a madman. Who was Oswald, Sirhan, Earl Ray; where did they come from, and why? Just some small-timer come to seek a moment of immortality, of fame, in death since it eluded him in life."

Franco came out of the kitchen with a tray of sandwiches. "Some sandwiches, boss."

"Okay, boss," Maria replied chidingly.

Franco smirked, a bit flustered. "How come you call *me* boss?"

"How come you call *him* boss?" Maria smiled.

"Ah, he's the boss," said Franco. "You want some tomato juice?"

"Okay."

"I'll have a beer," said Marc.

The phone rang.

Franco answered it in the kitchen. He walked into the living room with a plug-in phone and handed it to Marc. "It's for you," he said, plugging it in. "Your office."

Maria did not approve of phones as decorations in the living room. The world of commerce and big business fascination with telephones ended at their doorstep.

"Hello, Mister Conte?" asked Marguerite Elisan, Marc's secretary.

"Yes, Marguerite."

94

"You just received an emergency call from an attorney named Cahill."

"What's the emergency?"

"He said he wants you to represent a, wait a minute, I have the name here. Toni Wainwright. He's being held at the nineteenth precinct."

"Toni Wainwright is a woman," said Marc, remembering the name from having scanned the blazing headlines on the morning papers when he got home.

"I don't know. Mister Cahill just said Toni Wainwright. I didn't know it was a woman," said Marguerite. "Mister Cahill wants you to go over to the nineteenth precinct to represent her. He also said to tell you that money was no object."

"That sounds bad already. Where is this Mister Cahill now?"

"He said you could get him at the nineteenth precinct. Said he was going right over. He'd like you to go right over too."

"Okay." Marc looked puzzled as he replaced the phone carefully.

"Got to go and get someone out, right?" asked Maria.

Marc nodded. He walked over to Maria, sat next to her, and put his arms around her, kissing her forehead.

"Okay," she smiled. "I'll have dinner ready when you get back. Franco," she called. "You be sure to call when you two are on your way home," she admonished Franco. He nodded. She turned to Marc. "How come you can remember everything that happens in a courtroom and can't remember to call to say you're on your way home?"

"Want to leave something for Franco to do," he said. "God knows, he never does anything around here."

"Thanks a lot, *Mister Conte*," said Franco, a smirk on his face. "Does that sound better?"

Marc and Maria began to laugh. "No, actually it doesn't," said Marc.

Marc approached the nineteenth precinct, an old, red brick building with a short stairway leading to scarred wooden doors. Green glass lanterns were braced on either side of the entrance. Barricades lined the sidewalk across the street from the station house; behind the barricades Jewish Defense League demonstrators berated and jeered at the nearby Russian embassy about Soviet Jewry.

Marc entered the station house. Its interior was old, the walls and ceiling high and dusty, the ubiquitous light green paint peeling. A crowd of men, many holding cameras or pads, noisily surrounded the main desk to the right of the entrance. A Lieutenant was standing behind the desk, pacifying the newsmen, fielding their questions about the Wainwright killing. Marc walked directly to a staircase on the left which led up to the detectives' offices. A uniformed policeman was posted at the foot of the stairs. He raised one hand, gazing at Marc blankly.

"Nobody can go up," the policeman said.

"I'm an attorney," said Marc. "I want to go to the homicide squad office. A client of mine is being held up there."

"Sorry, Counselor, my orders are I can't let anyone up."

"My client is Toni Wainwright," Marc said.

The cop studied Marc more carefully now. He was a young cop, tall, beefy, with fairly long wavy hair and a thick mustache.

"Hold it a minute, Counselor," said the cop. "Hey, Phil. Phil," he called to another policeman, also young, with a thick, full mustache. The other policeman approached, his thumbs hooked into the thick cartridge belt girdling his waist. Marc thought momentarily how the two cops looked much like the photographs of the turn-of-the-twentieth-century cops, with flourishing antique mustaches. That which is supposed to be very new and mod, is merely a take-off of something quite old and not very different.

"What's up, Tom?" asked the second cop, looking at Marc with the condescending look that semi-officialdom seems to bestow.

"Tell the *lou* that the Counselor here represents Toni Wainwright. Should I let him up?"

The second cop pursed his lips. "You got a nice client there, Counselor. Not bad and plenty of dough. You'll make a good fee now."

Marc smiled patiently. He watched the second cop walk behind the main desk and approach the Lieutenant.

From the corner of his eye, Marc caught the images of men entering the station house. He turned. Walking directly toward him was Liam O'Connor, Chief Assistant District Attorney, and two D.A.'s detectives. O'Connor, with his burly figure and thick features, always reminded Marc of a bartender in an Irish gin mill. He should have had an apron bound high around his middle and a bow tie.

The desk Lieutenant waved and smiled as O'Connor strode directly to the stairway. O'Connor winked and waved back as the newsmen turned to see the newcomer. The reporters, sensing new blood, moved instantly toward the D.A.

O'Connor, obviously pleased, nonetheless shook his head, waving them back with his thick hand. "Not now, fellas, not now." He smiled a fast, toothy smile. "I'm too busy now. When I come down, I'll be better able to talk. Just be patient. Okay?" He continued toward the stairs. "Hello, Marc," he said blandly.

"Hello, Liam," Marc replied, equally bland.

O'Connor flashed his badge to the officers at the foot of the stairs. The reporters were swarming around the steps now.

"I'd like to talk to you a moment, Liam," Marc said.

"Later, Marc, I'm in a hurry now." O'Connor started up the stairs brusquely.

"If you want to talk to Mrs. Wainwright you ought to talk to me first," Marc called.

O'Connor stopped, nodding. He shrugged. "I should have known. Let Counselor Conte up, Officer."

The reporters were further aroused, their din increasing. "Hey, what's your name, Counselor?" called one of them.

"I know him, that's Conte," said one of the reporters who had overheard O'Connor.

Marc started up the stairs behind O'Connor and the two detectives.

The four men entered the homicide office. It was full of men. O'Connor nodded to several of the detectives. One shook his hand and smiled. The room was large, painted in the same light green and faded, dusty, peeling cream as the rest of the station house. There were several old, scarred desks, each with an old, manual typewriter. A prisoner's detention cage with thick mesh wire in place of bars stood in one corner. A fingerprint desk was suspended from the wall in another corner. The other two corners of the room were occupied by two small, partitioned offices. One belonged to the squad commander, a Lieutenant; the other, to the squad's clerical officer.

"Hello, Mister O'Connor," a small man in a rumpled gray suit announced. He was the squad commander, Lieutenant Balinsky. His short hair was streaked with gray, his craggy face looked tired. The other detectives nodded.

"Hello, fellas," O'Connor smiled. "Where's Mrs. Wainwright?"

"In the clerical office. You want to talk to her?" asked Lieutenant Balinsky.

"I'd like to talk to her first," Marc cut in.

The Lieutenant turned quickly to look at Marc.

"This dapper gumba is her lawyer, Marc Conte," said O'Connor.

"She's already got herself a couple of lawyers," Balinsky advised.

"They're holding the fort until I get here," said Marc. "And I'm Italian, Mister O'Connor," he shot out quickly, seriously. "If it's important to refer to that fact, you may. But don't call me a *gumba*, or I'll have to refer to you as a thick mick or a donkey."

The level of other conversations in the squad room dropped instantly. A number of detectives looked resentfully at this intruder, then to O'Connor.

O'Connor studied Marc's face. "I'm only kidding you, Marc. Come inside," he said, shrugging a semi-apology.

In a chair, beside another old desk, sat Toni Wainwright. She was pale, red-eyed, and looked even smaller than usual. She wore a blue sweater and blue slacks. Her fingers had several large rings; a gold chain dangled from her neck. A Black detective was handing her a cup of coffee. Standing beside Toni were two men, one, young, clean-cut with horn-rimmed glasses and a blue, two-button suit with a striped tie. He held a briefcase under his left arm. The other man was Cahill, also dressed conservatively. Toni looked at the men entering the room.

"This here is Assistant District Attorney O'Connor," Lieutenant Balinsky said to Toni. "And this here is a lawyer, Marc . . ." The Lieutenant looked at Marc.

"Conte."

The two men near Toni looked relieved. Marc walked to Toni. Her eyes were wide and quite red, rimmed with tears.

"Christ, it's about time," she scolded.

"Mrs. Wainwright, I came here directly, as soon as I was called. That was only twenty minutes ago."

"I feel as if I've been here for days."

"Your husband'll be where he is a lot longer," O'Connor injected caustically.

"It's all right, Mrs. Wainwright, the District Attorney isn't as big or bad as he wants to sound," said Marc, looking toward O'Connor.

"Oh yes he is," O'Connor shot back.

Marc frowned.

"We've been waiting for you, Mister Conte," said Cahill. "I'm James Cahill, from Cahill, Craven, Warren and Smith." He shook Marc's hand. "This is Mister Rutley." Rutley, in the dark blue suit, nodded, then shook Marc's hand.

"I'm sorry if I took long," Marc said. "But I wasn't in my office." He turned to O'Connor and the detectives. "May I talk to my client alone for a few minutes?"

"Come on, Marc," protested O'Connor. "This is an open and shut case. Let's not waste time with it. I've got a lot of other things to do, and I want to get going. She still has to be arraigned."

Marc saw Toni shudder at O'Connor's pronouncement.

"Mister O'Connor," Marc said sharply, "no case is open and shut. And if you want to play psychological games, I took abnormal psych in college too. So we're not impressed. Has Mrs. Wainwright been processed already, Lieutenant?" Marc asked.

"Oh, yeah," Balinsky replied. "We're finished with the prints and all. We sent them up to Albany already. They should be downtown soon."

"May I speak to you a moment," Cahill said to Marc.

"Surely."

Rutley remained with Mrs. Wainwright as Marc and Cahill stepped out of the small office and walked to one side of the large squad room.

"I don't know much about this sort of thing," Cahill admitted. "However, I took the liberty of having our appeals man check into the law on criminal procedure. And I've made arrangements for Judge Crawford to be here shortly." Cahill looked at his watch. "Any minute now. He can set the bail right here without even going to court. If that's okay with you?"

"Judge Crawford is going to come to the police station?" Marc asked with surprise.

"He's a long-time friend of friends. If you know what I mean."

"No, but that's okay, don't tell me," said Marc. "However, Mrs. Wainwright will still have to be arraigned, brought before a judge in the Criminal Court and have the charges read on the record, and have an adjourned date set."

"Oh? I thought that if we set bail here . . ."

"Mrs. Wainwright would be free?" Marc finished.

Cahill nodded.

"No. She might be bailed and free of custody, but she still has to go to court."

Cahill raised his eyebrows in dismay.

"But having bail set here will save her a great deal of discomfort," Marc assured him.

"Well, that's something then," said Cahill.

They walked back into the room where Toni Wainwright was sitting. O'Connor was stirring a cup of coffee.

"I understand Judge Crawford is on his way here to entertain a bail application and set bail for Mrs. Wainwright," Marc said to O'Connor.

"Crawford? Here?"

"That's right, Liam," replied Marc.

"We don't even have a fingerprint record on Mrs. Wainwright," protested O'Connor. "How can bail be set?"

"Do you really think Mrs. Wainwright has a record?" asked Marc.

"Who knows?" said O'Connor.

"What the hell is that supposed to mean?" Toni protested from behind Marc.

"Please, Mrs. Wainwright," said Marc, "there's no need to defend yourself from pointless remarks."

"You bet they are," she added.

"Crawford better get here before we're finished. Otherwise we're going to court with or without him. What the hell are you trying to pull, Marc?" O'Connor was red in his neck and under the chin now.

"Just protecting my client's rights."

O'Connor regained himself, shrugging with affected boredom. "I want to talk to your client, take a Q. and A. statement," he said to Marc. That merely meant questions and answers recorded by a D.A.'s stenographer.

"Mrs. Wainwright refuses to make any statements about anything at this time," said Marc. He watched O'Connor's face harden with annoyance. "Of course," Marc continued, "if you let me have a chance to speak to my client alone—your men can stay right outside the door—I'll be better able to ascertain if Mrs. Wainwright can give you a statement."

O'Connor's face streaked with disgust. "Let them have their little chit-chat," he said as he turned. He and the detectives started from the room.

The Black detective who had been giving Toni coffee winked at Marc as he left the room. "Nice going, Counselor," he whispered.

Marc walked to the door and began to shut it.

"Leave it open," said O'Connor.

"You think we'll try a daring escape?" asked Marc.

"Just following procedures," replied O'Connor.

Marc moved closer to Toni and the other lawyers. "Let's stand over here," he said, moving toward the far wall away from the door.

"What the hell is going on?" Toni demanded. "He said he's not going to wait for the Judge?"

"Mrs. Wainwright, the first thing is not to let O'Connor frighten you," said Marc.

"Too late," she said.

"I know you already are, but try. He wants you to be frightened so you'll panic. And please speak softly," he cautioned, gazing toward the doorway. O'Connor was leaning against the door frame, staring.

"I really only want to get the hell out of here," she replied, closing her eyes, biting her bottom lip. "And I am *really* frightened."

"Listen. The reason O'Connor wants to scare you, shake you up by saying it's an open and shut case," said Marc, "is to cause you to get frightened and confess to the crime. It's a bluff. He doesn't know what happened any more than I do. From what I understand so far, no one was with you at the time. Is that correct, Mrs. Wainwright?"

"I was alone, all alone, except for Bob." Her voice trailed off, her eyes closing tightly.

"I'm not asking questions to cause you discomfort," said Marc. "I just have to know something about the case."

"I'm okay," she said, wiping her eyes with the back of her hand. "It was just pretty awful. Horrible. Pounding, pounding, and then Bob came stumbling into, no, fell into the room like some wild beast. I don't remember what happened too clearly. It was worse than the worst nightmare I ever had."

"The only difference is that it was real," Marc added.

"Thanks a lot," she said.

"I have to work with facts," said Marc. "We don't have too much time right now. Just what did you tell the police so far?"

"Nothing at all, Mister Conte," replied Cahill. "We arrived here just as Mrs. Wainwright was brought from her apartment about noon. And I informed the police that no statement was to be made. The police have been extremely co-operative so far. Until O'Connor arrived, that is."

"Fine. However, Mrs. Wainwright, you were brought here a very long time after the police arrived at your home. What did you say to them during the time they were at your home?"

"They were in my house for hours," she said. "Searched every goddamn thing."

"What did you tell them?" Marc pursued.

"Just the truth. Just what happened. I was hysterical. How do I know?" she said impatiently.

"Mrs. Wainwright had to be placed under doctor's care a couple of hours this morning for hysteria and exhaustion," said Cahill. "Does that mean anything or help in any way?"

"Perhaps," said Marc. "Did the doctor come to the apartment?"

"Yes."

"What exactly did you tell the police?" Marc asked Mrs. Wainwright again.

"The same as I told you," Toni said flatly, impatient now. Cahill bent forward, listening. "Bob was pounding on the door. I didn't know it was Bob though. I didn't know what it was. Then I picked up the phone and started to call the police, you know, I dialed 911."

"Did you get them?" Marc asked.

"Yes. Well, they answered. I was screaming, trying to explain what was happening."

"I'll have to subpoena their records, to see what the police wrote down when you called," said Marc. "Go ahead."

"Then the door came in with a sound like, like, well, I don't know like what," Toni answered. "I never heard anything like it in my life. It scared the bejesus out of me. I dropped the phone and reached into the night table and took out the pistol that was there. I have a permit for it," she added.

"I was just going to ask that," said Marc.

"Then this person, breathing, stinking of alcohol—I should have known it was Bob just by that stink—came closer, closer. And that's really the last thing I remember. Oh, I remember, just vaguely, a flash of light and an explosion."

"That would be after the pistol fired," said Marc. "Did you recognize your husband up to that point?"

"I don't know," she said. "Thinking about it now, I think I must have. But I'm not sure I really did."

Marc studied Toni's face. "We'll go into more detail later. Right now let's talk about this arraignment that's coming up."

"What's that?" Toni asked.

"That means you have to go to court, and be formally charged—the charges will be read to you," said Marc.

"I thought we weren't going to court," she said, turning to Cahill.

Cahill looked sheepish. "Mister Conte says we must."

She gazed annoyedly at Cahill, then back to Marc. "And then?"

"Then you'll be given a date to return and then you'll go home," said Marc.

Toni frowned. "This is surely a pain in the ass."

"Is this little coffee klatsch over with yet?" intruded O'Connor. "Because I'd like to take a statement from your client now."

"Let me commune aloud for a moment, Mister O'Connor . . ."

"Commune? That's a cute word, Conte."

"We don't all have to be monosyllabic, O'Connor," replied Marc. "And since you're just fishing for evidence now," Marc continued, "and haven't any real evidence to go on, I can't, in good conscience, permit my client to make a statement which may afterward be used in court to nail down a case you don't have now. After all, Mister O'Connor, Mrs. Wainwright was the only person at the scene besides the deceased."

"You see, Mrs. Wainwright, how smart-ass attorneys can . . ."

103

"Mister O'Connor, talk to the detectives like that if you don't know any better, but not to my client," said Marc sharply.

"Excuse *me*," O'Connor said brusquely, staring at Marc. "I guess you never heard it before," he said to Toni. "As I was saying, how some lawyers can create for their clients more trouble than they had in the first place."

Toni looked at Marc questioningly.

O'Connor saw an opening. "If you have nothing to hide, you should make a statement," O'Connor said directly to Mrs. Wainwright. "After all, you don't think that me or my office, or the police would try to pull something over your eyes, try to frame you. Mrs. Wainwright, let me assure you, I'm only looking to help you." He smiled.

"He's looking to help you sink yourself," said Marc. "He's the prosecutor, and he's here to get evidence to help him do his job. My client is not making any statements."

"All right, look, that's her privilege," said O'Connor. "The Fifth Amendment gives that right. But only criminals hide behind it. It looks funny, you know," continued O'Connor, looking at Toni Wainwright. "What I mean is when someone with nothing to hide dodges behind the Fifth Amendment for no reason, it makes the District Attorney start to think maybe there *is* something she's hiding."

"My client is still not going to make a statement."

"You know, Counselor, if your client wants to make a statement, no matter what *you* say, she can make one. She doesn't have to be bulldozed by you." O'Connor looked to make sure Mrs. Wainwright got his message.

"That's quite correct," agreed Marc. "I'm advising my client not to make any statement. She's neither going to make your case nor any publicity for you."

"What's that supposed to mean?" flashed O'Connor angrily.

"Which? That Mrs. Wainwright is not making the case, or not making the publicity?"

"The publicity. You don't think for one moment that Mister Francis X. Byrnes's office is involved in or interested in publicity? Do you?"

"No, not the office itself," replied Marc.

"What are you implying, Counselor?" asked O'Connor.

"I'm not implying anything. I've said exactly what I wanted to say." Marc turned to Toni. "I guess they're going to keep us here, chit-chatting all day."

"Did you also advise Mrs. Wainwright that I'll put her in front of a grand jury under oath if she doesn't make a statement now?" threatened O'Connor.

"And Mrs. Wainwright, as a prospective defendant, will take the Fifth Amendment in that event too," countered Marc. "You know that's her privilege under the law."

Cahill was carefully following the verbal exchange.

"Well, if you want to embarrass your client like that, you can," O'Connor said, looking at Toni. "I can't understand why someone with nothing to hide has to use the same dodge as the most notorious criminals."

Toni turned to Marc. "Can I speak to you for a moment, alone?"

"Of course," O'Connor said, now smiling again. He looked at Marc, then turned, waving the policemen out of the room.

Toni watched the men leave. Cahill and Rutley stood next to Marc. Cahill had his arms folded, looking very serious.

"Doesn't what the D.A. says make sense?" Toni asked. "I haven't anything to hide. Why should I make it seem like I'm hiding something? Like a criminal. I mean, that's the thing all those gangsters you read about in the papers do."

"The fact is, that people accused of a crime need not testify or be witnesses against themselves, according to the Constitution," said Marc. "I don't want to give a course on legal proceedings, but the law purposely intended to make the Government, the prosecutor, prove a case, if he can. If he can't, the person who's accused doesn't have to prove anything. Let me just say as an aside that despite a Puritan ethic, it's just as lawful and right to benefit from the provisions of law as it is to be punished by the law. Now O'Connor's case is as thin as tissue paper. If you give him a statement, any kind of statement, indicating you did in fact shoot a pistol at your husband, you may give him just the evidence he needs to prove a case; if not a murder case, manslaughter. Without you, who does he have to testify as to anything that happened there?"

"There's just me," Toni admitted.

"I have a tendency to agree with Mrs. Wainwright," said Rutley.

"If that's the case, all she need do is tell it the way it actually happened. I don't believe Mister O'Connor would try to concoct a false case against Mrs. Wainwright. I mean, he is obviously a vulgarian, but concocting a case against an innocent person, I don't think even he'd do that. If you don't mind my saying so, you're making this thing out far too dramatically."

Cahill said nothing. He wanted to hear Marc's explanation.

Marc looked at Rutley. "Mister Rutley, how many homicide cases have you handled?"

"Your logic escapes me. I don't see what that has to do with it."

"How about you, Mister Cahill?" Marc asked.

Cahill shook his head.

"How would either of you like to try this one by yourselves?"

"I don't think this is the time or the place to have this sort of professional squabble, Mister Conte," Rutley protested. "Particularly in front of our client."

"Oh, yes it is," said Marc. "First of all, the squabble *you* started isn't professional. Next, you had your say in front of our client. And so will I. Those are the police. O'Connor is the Chief Assistant District Attorney. He is also dying to become the District Attorney and later move up even higher politically. He loves publicity. I'm telling you from my past experience that the man has blood poisoning, the poison being printer's ink. And if you think he's not going to prosecute this case under any and all circumstances—for publicity, if not for a conviction—you're out of your wonderful Ivy League mind."

"Now wait a minute . . ." protested Rutley.

"No, I'm not finished," said Marc. "This is a big, juicy case. O'Connor can smell the presses rolling already, with day after day of publicity about the beautiful socialite who killed her millionaire husband. Now, if he's going to prosecute this case, no matter what, even on the flimsiest of evidence, don't you think that perhaps he'd be delighted to have some real, down to earth, honest-to-God strong evidence in his quiver, evidence like the defendant's own statement that she had a gun in her hand, knew who it was that came into the room, they were all alone, and suddenly the next thing that happens is that the victim is dead. Don't you think that that sort of evidence would really help his case a great deal?"

"He could perhaps introduce the statement, I imagine," Rutley admitted reluctantly, "but certainly it eliminates murder, the intentional taking of life."

"Great. But what about manslaughter?" Marc asked. "The unintentional taking of life? Do you think Mrs. Wainwright could do twenty-five years in jail easily?"

Toni shuddered.

"If you are going to fight someone, does it make any sense to help him put on his armor?" Marc looked at Cahill.

Cahill stood silently.

"The Fifth Amendment is to help people protect themselves," Marc continued. "It's as American and constitutional as freedom of speech and freedom of religion. They're written in the same Bill of Rights. And anybody who thinks that there's something wrong with it, just doesn't know what it's all about. That man out there, that O'Connor, his job, as he sees it, is to put Mrs. Wainwright in jail. And I don't think it's necessary in order to be a good American to help put yourself in jail. I don't care what I or it looks like, Mister Rutley, but I'm protecting Mrs. Wainwright. That's my job." Marc turned to Toni.

"Let Mister Conte do what he wants," she said.

Marc turned toward the door where O'Connor was hovering. "My client continues to refuse to make any statement."

O'Connor turned away, waving a disgusted hand at Marc. "Arraign her and let me get the hell out of here and stop wasting my time." He began to walk directly through the crowd of detectives toward the stairs.

"Mister O'Connor," called Marc, "don't you want to be present to be heard on the question of bail when Judge Crawford gets here?"

"No judge is going to set bail without the D.A. being present to be heard," O'Connor said over his shoulder. "And I'm not going to be here."

"Perhaps when the Judge is informed that you were here and were told he was on his way and you refused to remain," Marc replied, "he might imagine that you didn't care what the bail was."

O'Conner wavered. "The Judge may not even be coming here. I haven't seen a Justice of the Supreme Court in a police station in years."

"Well, you're seeing one now," said Judge Crawford as he entered the homicide office, smiling, looking around the room. He was tall, red-faced, with gray hair slicked smooth and center-parted. He was as good a politician as O'Connor, maybe even better. After all, he had already worked his way up through the political ranks to Judge.

"Hello, Your Honor," O'Connor said sourly. "You're not really going to set bail here in the precinct, are you?"

"Why not?" asked the Judge. "Why should Mrs. Wainwright have to be brought down to the bull pen and sit in that filthy hole waiting for hours while you verify her fingerprints?" The Judge saw Toni standing at the door of the office. His eyes flicked momentarily down her figure and up again. He smiled reassuringly.

O'Connor looked at the Judge, a sour smirk turning the ends of his mouth down.

"You don't think it's necessary for Mrs. Wainwright to be incarcerated for no good reason, do you?" the Judge asked O'Connor. "Nor do you think there's anything wrong with a judge making a bail determination on firsthand information, do you Mister O'Connor?"

O'Connor said nothing, just watching the Judge, knowing the bail was going to be set no matter what he said.

"I know Mrs. Wainwright only from what I read," the Judge said smiling at her again. "But from what I know, I know she's not going to abscond from the jurisdiction."

Toni shook her head.

"And since the only purpose of bail is to insure the defendant's presence at court," the Judge continued, "I see no reason why we shouldn't set the bail right now and save Mrs. Wainwright the discomfort of sitting among all the junkies and prostitutes, and who knows what else, that are in the bull pen. Have you finished booking Mrs. Wainwright?" the Judge asked, looking around.

"Yes, sir," said Lieutenant Balinsky.

"Hello, Mister Cahill," the Judge said, seeing the older lawyer near Mrs. Wainwright. "Hello, Marc. Are you going to handle this case?"

"Yes, sir."

The Judge nodded approvingly. "A fine lawyer," the Judge said to Mrs. Wainwright. "Do you have any position to take in reference to the amount of bail, Mister O'Connor?"

"Yes. I don't think you should set it," O'Connor replied. "I think it leaves you open to criticism. It hasn't been done in years."

"If the administration of justice must bow to misplaced criticism or lack of precedent, we'd all, as the Court of Appeals said in some case or other, still have the law of the Plantagenets," replied the Judge benignly. "Do you have any reason to think that Mrs. Wainwright will not show up in court when she's supposed to?"

"I think of Mrs. Wainwright no differently than I would anyone else accused of the same crime," said O'Connor. "I think there should be no bail."

Marc stood silently by, not needing to gild the lily with the Judge apparently well disposed to Toni.

"Well, I, as indeed does the United States Supreme Court, believe in reasonable bail," said the Judge. "Do you have a recommendation on amount?"

"Two hundred fifty thousand," said O'Connor. "I kid you not about that, Judge. Mrs. Wainwright is in such a financial position, that any other bail would be meaningless."

"I think we must take Mrs. Wainwright's financial position into consideration," agreed the Judge. "However, two hundred fifty thousand dollars is a little out of line. Is your bondsman here, Mister Cahill?"

"Yes, sir. He's right over here," said Cahill, looking over the crowd that had now gravitated into a circle around the Judge.

"Here I am, Judge," said Sol Wachter, making his way through the crowd. He had arrived at the precinct shortly after Marc and O'Connor.

"Fine, fine. How are you, Sol? Are you prepared to sign a bond in the amount of fifty thousand dollars?" asked the Judge.

"My employer and the Stuyvesant Insurance Company have authorized me to write a bond in the amount of fifty thousand, yes, sir," said Wachter.

"Very well, I'm going to set bail in the amount of fifty thousand dollars," said the Judge. He watched Toni, smiling as he set the bail.

"She hasn't even been photographed or processed down at headquarters," complained O'Connor.

"I'm sure Mrs. Wainwright would be co-operative in going to headquarters for processing," said the Judge, looking at Marc. Marc nodded. "And then, when the processing is over, she can proceed on her own or with her lawyers to court for arraignment. It will, however, not be necessary for Mrs. Wainwright to be in custody since she's now on bail." The Judge looked toward Sol Wachter, who was sitting at one of the detectives' desks, writing.

"I'll be finished in just a couple of minutes, Your Honor," said Wachter.

"Fine, fine," replied the Judge.

"Thank you, Your Honor," said Toni.

"Don't thank me," said the Judge, looking into her eyes. "I'm only doing what I think is right."

Sol Wachter brought some papers for the Judge's signature. The Judge sat at the desk, read the papers carefully, and signed them.

"Is there anything else now, gentlemen?" asked the Judge.

All the lawyers, including O'Connor, looked to each other.

"The D.A. has to sign and approve the bond," said Wachter.

O'Connor's face brightened. "And I'm not going to do it."

"I took the liberty of phoning Mister Byrnes before I came," said the Judge softly. "We discussed the case. He seemed to know all about it already. And he said if you refused to sign the bond, I should ask you to phone him."

"Sandbagged, hanh, Your Honor?" O'Connor said sourly, taking the bond from Wachter's hands. He scribbled his signature.

"The bail is completed, Your Honor," said Wachter.

O'Connor turned and angrily made his way through the crowd of detectives toward the door.

"I'll go too, then," said the Judge. He shook hands and smiled again at Toni. Then he shook hands with Cahill, then Marc, then Rutley. The Judge made his way toward the door.

"I'm sure both O'Connor and the Judge will keep the press boys distracted for a while," Marc said to Cahill. He turned to the Lieutenant. "Is there any way out of here besides the front door?"

"That's a great idea," Toni said, perking up.

"May I see you for a second, Counselor?" the Lieutenant said, moving toward his private office.

"Certainly," replied Cahill. Rutley was right behind as they moved toward the Lieutenant.

"No, just Mister Conte," said the Lieutenant. "It's not about the case."

Cahill and Rutley stopped short, glancing at Toni. Marc followed the Lieutenant into his office.

The Lieutenant shut the door and turned. "Look, Counselor, I know you're all right. This other Counselor, the Wall Streeter and his little, wise-ass protégé, I don't know, except I know they don't know what it's all about. Now, the reason I wanted to talk to you is that me and my boys have been through a lot of trouble with this dame. She's been treated like a queen since she's been here. And she's got the mouth and manners of a Pier Six brawler. But I'm willing to help her get out through the back way. Even have a couple of the boys go with her. And they'll take real good care of her downtown. Even if she didn't get bailed, we wouldn't have put her inside, you know? I have been very considerate, so far. I didn't have to be, no more than to anyone else. You know that?"

Marc nodded.

"I knew you'd understand," said the Lieutenant. "Now the time is ripe, I figure to find out if these people are considerate enough to, you know, to reciprocate and do the considerate thing for me and the boys. It's only right," said the Lieutenant. "Especially, they want to avoid the newspaper guys."

"Let me talk to Mister Cahill for a moment," said Marc. "Can I talk to him in here, Lieutenant?"

The Lieutenant smiled. "Sure, sure. Should I get the boys going out the back way? It's a lot of trouble. I mean, it really is. Over a couple of roofs and everything. It's not dangerous," he assured Marc.

"Yes, I'm sure that's fine," said Marc.

The Lieutenant went out of his office and said something to Cahill. Cahill walked into the Lieutenant's office alone. Rutley, looking peeved, stayed in the squad room.

"Shut the door," said Marc.

Cahill looked at Marc, then out at the Lieutenant. "What's the matter?"

"It's all right," said Marc.

Cahill shut the door.

"The Lieutenant informed me that the police are going through a lot of trouble for Mrs. Wainwright," said Marc. "They're even going so far as to spirit her away from the reporters out the back way."

"I know, they've been very considerate," said Cahill. "I was thinking that I'd write a letter to the Commissioner, stating just that."

"I'm sure the Lieutenant and his men would appreciate that very much," said Marc. "However, I'm sure they'd also like something more immediate, more direct."

"What do you mean?"

"I mean, do you have a couple of hundred dollars in cash in your pocket?"

"What?" Cahill looked shocked.

"Mister Cahill, it's not a bribe. You're not asking the police not to do their sworn duty, are you? They are arresting your client, aren't they?"

Cahill stood watching Marc, weighing his thoughts.

"Do you think Mrs. Wainwright would prefer going through the crowd of reporters?" asked Marc.

"I'm sure she wouldn't," replied Cahill.

"Well, it's not part of the police job to help people over roof tops to escape the press. That's not what they're paid to do. If you want them to help you, help them. Otherwise, let's forget it and get out of here the front way now."

Cahill shrugged and took some bills out of his pocket. "Are you sure we won't be in trouble?"

"I'm sure. No one has said anything about money. No one saw anyone doing anything with money. There's just you and me here," Marc said, pulling open the center drawer in the Lieutenant's desk. "Drop it in here."

Cahill dropped the bills into the drawer and Marc shut it.

The two men walked out of the Lieutenant's office.

"Well, we're all set to go," said the Lieutenant. "Is everything okay?"

"Everything's okay," said Marc.

"Okay, fine. You lawyers don't have to be with us. We can meet you down at headquarters," said the Lieutenant.

"You mean no one is going to be with me?" said Toni.

"Rutley, you go with Mrs. Wainwright just in case she needs anything," Cahill directed. "That's okay, isn't it, Lieutenant?"

"Sure, sure," he said, "if that's what you want." The Lieutenant went into his office, shutting the door. He emerged again. "Okay, boys, let's go," he said.

X

MONDAY, AUGUST 14, 5:52 P.M.

"That wasn't too bad now, was it?" Marc asked Toni Wainwright. They were seated in the back of a large, black Rolls-Royce limousine, headed uptown on Park Avenue. James Cahill was seated at Toni Wainwright's other side. Rutley sat sideways on a jump seat in front of them.

"No, it wasn't bad," she replied. "It was horrible." Toni leaned forward to reach the bar console built into the partition separating the passenger compartment from the driver's seat. She poured more vodka into the glass she had already drained. "Get me some ice, will you?" she directed Rutley.

Rutley turned quickly and began searching for the ice tongs.

"Oh, Christ, your hands will do, your feet will do, anything, just give me some ice," she said impatiently.

Rutley took two cubes in a bare hand and put them into her glass.

"Are all court arraignments as ugly as mine?" Toni Wainwright asked Marc.

"No. Most are vastly more ugly," he replied. The limousine turned west on Sixty-third Street. "You didn't get to spend any time in the bull pen, the jail. Most defendants, men and women, spend at least a few hours there."

"I would have gone mad, simply mad." She sipped from her glass.

The black limousine slowed to a stop in front of the Hotel Louis Quinze. The doorman, recognizing Zack Lord's limousine, moved quickly to open the door, smiling broadly. Rutley was the first to get out. The doorman folded the jump seat, allowing Toni Wainwright to step out. Cahill was next, then Marc.

"Is this where Zack Lord has his office?" asked Marc.

"His New York office," Cahill acknowledged. "He happens to own the hotel."

"And, slowly but surely, it seems, the rest of New York?" Marc joked.

"Almost." Cahill nodded reverently.

As the small group moved toward the entrance, Marc noticed a black Cadillac coupe parked at the curb well forward in the NO PARKING area of the hotel entrance. A driver in civilian clothes sat behind the wheel reading a newspaper. The license plate was J A L—Joe Lacqua's car, thought Marc. Lacqua was the Democratic leader of New York County, one of the strongest political leaders in New York State.

The elevator doors opened at the twenty-ninth floor, revealing a private reception foyer decorated in ornate carved Louis Quinze furniture and lush, crimson Persian rugs. An attractive receptionist seated behind an ormolu-edged table-desk smiled and rose.

"Mister Lord is expecting you, Mrs. Wainwright, Mister Cahill," she said in proper British tones. "He suggested you wait in the conference room." The girl walked precisely and erectly ahead of them to a doorway at the left of the elevators. She opened the door for them, and stood to one side, still smiling pleasantly, nodding to each as they entered. The receptionist entered behind them, taking the lead again quickly, moving through an interior corridor, past several closed doors, to a door marked CONFERENCE ROOM. She opened the door and stood smartly as they entered. She looked around the room. "If there's anything you need, please just dial me on six-seven," she said, pointing to the phone. She smiled and turned.

"I know she's just got to have a broomstick up her ass," said Toni Wainwright as the door closed behind the receptionist. "I need a drink." She walked toward a bar built into the wall.

Zack Lord's conference room was decorated in light blue, with a luxuriously thick, dark blue rug spread across the floor. In the center of the room, a long, darkly inlaid and carved table stretched precisely between twelve carved, dark, straight-back chairs upholstered in blue velvet. At the head of the table was a high-backed swivel arm chair covered with dark blue crushed leather. To the left of the high-backed chair was a console table into which was built an array of buttons and switches. Two telephones hung side by side at the rear of the console.

Against the side walls of the room there were matching couches covered in blue brocade. Above each couch was huge woven tapestry depicting vast armies winding through an ancient countryside peopled with soldiers, mounted officers, women, dogs, horses, and cannon-on-wheels coursing along in blue and golden threads.

The four people in the conference room remained silent. Toni Wainwright sipped her drink. Cahill sat on one of the couches. Rutley stood. Marc sat on a side chair at the conference table.

"What happens now?" asked Toni as the silence, underscored by the sound of ice cubes clinking in her glass, grew too heavy. All looked at Marc.

"We have to wait to see if they get an indictment," said Marc. "It won't take O'Connor long to present a case like this to the grand jury. As a matter of fact, he'll make sure of that."

"Is it my imagination or does he hate me?" asked Toni.

"He doesn't hate you," replied Marc. "In fact, he's delighted with you and your case. It gives him a perfect opportunity to give full play to his normal, ordinary, politician's craving for attention. Show business and politics are very close to each other, not because they require the same talents, but because they are both havens for little, insecure people in search of applause. O'Connor's going to make sure that what he says about you publicly is really tough, and strong, and bold, all those other qualities that he feels the people of this great city would want to hear about in their District Attorney."

"But Byrnes is the District Attorney," said Toni. "O'Connor is just one of his assistants."

"Not for long, not if O'Connor has anything to do about it," said Marc. "Unfortunately, this case fell into his lap like manna from heaven. Byrnes is going after a judgeship at the Democratic Judicial Convention. If the Democrats give it to him, O'Connor will be in position to get the Democratic nod for D.A."

Silence prevailed again. Toni Wainwright rose and poured another drink for herself.

"As I understand it," said Rutley, "we cannot be present at the grand jury hearing?"

"Mrs. Wainwright could testify, if she cared to," said Marc, "but we cannot know what other witnesses testify to, or even who they are, or what other evidence is presented. It's a secret proceeding."

"What are the chances of Mrs. Wainwright's not being indicted?" asked Cahill.

"Since the D.A. can get an indictment, almost at will from the grand jury—depending on how he presents the case—I'd say less than slim," replied Marc.

A worried, distant look washed across Toni Wainwright's face.

"Don't worry," Marc said. "You may be embarrassed by the initial publicity, Mrs. Wainwright. That I can't eliminate. But O'Connor needs real evidence when he brings you to trial. And he just doesn't have enough in this case. We'll take the wind out of his sails when it comes to the important things."

"You're sure about that?" Toni Wainwright asked. "You're sure you can handle this case?"

"I'm sure."

A door near where Marc was standing opened. Everyone in the conference room turned. The man who opened the door hesitated at the door, still talking and laughing with people in the room beyond. Marc could only see the back of a man of medium height holding the door open. Beyond, Marc saw Joe Lacqua, the Chief, as he was called, the Democratic political boss, sitting on a couch, a cocktail glass in one hand, a cigarette in his other, laughing, saying something to the man at the door. There were other people in that room, all laughing now. Marc couldn't see the others.

Zack Lord is apparently already at work for Mrs. Wainwright, thought Marc, *busy placing some contracts.*

A contract has all sorts of connotations: legal, criminal, even political. In politics a contract may be an assignment from the political leader to one of his men in the clubhouse to do something for one of the constituents: help them fill out a tax form; find

116

them a job; call the housing department when the landlord doesn't provide heat. A political contract may also be a request by the political leader to an official—mayor, judge, D.A.—to make sure a decision is made, an outcome results, which favors the leader or one of his supporters.

Zack Lord entered the conference room, shutting the door behind him. He had a pale complexion, with almost colorless light blue eyes. His blond hair was slicked flat back. He wore a suit that was a medium, almost electric, blue, with a blue on blue herringbone weave. A pink shirt, and a tie with swirling abstract design on blue completed the outfit.

"Mister Conte," said Lord, walking directly to Marc, smiling a thin smile. The others in the room, including Toni, watched Zack. Cahill wiped the palm of his right hand on his pants leg as he rose in anticipation of shaking Zack's hand.

"Hello, Mister Lord," replied Marc. He felt Lord's hand close hard on his own, squeezing. Marc exerted slightly more hand pressure to equalize Lord's grip.

Lord studied Marc's face carefully as their hands squeezed, his eyes narrowing. His bottom lip curled outward as he nodded silently.

"Zack," Cahill interrupted respectfully, "we've handled the first steps of the case. Mister Conte and I have four men in the office researching the law right now." He walked over to Zack and Marc.

Lord nodded, without looking at Cahill. He turned abruptly toward Toni. "Are you all right, darling?" he asked.

"Fine," Toni replied, cradling her precious glass. "It was pretty crappy in the police station. And the jail! That was even worse."

"Of course it was. Of course," Lord said blandly. "But we have it all under control now." He smiled, actually sneering. "Everything that can be done, will be done. Everything," Lord emphasized, turning to Marc.

"I noticed," said Marc.

Zack studied Marc for a moment, puzzled. He looked to Cahill, then back to Marc. "What's that supposed to mean, Mister Conte?"

"That means I know you know some very influential people," said Marc.

Lord nodded, that thin sneer of a smile creasing his face again.

Lord's sense of affability was rather limited; his sense of timing was better, and he knew when to try to be pleasant, or when he should try to seem mysterious.

"I understand, Mister Conte, that you're a fine criminal lawyer," said Zack. It was said almost as a challenge. "I've gotten that from several sources."

"That was very kind of . . ."

"You'll be well paid for this case, well paid." Lord plunged on directly. "This is a case of total mistake. That should make it all the easier, Mister Conte. But I don't want you to waste any time on this."

"Mister Lord, I don't intend to waste time—yours, and especially mine."

"And, I don't tolerate failure," Lord said flatly, his eyes fixed on Marc's face.

"I don't enjoy failure either, Mister Lord," said Marc, returning Lord's stare. "But, if you want an absolute guarantee that I can walk Mrs. Wainwright out of the courtroom in this case, totally without blemish, absolutely without problem, you've got the wrong lawyer. I can't and I won't give it, regardless of the fee."

"That mean you don't think you can handle this case? That it's too big for you?" demanded Lord.

"Not at all. It means that anyone who gives you a one hundred per cent guarantee on the outcome of this or any other case is a liar or a fool, Mister Lord. I'll go in and fight right down the line with every weapon at my disposal. And I fight very well, as some of your sources must have already told you. But, the only thing I can guarantee is that nobody will do a better or more thorough job. As well, perhaps, but not better."

Lord was studying Marc, listening. "I'm an exacting man, Mister Conte."

"One other thing, Mister Lord," Marc continued. "I'm not a schoolboy, to be intimidated by you or anyone else. If you want me to handle the case, I will. If you don't, as you said, let's not waste time." Marc was being a bit abrupt. But he had decided Lord needed, probably respected, boldness and strength.

Cahill and Rutley watched Lord apprehensively.

Lord sneered his thin smile again. "You'll have plenty of help, Mister Conte. All kinds of help. From inside and outside the courthouse, including Jim's entire law staff. No expense is too great."

"I appreciate that, Mister Lord," Marc said. "May I suggest, however, for right now at least, that it won't do to have too many cooks working on this stew."

"Meaning?" asked Cahill tartly.

"Meaning," Marc said to Lord, "I appreciate Mister Cahill's staff looking up the law on criminal cases, but they're only going to discover things I have already looked up and been studying for years. Moreover, this is not a case to be decided on the law, but on the facts, the circumstances of the shooting. If I need investigation done, I can handle that myself with my own people. In other words, Mister Lord, I'm saying I don't want to have to check in and get clearance on how to handle the case."

"Just a minute, Mister Conte," said Cahill. "You're being a bit presumptuous, aren't you?"

"I don't mean to be," said Marc. "But, I might as well get this straight right now. I really won't answer to other attorneys who aren't in a position to evaluate. I have no objection to having Mister Cahill or anyone else informed of progress. But I have to make the final decisions."

Cahill became very red in the face. He turned to Lord. "This is preposterous. We've represented everything you've done for the last fifteen years."

Marc said nothing.

"I like to be the captain of my ship," said Lord, looking directly at Marc.

"This isn't exactly your ship," said Marc. "In the first place, it's Mrs. Wainwright's. In the second place, I doubt you've ever handled a ship like this before."

"Do I have anything to say about any of this?" Toni said, not too dryly.

Everyone turned to her. She sipped at her drink.

"Of course you do," said Lord.

"If he's got the balls to stand up to you as he's doing right now," she said to Lord—"if you'll pardon my French," she said to the others—"he's got to have something going for him. He'll do just fine."

"Mrs. Wainwright . . ." started Cahill.

"Oh, come on, Jim. You're not going to lose your fat retainer. Why screw around with something you don't know from a hole in the wall? Especially when it's my hole that's against the wall?"

There was silence.

"That settles that very directly," said Lord, turning to Cahill.

Cahill's jaw muscles twitched momentarily. He did not look at Marc. "As you wish, Zack."

"There is one other preliminary item to be discussed," said Marc. "Speaking of retainers. I don't know exactly with whom to discuss it, but it's a matter of agreeing on a fee and who's going to pay it."

"You don't think you have to worry about that," said Cahill dismissingly.

"No, but I do think I have to discuss it and have agreed upon right now," said Marc, looking to Toni Wainwright then Zack Lord. He had heard that *"Don't worry about it"* phrase too often from clients who would promise anything during their distress, only to forget or renege when extricated from the jaws of the cell. Besides, as in Vermont, good fences make for good neighbors.

"What is your fee?" asked Lord.

"Twenty-five thousand dollars, not including expenses or any appeal," replied Marc.

"Twenty-five thousand?" Toni Wainwright exclaimed. She looked to Zack Lord.

"That's a little steep, isn't it?" Cahill said for them.

"No. It's in line with the seriousness of the charges and the possible consequences," replied Marc. "Don't you think saving twenty-five years of your life is worth twenty-five thousand dollars?" he said to Toni Wainwright. "If you do want a bargain-priced lawyer, I'm sure you can find one," he added. "I'm not a businessman, I'm a lawyer, and I don't bargain."

"No bargaining, just asking," said Lord. "What if you're able to get rid of this case right away? Is the fee still the same?"

"Yes, sir," replied Marc. "It isn't the amount of time involved, the hours in court, it's the lifetime of study, the years of developing skill that's going on the line to defend Mrs. Wainwright. If I dispose of it quicker, it's still disposed of."

"Okay, done," said Lord. "Jim, make the arrangements."

Cahill nodded stiffly. "As you wish, Zack."

"You'll have additional help all the way down the line," Zack said to Marc. "I'll attend to that." He was nodding slightly.

"O'Connor is out to make himself a name here," Marc cautioned.

"We'll take care of that," said Zack. "His boss needs the Democratic nomination for judge. Matter of fact, he wants it badly. I don't imagine he'd like anyone to mess that up for him. And O'Connor's going to need all the Democratic help he can get to be the D.A."

Marc nodded acquiescence.

"What about publicity?" Toni asked Lord. "Mister Conte seems to think there'll be a lot of bad publicity. Especially with this O'Connor on the case."

"We'll take care of that too," said Lord. "A little oil takes care of most wheels." He smiled at Marc.

"Mister Lord," said Marc. "I'm just the trial man. Anything else, I don't want to know about. I'm not interested in politics or making contracts or contacts."

Lord nodded. "You take care of the trial. I'll handle the rest."

XI

WEDNESDAY, AUGUST 16, 1:15 P.M.

"How do you say we handle The Tombs prisoners who rioted?" Francis X. Byrnes, the District Attorney of New York County, asked his chief assistant, Liam O'Connor. They were seated in Byrnes's office having their daily conference concerning any new indictments handed down by the grand jury, the handling of pending cases, investigations, and the general running of the office.

Byrnes was short and small of build, with faded blue eyes peering from a bulldog face with a square jaw and thin mouth which seemed set in a scowl. He had joined the D.A.'s staff originally in 1934, when the salary was a token one dollar a year, and it was a privilege and a public service to be an assistant D.A. Besides that, serving an apprenticeship in the D.A.'s office gave one political muscle and a good springboard, if one wanted, into politics, onto the bench, or to some other government service. Byrnes actually had been too short for the Police Department, and, wanting to be in law enforcement, decided on a legal career and the D.A.'s staff. Somehow, sanctity and the protection of the innocent, the cold, calculated enforcement of the statutes were a sacred trust passed on from his father, who had been a police captain, to save the good people from the secular miscreants, the heathens, the wops, the sheenies, the polacks, the krauts, the spics, and the niggers.

"We're going to present the case to the grand jury today or tomorrow. Before the weekend, for sure," replied O'Connor. "We'll have them indicted and arraigned before Wednesday this coming week."

O'Connor had one leg crossed over the other, holding the ankle of the crossed leg so that it would not slide off the heft of the stationary leg. He wore short anklet socks which exposed his shin and part of his calf as he sat.

Byrnes's office was large and square, the walls painted a light, easy-on-the-eye, hospital green. The ceiling was white. His desk was plain and wooden. There was a large leather couch against one wall. Numerous certificates of election, a diploma, an admission to the Bar, and other awards hung on the wall over the couch. There were no other pictures, paintings, or evidence of human interest or endeavor to be seen in the office. This was a place of serious business, and wives and children were preserved for off the job.

"I want you to put every available assistant on the case," Byrnes instructed. His face wrinkled at the forehead and top of the nose as he pressed his fingertips like two flexed spiders. The wrinkled nose was one of Byrnes's two facial expressions. The other was the scowl. "Interview the guards, other witnesses. Do whatever has to be done. We have to have fast action. And a speedy trial. The public feels outrage, and more than that, fright. They think these prisoners can do what they want and get away with it."

"Don't worry about that, Chief," assured O'Connor. "I'll pull out all the stops."

Chief was the old Tammany Hall salutation for the top man.

Under the old Tammany regime, all the Democratic clubs were named with Indian names: Tammawah, Anawanda, Iroquois, even Tammany itself was Indian. And, naturally, the top man of the tribe was always the Chief. Byrnes was a Tammany man of the old tradition. On the job for more than forty years; right up through the ranks, from lowly assistant to Bureau Chief to the District Attorney himself. O'Connor, on the other hand, had been just a fledgling Indian when Tammany fell into disrepute and disrepair. But he still retained the old ways, the old respect he and his father before him had cherished.

If the truth be known, Byrnes was the Chief in name only. He had grown tired of late, and O'Connor kept his hand on the helm, informing Byrnes of everything, so at least he was aware of what was happening. Byrnes now just wanted his judgeship, a few years on the bench, and then to retire with his pension and his wife, Margaret Mary.

"Why not have them arraigned right after you get the indictment this Friday afternoon?" asked Byrnes.

"No good for the newspaper boys, Chief," replied O'Connor. "It'd be too late. And, besides, Saturday's not such a hot day for newspaper stories. Everyone's away. If we're going to go to town on this kind of thing, let the prisoners and the punks in the street know what they're up against if they attack a guard or a cop, then we need all the coverage we can get. I'll need time to arrange it, get extra copies made of our indictment papers. And the boys in the pressroom prefer stories early in the morning on Monday or Tuesday, so they catch all the editions."

Byrnes nodded slowly. "How many defendants are there going to be?"

"I'm not sure yet, Chief. Maybe a dozen, two dozen. I haven't gone over all the evidence yet."

"They all colored?"

"Mostly. Some Puertos too. And a couple of whites," answered O'Connor.

Byrnes nodded his scowl again. "What charges?"

"Attempted murder, assault, inciting to riot. I've got the Appeals Bureau looking into kidnaping and some other statutes."

Byrnes nodded, the wrinkle slowly creasing his forehead again. "Better have them check and double check that stuff," he suggested. "You don't want some bleeding-heart lawyer coming around with some fancy motion papers dismissing counts because they don't hold legal water. We'll get picketed for persecuting poor innocents."

"Poor innocents," scoffed O'Connor. "They're about as poor and innocent as the devil himself."

"Even so, I don't want any bad publicity right now, neither do you," said Byrnes, a tone of shared secrecy in his voice.

"Don't worry, Chief," said O'Connor. "The private citizens are howling about this riot. And the Mayor's talk about amnesty and all that other crap doesn't jibe too well with the voter. Davies still thinks that liberal crap is in vogue. He'll find out soon enough. The public'll be very sympathetic to the prosecution. You'll be the D.A. who puts the punks in their place, and I'll be the crusading prosecutor who'll get the daily trial publicity. That won't sit too badly with the voters when it comes to your Supreme Court seat." He winked at Byrnes. "And it won't hurt me as your replacement. The political leaders read the papers too."

"Those who can read."

O'Connor chuckled. He took a short, stubby cigar out of his coat pocket and unwrapped it.

"Who are you going to have present this riot case to the grand jury?" asked Byrnes.

"I'll do it myself, Chief," said O'Connor. He puffed on his cigar, a thick cloud of smoke enveloping his head momentarily.

The Chief nodded, satisfied. "Which judge you going to send the case to decide the motions and for trial?"

"Say no more, Chief," assured O'Connor. "I figure we send it to Crawford."

The Chief nodded again.

"He's been around long enough to know how to handle a case like this," O'Connor continued, giving Byrnes another wink. "Even if he had a contract to deliver on that Wainwright bail. I'd rather give it to him than let the case get in front of one of those sob sister reformers. Christ, you see this guy Haroldson, and some of the decisions he makes. They're off the wall. He's so busy being fair to everybody, he steps on his own prick."

Byrnes waved a disgusted hand through the air, shaking his head. The intercom buzzed. Byrnes picked it up and spoke softly into the receiver. "Okay. Put him on," he said. Brynes waited, then listened. "When?" he asked, a grave look on his face. He nodded. "Liam's right here. He'll get back to you."

"What's up, Chief?" O'Connor asked.

"That was Michael Scott, Captain over in the one-six precinct. He's at Roosevelt Hospital now. Compagna just died."

O'Connor said nothing, puffing on his cigar momentarily. A grim, pensive look spread over his face. "Well, that's no great loss; one less of those greasy gunslingers," he allowed. "I just hope it doesn't start a war where they'll leave their gumbas all over the sidewalks riddled with shotgun blasts."

"Maybe we ought to pick the gunsels up just in case. We could start a grand jury investigation of the shooting as an excuse, and pick all the dangerous ones up on subpoenas."

"Good idea, Chief. I'll call Dan Braverman in Queens—a lot of them live in Queens. Maybe he'll co-operate and have his staff get an investigation going too."

"The sooner the better," said Byrnes. He looked out at the weather again, then leaned back in his chair and glanced at the large wall clock through a spiral of O'Connor's smoke. He remembered a two o'clock appointment with his campaign fund raiser. Even though Byrnes was one of the candidates all the Democratic chiefs had backed for Supreme Court nomination, there was still need to raise substantial funds. Campaigns cost plenty these days.

"The FBI must not be too unhappy about Compagna," reflected O'Connor. "He really raked them over the coals with his Council, his pickets, and all the rest." O'Connor nodded as he savored the heavy smoke of his cigar. A smile played across his face at the FBI's discomfort.

"Compagna never did any of that against our office," said Byrnes, obviously pleased. "But why should he have? We always treat people square. If we've got a case, we get them. If we don't have a case, we don't frame them, we don't manufacture that conspiracy stuff the U.S. Attorneys love to use."

Byrnes relented for a moment, staring out the window. He allowed himself to think of the beach, and the surf down at Breezy Point, the waves rolling in, sliding across the surface in a sheet of foam; and his grandchildren running, leaving deep, moist footprints in the sand at the water's edge. It was too nice a day to be involved in all this gangbusters stuff. He was really ready for that Supreme Court bench. Let O'Connor get bloody hands on this job. He looked up at the clock again. It was close to 2 P.M. He wouldn't even have time for a sandwich before meeting with the fund raiser.

"That reminds me," Byrnes said abstractly, "this Wainwright case you mentioned. That's the one where the wife shot the husband. What does it look like?"

"It's okay, Chief. We only have circumstantial evidence to go on, but I'm sure it'll hang together enough for the grand jury."

"Well, don't stretch too hard to hold it together," Byrnes said. "I mean, if it's there, of course, by all means, you have to go after it. But, if it's a weak case . . ." He noticed O'Connor looking at him curiously. "If it's a weak case, it's a weak case."

"There any problem, Chief?"

"No, no problem," Byrnes replied. "Just there are a lot of big guns interested in the case—big money people who called county headquarters. So I don't want you to do anything to rock the boat unnecessarily."

"You're not telling me to lay down on this Wainwright case, are you, Chief?"

"Absolutely not," Byrnes said. "I just suggest you handle the case . . . just handle the case carefully taking into consideration the political ramifications."

O'Connor studied Byrnes who was again looking out the window as if some very important event was taking place on the sill.

XII

WEDNESDAY, AUGUST 16, 2:35 P.M.

The bridge man in Part AP-3 of the Criminal Court called the Maricyk case, then handed the court papers up to Judge Bamburg. The Judge read the papers as the defendant was escorted from the bull pen into the courtroom by arresting officer Schmidt.

Marc walked from the audience to the counsel table. He stood beside Maricyk, identified himself and gave his address so the stenotypist could record his appearance. Mrs. Maricyk was seated at the rear of the courtroom, watching anxiously.

"The defendant is ready for a hearing, if Your Honor pleases," said Marc.

The Judge looked to the assistant D.A. "Mister D.A.? What is the People's position in this case?"

The D.A. conferred with Schmidt in low whispers. "Your Honor, this matter has not been presented as yet to the grand jury."

"What do you want to do here?" the Judge asked the D.A. "The defendant says he's ready for a hearing. I don't like to keep men in jail without some sort of hearing. This defendant hasn't made bail yet, has he, Counselor?"

"No, sir," Marc responded.

"This is a jail case, Mister D.A. What about it?" said the Judge.

"I'd like one further adjournment," said the D.A.

"Bastard," whispered Maricyk to himself.

"Your Honor," said Marc, "the D.A. handling the matter in the arraignment part insisted on an adjournment the last time this matter was on because it might have been presented to the grand jury that day. It obviously wasn't. Now another adjournment is asked for by the People. I haven't heard of any reason for such adjournment, legal or otherwise. I suggest that this Court should not permit the People these delays intended only to frustrate the defendant's right to a hearing."

"Well, I don't know that that's the People's intention. However, if you are not prepared to hold a hearing today, Mister D.A., I'll entertain counsel's application to lower the defendant's bail."

"We'll let them have a hearing," the D.A. said with a shrug.

"Very well," said the Judge. "Go right in the back. The back-up part is open."

Behind the main courtroom of AP-3, in what had been a small office or judge's robing room, there is a small courtroom, AP-4, where cases from the front court are sent for hearing to determine if a crime has been committed or for non-jury trial if they are misdemeanors.

Marc entered AP-4's courtroom through a door to the side of

Judge Bamburg's bench. Inside, there was a small business desk at floor level behind which another Judge sat. Two uniformed court officers stood conversing near the judge's desk. A young female stenotypist sat with her machine at the side of the Judge. There was only room enough in the court for one spectator bench with a three-seat capacity. The window air conditioner was old and clackety. Schmidt brought Maricyk into the courtroom and sat him at the counsel table in front of the judge's desk. There was only one counsel table which had to be shared by both the prosecution, the defense, and the defendant.

"People against Maricyk," said one of the court officers, reading from the papers brought in from the front room.

"Let me have a couple of minutes, Judge," said the young, red-haired assistant D.A. assigned to AP-4. "I want to prepare the case."

"Go ahead," said the Judge. He sat back in his chair, gazing at the ceiling. It was peeling and bubbled.

"Officer," said the D.A., turning to Schmidt. He led Schmidt to a corridor outside the little courtroom, so that Schmidt might relate the facts of the case to him for the first time.

Marc waited at the counsel table next to Maricyk.

The court officers began talking about yesterday's baseball games.

"Who is this Judge?" Maricyk asked.

"Judge DeGeorge," Marc replied. "He had been Commissioner of Purchase."

"Any good?"

"He's pretty new. I don't know much about him," said Marc. He rose and walked over to one of the court officers who he knew slightly. "How's this Judge?" Marc whispered.

The officer turned his back to the judge's desk and rotated his hand from side to side. "He's not too bad on a plea. He doesn't like to send anyone to jail, yet. On a hearing, he holds most of the stuff in. You know, he's new."

"Thanks," said Marc, returning to his chair.

Maricyk inquired with a jut of his jaw.

"He apparently doesn't throw many cases out," said Marc. "But at least we'll be able to get a line on the D.A.'s case, hear what Schmidt is going to say."

"Do I have to say anything?" Maricyk asked. "What do I have to do?"

"Nothing," replied Marc. "We'll let them present their case, see if there's enough to convince the Judge that a crime has been committed."

"Officer," said the Judge. "See if you can turn the air conditioning higher. It's pretty close in here."

The court attendant touched the dials. The machine squawked and began pelting out a new, louder rhythm.

"Better leave it where it was," said the Judge. "Let's proceed."

The case was called. Schmidt took the stand, swore to tell the truth. The D.A. asked him to explain to the Judge what had occurred the night he arrested Maricyk.

Schmidt testified that he and his partner stopped Maricyk for an illegal U-turn. Schmidt also testified that Maricyk tried to talk him out of issuing a ticket. After Schmidt refused to hear Maricyk's plea, he testified, Maricyk became belligerent and tried to punch Schmidt. Thereupon, Schmidt arrested Maricyk and brought him to the station house.

"Now while at the station house, Officer," said the D.A. continuing, "did anything else occur?"

"Yes, the defendant said he'd make it worth my while if we just gave him some kind of disorderly conduct summons."

"What did you do then, if anything?" continued the D.A. "Explain it to the Court."

"I said, wait a minute, I want to talk to my partner about how much it'd be worth. Then I went outside, and told the sergeant. He gave me a small wire recorder, which I put under my jacket. I went back in, and the defendant kept talking about how he didn't need any trouble, he'd make it worth my while. So I asked him how much. And he said that was up to me, twenty bucks. I said, okay, where's the dough? He took it out of his pocket and tried to hand it to me."

"And then what happened?" asked the D.A.

The Judge was leaning back in his chair, listening. The stenotypist's moving fingers were recording everything that was said.

"I placed the defendant under arrest for attempted bribery."

"Do you have the recording of what the defendant said to you that night?" the Judge asked.

"Not with me. It's at the station house."

"But you do have the recording?" asked the D.A.

"I do."

"I have no further questions, Your Honor."

"Cross-examination, Counselor?" asked the Judge.

Marc rose. He knew it was pointless to cross-examine Schmidt. This wasn't a trial after all, and surely there was enough evidence on the record for the Judge to find a crime may indeed have been committed. As a practical matter, after hearing Schmidt testify about having recorded the bribe conversations, Marc realized that the best service he could render Maricyk was to get the D.A. to consent to a guilty plea to a reduced charge, and have Maricyk take such a plea before a reasonable judge.

Marc knew that more than ninety per cent of all criminal charges were disposed of through plea bargaining. Indeed, although many critics raise their voices in derision of such a system, if there were no dispositions of cases by the D.A. offering to the defendant a lower plea than the one originally charged, and if the defendant didn't, in turn, offer to have a plea of guilt entered against him to the lowered charge; if every case was disposed of only by trial, our courts would have to work around the clock and personnel—judges, D.A.s, lawyers, officers, stenographers, clerks —would have to be trebled, and still the overflow of untried cases each year would fill the jails to bursting.

And those who would suggest that pleas of guilty should be permitted, but not lesser pleas to lesser charges, should recognize as a fact of life that it would not interest a defendant to plead guilty to the top count or charge against him if the worst thing that could happen to him at a trial is to be convicted of the very same count. He might as well proceed to trial and take a chance. After all, he might win. And if he lost, he'd only be convicted of the top charge against him anyway.

Moreover, in a very substantial number of cases, it isn't that the D.A. is granting a unilateral favor to the defendant in permitting a plea to a lesser count—only the D.A., charged with the responsibility of prosecution, has the right to offer a lesser plea. For many a case is based on hazy evidence, or unsure witnesses, or illegal evidence, and if, indeed, a trial were to ensue, there might be a hung jury or an outright acquittal.

Since the outcome of trials is an uncertainty, for both prosecution and defense, and since the D.A.'s desire to permit the defendant to plead guilty to a lesser charge is directly tied in to the D.A.'s evaluation of his chances of success—the weaker the D.A.'s case, the more prone to a lesser plea he is, and vice versa—the D.A., in the ordinary instance of plea bargaining, is doing no more for the defendant than the defendant is doing for the People.

Most of the time, plea bargaining is a fair exchange, a good bargain which can usually be measured when neither side is completely pleased.

In Maricyk's case, Marc realized the D.A. had a strong case, and the D.A. would probably be less amenable to a lower plea.

"I have no questions of the witness," said Marc.

"Is that the People's entire case?" asked the Judge, looking at the D.A.

"Yes, sir."

"Do you have any witnesses?" the Judge asked Marc. He smiled pleasantly. He had an air of affability about him; particularly since he had a case before him that was solid, there were no complex issues to decide. He was astride the matter firmly.

"No, sir. The defense rests," Marc replied.

"Motions?" the Judge asked.

"Yes, sir. I move first to dismiss those charges alleging possession by the defendant of marijuana, on the grounds that there is absolutely no proof whatever in the record concerning any narcotics in this case."

"No, I'm going to deny that motion," the Judge said. He had a pleasant, don't-take-it-personally smile on his face. "There's enough here to hold this case for the grand jury."

"Your Honor," said Marc, "most respectfully, I suggest that there may be some evidence relating to an alleged attempted bribe, but I respectfully submit you can't hold a charge concerning marijuana in this case where the D.A. has failed totally to produce any evidence whatever concerning the same."

"Denied." The Judge smiled. "Any other motion?"

"May I ask Your Honor for the record on what grounds you are denying the defendant's motion to dismiss the marijuana charges?" Marc asked pointedly.

"Counselor, I've made my decision. You have an appeal available at the appropriate time if you so desire," replied the Judge. "Any other motions?"

Despite the fact that the Judge was being hard-nosed and seemingly legally obtuse, he was acutely aware at this precise moment, just as were Marc and the D.A., and even Maricyk, that Maricyk was stretched over a barrel by the evidence; that a jury, if they had any doubt of Maricyk's guilt after Schmidt testified, would be more than assured by the tape recordings. Thus, the Judge knew that it was 100 to 1 that Maricyk would plead guilty. It was also 100 to 1, therefore, that there would be no appeal by Maricyk. And, thus, what difference did it make what he decided, right or wrong, about marijuana, about anything at the hearing?

"Denied, Counselor," said the Judge. "I think there's enough to hold this attempted bribery, and that's what I'm going to do. This is a felony and must therefore go to the grand jury. If there's merit to what you say, the grand jury can dismiss it." He nodded with assurance. "The Supreme Court can throw it out if they want. I will not." The Judge wrote his decision on the papers before him.

"Will Your Honor consider a reduction of defendant's bail at this time?" asked Marc. "Particularly since the defendant and his family are totally incapable of meeting the present bail conditions. He hasn't been able to make bail since his arrest."

"What does the D.A. have to say about that?" asked the Judge. "Will you consent to lowering the bail?"

The young D.A. shook his head. "I'm not going to consent to anything, Judge."

"Your Honor, you do not need the consent of the D.A. to lower the bail," said Marc. "That's solely the Court's province. And I urge a reduction over the D.A.'s reluctance where the D.A.'s position is so arbitrary and totally without any relation to the absence of danger of this defendant not appearing to answer the charges. Since that's the only purpose of bail, to insure the defendant's presence at future proceedings, and since the D.A. hasn't even suggested there would be any danger of this defendant fleeing the jurisdiction and not answering the charges, I respectfully suggest a lower bail is eminently appropriate."

"I'm afraid, Counselor, that I'm not going to reduce the bail at this time," said the Judge. "You can make an application in the Supreme Court if you want to lower the bail."

"May we approach the bench, Your Honor?" Marc asked.

"Yes, surely."

The D.A. skirted one side of the counsel table, Marc the other. They met at the judge's bench.

"I'm just inquiring, Your Honor, if the D.A. is amenable to a disposition at this time," said Marc.

"This is certainly a case for disposition, Mister Conte," agreed the Judge. He looked to the D.A. "You willing to reduce the charges?"

In the Criminal Court, where there is jurisdiction over misdemeanors only, the felony charges have to be reduced to misdemeanor proportions, before the Court has any jurisdiction.

"No, sir," said the young D.A. "This is an out-and-out felony. I won't reduce it to a misdemeanor."

"That's all I can do, Counselor," the Judge said to Marc.

"Very well, sir."

"Hold the case for the grand jury," the Judge said aloud for the record. "You'll be notified when you're to appear in the Supreme Court."

"Thank you, sir," Marc said, turning toward the rear of the courtroom. Schmidt accompanied Maricyk back toward the bull pen to await return to The Tombs.

Mrs. Maricyk waved to her husband as he was escorted from the courtroom. She held her hand over her mouth to stifle her emotions as she turned to join Marc.

"What was that all about, Mister Conte?" asked Mrs. Maricyk. She was very upset. "I hope you don't think I'm dumb, I just don't know what's going on. I'm all confused."

"The Judge held the case for grand jury action," said Marc.

"When does that happen?" she asked. "I didn't hear no date."

"The D.A. schedules the grand jury," said Marc. "I've explained that we don't go to the grand jury unless Joey testifies. Other than that, the D.A. conducts the grand jury and then notifies us if Joey's indicted."

"They didn't even say anything about marijuana," said Mrs. Maricyk. "Just like you said. Joey's going to be indicted for that too?"

"I'm not sure," replied Marc. "He shouldn't be."

"How about what the Judge said about getting lower bail in the Supreme Court?" she asked.

"It's possible," Marc replied. "But I need the minutes of this hearing first to show the Judge in the Supreme Court."

"Do it, Mister Conte. Don't let him stay in jail so long. How long will that take to get the minutes?"

"That's difficult to say. The stenographers are so backlogged or inefficient, or a combination of both, that it'll take about a week to ten days to get the minutes. I imagine if we paid three times more than the regular price, they'd somehow find a way to speed it up."

Mrs. Maricyk closed her eyes hopelessly.

"Don't worry about the money," Marc said. "I've already told the stenographer I want the minutes."

"Don't worry about the fee, Mister Conte. You'll get it. I promise."

Marc nodded.

"Can't nothing be done, meanwhile?" she asked.

"Sure, I can apply without the minutes, and this same D.A. will appear upstairs to oppose a reduction. At least if a Supreme Court Judge reads the minutes, he can reduce the bail based on the legal grounds which appear in the record."

"This place stinks more all the time, Mister Conte. How can you stand it?"

"Because if everybody felt the way you do, nobody'd ever get out of jail."

XIII

THURSDAY, AUGUST 17, 1:30 A.M.

Jack O'Loughlin stood in the darkness of his living room still half asleep, dressing mechanically as he gazed out through the picture window at the dark, deserted street below. O'Loughlin lived on the upper floor of a brick two-family house on Colonial Road and

Seventy-third Street in Brooklyn. It was a good family kind of neighborhood. Nothing much ever happened on that tree-lined street in front of O'Loughlin's house, even at peak hours, save for an occasional pedestrian or a passing car. Nothing at all ever happened at this time of night. O'Loughlin twisted his wrist to pick up some reflected light from the street lamp. A few grains of sleep still clouded his eyes, so he had to stare at his watch a couple of seconds until he could make his eyes focus. It was 1:35 A.M.

O'Loughlin finished zippering his pants, then buckled the heavy leather belt he always wore around his waist. He reached down in the darkness and picked up the holster and pistol that were on the table. O'Loughlin cracked the cylinder and felt five live rounds into the chambers, then slipped the holster into the front of his waistband until a metal retaining clip on the holster caught the leather belt.

He heard a noise behind him. O'Loughlin turned. His wife was rocking the baby on her shoulder, trying to lull little Jamesy back to the sleep that the ringing phone had disturbed.

"What did they want this time?" his wife asked. She was thin, short; her head was covered in a mass of vari-sized curlers.

"They didn't say," O'Loughlin replied, donning a plaid, short-sleeved sport shirt. He left the tails of the shirt outside his pants to better conceal the pistol. "Maybe I better wear the jacket, just in case," he said almost to himself. He removed the pistol and holster, placing them back on the table, as he stuffed the shirt tails inside his pants.

"I'm going to bed," shrugged the wife. Little Jamesy was off again. "Don't forget we're going to Lally's racket tonight."

"I won't forget," said O'Loughlin. He put the pistol back in his waistband, then lifted a light wash-and-wear suit jacket from the back of a chair. He carried the jacket with one finger through the loop at the back of the neck; he'd put it on when he got to the D.A.'s office. O'Loughlin looked out the picture window again. Still deserted; not even the leaves were fluttering. He could feel perspiration already starting to soak into the shirt at the small of his back. One of these days, he was going to spring for an air conditioner for the apartment. Once he got past the sergeant's test, they'd be okay, he figured, for the hundredth, no, thousandth time. Sergeant's money was pretty good.

A dark Plymouth sedan cruised slowly toward O'Loughlin's house, its headlamps sweeping an ever advancing patch of lighted asphalt before it. Mickey's car, thought O'Loughlin, turning. He descended the flight of steps to the street quietly, so as not to wake up his in-laws. His wife's parents owned the house and lived downstairs; O'Loughlin and his wife and little Jamesy lived upstairs. Not rent free, O'Loughlin always reminded himself. The way he figured it, if he had a daughter, which he didn't, just yet, and he was retired as a Captain from the job with a pension, as his father-in-law was, and he had an empty apartment in his house, he sure as hell would let his daughter and her husband live there without gouging out the rent; especially when the daughter and her husband didn't have enough money saved, just yet, even for an air conditioner.

O'Loughlin opened the front door and walked to Mickey Cassidy's car that was at the curb.

"What the hell is this all about?" O'Loughlin asked as he hung his jacket on the hook over the rear door. He sat in the front seat next to Cassidy.

"What the hell do I know?" replied Cassidy. "I was down at Toolan's watching the movie on the late show and having a few good night brews when the wife called and told me they called."

"You were still sitting at Toolan's having some good night brews?" O'Loughlin looked at Cassidy. "You're okay, aren't you?"

"Are you kidding me or something?" asked Cassidy. "We only had a couple. Mostly bullshitting. We weren't doing any serious drinking." Cassidy guided the car onto the lower end of the Gowanus Highway, heading toward the Brooklyn-Queens Expressway and the Queens County D.A.'s office.

Both O'Loughlin and Cassidy were on the Queens D.A.'s squad. They were regular New York City police detectives, but their assignment was to the D.A.'s office. Which was a pretty good assignment, and you needed a pretty good rabbi, that is, connection, to get it. O'Loughlin's father-in-law was not only his landlord, he was his rabbi. Lately, however, with all the attention being given to organized crime, the D.A.'s squad was really stiff duty. Marty Braverman, the Queens D.A., was pushing all kinds of investigations through his rackets grand jury, directed against organized crime figures. Braverman wasn't going to let the Feds steal all the spotlight on the organized-crime stage, particularly in Queens.

"It must be something big," said Cassidy. "Aaronwald wouldn't even tell me what the hell it was all about."

"Who's Aaronwald?" asked O'Loughlin.

"He's another of them smart-ass Yids Braverman just moved up to rackets," Cassidy replied.

"Ain't that something?" said O'Loughlin. They were just passing Bush Terminal, which was dark; O'Loughlin remembered during World War II it only looked dark, but behind blackened windows they were working night and day in those factories. "The whole friggin' Queens D.A.'s office is Yids. You think at least Braverman would have somebody else on the staff. But everyone he puts on is a Yid."

"What d'ya mean?" replied Cassidy. "There's Riccuiti and Lewis."

"Oh, great, a wop and a nigger. I don't think there's an Irishman on the entire staff. Is there? Can you name an Irishman?"

Cassidy thought. "Not off hand."

"Fuckin' A."

From the highest part of the raised highway, they could see the downtown financial center in Manhattan, the darkened shadow of the Woolworth Building, the twin towers of the World Trade Center, still lighted, sending long, bright reflections slithering across the lower bay to Brooklyn. They could see ships anchored in the outer harbor waiting to have their cargoes unloaded. The clock in the tower of the Prudential Building, the two faces of which, from the angle of the highway, looked like the eyes of an owl, indicated 2 A.M.

"Two o'clock and still hot as a bastard," said Cassidy.

"You think that cheap bastard'd buy us an air conditioner," O'Loughlin griped.

"Who, Braverman?"

"No, my father-in-law."

"What in the name of Holy Mother Church does your father-in-law have to do with anything we're talking about?" asked Cassidy. He guided the car under the Brooklyn Bridge and along the Expressway toward Queens Boulevard.

"He's got to do with my apartment and the fact that his daughter and grandson don't even have an air conditioner. The cheap bastard."

"Not to mention his cheap bastard son-in-law," laughed Cassidy.

"Yeah, if I could afford it, I'd buy it," replied O'Loughlin.

"Give up every other of them brews you drink, and you'll have the money in no time," said Cassidy.

"It'll never be that hot," laughed O'Loughlin.

The small parking lot outside the D.A.'s office in Kew Gardens was filled to capacity with unmarked, dark colored police vehicles. So were the adjoining streets. Cassidy and O'Loughlin each silently made out all the license plates with the police serial numbers.

"Christ, the joint's crawling with cops," said O'Loughlin.

"A hell of a lot of cars over here." Cassidy surveyed, his eyes looking for an empty parking spot. "Ah, here we are, a very pretty little spot," he said softly as he and backed the car to the curb. "A little tight, maybe," he muttered to himself, maneuvering to get the car straight. "A neat little job of parking. Tight but neat."

"You wouldn't complain like that if you were talking about some dame?" said O'Loughlin.

"Just out of a warm bed with your dear wife and you're talking about other dames. No wonder that cheap bastard father-in-law of yours won't buy an air conditioner."

"It's not for me, Mickey. For his daughter and little Jamesy," laughed O'Loughlin.

"And what would she do, shut it off when you come home, Jocko? Jocko my own, you're talking to your old pal Mickey now."

They got out of the car and made their way up to the D.A.'s office, which was in a building behind the Supreme Court Building. Just to the rear of the D.A.'s building, was the Queens Branch of the Men's House of Detention. It was the Queens' version of The Tombs, far newer and more modern however, even had piped-in music; which from 6 A.M. to lights out was sheer torture. The three buildings formed the core complex of criminal justice in Queens. A policeman in uniform was sitting at the reception desk. He nodded to the two approaching detectives.

"What the hell's going on?" O'Loughlin asked the cop.

"You're about the hundredth guy who asked me," said the cop.

138

"And I'll tell you, like I told them. I don't know. It's all very hush-hush. Some kind of secret raid, I figure."

"Jesus Christ, a Jewish James Bond, no less, the good people of Queens have for their D.A.," said Cassidy.

The cop at the desk laughed.

The two detectives walked along the corridor which led to the Rackets Bureau offices. The closer they got, the more they could hear the noises of many men talking, laughing. As they turned the corridor, O'Loughlin and Cassidy saw a hallway full of detectives. All were in civilian clothes, some with just shirts, the tails out of their pants to hide their service revolvers, others with suit jackets and ties, some with shirts and jackets, no ties.

"Okay, okay, quiet down now," called Stan Greengold, chief of the Rackets Bureau. He was heavy set, with a thick, jowly face, and a space between his front teeth. Greengold was standing in the corridor, in the midst of the detectives. Another assistant, a new man, probably Aaronwald, thought O'Loughlin, stood next to Greengold, holding envelopes in his hand.

The hubbub diminished slightly.

"Okay, hold it down," repeated Greengold. "Let's get this over with. We have a lot of work to do tonight."

"What is it?" asked a faceless voice from the crowd.

"Yeah, what are we going to do that's so secret?" asked another.

"We're going to take over Borough Hall," replied a wag in the crowd. "This is a coup d'état," he said, purposely fracturing the French pronunciation.

"What's that, a kind of car?" yet another wag asked.

"Knock it off," admonished Greengold firmly.

The men began to settle down.

"We have assignments for each of your teams," said Greengold. "Each of you men were given partner's names. Has everyone met up with his partner here?" He looked around. No one said anything. "Fine, I guess that means you did. Now, each team will be given one of these envelopes." Greengold took one of the envelopes from Aaronwald and held it aloft. "In the envelope is an assignment. It's a subpoena the service of which you're to effectuate as soon as possible after you leave here. You are not to discuss your assignment with anyone, nor even open up your assignments until you're under way in your cars. The reason that we're doing it at this hour is that this is all part of an over-all plan and we're hoping that most of the people you have to apprehend will be in bed, and we'll catch them all before they have a chance to warn each other."

"And before the raiders have a chance to warn anybody else, hanh?" asked a sarcastic voice from the midst of the crowd.

"I don't think this is a press conference," said Greengold unflustered. "You each have an assignment, and you have to effectuate it immediately. So let's get going." He took all the envelopes and read from the first. "Ludwig and McCarthy."

Two detectives came forward and took the envelope. "You can go right out now and execute that. Leave as you get your assignments," he announced to the room. "O'Loughlin and Cassidy."

Mickey Cassidy took the envelope. He and O'Loughlin made their way back past the reception desk and rang for the elevator.

"What is it?" asked the cop at the desk.

"Can't open it until we're in the car," said Cassidy.

"Stop the shit," said the cop.

"Orders is orders," laughed O'Loughlin. "These guys learned a lot from the krauts in them concentration camps."

The elevator arrived and the two detectives descended to the ground floor. Once under way in the car, O'Loughlin opened the envelope. Cassidy stopped the car near a street lamp. The envelope contained a subpoena for Pasquale Pellegrino to appear before a Queens County grand jury forthwith.

"Patsy the Crusher," said Cassidy. "What the hell is up? Nothing new came in on him that I know of."

"You see the whole pile of envelopes?" asked O'Loughlin. "They must be pulling all the bent noses in Queens off the streets."

"What do you figure?"

"The Compagna killing," O'Loughlin replied. "What else? They must figure they'll get all these greaseballs so shook up enough with a grand jury investigation that they won't make a move and start a war over Compagna."

Cassidy thought for a moment, then nodded. "That must be it. A quick sweep of everybody so they know we're right on their ass. This way they'll be afraid to start shooting in the streets."

"Why the hell stop them?" said O'Loughlin. "Let them kill a few more of their own. Save us the trouble."

"Only one thing wrong with that," cautioned Cassidy as he started the car forward again.

"What's that?"

"If we let them do that, it'll take weeks to clean all the grease from the streets."

O'Loughlin laughed as they headed toward Brooklyn, where they knew The Crusher would most likely be. A grand jury subpoena was valid throughout the state, so they could serve The Crusher wherever they found him.

Cassidy was out of the car now. He had parked on a side street about fifty yards from the High Hat Lounge on Avenue T in Flatbush. O'Loughlin watched as Cassidy cautiously peeked into a side window of the bar, then made his way back to the car.

"He's in there," said Cassidy, leaning on the window frame of the car.

"Like shooting fish from a barrel."

"In a barrel," corrected Cassidy.

"In your ass."

"Up to your old trick, hey Jocko?" Cassidy laughed. "And you said you liked girls." He got back in the car, and drove into the shadows across Avenue T so they could simultaneously watch the front and side entrances of the High Hat.

"What time is it?" asked Cassidy.

"Quarter to three."

"Shouldn't be long now."

Both Cassidy and O'Loughlin knew The Crusher's entire file, knew where he lived in Queens, hung out in Brooklyn, had his hair cut, everything. They also knew better than to try to arrest him inside the High Hat Lounge, and perhaps start a fight, which, although they would ultimately win, perhaps, by calling for additional police help, might precipitate injury that was unnecessary. Especially since The Crusher would be out of his lair soon enough.

The neighborhood surrounding the High Hat Lounge was mostly residential. Everything was quiet and still in the breezeless heat except for the softly drifting sound of the jukebox in the High Hat, which could be heard whenever the door was opened or closed. Finally, at 3:05, Cassidy and O'Loughlin saw Patsy the Crusher come out. He stood on the sidewalk in front of the High

Hat with a short, thin man for a few minutes, talking. Sounds of laughter and indistinguishable conversation drifted to the unmarked police car. The two detectives watched as the small man and The Crusher parted, each going a separate way. The Crusher walked half a block and got into his car, a three-year-old Buick. People in The Crusher's financial position rarely owned new cars. They couldn't afford such a showing of wealth to the ever inquisitive Internal Revenue Service. The Crusher's car was on the same side of the street as the police car, headed in the same direction.

"Crusher didn't get issued a new license, did he?" asked Cassidy, as he watched The Crusher's car move away from the curb.

"Not that I know of," replied O'Loughlin. He smiled.

"Then he's committing the God-awful crime of driving with a suspended driver's license. A misdemeanor. Now we can even give him a toss. See if he's armed," said Cassidy. "Should I stop him?"

"Let him get a little farther away from the bar," said O'Loughlin.

They followed The Crusher's car several blocks. It stopped ahead at a red light.

"Pull in front of him," said O'Loughlin.

Cassidy drove next to, and then cut in front of, The Crusher.

The Crusher watched the other car and its occupants, at first disinterestedly. Then a look of recognition opened his eyes wider. His mouth frowned as Cassidy and O'Loughlin each got out of their car. Cassidy walked to The Crusher's side of the car. O'Loughlin moved to the passenger side, just ahead of the doors, so he could watch The Crusher through the windshield.

"What now?" The Crusher tossed out in his raspy voice as he lowered the electric window.

"License and registration," Cassidy asked coolly.

The Crusher studied Cassidy and his outstretched hand. "Let me just look in the glove compartment," said The Crusher, leaning to the passenger side of his car.

"I wouldn't try anything funny," said Cassidy tensely. He reached for his pistol. O'Loughlin braced.

"Officer, I'm surprised," chided The Crusher. "You think I'm foolish enough to go through some cops-and-robbers scene with you? I'm a peace-loving citizen." He laughed.

"License and registration," repeated Cassidy. "And don't make any fast moves."

The Crusher rummaged in the glove compartment and came out slowly with the car's registration. "I can only seem to find the registration, Officer."

"You know and we know you don't have a license, Patsy. What's the act all about?" said Cassidy.

The Crusher laughed. "I was looking, maybe I'd find an old one in there. What are you guys, demoted to riding traffic lights now? Making spot checks?"

"No license, Patsy?"

"But come on!" The Crusher complained. "You stop me at three-thirty in the morning to find out about my license?"

"We came to serve a subpoena," said Cassidy, handing the paper from the envelope to The Crusher. "But, now we find you committing a crime, driving without a proper driver's license. Out of the car, Patsy."

The Crusher studied Cassidy. "You gotta be kidding! Okay, you wanted to give me a subpoena. Okay, I got it. Now stop breaking my balls, get out of the way and let me get home."

"Out of the car, Patsy!"

"Hey, look, what are you breaking them on me for?" asked The Crusher. "You know I'll show at the grand jury whenever you want me. You're regular guys. You did your job, so let's forget about the rest of this for tonight. It's late."

"Are you getting out of the car?" Cassidy demanded.

"*Puttana*," exploded The Crusher, pounding the steering wheel with his beefy hand. He flung open his car door and got out. He stood about three inches taller than Cassidy. O'Loughlin was as tall as The Crusher, but was outweighed by about fifty pounds. The Crusher was angry, his mouth hard, the muscles in his neck bulging. "Okay, I'm out, now what the fuck do you want?"

"Open the car doors on the other side and the trunk," Cassidy instructed.

"Open your sister's ass," replied The Crusher.

O'Loughlin walked around the car to the side where Cassidy stood. He removed the keys from the ignition.

143

"Turn around, face the car, lean against it with your hands and feet spread," said Cassidy.

"Go and fuck yourself, hanh?"

O'Loughlin slipped his service revolver out of its holster and held it pointed at The Crusher. Cassidy did the same. The Crusher looked at them, grimaced angrily, and turned toward the car, leaning forward against it with outstretched arms. O'Loughlin kept his revolver trained on The Crusher as Cassidy searched him.

"Nothing," said Cassidy.

"Okay, copper? Can I get back in now?"

"Stay where you are," said O'Loughlin. He had taken a flashlight out of the police car, and now turned it on. He shone its beam inside The Crusher's car.

"There's nothing in there," said The Crusher. "You think I would carry anything knowing you guys are crawling all over the place?"

"Knowing there are a lot of gunsels on the street hunting for a lot of other gunsels because your boss Compagna got killed, yeah, maybe you would," said O'Loughlin.

"Come on," disclaimed The Crusher. "It was some fucking nigger. Who'd be looking for who?"

O'Loughlin's flashlight beam coursed over the seats in the car. Cassidy stood behind The Crusher, watching him. O'Loughlin leaned into the car, his flashlight probing under the seat.

"Hello, hello, what's this?" announced O'Loughlin, taking a brown paper bag out from under the front seat on the driver's side. Inside was a .38 caliber revolver.

"Patsy, you weren't telling us the truth," Cassidy chided.

"Not nice," added O'Loughlin. "We're going to have to arrest you."

"Come on, stop the shit so I can call my lawyer. I'm not begging you pricks for anything." The Crusher remained leaning on the car. He said nothing further.

"I guess we should advise him of his rights," said Cassidy.

"Stuff the rights up your ass," said The Crusher. "I'm not answering any questions. Just get me to the station so I can call my lawyer."

O'Loughlin searched around the interior of the car again. "Another paper bag under the passenger's seat," he announced. He removed the bag. It contained a .32 caliber automatic.

"Two guns?" said Cassidy. "My, my, Patsy, you're getting to be a bad boy."

"You're pushing your luck, wise guy," warned The Crusher.

"Don't threaten me, you guinea prick," Cassidy lashed back. "I'll blow a hole in the back of your head."

O'Loughlin searched the rest of the car, finding nothing else. He took the two pistols, being careful to handle them only through the paper bags so as not to spoil any fingerprints that might be on them, and placed them on the hood of the police car. He put a pen in the barrel of one, removed it from its bag, unloaded it, and replaced it in the bag. He did the same to the other.

"Okay, Patsy, get in our car," said Cassidy. "You drive. O'Loughlin'll be right next to you with his pistol in your ear. And I'll be right behind in your car. Try anything, and you'll have your head blown off before you can say Mussolini."

The Crusher turned, his face streaked with anger. "Look, you want to take me to the station house," he said, pointing a thick finger at Cassidy, "let's go. I'm not running nowhere. But I'm driving my own car down there. I'll follow you, or I'll go up in the front of you. But neither of you are driving my car. You don't even get in my car."

"You'll do what we tell you to do, Patsy," said Cassidy. "Don't start anything you can't finish."

"Oh, you think I can't finish it, hanh? Let me tell you, cocksucker," The Crusher shouted now at the top of his lungs. His chest swelled with rage. "You get in my car, go ahead, just get in my car." His eyes were wild as he glared at Cassidy.

Both O'Loughlin and Cassidy had their pistols trained on The Crusher now.

"Stand easy, Patsy," said O'Loughlin. "Don't make trouble. You'll end up dead."

"I want to see you get in my car," he rethreatened Cassidy, "and, you cocksucker, I'll kill you." The Crusher was purple in the face now. "Go ahead, get in the car. You'll get me. But I'll tear you apart first. You'll have to kill me. Go ahead. I want to see you get in my fucking car. Go ahead, wise fucking cop. Get in. Go ahead."

Lights were starting to light the windows of nearby houses. People appeared at the windows to watch the disturbance.

"Come on, you Irish prick. Get in my car. Let the people see how brave you are. You piece of shit."

"Mickey, what the hell's the difference," said O'Loughlin. He realized they'd have to kill The Crusher in front of all the now awakened neighborhood. "Let him drive his own car in front, we'll follow. If he makes one phony move, we can blow his brains out."

"Why the hell should this punk tell us what to do?" objected Cassidy.

"He's not having his own way," said O'Loughlin. "He's going with us to jail. Why start something here? Look at the windows. Who needs all the aggravation of a hearing with the Civilian Complaint Review Board if we kill him? Especially over who drives that piece of shit car."

"Go on, you fuck, get in and let me tear your fucking throat out. Come on."

"You lousy greaseball," said Cassidy softly. "When we're down at the station house, I want to see how tough you are."

"Oh, then you'll be tough, hanh? With fifty other Irish *cornuti* around, you lily-livered fuck."

"Don't get too carried away, wop," warned O'Loughlin. "You get in that car and drive real slow in front of us over to the precinct on Church Avenue. You know where that is, don't you?"

"I know."

"One mile an hour over twenty," O'Loughlin emphasized, "and I'll blow your fucking brains out for trying to escape. You don't even have to try. Just go one mile over twenty and you're dead, you punk."

The Crusher stared at O'Loughlin, then got into his car.

"One more word out of you, and you'll be dead," said Cassidy, white with rage. "Civilian Review Board, Jesus Christ himself, I don't care. One more word, just one more word . . ."

"Come on, Mickey," said O'Loughlin. "Let's just do our job."

XIV

Marc stood at the railing of his apartment terrace, watching the early morning sun slowly stretch its warm light across the Hudson River and the Jersey shore beyond. The weather was pleasantly mild, a little cooler than yesterday. Maria was still asleep.

The City, too, was still asleep, or at least dozing fitfully, which is as close to sleep as New York ever gets. The river was smooth and dark, deserted except for a single tug churning slowly down-river beside a flatbed barge loaded with railroad boxcars. A small spray of white water bounced low on the prow of the tug.

The Chinese glass chime Marc had hung on the sheltered side of the terrace danced and clinkled in the morning breeze. The sound reminded Marc of deserted early summer mornings long past, when, as a youngster at the beach house, he could hear that very same clinkling sound carried on the wind for long distances, to be discovered, after considerable meandering, chiming its pleasant notes in the quiet corner of some deserted porch or from under an awning awaiting the day's sun. It was a delicate sound which even a single voice could drown. It was a good sound, too, thought Marc. It meant peace and tranquillity; it was the quiet before the day's storm; it'd be the quiet after the day's storm. It was the music of the world at rest.

"Here's your coffee," Franco said softly, carrying a tray with two steaming cups of *cafe con leche* and some buttered rolls. He was usually the second riser in the household.

Marc turned and took a cup and a roll from the tray.

"What's the schedule for today?" asked Franco, as he put the tray on a nearby table. "You want me to go with you anywhere?"

Marc sipped the cafe. "Well, first we'll drop Mrs. Conte at her school. Then I want to go to the office for a while. After that, I'm going to see Mrs. Wainwright at her apartment around eleven. I want to get a little unhysterical information from her about the way her husband was killed."

Another tug, running alone, turned at the Battery and began making a quick run upriver.

"You want me to go with you?" asked Franco.

"Sure, why not? Maybe you'll come up with one of your great theories about who committed the crime or how he—or she—did it. Then you can throw the ball to Maria, and between the two of you, you'll come up with something absolutely wild."

"You have to admit our theories are good sometimes, right?" Franco smiled.

"They sure are." Marc smiled too. For it was true. Maria and Franco, on their own, sitting around at night, figured out harebrained, abstruse theories on the cases Marc was handling, which witness was telling the truth, where new evidence could be found, how to obtain it. And although usually their theories were way out in space, often the thinking moved Marc's investigation onto a side road which, with some patience, led to something important, something Marc hadn't thought about.

The phone rang.

Franco grimaced as he rushed to answer it before it disturbed Maria. He opened a metal box on the wall of the terrace. The phone was inside.

"Conte residence." He listened. "It's a cop. Patsy Pellegrino was arrested for weapons," he said, holding the phone receiver out to Marc.

Marc took the phone from Franco. "Hello. To whom am I speaking?"

"This is Detective Cassidy of the Queens D.A.'s squad, Counselor."

"The D.A.'s squad? Is this arrest on an indictment?" Marc inquired.

"No, Counselor," Cassidy replied. "It started really just as a simple service of a subpoena for the grand jury. But it ended up with possession of two loaded pistols."

Marc looked skyward at that. "What time do you think he'll be arraigned?"

"Gee, I don't know, Counselor. We're processing him now. His prints still have to be sent up to Albany for verification. Who knows how long that'll take. Sometimes two, sometimes six hours. It's hard to say, you know?"

"You figure about noon? That should leave enough time for everything," said Marc.

"I would think that ought to do it," agreed Cassidy. "We might be finished earlier though. You know, we can't tell how long it'll take."

"Well, I'll figure to be in court about noon," said Marc. "If it's any earlier, perhaps you can give me a ring at my office."

"I can't promise anything on that, Counselor. I'll try and work it out for you," said Cassidy. "If we get through earlier, we'll try and give you a ring."

"Fine," said Marc. "Let me say for the record that I don't want my client questioned or interrogated in any way without my being present."

"Say no more, Counselor," said Cassidy, laughing. "In the first place, we aren't going to question him. We don't have to. But if we did have a mind to, what's the sense, you know what I mean? I mean we're lucky if this guy gives us his name. You know, he's been around this mill before."

"Okay," said Marc. "I just have to earn my keep."

"Got ya, Counselor."

"Can I talk to my client for a moment?" asked Marc.

"Sure, Counselor. Hey Pellegrino," Cassidy called at the other end of the phone. "Your lawyer's on the wire."

There was a shuffling sound at the other phone. "Hello?" rasped out the voice of The Crusher.

"Hello, Patsy."

"Good morning, Counselor. I'm sorry to disturb your beauty rest, but I'm glad I got you. These guys come along and . . ."

"Let's not talk about it over the phone, Patsy."

"Right, right, I got ya, Counselor. When am I going to see you? You're going to be in court, aren't you?"

"I'll meet you there about noon. If the Judge calls the case before then, just tell him your lawyer is on the way and you want to wait."

"You think they'll do that?" The Crusher asked cautiously. "I'll feel a whole lot better if you're there when I get there, Counselor."

"I don't know exactly what time you'll get there," said Marc. "The detective said he'd try and call me if you get there earlier."

"I'll give this broken-down cop the dime," The Crusher said lightly.

"I'll take it," Marc heard someone say in the background at The Crusher's end.

"Listen, Counselor, do me a favor and give my wife a ring. I been out all night now. Tell her why, and tell her I'm okay. No sense getting a beef from my wife for no reason." The Crusher laughed. "And listen, tell her to call, she knows who, you know, and make arrangements for me. Tell her. She'll know. This way I can make bail right away. You gonna get me reasonable bail, at least, aren't you, Counselor?"

"I'm sure I can get the Judge to set bail, Patsy. I don't know how reasonable it'll be. But he'll set bail."

"I know you can do it, Counselor. I got all my confidence in you. As usual."

There was another shuffling the phone at The Crusher's end.

"Okay, Counselor?" asked Cassidy, getting back on the phone.

"Fine, thanks," said Marc. "See you in court."

"Right," said Cassidy.

"You'll have to wait a few minutes, Counselor," the policeman at the reception desk on the fifth floor of the Queens D.A.'s office said to Marc. "Mister Greengold said he'd be with you in a minute."

"Thanks," said Marc. He sat on a wooden bench against the light green wall. Occasionally, people would walk along the corridor in which Marc sat, some carrying papers, some whistling, others just walking. Almost all took a drink at a water cooler in the corner near Marc. Put a water fountain anywhere, and people suddenly realize a thirst they hadn't noticed before they saw the cooler.

"You can go in now, Counselor," said the policeman at the desk.

"Thanks." Marc rose and walked along the interior corridor, in the direction the policeman had pointed. Stan Greengold turned the corner of the corridor, walking toward Marc.

"Hi, Marc," said Greengold.

"Hello, Stan. How are you?"

Greengold shrugged. "What's the sense of kicking?"

"Will you tell me why the detectives brought Pellegrino here instead of directly to court for arraignment?" Marc asked. "When I talked to the detective this morning, he said he'd meet me in court, not here. If he hadn't called and told my office he would be here instead, I'd be sitting in court right now."

Greengold shrugged again. "I had nothing to do with it, believe me, Marc. The cops were ordered to bring him here first."

"Whose orders? For what?" Marc asked.

"Marc, I just do or die, or whatever that lousy poem said. I was told to tell the detectives to bring him over here, so I had them bring him over here."

"You didn't interrogate him. I advised the police . . ."

"Marc, I didn't interrogate him."

"Then why all this cloak-and-dagger aggravation?" Marc asked. "All you had to do was call me and I would have produced Pellegrino here any time you wanted. You knew I represented him."

"I knew, I knew," agreed Greengold. "And I know you would have brought him in. But orders came from the top."

"What for?" Marc repeated.

Greengold repeated his shrug.

"When is he going to be arraigned?"

"Right now," Greengold replied. "As soon as you and I finish, the detectives will take the two of you through the lobby. He goes in cuffs."

"The detectives? Cuffs? You think he's going to run? I want to talk to him alone."

"Can't let you do it," said Greengold.

"Why not?"

"Marc. I've got orders. He goes in cuffs."

"Stan, this whole procedure is a little far out."

"What do you want from me? I just work here."

At that moment, The Crusher was brought around the corner of the corridor, manacled, between the two detectives.

"For Christ's sake, Stan!"

"Marc, believe me—I'm not getting my jollies giving you and Pellegrino a hard time."

"Where's Braverman? I want to talk to Braverman. This is starting to smack of interference with my client's rights."

"Braverman's in a press conference right now," replied Green-gold.

"A press conference? No wonder we're having all this trick maneuvering! He's making a big splash about the Compagna killing and organized crime—with my client as the main attraction. This is an outrage. I really mean it, Stan. It's an outrage and a total lack of propriety. What is Braverman, a lawyer or an entertainer with press agents and publicity?"

Greengold shrugged. "I just follow orders."

"We've got to take him over now, Counselor," said O'Loughlin. "Hurry up so we can get the hell out of here," he whispered, leaning toward Marc. "We've been on the go since midnight."

"I been out a lot longer than that," said The Crusher. "Come on, Marc. Stop wasting your breath with these people so they can make a spectacle of me. Then we can all go home."

"I'll be back," Marc said to Greengold.

"Suit yourself," he replied. "Whatever good it's going to do you."

Marc, The Crusher, and the two detectives took the elevator down to the main floor. As soon as the doors of the elevator opened, Marc could see reporters and photographers clustering in the corridor leading to the courthouse. There were television crewmen with portable lights and cameras standing nearby. They immediately engulfed the small group from the elevator and backed along the corridor with them as they moved toward the other building. Cameras were not allowed inside the courthouse, so they were working quickly.

"What kind of bullshit is this?" demanded Pellegrino.

"You're a news story," replied Marc. "All about how Braverman is cleaning the streets of people who are in the midst of a gangland war."

"What war?" Pellegrino twirled as a photographer came close, flashing a strobe light in his face. "Get out of here, you bastard, I'll stick that camera up your ass."

Other reporters with microphones came close to the small group as they made their way through the crowd.

"Let us through," said O'Loughlin.

The reporters hurled questions at Pellegrino, about Compagna, about how he was killed, about how Pellegrino thought he was killed, if there would be a war, if he thought a rival gang had been responsible.

"No questions, please," Marc kept saying in vain. "No comments."

"No comments, you bastards," rasped Pellegrino. "What country is this, anyway? Germany? Stop harassing me, you Nazi bastards."

Another reporter came forward with a microphone.

"No questions, please," said Marc.

"Who do you think killed your boss, Compagna?" the reporter asked, ignoring Marc, thrusting the microphone at Pellegrino.

Pellegrino, helpless with both hands manacled, took a swipe at the microphone with a deft kick. He knocked it from the reporter's hand. The reporter held onto the cord, restraining the microphone from hitting the pavement. "Hey, watch out, you knocked my station sign off," the reporter complained.

"I'll knock you off," said The Crusher.

Finally, the detectives gained the door to the courthouse. They pushed The Crusher past the crowd through the door. The other three men walked in right behind him and shut the doors.

Judge Galloway set twenty-five thousand dollars bail on Pellegrino and adjourned the case to August 23. As Marc walked back to the spectator section of the courtroom, a bondsman got up from his seat in the courtroom and walked over to him.

"I'll be bailing him out in a couple of minutes, Counselor," said the bondsman. "I hope this guy don't take off."

"I doubt it," said Marc. "Tell the defendant I'll wait out in the hall."

"Okay."

The usual crowd was milling about the corridor: policemen, some in uniform, some in civilian clothes, were in abundance. Marc saw Cassidy and O'Loughlin come out of the courtroom with two other men. They stood near the doorway, talking. The other two men looked like detectives too.

In a few minutes, The Crusher and the bondsman came out of the courtroom. The Crusher smiled and started in Marc's direction. As he was walking, one of the men standing with Cassidy and O'Loughlin intercepted him and displayed what appeared to be a legal document.

"What? Are you kidding me?" The Crusher exclaimed angrily, loudly.

Marc walked over quickly.

"This motherless . . ." stammered The Crusher. He was choked with anger.

"This is the United States Marshal Salerno," introduced Cassidy. "This is Pellegrino's lawyer, Mister Conte."

"Counselor," said the Marshal, "we have a federal warrant for your client's arrest."

"What kind of railroad bullshit is this," rasped The Crusher.

"Take it easy, Patsy," said Marc. "What's the charge?" Marc asked the Marshal.

"Title Eighteen, Appendix Section Twelve Hundred and One and Twelve Hundred Two, Counselor," replied the other Marshal.

"What's that?" Marc asked.

"Illegal possession of firearms by a felon."

"We just answered a charge here on the alleged possession of those pistols," said Marc.

"I know, Counselor, but we have a warrant. We have to execute it."

"I'll execute you, you motherless bastard," shouted The Crusher.

"Hold it, Patsy," cautioned Marc. "May I talk to my client a moment?" he said to the Marshal.

"Sure, Counselor, just stay right here, though," said the second Marshal. They stepped back, leaving Marc and The Crusher alone.

"These lousy son of a bitches," railed The Crusher.

"Patsy, they have a warrant. There's no sense arguing with them. Let's argue with the Magistrate."

"But I just got bailed out on a gun charge. That bastard, Malone, is trying to railroad me. It's double jeopardy. It's a frame. It's got to be something. Do something."

"I can't do anything here in the corridor. Let's take that argument to the federal Magistrate."

"You want me to go with them?" asked The Crusher.

"I don't think we have much choice," said Marc. "I'll go right over to court and talk to Malone. At least there won't be a wait. He knows all about you."

"*Puttana*," cursed The Crusher. "Come on, come on, do your dirty work, you bastards," he said to the Marshal.

"What kind of bail are you going to ask for?" Marc asked Mike Malone as they stood to the side of the Magistrate's courtroom in the Eastern District Federal Courthouse.

"A hundred and fifty thousand," said Malone with silent relish.

"Come on, Mike. He just had trouble enough posting twenty-five thousand over in the state court on the same weapons charge."

"I tell you frankly, Marc, I'd prefer he didn't post it at all. That's why I'm asking such high bail."

"How come?" asked Marc. "Despite your personal feelings about him, you don't really think he'd skip out, do you?"

"No, actually I don't," replied Malone. "But I don't want a war on my hands over the Compagna killing either. And the best way to cut that possibility, is to get all the gunmen off the street."

"You mean, all this is because of that theory about Compagna being killed by people associated with Johnny *Botz* Santora?" asked Marc.

Malone nodded.

"If there was going to be a war, there would have been one already, wouldn't there? It's already a week since the shooting and nothing's happened."

"I know," said Malone. "But Compagna's only dead a couple of days."

"Mike, do you really believe that Johnny *Botz* engineered getting that Black guy to shoot Compagna?"

"Frankly, I don't, Marc. But Johnny *Botz* won't admit it. He figures, I guess, if everybody thinks he did it, he might as well get as much mileage out of it among the boys as he can. Meanwhile, somebody's liable to believe he really did and start getting gun happy."

"How about a hearing on this gun charge? I don't think it'll stand up. To be a federal crime, the pistols would have to be used in interstate commerce. You have anything on interstate commerce that makes this case different from the one already pending in the state court?"

"We'll have to see about that," said Malone. "For the time being he's here and I'm going to keep him here if I can."

"He's entitled to reasonable bail."

"Under the circumstances, a hundred fifty . . . all right, a hundred thousand is reasonable," replied Malone.

"And you people complain about the Supreme Court decisions being too lenient on defendants," Marc scoffed. "Despite them, you still seem to be doing exactly as you please."

"The decisions just need the proper interpretation." Malone smiled.

"And by the time I get out a writ of habeas corpus and appeal this unreasonable bail, you'll have accomplished what you want," said Marc.

"Something like that," Malone replied. "Look, Marc, today is Thursday. I'll consent to a bail reduction on, say, Monday. We just want to keep things cool for a little while. How's Monday?"

"Today is better than Monday," said Marc.

"I understand. Listen, let me give you a little clue about this client of yours. His troubles are just beginning. I just advise you in advance."

"Care to elaborate?"

"No. I can't."

The Magistrate entered the courtroom and sat behind his bench. He nodded to Malone to begin. The Magistrate was bald, with glasses.

"If Your Honor please," said Malone. "You have a fact sheet before you on this defendant. I can just say that he's a man with an extensive criminal background, he's a convicted felon, and he's been found in flagrant violation of law, possessing two pistols in his car. I'm going to ask that a hundred thousand dollars bail be set."

The Magistrate nodded to Marc. "Mister Conte. Let me suggest this in advance. I've already read the papers and it's apparent that the United States Attorney's application is based on solid ground. Go ahead, but let's not take too long. It's hot. See if you can turn that air conditioner up higher," he said to an attendant seated to the side of the bench.

"Are you saying that no matter what argument I use, you'll deny the bail application?" asked Marc.

"Certainly not. My mind is never made up in advance. But let's move along with it, shall we?"

"Your Honor," Marc began, "the United States Attorney is merely reciting words, giving lip service, as it were, to the language of the Supreme Court cases concerning bail applications. But I'm sure that there are absolutely no facts, nothing that actually indicates to the Government that Mister Pellegrino will in fact not appear on the return date for a hearing. I suggest that the United States Attorney's request is so unconscionable as to deny this defendant bail, reasonable or otherwise."

"I think you're wrong, Counselor," said the Magistrate. "I know what the bleeding hearts say. But I think that the purpose of bail is also to keep people off the street who deserve to be off the street."

"Your Honor, the United States Supreme Court, most respectfully, universally disagreed with your stated position," said Marc. "They indicate reasonable bail under all the circumstances should be set in all cases."

"If I'm wrong, you have your right to appeal," the Magistrate continued. "Meanwhile, the bail is set at one hundred thousand dollars." The Magistrate slipped his fingers into his collar and twisted his neck with heat annoyance. "It sure is hot in here."

"It sure is," Pellegrino said aloud, his face etched with anger. "Who can make a hundred thousand, Your Honor? I just made twenty-five in the state court."

"May I have a moment, Your Honor?" asked Marc. He turned toward Pellegrino.

"Certainly," the Magistrate said, taking out a handkerchief and wiping his brow. "Is that air conditioner all the way up?" he asked the attendant.

"Patsy, do you want me to represent you or do you want to do it yourself?" Marc whispered to Pellegrino.

"Come on, Counselor, don't get angry," said The Crusher. "I just get pissed off, with a prick like that on the bench. He don't even want to listen. Even if he's wrong, he tells you nice, right to your face, fuck you, and if you don't like it, up your ass. All in legal language, and everybody stands here and says, thank you."

Marc turned back to the Magistrate. "Your Honor, I'd like to set the bail review and perhaps the hearing at the same time. Can we set it down for the coming Tuesday?"

"Whenever you wish, Counselor. Tuesday, that's the twenty-second of August. Very well. August twenty-second."

The Marshal came up beside Pellegrino to lead him to the detention facilities.

"Thank you, Your Honor," said Pellegrino, putting his right hand over his genitalia and saluting the Magistrate.

"What is that?" boomed the Magistrate. "What do you think you're doing? Did you see that, Mister Malone?" he asked angrily.

"See what? I was looking at my notes, Your Honor," replied Malone, looking around.

"What's the matter, Your Honor?" asked Pellegrino.

"You animal," said the Judge.

"Because I'm itchy, Judge. I was just a little, pardon the expression, itchy, and scratched."

"The twenty-second," the Magistrate thundered.

XV

THURSDAY, AUGUST 17, 5:35 P.M.

Franco parked the car on Sixty-sixth Street, east of Fifth Avenue. From there, he and Marc walked toward Fifth Avenue and Toni Wainwright's apartment.

"Today is cooler and still it's sweltering," said Marc. "Especially when you get out of an air-conditioned car."

"Yeah," agreed Franco. "Poor Crusher, he's got to spend the night in the can. It must be really hot there. What a rotten deal."

"We'll make another bail application Tuesday," said Marc. "I'm sure we can do a little better for him then. You know, it's a real bitch, having to go along with the prosecutor's whims, because he's got the Judge's ear." He was silent again as they continued to walk. "What time is it now?"

"About five-thirty, five-forty," replied Franco.

"When I called this afternoon to tell Mrs. Wainwright we were in court, she said to come over at six. I guess it's all right if we're a little early."

"Rich girls look any different with their hair in curlers than poor girls?" asked Franco.

"How is it you get to meet the women in every case?" Marc asked lightly.

"I guess you bring me along because you want to make a good impression on them," Franco replied. "Kind of a mature impression. Besides, you want me to get facts so the Mrs. and me can develop one of our super-duper theories."

Both men laughed as they entered the lobby of the Wainwright apartment building. The doorman, in gray uniform and white winged collar, smiled and inquired who they wished to visit.

"Mrs. Wainwright," replied Marc.

"Very good, sir. Just a moment," said the doorman. He walked to a phone at the side of the lobby and picked up the receiver. "Who's calling, sir?"

"Mister Conte and Mister Poveromo," replied Marc.

The doorman spoke into the phone.

"Don't kid me about your theories," Marc joked. "You just want to get a good look at Toni Wainwright."

"That too." Franco smiled. "Why should you have all the good times without me?"

"You may go up, sir," said the doorman. "Eighteenth floor."

"Thank you."

A maid showed Marc and Franco into Toni Wainwright's living room. It was very large, and white, decorated in modern straight lines of glass and chrome, with white geometric furniture. On the walls were many modern, non-objective paintings lit by small gallery spotlights hung from the ceiling. On the floor near a full grand piano was a life-size modern sculpture of a nude, seated man. A glass-topped cocktail table stretched in front of the entire length of the couch; lamps hung from the ceiling on either side.

The maid opened a double door in the wall, revealing the small, mirrored cocktail bar.

"Mrs. Wainwright will be with you shortly," said the maid as she left the room. "She said to make yourselves a drink."

Franco made a vodka and tonic for Marc and one for himself. He sat on a side chair, as Marc studied one of the paintings on the wall, twisting his head from the vertical to the horizontal. The painting was a mass of lines and color, seemingly without rhyme or purpose.

"This is like living in a museum," said Franco. "You figure these pictures were expensive?"

"I'm sure they were. Very," replied Marc.

"It's bad enough they don't make any sense, but if they cost a bundle too, it's even worse."

Twenty minutes later the two of them were still waiting for Mrs. Wainwright to appear. Franco fixed another drink for himself. Marc's was still almost full. Finally, they heard footsteps.

"I'm very rushed. I'm sorry," said Toni Wainwright breathlessly, sweeping into the room. Her face was heavily made up, almost as if she were wearing a mask. She wore a silk dressing gown, belted at the waist. It was long and green, embroidered with little gold figures. She wore nothing underneath, which was obvious from the view of her décolletage. "The hairdresser just finished me, and I still have to get dressed. Can we make this brief? I'm going to the Children's Relief Gala tonight. I bought a table and now I'm going to be late for my own guests." She sat on the couch.

The way she spoke, Marc knew she had had a couple of drinks while she was being prepared by the hairdresser.

"I guess we can make it brief," said Marc. "I wanted to talk about the case. Especially about the actual scene when your husband was shot."

"I'm really not going to have much time to talk," she said brusquely. Now she crossed her legs and the green gown opened over her bare legs to mid-thigh. She put a cigarette in her mouth, looking at Franco somewhat impatiently.

"I'll get it," said Marc, taking a lighter from the glass table.

"Thank you. Your friend seems too involved with my gin to light a lady's cigarette," she said.

"It's vodka."

Mrs. Wainwright looked ceilingward with impatient disdain. Franco studied her, his jaw muscles starting to tighten. He glanced over at Marc. Their eyes met, and Marc shook his head.

"I'm really sorry for the hurry," said Mrs. Wainwright. "I forgot all about this benefit tonight. Old George Shaw is my escort." She shrugged, almost to herself. "George is a pain in the ass. But he does have fifty million dollars and is *so* very social. Oh, I guess you wouldn't know that," she said, aware of Marc and Franco again. She puffed on her cigarette. "Can you fix me a drink?" she said over her shoulder toward Franco.

Franco, his pique still aroused from her last remark, did not move.

"Sure," said Marc. "What would you like?" He nodded to Franco, winking to ease him up.

"A very dry martini. Do you always speak for your friend?" Toni Wainwright asked caustically.

"Sometimes." Marc smiled patiently. "Since you're in a hurry, let me ask you some quick questions."

"I really can't tell you anything more than I already have. I told you everything. Am I going to get that drink?"

"I'm making it."

"Oh dear, I think your friend doesn't like me," she said, turning to Marc, a coy smile on her face.

"About Mister Wainwright," Marc pressed.

"I was asleep, or drunk, or both. I don't know anything about it. Thank you, dear boy." She smiled, leaning forward purposely as she took the drink from Franco. Her décolletage opened fuller as she did, as she knew it would. "All I can tell you is that Bob was a shit and spoiled my dinner party that night."

"When you say Bob, you mean Mister Wainwright, your husband?" asked Marc.

"What other shit are we talking about, dear boy," she replied. "What time is it? Tell me what time it is," she said to Marc.

"Six twenty-five."

"Oh, Jesus Christ," she brought her drink down hard on the glass table. "I have to get going. I'm sorry, I can't talk any more. You'll have to call another time. Do call another time," she repeated to Marc. "When just *we two* can have dinner or something."

"All right, if you have to run," said Marc. "Just let me ask you a couple of things quickly."

"Come inside with me then," she said, starting toward the door.

"No, I'd like to get the questioning over, and then you can get your dressing done by yourself," he replied firmly now. He had had enough of her cuteness.

"Afraid of a little girl like me?" she asked.

"Hardly," said Marc blankly. "Where did you get the pistol? You said you have a license for it. How long had you had it?"

"Not afraid of me, hanh," she said, looking at him saucily from the side of her eye.

"Mrs. Wainwright, let's be serious. Where did you get the pistol, and how long had you had it?" Marc repeated.

"Zack Lord gave it to me. We went out to Colorado. We both have some cattle holdings in Colorado, you know, for tax deductions and all that?"

"Is that where you got the pistol?"

"Yes. Zack bought them, and had them shipped to a dealer here in New York," she replied.

"Them?" Franco interjected from his chair to the side.

"Did he buy more than one pistol?" Marc picked up.

"There were two," she replied. "Zack bought one for himself and gave one to me for a present."

"Were they both the same?" Marc probed further.

"Exactly the same. Twenty-five automatic calibers, or something like that. They were made of solid silver, with scroll work and pearl handles. Now can I go? I have to pee."

Franco stared at her.

"When did he buy the pistols?" Marc asked, ignoring her indelicacy.

"About six months ago," she answered. "Look, I really have to get going. I don't have any more time for this."

"Mrs. Wainwright," Marc said impatiently now. "If you don't co-operate, you won't have time for anything else. You'll be behind bars for twenty-five years, and they'll be running benefits for *you.*"

She stared at Marc, then nodded slightly. "Go ahead, what else?"

"You say you had the pistol about six months?" Marc repeated.

"That's about how long Zack and I have been seeing each other. Oh, I knew him longer than that, of course. Saw each other for drinks occasionally. But Bob and I separated, say, about eight months ago. And Zack and I began to see each other more openly about six months ago."

"And that's when you went to Colorado?" asked Marc.

"Shortly after we began seeing each other regularly, we went out to Colorado, to a cattle ranch, for a weekend in the big country, you know. And Zack bought the pistols then."

"Where is Zack tonight?" asked Marc. "Is he going to this benefit?"

"No. He's in Florida," she replied. "He had some contracts or something he had to work on with a couple of men from Texas. Why they met in Florida is beyond me. He's working on that damn octopus of his."

"Octopus?" asked Marc.

"His mutual fund, conglomerate, corporation, holding company, or whatever the hell it is," she said. "That's the company that owns all of his companies. Seems he's swallowed up so much, so fast, he needs a little time for digestion."

"Is Zack having business difficulties?" Marc asked.

"No, his holdings are growing every day. Zack's getting richer and richer. I think one of these days we're going to have to ask permission to live on his world." She puffed on her cigarette. "Bob —my husband—was always saying how he thought Zack's whole empire was going to bust apart one day," she added. "But Bob was jealous. He was lousy at being jealous. He was lousy at everything," she added. "And now, I *really* must pee. Give me a call and we'll talk for hours another day." Without another word, Mrs. Wainwright disappeared quickly out of the room, her green robe flowing behind.

"That nasty little bitch," Franco murmured.

"Cool it," said Marc as they made their way to the front door. The elevator arrived and they rode silently to the street level.

"Another minute of that smart-aleck talk and I was going to kick her in the ass," Franco splurted as they reached the sidewalk.

"Take it easy, Franco. She's a client, not a friend. We don't get involved with clients because we like the pleasure of their company."

"I guess that's right," said Franco.

They were both silent as they continued to walk toward the

car. When they reached the car, Franco opened the door for Marc and then got into the driver's side.

"You know, I've been thinking," said Franco.

"Go ahead," said Marc expectantly.

"Well, you brought me along so I'd get some ideas, right?"

"Right."

"Okay, then, here we go," said Franco. "First, she's a nasty bitch."

"That I figured out by myself."

"Okay, next. Even if she's a nasty bitch, that don't mean she ought to get hung with a rap that ain't—isn't hers."

"I'm with you so far," said Marc. "Now what's the theory? Or do you want to wait to discuss it with Mrs. Conte?"

"We can discuss it some more later," he said. "But I don't get the feeling that she killed him. I don't know why. But that's the feeling I get. What I do feel is that this nasty bitch gets drunk a lot. We know she was drunk the night her husband was killed; really drunk, is how she said it. Now if her being really drunk is a lot worse than she is now, then she wouldn't even know what she was doing or where she was when she's like that. People who know her would probably know that too. So when she was really drunk, like that night her husband was killed, someone who knew her could have knocked off her husband while she was passed out and put the gun in her hand."

"That's really good," said Marc irreverently. "*Except*, how did the killer in your theory get *Mister* Wainwright to Toni Wainwright's apartment on this particular night? How did the killer then get in himself or herself? How did the killer get Toni Wainwright's pistol to kill Wainwright with? And one final question, why?"

"I don't know those answers," said Franco. "Not yet . . . I've got to talk to Mrs. Conte about that. But Mrs. Wainwright wouldn't know the difference if somebody did kill her husband even if she was there, if she was passed out drunk."

"That may be true, but it's the rest of the idea that disturbs me," said Marc.

"And how about that Zack Lord having the same pistol?" asked Franco. "That's something we've got to kick around some more."

"Interesting," said Marc. "But ballistics will probably indicate that Mrs. Wainwright's pistol fired the fatal shot. Of course, we don't know much about ballistics, do we?"

"You think I may be onto something, hanh?"

"No, I was just thinking about the fact that a ballistics man could get on the stand and testify that a bullet came out of a particular pistol, say Mrs. Wainwright's. And then, because we haven't done much research into the subject of ballistics, we'd have to accept it, as the jury, judge, and everyone else does now. But supposing ballistics isn't so accurate a science, or supposing the ballistics man isn't so sharp. Maybe he makes a mistake. But I don't know it, because I'm not up on the subject." Marc thought quietly for a moment. "I think we'd better do some checking into ballistics."

"And how about my theory?" asked Franco.

"Talk to Mrs. Conte and come up with some of the answers to the problems in your theory. Then you'll have something."

"Thanks a lot."

XVI

SATURDAY, AUGUST 19, 1:30 P.M.

Pescadorito's hull lifted and fell through the gently rolling tide of Gravesend Bay as the boat passed beneath the vast span of the Verrazano Bridge. The bridge, arching from Brooklyn to Staten Island, over that part of New York Harbor known as The Narrows is the longest suspension bridge in the world. And yet, the dazzling effect of the bridge is somewhat diluted by ten other major bridges within a five-mile radius.

Franco was at *Pescadorito*'s helm. He wore jeans and a striped polo shirt. It was a hot day, and the sky was completely cloudless.

Maria was on the fore deck in a white bikini. She was lying down, sunning herself, her eyes closed. Her arms were braced on each side of her as the boat rolled on the ever larger waves. They were headed out to the ocean.

Marc was reading the New York *Times*. He wore bell bottomed jeans; no shirt.

"What are you doing?" Maria asked, not opening her eyes.

"Just reading the paper."

"How come? I thought we came out here to get away from all the horrors they report in the papers."

"Just checking," said Marc. "I'm reading about this fellow who was arrested in Brooklyn last night, charged with killing a seven-year-old girl."

"I heard that on the radio this morning," said Maria. "That the case where he molested her and then tried to decompose her body in a pit of lye?"

"Those are the charges." Marc continued his reading.

"I know everybody's entitled to a fair trial and all that," said Maria calmly, her eyes still closed. "But a person like that is really sick. I don't advocate anything violent, but they ought to give him a frontal lobotomy or something, turn him into a harmless vegetable."

"That's a hell of a thing." Marc put the paper aside. "What could be more violent than that?"

"Molesting and killing a seven-year-old girl and trying to get rid of the body in a pit of lye, that's what," Maria said emphatically, sitting up. She wore a printed cloth band about the top of her head.

The wind was increasing as they neared the open water. The boat was heeling over sharply now. The breeze pushed Maria's hair back off her face.

"It's a pretty crummy crime," admitted Marc. "This fellow's going to have one hell of a time getting a fair trial."

"I don't get the impression you're starting to think about defending him, do I?" she asked with obvious displeasure.

"You sound pretty strongly on the subject. Why shouldn't the man be defended?"

"Because it's more than a pretty crummy crime, as you described it. It's horrible . . . a seven-year-old child."

"Your reaction is all the more reason that the fellow needs a strong, objective defense," said Marc. "You, after all, darling, are a pretty reasonable person—most of the time—and even you are outraged. Can you imagine how some of the cops that arrested him feel? Can you imagine how the people in Brooklyn who are going to be on the jury will feel?"

"Come on, Marc. Don't get any ideas about defending him."

"Why not?"

"Because. It's just horrible. That poor little girl."

"You sound like all the strangers who ask me whether I'd defend someone if I knew for sure that he was really guilty," said Marc.

"I know, and your answer is that whatever crime he's committed your job is *not* to get him off, but just to see that he gets a fair trial. But this crime is horrible. Who cares if this filthy animal gets a fair trial as long as he's off the streets."

"I care," said Marc. "The more I listen to you, the more I realize maybe I should volunteer my services. I can just imagine what Franco would say about this case."

Maria turned. "Franco."

Franco saw her turn toward him and say something. He motioned with his head to indicate he couldn't hear. Both his hands were on the wheel.

"What do you think about the case this morning in the paper, about the little girl?" Maria called.

Franco cupped one hand around an ear; he still couldn't hear her.

"What do you think about the case where the little girl was killed this morning?" she called louder now.

Franco shook his head. He couldn't hear over the sound of the rushing waters and the wind. They were out past Breezy Point jetty now. Sandy Hook loomed over the starboard bow.

"Go and ask him, please," Maria urged. "I want to see his reaction."

"Okay. I'm curious myself." Marc walked aft.

"What's the matter?" Franco asked.

"Nothing. Maria just wanted to know what you thought about the fellow who's accused of killing that little girl in Brooklyn this morning?"

Franco looked forward to Maria and put one hand around his own throat, letting his tongue dangle out of his mouth. He pointed to the top of the mast.

"First, I'd cut the bastard's balls off and stuff them in his

167

mouth," Franco said quietly to Marc. "Then I'd hang his ass from the tallest thing I could find."

"That's what I thought you'd say," said Marc. He made his way carefully back to where Maria was sitting.

"You'd better not defend that animal, Marc Conte," Maria said firmly.

"Look darling, I personally think the crime is outrageous, okay? Professionally, however, it's something else."

"What else?"

"Professionally, it's a crime, like any other crime, which has legislated elements which the D.A. must prove in order to obtain a conviction. A defense lawyer can't think of it as a terrible thing. It's a crime, a crime created by men in the Legislature in Albany, put into effect by men—the D.A., and a judge, and a jury. And someone has to resist the rushing flow of bad publicity and make the D.A. prove his case according to the law."

"Darling," said Maria. "I know what you mean. I agree with you most of the time. But this . . ."

"This is exactly what I've always been talking about. The kind of case where no one wants to touch the defendant with a ten-foot-pole. Not even me, really. But someone has to protect him. Not because he's innocent. Not because he's a marvelous person. Not because I'd want to get him off. That's not the defense lawyer's job even though most people think that it is. But this man needs someone to defend him just to make sure that he gets a fair trial; that all the T's are crossed and all the I's dotted, and the law complied with right down the line. If that's done, and he's convicted, then I'd have no complaint. What would you say if after a full, impartial jury trial, the jury decides that the man is actually not guilty, say because it's a mistaken identity, or some other reason?"

"That would be different."

"Well, how the hell are you going to find that out if he doesn't get a fair trial?" asked Marc.

Maria looked at him, her mouth softening into a smile. "I guess you're right. But it's such a horrible thing . . ."

"I absolutely agree. But perhaps after a trial, he'll be found to have committed not murder, but, say, manslaughter in the first degree. The difference between life in prison and twenty-five years. Shouldn't he be convicted of what he's committed? Not a whit more, not a whit less?"

"Yes."

"Well then let the D.A. earn his salary, and whatever the jury says goes, guilty or not guilty. Is there anything fairer than that?"

"No."

"You think it should be different than that?"

"No."

Marc leaned over and kissed the end of Maria's nose.

"Are you going to volunteer to represent this fellow?" she asked.

"Why do you ask that?"

"Because I know you."

"I'm sure the court will appoint someone who knows how to handle the case," said Marc.

Maria put her arms around Marc's neck, leaning her forehead against his, looking into his eyes, gently reproving him. "Only if it's absolutely necessary. Please. I mean, there *are* other lawyers. You didn't invent the system, you know."

"I know."

Maria kissed him, her mouth soft and warm. Marc's tongue gently flicked at her lips. Her tongue in turn touched the tip of his.

"Did I tell you this morning how fantastically you fill out that bikini," Marc said, his forehead still pressed gently against hers.

The air was fresh and smelled of the clean sea now.

"No."

"You have some everything, baby," he said, kissing her again. "Some legs, some ass, some beautiful, round belly, some . . . shall I go on?"

"Did I tell you," she said, looking back toward the helm to be sure Franco was busy, "that I noticed that you weren't wearing anything under those pants?" Her hand gently slid up his thigh and touched the firm bulge at his crotch.

"Why you little devil." Marc smiled. He took her arm and moved her so that she lay back on the deck again. He lay close beside her. They kissed warmly, passionately. Maria's tongue slid into Marc's mouth. Their legs intertwined. The heaving of the boat rocked him against her legs.

"Let's go below," she said gently as their lips parted.

"Right here on deck?"

"Very cute."

Marc stood, and helped Maria to her feet. They both moved along the side of the cabin to the cockpit. Marc patted her rear end as she moved ahead of him. She flicked her hand at his to stop him as they reached Franco.

"We're going below. I'm going to sleep for a while," Marc said to Franco. "You be okay here by yourself for a while?"

"Sure."

Marc followed Maria below. She moved directly through the main salon into the forward cabin. As she arrived there, she turned to embrace Marc who was directly behind her. They stood, their bodies now pressed warmly against each other, kissing. Marc shut the cabin door with his foot.

"You turn me on like an electric light bulb," she said as she stopped kissing him so she could gather air.

"And you me," he said, his hands sliding up her back and undoing her bra. It fell to the floor. Her breasts, firm and taut, were quite light compared to the tan of the rest of her. Her nipples were pointed and erect. Fingers of each of his hands gently brushed across both her nipples as they kissed again.

"You have such fantastic hands," she said, her eyes closed ecstatically as Marc continued to rub her nipples.

Maria's hand went into the waistband of Marc's pants moving down until she grasped him firmly, caressingly.

"You have fantastic hands too," Marc said. His mouth found hers again, and they silently caressed and fondled each other as they kissed. The rocking of the ship was timed, it seemed, or they timed themselves, so that they were rocking against each other excitingly.

Marc's hands moved down and he hooked his index fingers into each side of her bikini bottoms. The pants slid beneath his fingers until, after they cleared her wide hips, revealed all the whiteness and darkness and softness beneath. Marc moved forward, as they still kissed, toward the bunk. He reached down now and picked Maria up in his arms, lifting her onto the soft mattress of the bunk.

Maria's hands unlaced Marc's pants. They, too, fell to the floor, revealing him naked and aroused and aching for her. He climbed onto the bunk. They kissed again, their bodies hot, their legs intertwined.

Marc's hands gently ran over her breasts as they kissed, then slowly slid down her chest to her stomach, and then lower still until he caressed her completely.

"Oh, Marc," she gasped in his ear. "Oh, ohhh . . ."

Her hands had enveloped him, arousing him, exciting him, pulling at him. And all that could be heard now was the rushing of the water beneath the boat, and the gentle rocking, and the occasionally shifting of the sail on the mast as *Pescadorito* cut its way smoothly through the sea.

XVII

MONDAY, AUGUST 21, 9:15 A.M.

Marc was at his office desk looking over his check book and a list of accounts receivable. He still hadn't charged Mrs. Maricyk any fee. He didn't want to press her too hard, especially since she was trying to raise bail money. He probably would only ask her for a thousand dollars, maybe less. He tried to adjust his fees so a defendant without much money or with no money could still be helped yet not insulted or humbled. The wealthier people paid more, but to them, their freedom was worth it, and they didn't give a damn that they were paying more so Marc could afford to help the little guy too.

Sunlight streamed through the windows; the kind of sunlight early fall always brings, not as hot, but brighter, whiter, as the sun held lower in the sky. The weather was considerably cooler today. A buzzer sounded.

"Yes?" said Marc, picking up the intercom.

"Mister Fox is here to see you," Marguerite announced.

"Bring him in," said Marc. He read the last remaining entries on the check book, then closed the book.

Lawrence V. Fox was an attorney. He handled mostly minor

criminal cases, and could be seen daily hustling through the corridors of the Criminal Courts Building. Indeed, when many criminal attorneys were sought to handle minor gambling, prostitution, pickpocket cases, they referred the case to Fox. There was usually not much fee involved in such matters, but Fox capitalized on volume work. He rarely went to trial; usually the case was disposed of by way of plea and fine. The door opened, and Marguerite showed Mister Fox into Marc's office.

"Hiya, Marc," said Fox, smiling, reaching out to shake Marc's hand. He was of medium height, his gray hair combed into a pompadour. His clothes were kind of flashy-sharp, like a small-time gambler's. Fox was quick-moving, doing everything with a kind of nervous, compulsive rapidity.

"Hello, Larry," replied Marc, standing. "Here, Marguerite," he said, taking some papers from the side of his desk. "Type these Wainwright papers in final form and serve them on the D.A. right away. Make the motion returnable next Tuesday. And here," he said, taking the draft of another set of motion papers from his desk. "Take the motion to suppress the recordings in the Maricyk case and make it up. Serve both motions for the same day."

Even though Marc had decided to seek a lesser plea for Maricyk, he had to continue to prepare for a trial. The D.A. might not offer a plea Marc thought acceptable. And, besides, to keep some leverage, Marc couldn't throw in the sponge now. He had to play it as if it was for real.

"Yes, sir," Marguerite said, taking the papers, then turning to leave the room. She shut the door behind her.

"Always work, hanh, Marc?" said Fox, smiling quickly. He sat in the chair just in front of Marc's desk, crossing his legs.

"Yes," agreed Marc. "There's always something else to be done."

Fox uncrossed his legs as he studied the pictures on the walls, the diplomas, the certificates behind Marc. "Nice office," he said. Even while seated, he seemed to be moving.

"Thanks. How've you been?" asked Marc.

Fox waved his hand through the air several times quickly. He frowned. "With all this Legal Aid crap, business stinks. Nowadays, the judges ask the defendant *You have any money?*; naturally the defendant says no, and then they give him Legal Aid just like that without even checking the guy out. In the old days, you had to really not have any money to get Legal Aid. This way, it's really cut into the business. Don't you find it that way?"

"I've noticed the judges doing that," Marc replied politely.

"Are you kidding?" said Fox, weaving back and forth on the chair. "Now they have, who knows, forty, fifty, Legal Aid lawyers just in 100 Centre alone. There's three or four in every court. Sure it's cut into business. Maybe you don't know. You handle different kinds of stuff. Me, I grab a quick fee, wham, bam, thank you ma'am, finished. But that business is shot, too. Gambling used to be good. Ten cases a night. And the prostitution cases. And the fag cases. All the little shit that nobody else wanted, I'd make a good buck, I mean, a real good buck on it, Marc." He winked at Marc for emphasis.

"That's fine, Larry."

"But all that practice is down the drain, Marc," Fox continued. "What with this Legal Aid on one side and Mayor Davies and all his ass-hole policies on the other. Gamblers aren't arrested anymore; prostitutes you fall over them in the streets; fags almost have a union or something now. They organize and picket. You can hardly make a living nowadays." He grew silent, staring at a spot of sunlight on the floor.

"What can I help you with, Larry?" Marc asked, after a rather long silence.

Fox started nodding his head quickly. "I got myself an indictment."

"You were indicted personally?" Marc was surprised.

Fox nodded again. "Yeah. Didn't you hear about it?"

"No, I didn't," replied Marc. "I'm sorry."

Fox was staring abstractedly at the floor. "Yeah. I got myself indicted for bribery."

"Who were you supposed to have bribed?"

"A cop."

Marc leaned back in his chair, looking steadily at Fox. "How long ago was this?"

"What, the indictment or the bribery?"

"Both."

"The bribery was supposed to be about two months ago," Fox replied. "In the beginning of June. The indictment, they came

173

down with about two weeks ago. I didn't retain any lawyer yet. I handled the arraignment myself. I mean, if I couldn't enter a plea of Not Guilty for myself, I might as well hang up. So I saved a few bucks, right?"

"What's supposed to have happened?" asked Marc.

"I was handling a small junk case, you know? Marijuana," said Fox. "I'll tell you confidentially," he said, automatically looking over his shoulder. "These kids were really dealing in pretty large amounts of marijuana. No hard shit. Only marijuana."

"Go ahead."

"Well, these kids have a whole operation going, you know?" He stole another glance over his shoulder. "Heavy weights of stuff. I'm not representing any of them at the time, or anything. But one of the guys is a fruit I took care of a couple of times. Meatball cases. So he gets busted by the cops for marijuana. It was a real meatball case, too. A real nothing. They only caught him with, who knows, a few ounces, a half pound."

"And you handled his case?" Marc probed.

"Yeah. Just the fruit. He was the only one arrested. The others are all from out of town, California. So he recommends me to them, and they pay me a good fee to represent him. Now I see fireworks in my head when I think maybe I do a dynamite job on the fruit's case and they retain me to take on all their cases here. Nice piece of business, you know what I mean?" He looked at Marc, his eyebrows raised, nodding quickly. "I could cash in on these kids. Especially the way kids smoke grass today. We were born twenty years too late, hanh, Marc? The way these kids live— laid, parlayed, everything goes."

"How'd you come to get indicted?"

Fox shrugged and grimaced simultaneously. "The cop on the arrest, I was talking to him. See, I made a motion to suppress. And we're going to have this hearing, you know? And I talk to the cop outside the court and tell him that he don't have to go out of his way, you know, break his neck, to make a case here. I more or less told him the facts of life."

"And those facts included money, I suppose?" said Marc.

"Well, I told him there was a little sugar available, you know? He knew what I meant. He says 'okay.' But then he says the case had to be adjourned this day. So I say, 'okay.' I should have figured the fink was going to fuck me around. But everything is going good. So I figure what the hell. Besides, Judge Crown is sitting. He's in the Part for a whole month. So I figure, sure, give this guy a two-week adjournment. Crown'll still be sitting. You know he's a good guy for a lawyer to appear before, right?"

"And the next time the cop came to court," said Marc, "you spoke to him and he was wired with a tape recorder, is that it?"

"That's it," Fox said. "Screwed, blued, and tattooed, all at once. The son of a bitch cop has a wire on him; he tapes the conversation and then some other bastard cops that were staked out nearby, they come over and arrest me. Right in the courthouse."

Marc leaned forward, his elbows on the desk, his chin resting on his hands. "Larry, I can't imagine how much any client could pay—and don't tell me how much you were paid—I just can't imagine anyone being able to pay a lawyer enough to put himself, his career, his profession, his license on the line by offering a bribe, by getting involved in a crime."

"Believe me, these kids were paying me real good. And it wasn't just one case, Marc. It was the future. I was going to make them a package deal. When someone they sold to got busted, I'd handle that too. Not big cases, but all together, it would add up to a big thing, Marc. It really would."

"I've often wondered, Larry, what kind of money could make me get involved in a crime," Marc mused aloud. "I figured anything in five figures would be an insult, so we forget that."

Fox stared at Marc.

"And six figures, well in a few good years, you can make that in practice yourself without risking the loss of your license or getting disbarred. So, it'd have to be in the high six figures or millions for me to get involved. But then what would I do with millions?"

Fox was studying Marc, his mouth open hungrily.

"As soon as I bought a big yacht or a private plane, the Internal Revenue would be on my back. The only thing I could do is bury the millions in the ground," Marc went on. "And what the hell good would it be to have millions in the ground? So, here I am, and I can't be bribed or bought. And I look at you and I say, Larry, how the hell could you get yourself into this predicament?"

"Hey, Marc, stop with the preaching bullshit," said Fox. "All right, you wouldn't do it. I did it. I'm in. Now will you defend me? Or is that beneath you too?"

"I'll defend you, if you want," said Marc. "I don't have to approve of the crime in order to defend a case."

"That's all I ask," said Fox. "I know you're the best. You'll do a job. You won't charge me too much, though, will you?"

"You know, you're incredible," said Marc. "First you put yourself on the line for a client in an incredible way. Just for a few bucks. And now, when your whole career is on the line, you want to get a bargain price too. Don't you think about anything except money?"

Fox shifted his eyes away from Marc. He tried a skimpy smile. "Sure I do. But at the moment, I can't remember what it is."

"It'll cost you five thousand," said Marc.

"Five thousand? Are you kidding. I'm a brother lawyer, Marc. Take it easy."

"That's why it's only five thousand. If I thought you didn't have it, I'd defend you for nothing. But you've got plenty, Larry. Remember all those good bucks you made on all those little cases. You stop playing the horses for a week and you'll have it saved."

Fox looked at Marc with a grimace that turned into a hard smile. "Okay. Give me a little while to put it together, okay?"

"Of course."

XVIII

TUESDAY, AUGUST 22, 10:40 A.M.

Marc stood at the judge's bench in Part 35 speaking with Judge Bernard Haroldson. Judge Haroldson was formerly a New York County Assistant D.A., later a Health Commissioner in the Impellitteri city administration, and, finally, a Supreme Court Justice. He was, in addition to being a good Democrat who made his way up through the ranks in proper order, a fine judge who not only knew the law but applied it fairly between the prosecution and the defense. D.A.s and defense lawyers alike who were looking for an edge were bluntly disappointed in Judge Haroldson's courtroom.

While waiting for a prisoner to be brought to the courtroom from the bull pen, the Judge had asked Marc to approach the bench.

"How about a hint as to what your decision on the motion to suppress in the Samon case is?" asked Marc.

"What do you think this is, Marc"—the Judge was smiling—"the coming attractions at the movies?"

"No, but you've already said you made the decision. It's just that your secretary hasn't finished typing it. You could tell me what it is. I wouldn't tell anyone."

The Judge laughed.

Marc's client, Percival Samon, a young Black man, had been arrested by the police after they entered his apartment with a search warrant which authorized them to search for untaxed cigarettes. The New York State authorities were in the throes of a drive to stamp out the trade in cigarettes which were purchased in North Carolina, where the tax is minimal, then smuggled into New York and offered for sale at low, taxless prices. They obtained information that Samon was allegedly retailing the untaxed smokes. They swore out a search warrant, but when they arrived in Samon's apartment, they didn't find any cigarettes. They did find, however, several valuable paintings wrapped in cardboard; and in another room, tickets which looked like gallery tags for the same paintings. They arrested Samon on the spot, and after several hours at the station house, the police finally discovered that the paintings had indeed been stolen from the Parisian Art Galleries some months before, and were worth $12,000. Samon was booked for possession of stolen property.

"I may change my mind after I see the final decision typed," said the Judge. "You know, I've done that. I've done research and dictated a decision. And before I see the final version typed, I find a new case or I've changed my mind for some other reason."

"You mean, the decision depends on how fast your secretary types?"

"No, not at all. It's just that in reading it over, I may find I want to decide the case some other way. Now you wouldn't want me to tell you one thing, and then sign an opinion completely different, would you?"

"No. So tell me the final decision, and don't change your mind."

The Judge smiled again. "You brought up a most interesting point in this case, Marc."

"Well, I just found that People versus Brown, 22 New York 2nd to be on all fours with the Samon case," replied Marc.

On all fours in legal parlance means that the Brown case, to which Marc referred, and the present case were legally the same from every point of view, just as an animal might resemble another animal from every point of view, from all four sides, on all four legs.

"I'm not sure it's on all fours," the Judge said thoughtfully.

"How come?" asked Marc. "The Brown decision says that a search warrant must specifically indicate what the police are to look for. And if they find something else they believe to be fruits of another crime, they must secure the place and obtain another search warrant. Isn't that what happened here? They were supposed to look for untaxed cigarettes and they arrested Samon for paintings?"

"You're not saying the police can't seize contraband in open view, are you?" asked the Judge.

"No. But paintings are not contraband. Weapons are. Drugs are. But paintings may or may not be. That's why the cops need a search warrant."

Judge Haroldson shrugged noncommittally. He glanced over to the clerk and saw that the prisoner for whom he was waiting had arrived. "Still looking for a preview aren't you, Marc? And you think you're going to suck me into telling you. Come back in an hour and I'll have the final version for you."

"You're sure a tough guy to get any information out of, Judge."

"You wouldn't want me to change my mind and not suppress what I've already decided to suppress, would you?" the Judge asked, winking.

Marc smiled. "No, I can wait."

"Fine."

"Judge, can I just say that it is always extremely refreshing to appear before you."

"Thanks."

"The only reason I say that, Your Honor," Marc continued, "is that there are so many knocks put on judges these days; I find it important to let the good judges know there are people out here who appreciate them. A lot of other judges would have hidden behind some flimsy excuse to find the search in the Samon case valid, and thus force a guilty plea."

"Thank you, Marc," the Judge said. He motioned the clerk to hold off calling the prisoner's case. "I see my function as a judge to be an impartial arbiter between prosecution and defense. Not a participant. And not as a legislator either. The entire system works best when each of us performs his own function. I only put the laws into effect. If better laws are needed, the legislators have to make them."

"I'm glad some people on your side of the bench see the same thing some of us on this side see, Your Honor," said Marc. "I can't fathom how cops or D.A.s select the laws defining crimes as sacred, and, therefore, important to enforce. But they find the procedure laws defining the proper methods of obtaining evidence, and the rights of citizens against unreasonable searches, or the laws protecting people against involuntary confessions to just interfere with the cop's sacred duty. They just ignore the procedure laws to enforce the penal laws."

"Not in my court, Marc," the Judge said emphatically. "All the law is sacred here. It's not only important that the law is enforced, but that it is enforced in the right way, legally, according to the letter of *all* laws. Those protecting the defendants as well as those damning the defendants."

"Terrific, Judge," said Marc. "I couldn't have said it better myself."

The Judge smiled. "Now will you get out of here so I can try to render substantial justice to defendants other than yours."

Marc made his way toward Part 30, one of the two Parts in New York County in which felony arraignments were processed after the grand jury handed down an indictment. Both the Toni Wainwright case and the Maricyk case were on today's arraignment calendar. Several reporters were lounging in the corridor outside Part 30, smoking, glancing occasionally through the oval glass panels into the courtroom. Marc walked past the reporters and entered the courtroom. Judge Brana, heavy-set and wearing glasses, presided. Toni Wainwright was seated next to Messrs. Cahill and Rutley in the second row from the front. Mrs. Maricyk was seated by herself at the rear of the courtroom. Marc slipped into the seat next to Mrs. Maricyk. She turned to Marc, touched his arm, and smiled in relief.

"I was afraid you weren't going to get here on time," she whispered.

"I wouldn't let you down."

"Are you going to try to get Joey out on bail today, Mister Conte?"

"I'm sure going to try."

"Oh, please, Mister Conte. Joey looks so bad. I seen him last night. He looks awful. And I just can't get collateral for the bail. That lousy bondsman won't take nothing but a deed or a bankbook. I don't have neither of them. Please get him low bail today, Mister Conte."

"I'll try. They're calling Joey's case now," Marc said, rising. He walked to the front of the courtroom. Joey Maricyk came out of the bull pen accompanied by a court officer. He waved discreetly to his wife. Marc gave his name and address to the court stenographer for the record.

"Are you Joseph Maricyk?" asked the clerk.

The defendant nodded.

"You have to speak up," said the clerk.

"Yes."

"Is Mister Conte standing beside you, your attorney?"

"Yes."

"Will you step up here, gentlemen," said the Judge.

The assistant D.A. in charge of the Part, a young man with glasses, walked up to the judge's bench. So did Marc.

"Any possibility of a disposition here?" asked the Judge.

"The file jacket is marked an E felony," the assistant said to the Judge. "We'll accept that plea if Counsel wishes."

The Judge looked at Marc. "What do you say, Mister Conte?"

"I might be able to work out a disposition," said Marc. "But not to an E felony."

"That's the best the office is willing to make, Judge," said the D.A. "This is an attempted bribe."

"That's questionable, Judge," said Marc. "Particularly in view of the fact that the defendant was worked over by the police with an ax handle. I have the proof in the record at arraignment. Here are the minutes." Marc handed a transcript of the hearing to the Judge.

The Judge scanned the pages of testimony. "I do see what you're saying in the minutes," he said. "But I can't force the D.A. to give you any plea other than what he's offering. I'd like to dispose of this if we can. How about if I give your client a suspended sentence? He won't do any jail time. That I do have control over, Mister Conte."

"Let him take the felony," said the D.A. "What the hell, it's only an E. The Judge will give him a walk. How can he be hurt?"

"I can't let a client take a plea and get a felony record, just to get rid of a case," said Marc, "even if he doesn't go to jail."

"How about interference with the administration of justice as an A misdemeanor if the defendant doesn't press charges against the police or anyone else?" said the Judge. "What do you say, Mister D.A.?"

Judge Brana liked to dispose of cases. He seemed to get satisfaction knowing at the end of each month, each year, that he was the judge, statistically, who disposed of more cases than any other judge in the state.

As far as statistics were concerned, Marc knew the gathering of statistics to be a highly sophisticated game played in the courts and by the police. While the statistics relating to the incidence of crime is high, thus requiring continued legislative appropriations, the police carry cases on the books at the precinct level as less severe than the actual crimes. Thus, an armed robbery may be carried as a larceny; a rape as an assault; an assault as disorderly conduct. Perhaps, the police brass and other authorities decided that the false sense of security engendered by inaccurate statistics subserves the interests of the People, as if the facts and dangers which actually exist in the streets will seem better if they're distorted in print. In court, the statistics game is played with dispositions of cases. A number of cases are assigned to a Part. That Part may decide a motion only, then refer the case to another Part for trial. Yet that counts as a disposition, and when Judge Goldman spoke at Vinnie Bauer's induction ceremony, he was absolutely correct. Statistically, more cases are being disposed of, and the machinery is working well. That some of the machinery of justice is merely spinning wheels is overshadowed by the statistical fact that taxpayers rebel at supporting the court system, the D.A.'s budget, the police salaries. But as long as statistics prove life is safer, the courts are working well, the judges are busy, the D.A.s persevering, they can continue to exist.

One of the most accurate statistics of crime, however, relates to homicides. Because you can't hide bodies. Except, of course, in high-crime areas where many a body is found in an alley and marked "Natural Causes: Case Closed."

"No can do, Judge," the D.A. said to Judge Brana, shaking his head. "Maricyk takes a plea to a felony or nothing."

"Sorry, Marc. I'd really like to help you out." The Judge shrugged. "Okay, if that's the best you'll do, Mister D.A."

The D.A. nodded.

"Step back, gentlemen."

The two lawyers returned to their respective counsel tables.

"How does your client plead, Mister Conte?" asked the clerk.

"Not guilty," said Marc.

"Enter a not guilty plea," said the Judge. "August 29, Part 39."

"August 29, Part 39," repeated the clerk.

"Can you get me bail today, Mister Conte?" asked Maricyk. "I'm going crazy in there. See if you can get it lowered."

"Your Honor," said Marc. "My client has been in jail for more than two weeks now and is unable to make a bail of thirty-five hundred dollars. Will Your Honor entertain an application to reduce the bail?"

"What's your position, Mister D.A.?" asked the Judge.

"The People oppose any such application," said the D.A.

"I won't lower the bail without the D.A.'s consent," said the Judge.

"May I suggest to Your Honor that since the present bail is beyond the means of the defendant, it's tantamount to no bail at all."

"I'm sorry," said the Judge. "That bail is little enough. Call the next case."

The court officer escorted Maricyk back toward the bull pen.

"Would Your Honor be kind enough to permit the clerk to call the Toni Wainwright case?" asked Marc. "It's another matter I have before you on today's calendar."

"Certainly."

"People versus Toni Wainwright, indictment number three, eight, seven, two," called the clerk.

Toni Wainwright rose and walked to the front of the courtroom to join Marc. Cahill and Rutley sat attentively in their seats.

The newspapermen on vigil at the glass panels in the rear doors now entered the courtroom, moving in a horde down the side aisle, standing as close to the front as possible, their pencils and pads at the ready.

Toni Wainwright stood nervously at the defendant's rail, watching the Judge. Marc stood at the rail with her.

"Too busy with the floozy to talk to your client," she whispered harshly.

Marc leveled an angry gaze at Mrs. Wainwright. "You'll plead not guilty when the clerk asks how you plead," Marc said flatly.

"If Your Honor please," said the assistant D.A., "Mister O'Connor is coming down to handle this matter personally. May we have a second call on it?"

Marc decided not to waste time arguing.

"Yes, certainly," said the Judge.

Marc walked next to Mrs. Wainwright back toward the spectators. The reporters started to drift out of the courtroom to resume their smoking positions outside the door.

"What's going to happen to Joey now?" asked Mrs. Maricyk, walking up to Marc.

Toni Wainwright and Mrs. Maricyk looked at each other carefully. Mrs. Maricyk studied the gold earrings and the necklace Toni wore. Either of those items could bail her husband out in minutes.

"I'm going to make out a writ of habeas corpus," Marc whispered.

"What's that?" Mrs. Maricyk asked.

Toni Wainwright stood silently next to Marc.

"It's a court proceeding to get Joey's bail reduced," Marc replied.

"Can you get him out today?"

"No. First the papers have to be drafted. A habeas corpus is a civil proceeding. I have to start it in the civil division of the Supreme Court. Then if the judge there denies the habeas corpus, we can appeal to the Appellate Division."

"It sounds complicated. How long does all this take?"

"At the very least, two or three days."

"Counselor," said a court officer, walking down the aisle toward Marc. "Can you talk outside, please. The Judge wants everyone to sit down and be quiet."

"Surely. Wait for me a few minutes," Marc said to Mrs. Maricyk. "Let me get this other case over with."

Mrs. Maricyk waved her arm annoyedly in the general direction of the judge's bench. "I can't stand the stink around here, Mister Conte. I know it's not your fault. But I get nauseous in this place."

"Let's all sit down," suggested Marc. He sat in one of the audience benches, Mrs. Maricyk on one side, Mrs. Wainwright on the other.

The clerk called another case, and a defendant was brought before the Court.

O'Connor walked brusquely into the courtroom. He nodded to Marc as he walked up the aisle and took a seat at the District Attorney's table.

"That was a pleasant greeting," whispered Toni Wainwright. "Why has he got a hair in his ass?"

Marc looked at Mrs. Wainwright. "I'm not sure exactly how to answer a question put that way."

The defendant now at the bar pleaded guilty to a crime.

"I gotta go, Mister Conte," Mrs. Maricyk said, rising. "I had enough of this place for today."

"I'll only be a few more minutes," said Marc.

She shook her head as she walked out of the courtroom.

The clerk called the Wainwright case again. O'Connor rose and stood before the judge's bench. Marc and Mrs. Wainwright rose and walked toward the front. The entire staff of newsmen reentered the courtroom, again lining the walls near the front.

"Is your name Toni Wainwright?" asked the clerk.

"It is," she replied as she stood nervously at the railing.

"And is Mister Marc Conte standing beside you your lawyer?"

"It is. I mean, he is."

"I assume, gentlemen, this matter won't be disposed of today?" said the Judge.

O'Connor looked at Marc.

"No disposition, Your Honor," Marc said to the Judge. "This matter has to be tried."

"Very well," replied the Judge. "Let's arraign the defendant."

"You are charged with the crime of manslaughter in the first degree, how do you plead?" the clerk asked Mrs. Wainwright.

She looked at Marc.

"Not guilty," he whispered.

"Not guilty."

"Date, Your Honor?" asked the clerk.

"August 29," the Judge replied. "Part 39."

"August 29, Part 39," repeated the clerk as he made a note on the court file.

"Your Honor," said O'Connor, "I want to make a bail application at this time."

"Very well."

"Your Honor, this is a most serious, a most terrible crime," O'Connor began, waxing dramatic for the reporters who were scribbling onto their pads. "And while I realize that Mrs. Wainwright has never been in conflict with the law before, the law should apply equally between both rich and poor. The fact that Mrs. Wainwright is wealthy should not in any fashion give her greater privilege or wider latitude in obtaining bail or committing a crime. Neither Mrs. Wainwright, nor anyone else, should be able to afford a better system of justice. The law must be impartially meted out." O'Connor's voice was rising to his occasion. "And I believe that the bail should be increased to a hundred thousand dollars at this time."

"May I be heard, Your Honor," said Marc. Outwardly, at least, he was calm and controlled.

The Judge nodded.

Marc began: "Mister O'Connor's outrageous bit of circus drama is . . ."

"Wait a minute," said O'Connor, "what's this circus stuff . . ."

"Your Honor, I didn't interrupt Mister O'Connor when he wanted to make his statement. May I have the same courtesy?"

"Yes, certainly," said the Judge. "Mister O'Connor, I'll give you another opportunity if you so desire." The Judge's fairness was now on display, as the reporters were avidly writing every word.

"The speech by the District Attorney was intended for the ears of the reporters, apparently for . . ."

"Now, Judge, I'm not going to let him say . . ."

"Mister O'Connor, Mister Conte is speaking. You may answer him when he finishes," said the Judge sharply. "Let's keep a little decorum here."

"But I refuse to be told that I'm a circus performer making a publicity speech." O'Connor was red around the neck, white in the cheeks, as his anger mounted.

"Wait your turn, Mister O'Connor. I'm sure you can meanwhile think of something nasty to say about Mister Conte. But don't say it," the Judge cautioned, smiling warily. "And, Mister Conte, get to the legal point, directly."

"Yes, Your Honor. The factor of money has nothing to do with the bail on which Mrs. Wainwright is presently at liberty. Judge Crawford determined the bail in this case based on several factors; Mrs. Wainwright's lack of prior difficulties with the law, her roots in the community, the possibility of her not appearing before the court to answer these charges; and, in addition, the District Attorney's potential for success," Marc said cuttingly. "With these factors in mind, Your Honor, Judge Crawford set the present bail figure. Which is as it should be, Your Honor, in this defendant's case, in every defendant's case, as the law requires. Mister O'Connor's speech for higher bail has nothing whatever to do with the reality of this situation, and I again say, his speech is just some boiler plate for the benefit of the press. Particularly is this true, Your Honor, as you are a Supreme Court Justice and do not have the power to sit as an Appellate court to review the action of Judge Crawford who is also a Supreme Court Justice of equal jurisdiction. Mister O'Connor is aware of that, and yet he makes a useless motion. I must repeat that the only reason he's making this useless motion can be for reporters to hear."

"Your Honor, I just can't stand by idly and let Mister Conte accuse the District Attorney's office of publicity grandstanding."

"Oh, not the office, Your Honor," said Marc. "Just Mister O'Connor."

"Gentlemen, may I now have something to say without being

interrupted?" asked the Judge. He looked from O'Connor to Marc. "Judge Crawford did set the bail in this case. And, as Mister Conte correctly points out, Judge Crawford is, as I am, a Supreme Court Judge. I cannot overrule his decision, nor do I believe that it is proper that I even consider this application. I must suggest that this matter of bail for Mrs. Wainwright be taken up again with Judge Crawford if you so desire, Mister O'Connor."

"Your Honor has jurisdiction to set the bail now that this matter has come before Your Honor for arraignment," said O'Connor.

"I do not have the jurisdiction to overrule Judge Crawford," said the Judge.

"Unless, of course," Marc said, now wanting to twist the knife in O'Connor's hand before the press, "there is new information that the District Attorney has to show that Mrs. Wainwright is a poorer bail risk than she was when the bail was set?"

"Mister O'Connor?" the Judge inquired.

"I'll take this up with Judge Crawford, Your Honor, if you say he is the one with the jurisdiction."

"Very well, present bail continued," said the Judge.

Marc and Mrs. Wainwright walked away from the bench.

"Whew. That O'Connor is awful," said Toni Wainwright.

O'Connor walked along the middle aisle, making his way toward the back door and the crowd of reporters now huddled there. "You have a lot of nerve with the circus bit," O'Connor complained to Marc as he walked past him.

"It's all part of the day's work," replied Marc. "You have a job to do, and so do I. Now how about co-operating with me and giving me a voluntary bill of particulars in this case?" Marc asked. He waited for O'Connor to blow up.

"Co-operation? Hell'll freeze first," O'Connor replied. "You make your motion, and I'll oppose it." He stormed off toward the back.

"How come he hates us?" asked Mrs. Wainwright.

"He doesn't," replied Marc.

"He does seem unusually overwrought about this case," said Rutley, who, along with Cahill, had joined Marc and Mrs. Wainwright.

"He's just making a play for the newsmen," said Marc. "He knew that's what the Judge would say about the bail, but he wanted to make the play anyway."

"Do we have to go through the crowd of newspaper people?" asked Mrs. Wainwright.

"There are very few exits from this building," said Marc. "The press will have them all covered. There's no need to run away, however. You haven't done anything."

"I know, but I don't want to go through all their questions, or be on everybody's television screen tonight as the rich husband killer."

"Mister Cahill," said Marc, "could you get Judge Crawford to do another favor for you?"

"Yes, I'm sure if the Judge could do anything for us, he will," replied Cahill.

"Perhaps if you go to the Judge's chambers on the seventeenth floor, either the Judge or his secretary will be there. The judges have a private entrance on the side street, Leonard Street, and they have a private elevator going down to that entrance. If Judge Crawford will co-operate, you can all go up to the seventeenth floor in the judges' elevator behind this courtroom. From there you can take the other private elevator down to the side street."

"That's great," said Toni Wainwright. "Do it, Jim."

"Why don't we all go together," said Cahill.

"Perhaps it's better that Mrs. Wainwright waits here until the coast is clear," said Marc. "It might embarrass the Judge if we all went to his chambers, particularly since Mrs. Wainwright is a defendant."

"Right," said Cahill, turning. "Oh, Rutley, go down to the car and tell the driver to be ready to move around to Leonard Street." Cahill walked toward the back.

"Your keeper is here," Mrs. Wainwright said to Marc.

Marc looked around. Franco had entered the court. Marc waved and walked to the back. The two of them stepped into the corridor. O'Connor was there, talking to three reporters. One of the reporters came over to Marc.

"When is Mrs. Wainwright coming out?" the reporter asked.

"Couple of minutes," Marc replied.

"What kind of defense are you going to have in this case?" the same reporter asked.

"I can't comment on a pending case," Marc said flatly. "Excuse me, will you? Anything the matter?" he asked Franco.

"Nothing. I just wanted to make sure you were still here," he replied. "I went away for a bit while you were here, and I wanted to be sure I didn't miss you."

"I'm almost finished."

"I got some interesting information," Franco added.

"What is it?"

"Your wife asked me to go out to Butler aviation, the private air field over at La Guardia airport," said Franco.

"Yes?"

"That's where I was just now. I checked out Zack Lord's plane for the evening of the fourteenth of August, the night Wainwright was killed. His plane didn't leave until two-thirty in the morning. About an hour or so *after* Wainwright was killed." Franco waited for Marc to react. He was pleased with himself.

"Two-thirty?" Marc repeated. "You think that ties in with your concept about someone else—maybe Zack Lord—shooting Wainwright while his wife was drunk out of her head?"

"It could," said Franco. "You told us to work on it. That's what we're doing."

Marc smiled.

"What are you smiling about?" Franco asked. "I do something dumb?"

"No. I'm just smiling because if I leave it to you and Maria you'll come up with something wild. And make it sound logical to boot. Coming out of your mouth, the possible rises out of the impossible. But objectively, what does it really mean? So Lord didn't leave until two-thirty. The other things we discussed, the why, the how, getting Wainwright to go there in the first place. These are the imponderables of real significance."

"Give us some time, we're working on them," said Franco.

Marc laughed. "Don't get lost now. I'm almost finished. Then we're going to the Federal District Court in Brooklyn. I have to make a new bail application for The Crusher. Now that he's spent the weekend without making bail, maybe I can get it down from a hundred thousand."

"I'll be right out front," replied Franco. "What do you really think about this Zack Lord thing?"

"I don't know. It's really crazy, of course. But follow it up and see where it leads. Later on I'm going to see Mrs. Wainwright again. Alone," he added. "I hope to find her sober this time."

"Fat chance," said Franco.

XIX

TUESDAY, AUGUST 22, 4:15 P.M.

Marc and Michael Malone, the assistant U.S. Attorney, stood outside the Magistrate's courtroom in the Federal District Courthouse. Malone was smoking a cigarette. He and Marc both kept glancing into the courtroom to see if the Magistrate was still conducting a previous arraignment.

"You think Pellegrino will get a hearing here today?" Marc asked, not really expecting an affirmative answer.

"Not today, Marc," said Malone. "This is only on for a bail application." He took a puff on his cigarette. His eyes narrowed as the smoke swirled upward.

Marc pushed the door to the courtroom open slightly, peered in, then let the door shut again.

"When was the last time you were involved in a hearing in this court?" Marc asked.

"I can't remember," Malone said with a slight smile.

"I can't remember when I was either," said Marc. "I don't think I ever had a preliminary hearing in the Federal Court."

"We usually indict before the hearing."

"What's the sense of having a preliminary hearing procedure outlined in the law, when in fact it's just there for the hell of it? Nobody ever gets a hearing around here," said Marc.

"The grand jury is your hearing, Marc," Malone said. "You don't really need a Magistrate's hearing too."

"How come, if the federal system is so fair, you refuse to let the defendant have a hearing so he'll know exactly what evidence he's faced with?" asked Marc. He was feeling argumentative as he waited.

"Do you get hearings over in the State Court?" Malone asked.

"Yes, fairly often," Marc replied. "At least you've got a shot at one over there."

"I think this court is much fairer than the state courts anyway," said Malone. "It's run better, more lawyerlike, more dignity. And when you get an indictment here, the defendant knows he's not going to get the courthouse in plea bargaining. Over here, you have to face the music."

"You must think you're still in grammar school—where neatness counts. The state courts have twenty times the cases you have over here."

Malone shrugged.

"Do you think merely because you're less flexible than a D.A. that that makes this court fairer?"

"It's not inflexibility, Marc."

"Oh yes it is," Marc countered. "You get an indictment, and then you sit like prima donnas and refuse to discuss the plea, the sentence, and if the defendant doesn't cop out, you go out of your way to sink him with an all-embracing count of conspiracy to commit a crime."

"What's wrong with conspiracy as an indictable offense?"

"Everything—when it's used as a substitute for solid evidence of a crime," said Marc. "Clarence Darrow, who I'm not so crazy about in the first place, was very correct when he said conspiracy, the crime of thinking about doing something, has been the dearest weapon of every tyrant in recorded history. The way the judges around here charge the jury, the audience is lucky they're not convicted of conspiracy."

Malone peered into the courtroom again. "Let's go," he said, dropping his cigarette to the floor. "I'll go along with thirty-five thousand dollars bail, if that'll help you out," Malone whispered.

"Are we playing games?" asked Marc. "If it's so unimportant, make it five thousand."

"I can't do that just now, Marc." Malone was holding the door half open as they spoke. "Things aren't that cool in the streets yet. You know why this is being done. Do you want it, or do you want to argue in front of the Magistrate?"

"I know he's not going to do me any favors. Make it twenty-five, and I'll go along with it for today."

"Make it twenty-five then," agreed Malone. He pushed the door open to the courtroom.

"Where to now?" asked Franco as he drove back toward Manhattan across the Brooklyn Bridge.

"I told you I made an appointment to talk with Mrs. Wainwright this afternoon," said Marc. "I have to have more information from her."

"You also said I didn't have to go with you, again. Right?" asked Franco.

Marc laughed. "Not if you don't want to."

"Nah. The two of us don't get along too good." Franco cursed softly as another car, speeding to Manhattan, cut too closely in front of them. "You think now that the bail was lowered to twenty-five, that The Crusher's going to hit the street?"

"I don't know," replied Marc. "Patsy said he'd try to make it today. If he can't, I'll just make another application in a couple of days to get it reduced even further. The way Malone is acting right now, that may not be too difficult."

Franco nodded slowly. "They got it by the balls, those Feds, don't they. They can get whatever they want, even put you in jail a few days to cool you off, and everybody else's got to like it."

Marc was silent. He was thinking how true, and at the same time, how frightening such a prospect was. A government which reveled in law and order, which could brand certain people criminal by means of publicity, which could break into homes, trammel constitutional privileges, was too close to Nazism for comfort. Hitler was put in office on a platform of law and order, on promises to clean up crime in the streets. Every time Marc heard the terms law and order, crime in the streets, he remembered Hitler. He also thought, however, that as long as he and other defense attorneys could keep talking, defending, the system was reasonably okay. They would be among the first to be quieted; but then it would be too late.

As the car neared Manhattan, City Hall loomed majestically across the park at the foot of the bridge. Franco turned the car onto the cloverleaf that led to the East River Drive.

"Remind me, Franco, to see George Tishler in the next couple of days. I have some information he wanted about the courts."

"Okay, boss," Franco said. "And, okay," he added quickly, "I won't call you boss." He and Marc both laughed. "You want me to drop you off at Mrs. Wainwright's apartment?"

"No. She said she was going to be shopping. So I made an appointment to meet her at five-thirty at Bob Dick's."

"That's that little restaurant on Fifty-sixth Street off Park?" asked Franco.

"Right."

"You think it's a good idea meeting this one at a restaurant where there's liquor?"

"I'll talk fast," Marc kidded.

The car rolled along easily on the highway until they slowed into some heavy traffic at Twenty-third Street, which was bumper to bumper, until Thirty-fifth Street, where there was a stalled car with its hood up. A woman was at the rear of the car waving a handkerchief to the oncoming traffic. A man had his head inside the motor compartment. Once past, traffic rolled more quickly, until another stalled car under the tunnel at Fifty-fifth Street slowed them again. Finally, they reached the Sixty-third Street exit where they headed across and then downtown.

"You want me to wait for you?" asked Franco, as he stopped the car in front of Bob Dick's canopy. He looked at his watch. "It's a quarter to six now."

"No, I don't know how long this is going to take. I'd rather you tidy up the boat for tomorrow instead. I'll take a cab home when I'm finished."

"Better watch this one," cautioned Franco. "She's like the original snake."

"I will," Marc smiled. He got out of the car and walked to the front entrance of the restaurant. Once inside, there was a short stairway leading up, then a turn to the left. The bar was on the left. Tables lined the right side. In the back, there was a doorway leading to a dining room. Marc peered into the darkness which was hardly pierced by occasional amber wall lighting. As he waited for his eyes to adjust, he could see only shadows and silhouettes, and hear murmurs of conversation.

"Marc, Marc," he heard a female voice call.

He looked in the direction of the sound, then saw a shadow waving to him. Toni Wainwright was sitting at a table near the back with an attractive blond woman about thirty-five years old.

"Hello, Mister Lawyer," said Toni.

"Hello," said Marc. He gauged from her voice and manner that Mrs. Wainwright was probably only on her second drink; still sane and safe. He resolved to keep her, if he could, that is, from drinking too heavily until he finished with his questions. Either that or talk faster, he thought, kidding himself.

"This is Shani Dunlop," Toni Wainwright introduced the blonde. "Shani, this is my legal eagle, Marc Conte."

Shani smiled. She was heavily bosomed, and her face had indications that she had been a beautiful woman. While still quite attractive, her face was beginning to puff up from drinking.

"Sit down, sit down," Mrs. Wainwright said, smiling widely. Marc sat. She put her arm on his back, patting it. "This man is the greatest lawyer in the whole U.S. of A.," she said to Shani. "Mauro, Mauro," she called to the waiter. "A drink for the barrister. And another for us."

Marc ordered a drink, which was shortly delivered along with fresh drinks for Toni Wainwright and Shani.

"Now, what did you have to see me about?" asked Toni Wainwright. "Not that I don't want to see you even if you didn't have to talk about the case," she added. She and Shani laughed girlishly.

"No offense, Shani," said Marc. "Do you want to talk about it in front of Shani?" he asked Mrs. Wainwright.

"Of course. Shani knows almost as much about me as my mirror."

"Okay," said Marc. "I wanted to talk to you about the night your husband was killed. And about Zack Lord."

"I've told you about the night Bob was killed about five times already. There's nothing new," Mrs. Wainwright said.

"I know. It may seem useless to you, but I like to keep going over it again and again, listening to anything that I might have missed, something you may have forgotten," said Marc.

A tall, lumbering man with fair hair, came over to their table, a drink in his hand. From his face, Marc saw that the man had already held several drinks in that hand today.

"Well, if it isn't old thimble belly himself," Toni Wainwright said to the man.

"Who's your loudmouth friend, Shani?" the man cut sarcastically. "She's got a big mouth for a little broad."

"She always speaks well of you," Shani laughed. She finished her drink in one gulp.

"Marc Conte, my lawyer, say hello to Brad Stone," said Toni Wainwright.

Marc stood and shook hands with Stone. Stone had a large ham hock of a hand, strong and meaty.

"Pleasure, Counselor," said Stone. "Sit down, sit down, I want to stand. How's the case going?"

"Fine," said Marc.

The conversation was halted now as Stone stood draining his drink.

"Come on, Brad," said Shani. "How about you and I have a drink at the bar?" She rose and winked at Toni Wainwright.

"Oh, oh. Confidential stuff, eh? Okay, let's see if we can find ourselves a little trouble," said Stone.

"See you later," Shani said to Toni Wainwright and Marc.

"Now what is it you want out of my life?" Toni Wainwright asked Marc as she drained her glass. "Wait, before you tell me let's have another drink."

"I'd rather if, for a few minutes more, we'd stay off the drinks and concentrate on the facts in this case," said Marc.

Toni stared at him. "Are you going to order me a drink, or do I have to do it myself? Mauro," she called, turning to the waiter without waiting for a reply.

"Yes, Mrs. Wainwright?"

"Get me a very, very dry Beefeater martini, straight up."

"Yes, ma'am."

"I don't like being treated like a little girl," said Toni Wainwright.

"I wasn't treating you like a little girl. I just want to work without interruption or distraction. If that sounds to you like you're a little girl, I think you're mistaken."

The waiter brought her drink. She took it directly from the tray and began to sip at it.

"I've got a drink now, no thanks to you," she said caustically.

"Now let's get on to what you want to know so we can be finished with it."

"Fine," said Marc. "Tell me about the actual shooting. Tell me what happened."

"I told you. I saw this shadow come into the room—after it broke my door into a million pieces."

"Then you said the shadow came at you," added Marc. "And you moved backwards. You had the pistol. Then you realized it was your husband. Then everything went black, and then there was the tremendous explosion and the flash of light."

"That's right. Why do I have to go over this again and again? You know the whole story already."

"Because this way I can ask you questions about what happened," said Marc. "Questions that I can't answer by myself."

"For instance?"

"For instance, are you sure that the explosion and the flash of light came *after* and not before everything went black?"

Toni Wainwright thought for a moment. "Yes, everything went black, and then the explosion and the flash of light. Now that I think of it, I don't know how. What does that mean?"

"I don't know yet. Did anyone else have a set of keys to your apartment, besides yourself?"

"Zack. He's the only one. Except for the maids."

"What about Bob Wainwright, your husband?" Marc asked.

"No, he didn't have a key to the new locks. I had them changed after he left."

"How about the building manager? Does he have a key?"

"Yes, the building has a key too."

"Tell me some more about Zack Lord," said Marc.

She puffed a cigarette impatiently. "Zack is very green if not very blue. That is, he's very wealthy, although not very social. That doesn't mean he isn't nice to be with, by the way," she said. "It means his name isn't in the social register. What else is there to tell you? He's in mutual funds, and his mutual funds own all kinds of businesses and corporations. That's about all I can tell you, except his empire is about one billion big."

"You said something the last time we spoke about your husband saying that Zack Lord's empire was going to crumble and fall apart some day."

196

"That's right, he did. He was always saying that Zack over-extended himself too fast and it would blow up in his face one of these days. But he was only jealous. I also told you that. He was lousy at being jealous."

"Besides being jealous, as you say," probed Marc, "did your husband ever give a reason why he said these things about Lord's business?"

"Well, first of all," she said, "Zack got his first real money to expand, go public, whatever the hell he did, from Wainwright and Company."

"Your husband's company handled the underwriting for Zack Lord's operations?"

"Originally, yes."

"And then?"

"After that, Zack was making deals all over the place," she said. "He didn't need any money. He was dealing in swapping stock with other companies."

"When was this?" asked Marc. "The first underwriting."

"About two, two and a half years ago."

"So your husband had more information about Zack Lord's finances than just casual conversation."

"Absolutely. Bob knew Zack's entire operation. And, as a result of the original underwriting, Wainwright and Company owned a large portion of Zack Lord's operations. Aren't you drinking anything?" she asked as she finished her drink.

"I'm still nursing this one."

"Well, I'll have another."

Marc said politely as he could: "Maybe we can finish this conversation quickly, so I don't interfere with the rest of your evening."

"Oh, you're all right, as long as you don't start your temperance preaching," she said. "Are you Catholic?"

The liquor was becoming more apparent; and Marc wanted to finish even more quickly now as Mrs. Wainwright opened into one of the drunkard's classic conversations.

"Yes, I am, if that makes any difference," Marc replied. "Now, did your husband ever give any reason for his opinion about Zack Lord's business?"

"I thought you were Catholic," she continued. "Very Catholic, aren't you?"

"Mrs. Wainwright, whatever I am, except for being a trial lawyer, is of no significance in this case. You're the one who's indicted, not me."

"Oh, is that so," she said. She turned away from Marc. She was petulant now, brooding, silently sipping her drink.

Marc was quiet, too, thinking about what Toni Wainwright said about Zack Lord. Here was Lord's billion-dollar enterprise, which Bob Wainwright had not only helped to put together, but which he had also said was about to fall apart. Supposing it was. Supposing Bob Wainwright knew something about Lord's operation that indicated it was about to blow apart. Suppose, he . . . Marc had to check himself. He found himself getting carried away with one of his wife's and Franco's fanciful theories. And there was nothing to hold the idea together. He'd check it out, of course, he assured himself. But, not with Toni Wainwright. And not this evening, for sure.

"Mrs. Wainwright, I'm going to be going," Marc announced. "I have an appointment later."

"Another appointment? I thought we were going to have dinner?" she said, turning back toward Marc.

"Not that I knew about. I have to meet some people, strictly business, of course," Marc made up as he spoke. "Do you want to stay here or would you like me to drop you somewhere?"

"You'll take me home, like any proper young man," Toni Wainwright said coyly. "You'll take me right to my doorstep."

"Fine." Marc paid the check, and he and Toni Wainwright walked out to the street, where Marc signaled a cab. As the cab drove uptown on Park Avenue, Marc watched the people and cars moving through the fading daylight. It was a pleasant evening, warm; there was a mild breeze and not much humidity. Suddenly, Marc felt a movement next to him. He turned. Toni Wainwright's face was directly next to his, and moving closer. Her mouth was upon his in a moment, and her tongue was slithering into his mouth. She slipped her hand behind his head, clutching the back of his head to hold him closer while she kissed him.

Marc pulled himself away, holding Toni Wainwright at arm's length. "What the hell are you doing?" He was angry.

"Afraid of a little girl like me?" she asked.

"Mrs. Wainwright, thank you very much, but no thanks," said Marc.

"It's because you're Catholic, that's what it is, isn't it? You're Catholic."

Before Marc could answer the cab stopped. They were at Toni Wainwright's building. The doorman came out and opened the cab door. Marc got out of the cab to say good night.

"Oh no. You don't think you're getting away just like that, do you?" said Toni Wainwright. "You've got to take me to my door and see me safely home like any self-respecting gentleman would."

"No, I don't think so," said Marc.

"Oh yes you will," she demanded in a resounding, loud voice. "You'll take me home, right to my door."

People walking on the street stopped to look.

The doorman looked at Marc helplessly.

"Well?" she nearly shouted.

"Okay," said Marc. To avoid what was developing into a scene, he would drop her at her door.

"Here are the keys," Toni Wainwright said, as they got off the elevator. Marc unlocked the door. Just as he did, a maid appeared.

"Oh, it's you, Mrs.," said the maid. She spoke with what seemed to be a Scandinavian or German accent.

"Yes, it's me. Who did you expect, anyway?"

"Very well, Mrs.," said the maid. "I just wanted to be sure you were all right."

"I'm fine, I'm fine," Mrs. Wainwright said. "Mary, take care of Mister Conte, fix him a drink, show him where everything is—well, not everything," she said with a leer. The woman looked at her blankly. "I'll be right out."

Toni Wainwright walked through a door and disappeared into another part of the apartment.

Relieved, Marc began to make his retreat.

"Right this way, gentleman," said Mary.

Marc stood still at the door. The maid was looking at him, waiting. Somehow she reminded him of something. "Mary, were you on duty the evening that Mister Wainwright was shot?"

Mary hesitated, uncomfortable, standing in the hallway when Mrs. Wainwright directed her to show Marc to the library.

Marc walked forward with her as she moved to the library.

"Were you on duty that night, Mary?" he asked again.

"I guess it's all right to talk to you," she said finally. "Mrs. Wainwright told all of us not to talk to people about that night. But I know that you are the lawyer. So I'm sure that Mrs. Wainwright wants us to talk to you. Yes, gentleman, I was on duty." She opened the bar and showed Marc where the ice was.

"I just want to talk to you," Marc said, declining a drink. "How many servants are there all together?"

"Most of the time, there are three. The cook, Mademoiselle, and myself," said Mary. She stood to the side, uncomfortable, watching Marc.

"Mademoiselle, is that the children's nurse?"

"That's right, sir."

"You say ordinarily there are three in help. Were there more or less the evening that Mister Wainwright was killed?" asked Marc.

"More. Margaret, my sister, she came to help with the dinner party," said Mary. "There was me, and Margaret, and Mademoiselle. And cook. There were four altogether."

"Now, think about this," said Marc. "Were you up, did you hear anything, see anything that night, after the guests left? Did you hear anything when Mister Wainwright arrived?"

"No, sir. Margaret and me, we were asleep. We didn't hear anything," she replied. "We were so tired from cleaning up, we fell right asleep, and slept through everything. See, Margaret and me, we cleaned everything and put all the dishes in the dishwasher, all the silver away, everything. After all, you're not going to see cook or Mademoiselle doing that kind of work, are you? So, Margaret and me, we had to do everything by ourselves. And, I say, by the time we were finished all of that, we were exhausted. It was a big party Madam had that night."

"How did you find out about Mister Wainwright being shot then?" asked Marc.

"Mademoiselle woke us up. Margaret slept in my room that night. She was so tired, you know, from the cleaning up and all. We did all the cleaning . . ."

"I know, we went through that already," said Marc smiling.

"Well, it may be a smiling matter, but it sure was a lot of work, too, Mister."

"I'm sure it was, Mary. Now tell me about when you first found out about anything having to do with Mister Wainwright being shot."

"As I said, Margaret was sleeping in my room. And we didn't hear anything. Mademoiselle came into the room and said there was some trouble up in the front. She said she just woke up and she saw policemen, a lot of them, up front."

"How long was Mademoiselle up before she woke you up?" asked Marc. "As far as you know?"

"I don't know. I know she was awake when the police arrived. Margaret and me, we didn't know anything about it until after that."

"So neither you, nor your sister Margaret, nor Mademoiselle, saw or heard anything until about the time that the police arrived and Mister Wainwright was already dead, is that right?" Marc asked.

"That's right, sir."

"And Mademoiselle was up before that but you don't know how long?"

"That's right, sir."

"Fine. Now what about the cook?" Marc asked.

"Now, cook, see, she was finished right after the meal was served, so she was plenty rested, not like Margaret and me."

"Fine," said Marc. "Do you know if cook saw or heard anything?"

"She did," replied Mary. "She don't sleep too good, anyway. She's always getting up in the night, going to the ladies room and all that. Woman trouble, one thing and another, you know."

"Did she get up the night Mister Wainwright was killed?" Marc pressed.

"Yes, sir, she did. She told me afterward that she was up and heard something inside. She went up front to see, and then she was frightened, and she was hiding in the dining room, looking across to where the library and Madam's wing is. And, she heard or saw something. I don't want to say for sure. I can't speak for cook, you know. But I know that she was awake. Maybe she didn't see anything. But I know cook was awake."

"What's the cook's name?" asked Marc.

"Hattie. Hattie Adams."

"Is she here now?" asked Marc. "Is she still working here?"

"She is not."

"She doesn't work here anymore?" asked Marc. "Is that what you're saying?"

"That's right, sir."

"Did she get fired?" asked Marc.

"No, sir. She doesn't work here anymore, right now. She's on vacation. Be on vacation for another three weeks. She's been with Madam for many years, you see. She gets a long vacation. I been here only four years, so I don't get the kind of vacation Hattie gets."

"Do you know where I can get in touch with Hattie Adams?" asked Marc. "Do you know where she lives?"

"Yes, sir. She lives on 107th Street," replied Mary.

"On the east or west side, do you know?"

"No, sir. I try not to butt into other people's business, if you know what I mean. That's the best policy, sir, if I may be so bold."

"I certainly agree, Mary."

"Yes, sir."

"Do you know if cook is out of the city on vacation?"

"I wouldn't . . ."

Toni Wainwright came sweeping into the room. She was wearing her flowing green robe, with the deep décolletage. The bottom part of the robe parted for her legs, as she walked.

"Flirting with my guest, Mary?" Toni demanded, not entirely joking.

"No, ma'am. Mister Attorney was asking me some questions about the night poor Mister Wainwright had his accident." Mary looked sheepishly toward Toni Wainwright. "Excuse me, ma'am. I be leaving unless there's something else for me to do?"

"No."

Mary nodded and left.

"How about fixing me a drink," said Mrs. Wainwright.

"I was just about to leave," said Marc.

"Well, you can fix me a drink before you go, can't you?"

"I guess so." Marc walked to the bar. "What are you drinking?"

"A very dry, and I mean, very dry, Beefeater martini."

Marc mixed the drink. By the time he had turned to hand her

the drink, Toni Wainwright was lying at full length on the couch. She was naked. Her robe was on the floor.

"What's the matter, Marc? Haven't you ever seen a hard-on before." She laughed. "That's a punch line from a joke," she explained.

"I know the joke." Marc looked at Toni. She was small, muscular, with almost boylike wiryness, except for her breasts, which were long, thin, and flat, wide apart, with large, pale nipples.

"Now about my drink?" she asked.

Marc handed her the drink. She reached out, but rather than taking the drink, she pulled Marc by the wrist toward her, pulling him off balance into a sitting position on the couch. Her arms went around him, as her mouth found his, her tongue starting to press its way into his mouth. Marc reached out to put her drink down. As he succeeded in putting the glass on a small table beside the couch, he grabbed Toni Wainwright by the shoulders, pushing her away from himself.

"I thought we just went through this, a little more dressed, perhaps, in the cab. It's not my scene."

"Aren't you man enough to do anything about this?" she said.

"Don't start that manly ploy with me. I won't be embarrassed into making it with you to prove my masculinity," Marc said flatly. He rose to his feet. "I'm married, very pleasantly so, and I don't appreciate the wrestling."

Toni Wainwright stood on the couch, next to Marc. She put her arms around his neck, pressing and moving her naked body against him.

"Come on, ease up, lawyer man," she said coyly. "Your wife won't know, so what's the difference? I bet you're groovy in the sack."

"I don't mean to be ungrateful, or anything like that," said Marc. "But I'm really not interested in other women. There's no point to this."

"No point?" said Toni Wainwright, angry now. "Here I am practically throwing myself at you, and you're telling me there's no point. What the hell do you think I am, a ham sandwich?"

"No, I'm sure you're not that," said Marc.

She took her arms from around him, putting her hands on her

naked hips. "Go ahead, get the fuck out of here, little lawyer boy. Get out of here." She reached out to slap him.

Marc dodged and reached out himself, grabbing her wrist and pulling her forward off the couch. He twisted his body to the left. Before Toni Wainwright knew what happened, she was spread across Marc's shoulders in a fireman's carry.

"Put me down, you son of a bitch," she screamed, her feet pumping the air, her free hand hitting him on the head.

Marc turned and walked out of the library. "Which way is the bedroom?" he asked.

"Oh, goody, I'm going to get fucked," she said, stopping her struggle. "It's in through the door straight ahead," she said. "Do you have a big cock? Tell me. Do you?"

Marc walked silently into the large bedroom, stopping to look around. He saw a side door and walked toward it. As he thought, it was the bathroom. He entered, and while still holding her on his shoulders with one hand, reached across the tub and turned on the shower.

"Oh no you don't, you rat bastard," Toni screamed, struggling more violently now.

"Oh yes I do," Marc replied. The water was splattering full force and cold. He slipped Toni off his shoulders and in one movement had her standing under the shower.

"You fuck, you lousy, no good fuck," she screamed, water streaming over her head. She kicked at him, missing him with her foot, but splashing him with water. Marc moved quickly toward the bathroom door, shutting it behind him. He could hear her still cursing beyond. He moved quickly out of the bedroom, also shutting that door behind him, walked out to the foyer and opened the entrance door. He rang for the elevator, then shut the entrance door behind him. He took some bills out of his pocket, selecting a ten. He held the ten in one hand, holding the doorknob of the entrance in his other hand. He could hear Toni Wainwright moving inside now, still cursing. She was screaming, looking for him in the library. Marc could hear the elevator starting its trip up.

"Hurry, hurry," he thought.

"Where are you, you motherless bastard?" Toni was screaming

inside. He heard her coming toward the entrance door. The elevator was getting closer. Toni tried to open the front door. Marc held on to the knob. The elevator door opened. The elevator man stood amazed at the sight of the man holding the door shut, and the shouts and curses coming from inside the apartment.

"Here's ten bucks," said Marc, reaching the ten-dollar bill toward the elevator man. "Now I want to get the hell out of here. She's so bombed she won't even remember this happened, so don't worry about her."

"Yes, sir. I know the condition, sir," said the elevator man. He was relaxed now, and ready to help.

"Just stand aside and I'm going to let go of the door. Shut those elevator doors as quick as you can, and let's move it out of here. Ready?"

"Ready."

"Go," shouted Marc, dashing for the elevator. The doors, which were already moving, slid shut behind him. The elevator man threw the switch.

"Come on back, you rotten faggot, you lousy bastard. You guinea fuck."

Marc laughed. So did the elevator man, as they were accompanied all the way to the ground floor with a stream of curses that echoed through the entire building.

XX

THURSDAY, AUGUST 24, 11:45 A.M.

"How's everything, Marc?" George Tishler asked as he removed the ever present papers and reports from the chair beside his desk. "Here, sit here."

"Everything's okay," Marc replied as he sat. "How're you doing?"

George frowned. "Have you been reading the blasts the newspapers are taking at the Mayor now?"

"You mean about all the money the Mayor's supposed to be

squandering on outside experts and per diem workers on his staff and all that sort of thing?" asked Marc.

"That's it," said George. "The bastards. I don't understand what they want, these media people. Here's the most dynamic and progressive mayor this town has had in fifty years and still they blast him constantly."

"What they want, George, is to sell newspapers or commercial air time," said Marc. "You don't really think the reporters are poet laureates in quest of artistic perfection, do you?"

George shook his head in exasperation. "I'd like to say, let's talk about something pleasant instead. But I'm curious to hear what's happening with your snooping around the courts."

"After thinking about it for a while," Marc began, "I've come to the conclusion that basically there's nothing wrong with the court system, the justice system as you call it."

"That's good," said George.

"The real problem," Marc continued, "as in all human equations, is the implementation of the system by the people charged with responsibility for putting the system to work."

"That's bad," said George. "What and who exactly do you mean? The judges?"

"To a great extent it has to do with the judges. But it's not as simple, or as limited, as that. An entirely strange, warped sense of values infects the attitudes of the personnel in the courts, including the judges."

"Can you run that down a little more clearly for me, Marc?"

"I'll try. I don't know if this is new or if it's always existed, but I think you could say it's kind of a cavalier attitude toward defendants, a kind of callous attitude, really," said Marc. "Perhaps, here in New York, with so many cases, and so many defendants, after a while, one case looks just like every other, it all becomes the same, and some of the personnel—including the judges—become insensitive to the fact that they're not dealing with an inventory of machine parts or frying pans, but rather with human lives."

"Are the judges insensitive?" George asked.

"To this extent, they are," said Marc. "First of all, all day long the court hears defendants claim their innocence even in the face of overwhelming evidence."

"That's their constitutional right," said George, "and also the name of the game."

"True," said Marc. "But the judges, most of whom come from a prosecutorial background, or a court connected background, have become callous to a defendant's protestations of innocence, and tend to help the prosecutor in ridding the street of vermin."

"You really think the judges lean toward the D.A.?"

"Don't call it leaning necessarily," said Marc. "I just think that many of them have lost sight of or never knew that the defense counsel represents the people, the forces of good, as much as the D.A. does."

"Now you've really lost me," said George. "How does the defense counsel represent the people?"

"The people, the citizens of the state, are interested—or should be—not in mere conviction statistics but in fairness and true justice."

George nodded.

"And although they perform different functions, both the prosecutor *and* the defense lawyer are equal, integral parts of the system the people have put into effect to obtain those fair trials, to obtain that fairness and justice. Both defense and prosecution were created by the same laws, to uncover the facts, the evidence in each case, even though each is required to look for different facts and different evidence. The prosecutor finds evidence against the defendant; the defense lawyer in favor of the defendant. And all so the jury can sift all the facts."

"That's fine, Marc. And correct," George added. "What problems are the judges having with that?"

"It's a subtle kind of allegiance, George. Perhaps, because of a government-oriented background, perhaps because they receive their pay check from the city, or the state, the same as the D.A., many judges feel they're on the same team as the D.A.; that they have some extra obligation to help the D.A. obtain a conviction."

"They help the D.A.?"

"Sometimes directly, absolutely," said Marc. "And sometimes indirectly because they haven't the balls to throw out a case that should be thrown out. They sort of feel guilty enforcing the law and deciding an issue according to the law if it means dismissing the charges against a defendant."

"So, you're saying that by not doing a proper job, the courts are actually enhancing the D.A.'s prosecution," said George.

"That's right," agreed Marc. "Instead of being completely impartial, making sure that the rules of evidence are meticulously and fairly observed by both sides, some judges hold the D.A.'s hand, pick up with questioning where an inexperienced D.A. leaves off, repeat testimony and emphasize accusations, make rulings that favor the D.A.'s case. That's not right, George."

"No, it's not," agreed George. "The defendant is a citizen entitled to all the protections the law allows until he's proven guilty."

"That's right, George," said Marc. "The system would work a hundred per cent better if the judges called it just as they see it and when they see it. In other words, don't give the defendants a break, don't give the D.A. a break. Call it like it is, wherever the chips fall. Unfortunately, when the chips are going to fall against the D.A., some judges give them a little extra help. That kind of judge isn't doing anybody any good, George."

"It's tough getting the right guys on the bench, Marc," George said. "It really is. A lot of lawyers don't want to get involved, the work's tough and the money isn't great. It's impossible to get enough funds to give them a proper salary without raising taxes. And you know the people'd go berserk if we had to raise taxes again. We don't even have enough funds to provide proper courtrooms in which to sit. And, now, besides the lousy pay and working conditions, these days with every newspaper guy looking down every judge's neck every minute, it's a grueling job. They want you on the bench from 9:30 in the morning to 5:00 in the evening. If you have to look up the law to make a decision, do it on your own time before or after court. So how can we recruit judges from the private sector, private lawyers?"

"That's a major factor in the problem, George," said Marc. "Far too many of the judges on the bench are ex-D.A.s or political hacks of some sort, ex-commissioners, judge's secretaries, or something or other. They're, most of them, government workers, who have been on the public tit for years—present company excluded of course, George," Marc laughed.

"Of course," George laughed, not as easily as Marc.

"And they're so used to sucking on that public tit, they couldn't earn a living without it. They want it to continue forever. And so they figure they've got to protect it, shield it. And what group endangers their sucking more than the social rebels who are accused of crime?"

"What you say may make a lot of sense, Marc. But this is no different than anything else. When you have to pick a man to do a job, you look around, and who do you see. You see the men around you, naturally. And you pick first from that group. When it comes to judges, I look around, and there are all sorts of men, mostly government-oriented, as you say, D.A.s, judges' confidential secretaries, commissioners. They're the first ones who are tapped, not because they're better, but because they're there. The judge makers are a very small community, Marc. Maybe a hundred men in all, and everyone knows everyone else. If it comes to them approving someone they know, who's been around, or a stranger, naturally they pick the one they know."

"That's how you get imbeciles, George. That constant inbreeding weakens the species. That's what's happening to the judiciary. With all the lawyers there are in New York, brilliant lawyers, shrewd lawyers, fair lawyers, you should stop pulling judges out of the nearby bushes, merely because they've been there a long time."

George nodded, not convinced. "You've also got to remember, Marc, that from a practical and political point of view, a lot of appointments the Mayor makes, he makes because the political leaders whose support the Mayor needs, make recommendations."

"And who do the leaders send over: qualified legal scholars or their brothers-in-law?"

"I want you to know," George said lightly, laughing, "that a lot of politicians' brothers-in-law are astute legal scholars. That, of course, makes it easy."

They both laughed.

"Really, though, Marc, since I've been in charge of screening the judicial candidates the Mayor appoints, we've been getting pretty good candidates. I've been working like a bastard on it. I'll admit some of the judges who were appointed before us leave something to be desired. But now it's better, much better."

"Some of the old-timers leave more than just a little to be desired, George. You have some men like Crawford. He's the D.A.'s hatchet man. Whatever the D.A. wants, in order to obtain a conviction, Crawford will figure out how to give them. Aren't they slipping The Tombs riot trials to Crawford?"

George shrugged. "Wasn't he picked on the regular rotation?"

"There is no regular rotation!" Marc scoffed. "In the Federal Court there's actually a system of blindly picking a judge from a revolving cylinder of names—but then they screw you other ways. The only rotation in the state courts is in the mind of some of the D.A.s when they wonder which judge can do the best job to obtain a conviction."

"That's pretty scathing criticism of our system, Marc."

"Not the system, George, just some of the people involved in running the system."

"The bitch of it all is, Marc, that you're probably right. But we're dealing with human beings, not machines. We can't reach out and tap a computer to give us perfect judges."

"I'll buy that," said Marc.

George, still with his arms across his chest, leaning back in his chair, mused for some moments. "I still think your being screened by the Judiciary Committee would be a great idea. We really need a guy like you."

"I thought you forgot about that crazy idea."

"Forget it, hell," George said. "If what you say is true—and I don't doubt that there is truth to it—what we need are better men, men who can go right down the middle, as you say. Men who know the law and are willing to enforce it. Well, you're a good man, Marc. You know your stuff, know the law, you have a feel for what happens in the courthouse. You'd make a terrific judge."

"George, I really think there's a need for the work I do," Marc replied. "Besides, I've told you, I'm not a politician."

"If every good man we want says the same thing, Marc, then all we have to fall back on are the political hacks you describe as groveling around beneath the table to get some droppings from the public tit. You can't talk out of both sides of your mouth now," said George. "If we need good men, and you're a good man, then why not do something affirmative about it. Let me put your name in to be screened by the Mayor's Committee on the Judiciary. You don't have to take it. You might not even pass muster, although I doubt that. Let me at least submit your name."

Marc studied George for a moment. He shrugged. "Okay, George. I'm not making any decision right now, one way or the other. Let's just see what happens."

XXI

The day was bright and warm. Sun poured through the windows of the Conte apartment. The terrace was bathed in light as a slight breeze lifted the branches of the trees gently. Marc sat at the table reading a newspaper. He had just finished his eggs and kippers. Maria was leaning back on a chaise longue, her eyes closed, her face lifted to the sun.

"Are we off sailing this morning?" asked Maria, not opening her eyes.

"Yes, but not right away," Marc replied, looking up. "I want to take a walk over to West Street first."

West Street bordered the Hudson River. It was also the street on which, at Eleventh Street, was located the Federal Detention Headquarters, the federal equivalent of The Tombs. Except that West Street was a country club compared to The Tombs.

"Who's over there?" asked Maria, still not opening her eyes.

"The Crusher."

"I thought you finally got his bail reduced to ten thousand yesterday. Didn't you say he was going to be able to make that bail?"

"I did," Marc replied. "But it was so late in the day yesterday when bail was fixed, the bondsman couldn't get all the papers signed and filed in time. The Crusher's supposed to get out first thing this morning. I just want to make sure he doesn't get any more of a runaround."

"And then we're off sailing?" asked Maria.

"No, I have to see Hattie Adams after that," said Marc.

"That Toni Wainwright's cook?" Maria asked, opening her eyes.

Marc nodded.

"Checking out our theory, are you? You figure we're really onto something?"

"Let's say we shouldn't ignore the possibilities."

Maria shook her head in feigned annoyance. "Can't give anyone credit, can you? That's really cheap."

Marc laughed.

"Franco, Franco," Maria called.

Franco came out of the house. "I'm here, Mrs. Conte."

"The big fish is beginning to bite," she said, pointing to Marc.

Franco smiled, rubbing his hands together gleefully. "Naturally, naturally. I knew we had the right track."

"Not so fast, Sherlock and Dr. Watson," said Marc. "I just said I wanted to see Hattie Adams to be cautious, to cover every base. It doesn't mean your wild theories are anything more than that, wild theories."

Maria and Franco looked at each other.

"I always hated a sore loser," Maria said.

"I'm with you, Mrs. Boss."

Marc looked from Franco to Maria. What a delight she is, he thought. Bright, loving, groovy-looking, and physically we're so compatible, there has to be something wrong. Or very right! Marc looked back at his newspaper. He glanced at Maria once again for a moment, admiringly. The best thing was that she wasn't a member of the wives' club; that group fiercely and mortally engaged in a combat against that oppressive vulgarian known as the husband.

"I want to go with you," Maria said.

"Where?"

"To the cook's," she replied.

Marc thought for a bit. He nodded. "Only if you promise to remain silent unless I need you to speak Spanish to someone to get directions in East Harlem."

"May Franco and I speak in the car?"

"Not too much."

"Okay."

Marc returned to his paper. Maria watched him for several minutes pensively. "I also want to go with you when you see Mrs. Wainwright one of these times," she said seriously.

Marc looked up. "What for?"

"Just simple female curiosity," she replied. "I've heard about her, read about her, and sometimes I get to thinking about your going up to her apartment to interview her. I get jealous."

"You don't have a thing to worry about," said Franco. "She's rotten."

"I still want to go."

"Honey, with all the time I have when we're both working and not together, and all the women there are in the world who are more than available, if I were interested in another woman, I wouldn't have to fool around with a client you know about. And, besides, if you had to worry about me being interested in other women, there'd be something wrong with our relationship." Marc stood and walked over to Maria's chaise. He sat next to her.

Franco turned and went back into the house.

"I know, I know," Maria said, putting her arms around Marc's neck. "If you have to worry about someone you love being interested in someone else, then you're in love with the wrong person, because they couldn't love you and be interested in someone else. I know all that. But I still get jealous."

"I'm glad," said Marc.

As Franco stopped the car in front of the West Street jail, Marc noticed several people standing on the sidewalk in front of the steel doored entrance. He recognized Pellegrino's wife, two of his sons, another man, and Pellegrino. The Crusher was laughing loudly, walking with his arms around one of his sons on one side and his wife on the other.

"Looks like he made it," said Franco.

"Is that tall one The Crusher?" Maria asked.

"Yes to both of you," replied Marc as he got out of the car. "I'll be right back."

"Hey, here's the greatest counselor in the world. Come on over here, Counselor," Pellegrino exclaimed, crouching playfully, coming at Marc. He snared Marc around the waist, and lifted him high in the air. He twirled in a circle, Marc still in his arms. "One thing I always say, you pay the bondsman and the lawyer first, because they're always the ones you need when the going gets rough. Right, Philly?"

"Right," grunted Pellegrino's friend with the large nose, and five o'clock shadow. He wore a patterned sports shirt, the shirt tail outside his pants.

The Crusher let Marc down. "What are you doing here, Counselor?"

"I came to see if everything went all right."

"See that? See that?" The Crusher said, turning to the others. "Didn't I tell you he was the greatest in the world? Saturday morning, what time is it?"

"Nine-fifteen," said one of The Crusher's sons.

"Nine-fifteen on a Saturday morning, in the summer, and here's the Counselor worried about his client. How many other guys do that, Philly?"

Philly stuck out his bottom lip and shook his head. "None."

The Crusher turned back to Marc. "You know, Counselor, no matter what happens, I'm with you all the way. And you know, Counselor," he said, leaning close now to Marc, speaking more softly, "anything, *anything* you want, you just"—The Crusher pointed to himself—"you just get me and it's done. *Anything.* You get me?"

"I get you, Patsy," said Marc. "Well, as long as everything is okay, I guess I'll go now."

"Thanks a lot, Mister Conte," said Mrs. Pellegrino. She smiled demurely.

"Yeah, she missed all the aggravation I give her, right, baby?" The Crusher asked raucously. He slapped her playfully on the bottom.

Mrs. Pellegrino looked at The Crusher sharply. He shrugged playfully.

"Okay, Counselor," said The Crusher. "I'll call you when?"

"Monday or Tuesday. We have to be in court on Wednesday, August 30."

"What case is that on the thirtieth?" The Crusher asked, smiling. "I got so many cases," he said proudly to Philly, "I don't even know which one is which any more."

Philly chuckled silently.

"The gun case in the State Court is on the calendar on the thirtieth; that's next Wednesday," said Marc.

"I thought we was already arraigned on that case in the State Court," said The Crusher.

"That was in the Criminal Court. Now that you've been indicted, it starts all over again in the Supreme Court."

"Whatever you say, Counselor," said The Crusher. He crouched playfully, coming at Marc again.

"Not again, Patsy," said Marc, backing off.

The Crusher laughed. "Okay, I'll talk to you in a couple of days. Thanks a lot, hanh?" He shook Marc's hand. "And don't worry about a thing. I'll put everything together for you in a couple of days." He winked.

"That's not necessary, Patsy," said Marc. "The Federal Court and the State Court are each paying for your cases because you're indigent."

"I know," he said laughing. "But I got to do the right thing by you. Just a little something on the side."

"No, Patsy. I can't accept it. The court is paying me. That's enough."

The Crusher looked surprised. "What a lawyer, right?" he said to Philly. He nodded in agreement. "I'll talk to you, Counselor, all right?"

"Right," said Marc. He got back in the car.

"Now where?" asked Maria.

"A Hundred and Seventh Street and Fifth Avenue."

"Why are we in this lousy neighborhood?" Franco asked as he drove through East Harlem. Acrid smells rose in the streets and poured from the buildings. "We could have seen the cook at Toni Wainwright's."

"I wanted to see Hattie in her own home," Marc said.

"How come?"

"I thought it would be better to talk with her away from Toni Wainwright's. Sometimes it's easier to get at the real story when the person questioned feels safe, in a familiar atmosphere."

Maria asked, "You think this Hattie knows the real story?"

"I don't know. But Hattie is the only person in the world, beside Mrs. Wainwright, who was there to see or hear anything the night Wainwright was killed."

"As far as we know *now*," added Maria. "Remember, we're still working on our theory that there may have been someone else there who did more than hear what was going on."

"Right you are," said Marc. "And besides, Mrs. Wainwright may not be giving us an accurate account of what occurred. She may have been so out of it, she doesn't actually remember what really happened."

"Maybe she's giving us a line," said Franco.

"That's also a possibility," said Marc. "That's why I wanted to see Hattie away from Mrs. Wainwright's."

"Hattie's house is over there," said Franco. He pointed to a house on the north side of 107th Street close to Fifth Avenue. He parked the car. A fire hydrant near the corner of Madison was open, and a thick stream of water was flowing from it onto the gutter, coursing rapidly to the sewer. Kids were taking turns holding a large tin can, open at each end in the flowing stream just in time to direct a heavy blast of water at passing cars. In the buildings people were leaning on pillows on their window sills shouting in Spanish or English, urging the kids to flood the cars.

"Here we go again," said Franco.

Inside Hattie's building, the acrid smell of urine, garbage, oily cooking, mustiness, humidity, and rotting plaster, broiled to intensity in the summer heat, was almost overpowering.

Marc looked at the mailboxes on the wall to find one with the name Adams. The mailboxes were scarred, scrawled on, bent open to be looted, but there were no names in any of their name slots.

Maria spoke in Spanish to a man in a strap undershirt coming down the stairs. He wore a gold cross on a chain around his neck and a panama hat on his head. He smiled courteously to Maria and pointed over his shoulder up the stairs.

"Up this way," said Maria.

"Where does she live?" asked Marc.

"Third floor."

Franco knocked on the door of apartment 3R.

"Who is it?" a woman's voice muffled through the closed door.

"Marc Conte, Mrs. Wainwright's lawyer."

The door was opened as far as the inside chain allowed. A short, heavy-set, Black woman peered out.

"I'm Mister Conte, Mrs. Wainwright's lawyer," Marc said. "Are you Hattie Adams?"

She looked at them in silence. "That's right," she finally allowed.

"Who is it?" asked a male voice from the background of the apartment.

"Hush," said Hattie, half turning. "You Miss Toni's lawyer?" she asked hesitantly, the chain still holding the door shut.

"That's right," said Marc. "This is my wife and my investigator. We'd like to talk with you for a couple of minutes. I would have called you at Mrs. Wainwright's, but they told me you were on vacation."

Hattie nodded, looked them over again, studied Marc's face, then looked at Maria and Franco. She slid the chain open. "I guess you are," she smiled now. "Miss Toni said how her lawyer was nice-looking. You better not say I told you that," she said chuckling.

Maria looked at Marc with a sly smile.

The room they entered was the kitchen. There was a porcelain-topped table in the center, a refrigerator, a stove, and a sink. Beyond, they could see a living room. A bedroom, separated from the kitchen and living room by a curtain, was off to the side. Through a slit in the bedroom curtain, Marc saw a man brushing his hair in a dresser mirror.

Hattie led the three of them into the living room. She took a newspaper and some magazines off the couch, replaced an antimacassar that had fallen from the arm of the couch, and asked them to sit. She turned off the television.

"How come you want to see me?" asked Hattie.

"I just wanted to ask you a few questions," said Marc.

The man from the bedroom, dressed in a T-shirt and trousers, scuff slippers without socks, came into the living room.

"This here's my husband," said Hattie. "Charles, this is Miss Toni's lawyer, Mister Conte. And this is his wife, and this is . . ."

"Franco," said Franco, shaking hands.

"Can I get you a little something to drink?" asked Charles, lifting his right hand, his thumb and index finger indicating an inch shot.

"Too early in the morning for me," said Marc.

"Me too," said Maria.

Franco shook his head.

Charles sat on the couch, next to Hattie, watching. He offered a Benson and Hedges cigarette box to the others. No one wanted to smoke. Charles fitted a cigarette into a plastic holder and lit it.

"Hattie, tell me about the night Mister Wainwright was killed," said Marc.

She pursed her lips and shrugged. "I can't tell you much. I was asleep most of the time."

"Did you hear anything at all?" Marc asked.

She shook her head. "I didn't hear no talking. I did hear plenty of noises. At first, I thought the dead was coming to take me," she recalled ominously. "I was in my room, in the back of Miss Toni's. And I hear this terrible pounding. Then I sat up, and just listened. It was real all right, I said to myself. I put on my robe, and went out through the kitchen into the dining room. I hid behind the door, watching out to where Miss Toni's room was."

"Did you see who was doing the pounding?" asked Marc.

"No, that was all over by then."

"Could you see Mrs. Wainwright's door?" asked Marc.

"That was all broken in. I couldn't see nothing beyond it. It was all dark in there."

"What happened next?"

"Then I heard this here explosion," Hattie explained. "It was something terrible. I near fell down just from the sound. It was a gun, all right. I got me into the nearest corner and sat on the floor and just stayed there, praying. I hear some movement in there, like footsteps. Didn't see nothing. I thought, maybe Miss Toni was hurt. So I crawled and looked around the corner. And I still didn't see nothing. I didn't even hear nothing no more. So I creeped over there on my hands and knees, over there where the door was broken, and I listened. I called, *Miss Toni, Miss Toni.* And I heard a man's voice. I didn't recognize it to be Mister Bob, 'cause it was kind or more like moaning. He called *Zack, Zack.* And then . . ."

"He called what?" Maria asked with sharp surprise.

"Zack. He just said Zack a couple of times," Hattie repeated. "That was all I heard. Then I ran inside and called the police. That's all I know."

Maria looked at Marc, then Franco.

"You didn't see anyone, or hear anything, other than Mister Wainwright calling Zack?" Marc asked.

"I heard some footsteps, someone walking around just after the explosion."

"Did you tell all of this to the police?" Marc asked.

"No." She shook her head.

"How come?"

"Because I didn't know if I was supposed to or not. So I just kept quiet. I figured Miss Toni'd get herself a good lawyer—now don't you tell her I told you she said her lawyer was good-looking. I figured I'd tell the lawyer 'cause I'm not going to get Miss Toni in no more trouble than she's got."

"Did the police question you?" asked Marc.

"Sure, that night. They asked all of us all kinds of questions."

"And you didn't tell them about the footsteps or the voice calling Zack?"

Hattie shook her head.

"I want to write all of this into a statement for you to sign, Hattie," said Marc. He took out some large folded pages from his pocket.

"How come she has to sign something?" asked Charles.

"That's just to save you any more bother," replied Marc. "Even if a person doesn't know anything about a case, I like them to sign a statement. This way, I don't forget what they said, and I don't have to come back and bother them again." Marc failed to add that when a potential witness signed a negative statement, that potential witness couldn't easily change his or her story later on and be helpful to the D.A. with evidence they couldn't remember for Marc.

Hattie carefully and slowly read the statement Marc prepared. She read it over twice, her lips forming each word as she read, then signed it.

"Okay, Holmes and Watson," said Marc as they walked down the stairs. "I know neither of you could have come this far down the stairs without already hatching out a scheme. What's in your heads?"

"You notice how he always makes wisecracks?" said Maria. "But he always asks too."

"Every time," agreed Franco.

Marc smiled. "Well, what do you think?"

"I'm more convinced than before that Zack Lord must have had something to do with it," said Maria. "Wainwright called out his name. He must have been there. It must have been he who shot Wainwright."

"And how about the walking movement? That's when Lord slipped out of the room," Franco added. "We know Toni Wainwright fainted before the explosion. So she wasn't the one walking around."

"There was definitely someone else there," said Maria.

"I must admit we have a little more about another person now," said Marc. "But as far as Zack Lord is concerned, how did he know that Wainwright was going to go to the apartment? Wainwright wasn't living there at the time. So how could Lord or anyone else know Wainwright would be there to be killed? And second, how would Lord have gotten into and out of the apartment without being seen? Forget the keys. We know he had a set. But how did he get up to and down from her apartment on the eighteenth floor without someone seeing him?"

"I don't know," said Maria. "But what about Wainwright calling out Lord's name?"

"Didn't Toni Wainwright already say that when Wainwright came into her room in the dark, he was calling her a whore, and calling for Zack, looking for him in the bed?" said Marc.

Maria nodded thoughtfully.

"How did *Wainwright* get into the apartment then?" Franco asked. "Mrs. Wainwright told you that Wainwright *didn't* have a key. So, somebody had to let him in, right?" He looked at Maria.

"Right," she answered.

"And we know it wasn't Mrs. Wainwright or any of her servants," Franco continued. "So, how did he get in?" He awaited an answer. Marc thought. "Someone with a key could get in and let Wainwright in," Franco added finally. "That's how."

Marc hesitated. "No one saw Lord go in or out of the building."

"Come on, let's get out of this hallway," said Maria, giving in to an urge to hold her nose. "Let's talk in the car."

"I think we ought to talk to those elevator guys at Mrs. Wainwright's apartment," said Franco. "I still say Lord could have been the one who shot Wainwright."

"Keep working on it," said Marc. "But it's still too much of a blind alley. Too many dead ends with no answers."

"And too good a possibility to let go," said Maria.

"How handsome you are, Counselor," Maria said tauntingly. "Isn't it nice your clients think you're handsome?"

"Don't you?"

"And that's enough," she said, still teasing. She put her arm around Marc's waist. "You're my baby, remember?"

"I do," Marc said. "And I will."

XXII

TUESDAY, AUGUST 29, 10:17 A.M.

Marc stood inside a phone booth on the thirteenth floor of the Criminal Courts Building. He had the phone receiver to his ear, listening to Marguerite read off the list of calls he had received in the office this morning. There was nothing urgent. Marc said he would be back in the office as soon as he finished with the Maricyk and Wainwright cases in Part 39.

Justice Arthur Kahn was presiding in Part 39. Usually Justice Kahn sat in the civil term of the Supreme Court. But during the summer months, when the number of civil trials dwindled, judges who usually did not sit in criminal term were rotated there so they could gain experience in criminal matters.

Judge Kahn was tall, and his grayed temples and gold half-glasses contrasted elegantly against black robes. He was the very picture of a man of judicious mien. Which was exactly what he was not. Judge Kahn was a favorite of criminal defense lawyers when pleading clients guilty; he was quite lenient on sentencing. But, Judge Kahn was the last judge sought or desired for trials or hearings; he was ignorant of the law, insecure, impatient, irascible, verging on the paranoid. His elevation to the bench of the New York State Supreme Court was over the disapproval of every Bar association in the City. His wife's family, however, was well endowed with campaign contributions for the coffers of the Republican Party, and so a judge was made. Or at least someone who was called judge. And that calling to some, is far more important than the position itself.

Marc walked to the front of the courtroom and sat in the first row of seats to wait the call of his cases. Mrs. Wainwright was not in court today. Marc had advised her that her presence wasn't necessary because the only thing pending in her case today was a motion for a bill of particulars—simply, a further specification of the details of the charges pending against her. Since the courts permitted an indictment to state merely the bare bones of a case— *the defendant caused the death of one Lafayette Wainwright on the seventh day of August by shooting him with a gun*—Marc had moved to have the D.A. supply further information about the exact time and place of the crime, the type of weapon used, the autopsy report, the ballistics report. If the Wainwright case was going to trial—and Marc was sure it was, at this point—he needed details about the Wainwright death.

Just as Marc knew he would go to trial on the Wainwright case, he also knew he wasn't going to trial on the Maricyk case. Seeing Judge Kahn on the bench today, Marc decided to push to have a hearing on Maricyk's motion to suppress evidence. Not that Marc actually intended to have the hearing. He was using the motion to gain leverage for a lessened charge to which Maricyk might plead.

"And if Your Honor please," intoned James O'Reilly, the most punctilious of the court clerks, "on line fifteen of the second page of Your Honor's pleading calendar there appears the name of Oscar Johnson, also known as Ali Al-Kobar, defendant, who is on this occasion representing himself as defendant *pro se* on a motion to suppress evidence."

"Come on, come on, Mister O'Reilly," exclaimed Judge Kahn impatiently. "Let's do get on with it. We've a long calendar to call, and I'm on trial. I have a jury waiting. Let's do move along."

Oscar Johnson was escorted from the bull pen by a court officer. He stood at the defense counsel table, his shaved head glistening beneath the court's lights. He put a portfolio filled with papers and legal books on the table.

"Is your name Oscar Johnson," asked O'Reilly, "the defendant named by the People in this indictment, number one thousand four hundred and thirty nine?"

"Mister O'Reilly," the Judge cut in before Johnson could say anything, "can't you forget all the rococo language and just call the cases as quickly as possible?" The Judge looked at O'Reilly over the rim of his glasses.

"I shall endeavor to follow Your Honor's suggestion," said O'Reilly, rising to his feet.

"Will you please sit back down at your desk, and not take all day with the calendar," snapped the Judge. "We do not need a dialogue on this too." The Judge rose, walking around the small confines of his bench platform. He removed his glasses, tossing them on his desk.

"I am merely doing that required by law and the directives of the Appellate Division, Your Honor," said O'Reilly calmly. "I am merely performing my duty as best I know Your Honor would wish me to, both to protect the record and the defendant."

"How about the People?" piped in the young assistant District Attorney. He was thin with dark, curly hair.

"And of course, the People," said O'Reilly. "Shall I proceed, Your Honor?"

"I'd be delighted if you would," the Judge said.

O'Reilly sat back at his desk. "Is your name, sir, Oscar Johnson, the defendant . . ."

"Mister O'Reilly," interrupted the Judge again, his head giving a nervous little tic to one side, "I asked you to call the cases with expedition. And now it seems that the only expedition you have ever heard about is to Africa. Now . . ." The Judge's face suddenly grew red with anger. "Is that a smirk I see on your face, Mister O'Reilly?"

"Certainly not, Your Honor," replied O'Reilly, standing again. "You know that I have nothing but respect for Your Honor and the office that Your Honor so judiciously holds."

"Now stop that folderol with me, Mister O'Reilly," the Judge lashed out. "Are you trying to lock horns with me?"

"Certainly not, Your Honor."

"Well, don't try to. For I'll prevail. I assure you of that, Mister O'Reilly. I'll prevail." The Judge had his hand raised, a finger pointing ceilingward.

"I'm sure Your Honor would. And I assure Your Honor that I do not have any intentions of so doing." O'Reilly's strength lay in the fact that he was civil service and his calling of the calendar was letter perfect according to law and the court regulations. He knew this and so did the Judge.

"Then let's go, let's handle this calendar with dispatch. Let's try dispatch instead of expedition this time."

"Very well, Your Honor. Shall I arraign the defendant for the record?"

"You've done that twice already, for heaven's sake. Is there any doubt at this point that this is Oscar Johnson, the defendant?"

"My name is not Johnson, it's Ali Al-Kobar," Johnson interrupted with disdain. "I don't have no slave name."

The Judge shook his head in exasperation and twirled his seat until he faced the wall.

"I'm being persecuted on a political charge here," Johnson continued loudly. "We were demonstrating against the offensive conditions of that pigsty called The Tombs and now we're being persecuted for a crime because we demand being treated like human beings."

"Right on," shouted someone from the court audience.

"None of that," the Judge snapped, twirling forward again. He pounded his palm on the bench. "I'll clear the courtroom."

There was a group of young people, sitting in the back of the courtroom listening to the preliminary proceedings of The Tombs riot trial. Marc recognized the pretty blond girl who had been demonstrating outside the court the day of the riots. What was her name again? Andrea something, Marc recalled. He remembered she had asked him for his card. Apparently she remembered too; she smiled at Marc.

"Mister Oscar Johnson also known as Ali Al-Kobar," said O'Reilly, unflapped. He spoke slowly, carefully. "You have not been properly or completely arraigned. Please be kind enough to listen to my admonitions and instructions as to your rights before you speak further."

Johnson was silent.

O'Reilly nodded. "Now, do you have an attorney, Mister Johnson? If you do not, as you are entitled to an attorney at all stages . . ."

"Mister Johnson," the Judge cut in, speaking directly to the defendant.

"Ali Al-Kobar," Johnson demanded.

"Fine, fine," said the Judge quickly. "Whatever you want to call yourself is satisfactory to the Court. As long as we get on with it. You are entitled to a lawyer, I'll appoint an attorney, if necessary, at the county's expense for you. Do you understand?"

"I already had me a Legal Aid lawyer, Your Honor," said Al-Kobar. "He was no good. He didn't even want to come to see me to discuss my case. He didn't know nothing about it. I want my own lawyer."

"Can you afford to retain your own lawyer, Mister Johnson?" asked the Judge.

"Al-Kobar," Johnson insisted.

"I meant Al-Kobar," said the Judge curtly.

"I been laying up here in The Tombs for a long time, Judge," said Al-Kobar. "Even before The Tombs trouble. I don't have no money to pay a lawyer. Does that mean that a poor Black man charged with a political crime for wanting to be treated like a human being, that he is prejudiced as a result of his state of fundlessness?"

"It means nothing of the sort, sir," retorted the Judge. "And I want you to know and the record to reflect clearly that no one is prejudiced in my court because of race, creed, color, or condition of finances." The Judge was looking straight down at the defendant. "You'll have a lawyer appointed. A private lawyer, not a Legal Aid lawyer. Is that what you want?"

"I want my own lawyer," said the defendant.

"And you'll have one. And we'll do this expeditiously, Mister Al-Kobar. Was I correct that time?" the Judge probed cuttingly.

The defendant stared defiantly at the Judge.

"You're one of The Tombs riot defendants," said the Judge. "And the case is being prepared for trial for the September term. Is that right, Mister D.A.?"

"That's what Mister O'Connor said, Your Honor," replied the young D.A.

"Yes," agreed the Judge. "And you, Mister Al-Kobar, have a motion to suppress evidence pending. That will be handled by the trial judge just prior to the trial."

"What if I win the motion?" asked Al-Kobar. "Or are you prejudging the motion, Your Honor?"

"I'm doing nothing of the sort," the Judge said angrily. "I'm not even going to be the trial judge. I'm just going to make sure you have a lawyer. Now I will certainly provide you with the opportunity to be represented, as is your right, as I have already stated, but it must be done with expedition. There are two other defendants in your case, which is the first of the riot cases, and you are charged with initiating the riots in The Tombs. Now this is a matter of grave concern to the public. The District Attorney wants to proceed with the trial without delay."

"It is a matter of grave concern to me too, Judge," said the defendant. "I want an attorney of my own choosing."

"Now just a minute. Just a minute," said the Judge. "The Court will appoint an attorney for you. Those judges in the Appellate Division have been judges longer than you've been out of your diapers, so I think they can pick a better lawyer for you than you could for yourself."

"I don't want no lawyer then," said Al-Kobar curtly. "I want a lawyer of my own choice, or I don't want one at all."

"You're not going to impose your will on this court, Mister Al-Kobar. Let me assure you of that," said the Judge. "And you're not going to play games with this court. I know how it's done. I've been around. You try your own case, handle your own defense and then when the case goes up on appeal, you get a reversal because you should have had an attorney. Not in this court, mister. You're going to have a lawyer and a trial with all the trimmings. Your rights are going to be safeguarded all the way down the line."

"May I be heard, Your Honor?" asked the defendant. He was hostile and belligerent now.

The Judge studied Al-Kobar. "You may," he said. He swiveled half around, looking at the side wall.

Al-Kobar began to speak. He spoke about his rights, about being poor, Black, prejudiced by the fascist system, unable to defend himself in court. Someone from the audience cheered loudly. The Judge pounded on the bench. The courtroom became silent. Al-Kobar continued. The Judge now picked up the *Law Journal* which contained all the court calendars in the City, as well as all the decisions that had been made in all courts the day before, and other news items of importance to judges and practicing attorneys. Al-Kobar was still speaking, saying whatever he wished for the record. The stenographer was calmly recording everything said. The defendant began declaiming now against tyranny, oppression, and racism. Whatever he said, however, wasn't about to change Judge Kahn's opinion about anything. The clerk and court officers lounged back and relaxed while the defendant made his speech.

"You aren't even listening," the defendant complained angrily to the Judge. "I want the record to show that the Judge is looking away, reading a newspaper, while I'm here pleading for my life and the lives of all poor Blacks and other poor people caught in this fascistic society."

The Judge whirled on his seat, tossing the *Law Journal* aside. "You have the audacity to say for the record that I'm not paying attention to what you're saying?" he boomed. "Is that your opinion? Is it?"

"Yes it is. Those are the facts," said Al-Kobar.

"Right on," called a voice from the audience.

"I just want the record to reflect the following facts," the Judge continued, ignoring the outburst this time. He proceeded to repeat, almost verbatim, everything Al-Kobar had said concerning fascism, racism, Black people, and all other subjects the defendant had mentioned. The Judge stared directly at the defendant as he repeated what had been said. "Now, is that what you said, in words or substance?" he demanded of Al-Kobar.

The defendant glared back.

"I asked you a question, Mister Al-Kobar."

"That's right, Your Honor," Al-Kobar grudged. "That's what I said, and you *weren't* paying any attention to me."

"You heard me repeat it, didn't you?" the Judge asked. "Your jailhouse law degree ought to include a course in the errors of presumption."

"Can I speak, Your Honor, or are we going to continue to exchange verbal assaults? And I repeat you paid no attention to what I said."

The Judge frowned impatiently. "The record speaks for itself. Go ahead. You want to say something else for the record?"

"Yes, I do."

"Go ahead. Say whatever you want." The Judge picked up his *Law Journal* and swiveled again.

O'Connor strode into the courtroom and up the aisle to the well of the courtroom. He saw Al-Kobar at the defense table, and walked to the prosecutor's table, standing there, his arms folded across his chest as he listened.

Ali Al-Kobar continued speaking for the record, now decrying the judicial system; a poor man, especially a poor Black man, could not get justice in America, he said. The Judge continued to read his *Law Journal*. The court officers and the clerk chatted quietly among themselves. The young people in the courtroom were straining to hear every word, nodding in silent agreement. Finally, the defendant talked himself out.

The Judge turned front again. "Put the case on one week from today. Remand the defendant. Have the Appellate Division appoint counsel. Call the next case."

The court officer accompanied a scowling Al-Kobar back to the bull pen. Just before he disappeared through the door Al-Kobar gave the raised fist salute of the revolution. Marc saw the pretty girl in the hippie group return the salute.

O'Connor walked to the empty jury box and sat.

"The case of Joseph Maricyk is next, Your Honor," intoned O'Reilly. "On behalf of the defendant is the eminent and erudite Mister Marc . . ."

"Don't listen to him any more," the Judge directed the court reporter annoyedly. "Just let him keep talking. I'll call the calendar. Maricyk!"

Maricyk was brought out from the bull pen. He waved to his wife.

"What's your pleasure on this case, gentlemen?" said the Judge.

The assistant D.A. in charge of the Part looked at Marc.

"The defendant is ready for a suppression hearing, Judge," said Marc.

The Judge nodded. "After the call of the calendar, if you're ready, Mister D.A.," he said.

"We'll be ready, Judge. It'll only take a few minutes to get prepared."

"Fine," said the Judge. "Wait awhile and we'll get going."

"Would you call the Wainwright case, Judge?" said Marc. "I'm on that too."

"Certainly. Wainwright," the Judge announced. "Where's the defendant?"

O'Connor walked to the prosecutor's table. The Judge nodded to him.

"This is only a motion for a bill of particulars," said Marc. "The defendant isn't here."

"Very well, we don't need the defendant then," said the Judge, looking at Marc's motion papers, which O'Reilly had handed up to the bench. "Can you gentlemen agree on some of the particulars so that we only have to litigate the ones you can't agree on?"

"Your Honor," said O'Connor, reading from his copy of the papers he held in his hand, "we'll give him the time, the place, and the autopsy report. All the rest of the matters requested in these papers are evidentiary in nature, and we refuse."

"Mister Conte," said the Judge. "I'll hear you. You know, of course, you're not entitled to evidentiary matters."

"Your Honor, I do not believe that photographs of the scene of the crime are evidentiary. They are objective facts no longer in existence. The deceased's body has, of course, been removed, the physical scene has been changed. But the police have photographs of the scene. I'd like to see them. I say I have a right to see them. They might be of help to me in formulating a defense. The People won't be prejudiced if I see them, I might add, since I certainly can't alter or change the photographs or the scene that existed that night."

"Denied."

"And the ballistics information," Marc continued, not surprised at the Judge's ruling. "Ballistics evidence is not evidentiary either. It, too, is objective fact which existed at the time of the crime, evidence which should be available to both sides, so that the truth can be developed. To permit the District Attorney to keep these facts hidden from the defendant is to permit the motor of justice to operate on half its cylinders, to condemn a defendant to defending himself from the onslaught of a tiger with a paper shield."

"Denied."

"Your Honor," Marc continued, "it isn't fair or just that the People have access to the scene of the crime, take possession of all the evidence there and withhold it totally from the defendant."

"I have made my ruling, Mister Conte. The matters you seek are evidentiary in nature. If you don't like my decision, you can appeal. You have any other point you wish to mention?" the Judge said brusquely.

"Just that it's too late at an appeal after a trial for a defendant to complain about not knowing about the evidence."

"Are you going to give me a lecture on the law, Mister Conte?"

"Certainly not, sir," said Marc. "Just putting my statement and objections on the record."

"You have. Come up here on that other case—the Maricyk case," said the Judge. "Can we dispose of that without a hearing?" he asked as the two lawyers stood at the bench.

O'Connor shrugged. "I'm not on that, Judge. But I'll handle it." O'Connor took the file jacket on Maricyk's case from the prosecutor's table. He read the fact sheet as Marc explained his version of what had happened during and after Maricyk was arrested. Marc was careful to mention the injuries Maricyk mysteriously sustained.

"What about the charges that the policeman brutalized this defendant, Mister O'Connor?" asked the Judge.

"That's an old saw, Judge. It doesn't cut as far as I'm concerned."

"Ask Mister O'Connor for the mug shots of Maricyk taken after he was arrested, Judge," said Marc. "See if they look like a man who was just out for a quiet drive."

"You have them there, Mister O'Connor?"

O'Connor went through the file and handed the mug shots and a full-length photograph of Maricyk up to the Judge.

The Judge studied them. "The defendant does look marked up," he agreed.

"On the record in the Criminal Court, when he was first arraigned," said Marc, "I enumerated his bruises and contusions. Mister O'Connor wasn't there. But Judge Rathmore acknowledged the marks. Here are the minutes," said Marc, handing the papers up to the Judge. "My client has already complained to the Police Civilian Complaint Review Board."

The Judge leafed through the minutes, then looked to O'Connor. "Mister O'Connor, we're not dealing with a really serious situation here. A traffic infraction started all of this. I mean, it's not like he was trying to bribe the cop to not arrest him for a murder or robbery. He's only charged with an E felony. How about disposing of this as a misdemeanor?"

"A bribe, a bribe, Judge?" asked O'Connor.

"I know," said the Judge. "But his isn't the cleanest case in the world. Look at those pictures. Look at them yourself."

O'Connor looked. He was unimpressed.

"What if the defendant drops the Civilian Review Board case against the cop?" the Judge asked O'Connor. "Your client Maricyk is willing to do that?" he asked Marc.

"If he pleads guilty to, say, an attempt to resist arrest as a misdemeanor," said Marc, "he couldn't very well complain about injuries sustained when the cop tried to restrain him."

"That's right too," said the Judge. "What do you say, Mister O'Connor?"

"I don't like it," said O'Connor. "But, if he drops the charges against the cop, we'll agree to let him plead to a misdemeanor."

And so Maricyk pleaded guilty, indicating on the record that he was dropping the complaint against Schmidt and waived any further suit against the police or the City of New York.

"Fine. I'll only ask for a short form probation report," said the Judge. "Let's put sentencing down for September 11."

And, thus, another case was disposed of, a plea was entered, a defendant guilty, and, after all the facts sifted down, it came out just about right, thought Marc. Maricyk didn't get away with the courthouse, neither did the D.A. or the cop. The people could sleep safely one more night. Not so Mrs. Maricyk, thought Marc as he looked to the audience. She was sitting on the edge of her seat. Marc knew she would have plenty of questions to ask him.

XXIII

WEDNESDAY, AUGUST 30, 11:03 A.M.

Marc sat in a small area just off the huge, marble and columned entrance corridor of the prestigious Association of the Bar of the City of New York. He was absently reading a copy of the *Law Journal*. Across from him sat a short, thin man with a mustache reading the *Wall Street Journal*. A little farther away, another man seated on a wooden backed chair smoked a cigar. There was no door to the sitting area, and the three of them had a full view of the main corridor and the large, wooden doors across that corridor which led to the Dag Hammarskjöld Conference Room.

The Mayor's Committee on the Judiciary was in session behind those doors. This Committee served, without compensation, by appointment of the Mayor, to screen proposed judicial appointees. Most of the members of the Committee were lawyers. And each one represented, in some fashion, a segment of the diverse ethnic, economic, social, religious, racial, groups of which the City was composed.

A door to the Dag Hammarskjöld room opened. The three men in the sitting area turned as a man with blond hair emerged and walked toward them. He wore round tortoise-shell glasses and a vest across which hung a gold chain.

"Luis Del Gato?" the blond man inquired.

"Yes," said the man smoking the cigar. He rose hastily and stubbed out the cigar in an ash tray.

"I'm George Emerson," said the blond man. He shook hands with Luis Del Gato. "The Committee would like to see you now, Mister Del Gato. If you'll just follow me." He turned and started back toward the conference room.

"Good luck," said the little man with the mustache seated across from Marc.

Del Gato raised his eyebrows as if to say, here-goes-nothing. "Thanks. I need it," he remarked as he followed Emerson.

Marc and the man with the mustache watched Del Gato disappear into the conference room to be interviewed. They looked at each other, then resumed their reading.

Marc and the others had already been interviewed by a three man subcommittee of the Mayor's Committee on the Judiciary. The subcommittee had approved their qualifications. Now Marc and the others were to appear before the full Committee for final approval. If the full Committee approved Marc as qualified, he would still have to appear before the Judiciary Committee of the New York County Lawyers Association, and then the joint Judiciary and Criminal Courts Committees of the Association of the Bar of the City of New York.

These screening processes were intended to select the best, most qualified men for judicial appointments. Of course, the Mayor, or, depending on the particular judgeship, the Governor, or the President of the United States, could ignore the findings of the committees and appoint a totally unapproved, even disapproved, person to the bench. Such was the case when Judge Kahn was appointed by the Governor to the Supreme Court bench. But then, Judge Kahn and his wife had other substantial qualifications that certainly spoke well for him as a prospective candidate for the bench.

"They have plenty of interviews today," the little man with the mustache said to Marc. He had put down the *Wall Street Journal.*

"Seems that way," Marc said cordially. "I saw the list when I checked in."

"What time are you supposed to be interviewed?" the man asked.

"Eleven o'clock. They're running late."

"I can't figure why they're interviewing in the morning," said the man. "Don't they think we have to make a living?"

"I know what you mean." Marc smiled. "I have to be in court in Brooklyn in a little while."

"Sure. All of us do. I have four matters I could be working on right now, you get me? I'm losing maybe three, four hundred dollars just sitting here this morning."

Marc didn't react.

"I'm George Seigel," said the man, reaching out to shake Marc's hand.

"Marc Conte. Glad to meet you." Marc leaned forward. "Any relation to the actor?" Marc said jokingly.

"A lot of people ask me that," Seigel said. "I'm not, though, you get me? My brother is Harry Seigel." He looked for Marc's reaction.

Marc's face showed he didn't know Harry Seigel.

"He's the Democratic leader over in the Washington Heights area, Inwood, over there," Seigel supplied.

"Oh, that Harry Seigel," said Marc, not really knowing Harry Seigel.

The man nodded, smiling. "Harry, my brother, asked me to come over and be interviewed. I told him, I said, *Harry, I don't want it*, you know? Not that they'll give it to me, you get me? But if Harry wants me to come over, I said to myself, I'll come over. So here I am. I have an eleven-thirty appointment with the Committee. I'm a little early. I figured, if I'm going to kill the morning, I might as well get here on time, you get me?"

"They seem to be running a little late," Marc repeated.

"Wouldn't you know," Seigel said with a frown. "That Del Gato who just went in," Seigel said, nodding toward the conference room. "He's got a good shot at an appointment."

"I don't know him," said Marc.

"What's to know? He's Puerto Rican. The Mayor's looking all over for Puerto Ricans to put on the bench. He's got plenty of pressure from the Puerto Rican community because he don't put them on the bench. I mean, how the hell can he, you get me? How many Puerto Rican lawyers are there anyway? And of those, how many could even sit on the bench? They're good for some closings on *bodegas* and such, you get me? But they don't think like we do. They still have to assimilate. So here's a guy the Mayor'd die to put on the bench. He'd be off the hook for a while. What club are you with?"

"I'm not with a club," replied Marc. "George Tishler asked me to be interviewed. That's how I got here."

Seigel gauged Marc for a moment. "Oh? Tishler's pretty important in the appointments. I mean, he's the Mayor's man for judgeships. Tishler says okay, it's okay. You got yourself a good rabbi." Seigel studied Marc again. "You're Italian?"

"Yes."

"The Mayor needs Italians too. Nothing personal about Italians, you get me. It's just that he hasn't appointed one in a while. Almost as good a shot as the Puerto Rican—in chances, if you know what I mean?"

"Sure," said Marc. "You a Jew?" He saw Seigel draw back with a wariness that most Jewish people have when asked if they are Jewish. It's almost as if asking that question were an accusation.

"Why do you ask?" Seigel said. He was studying Marc again.

"Doesn't the Mayor need Jews?"

"Oh." He smiled. "He's already got a bushel of them on the bench." Seigel relaxed a little. "I'm not really interested in being a judge, if you get me?"

"How come?" Marc asked politely.

"I mean, who needs it, you know?" said Seigel. "The money stinks. What is it, thirty-three thousand five hundred. Is that money?"

"It sure is," replied Marc. "When you don't have office rent to pay, no secretary, no overhead."

"Yeah, sure," said Seigel, "but still." He paused. "And besides . . ." Seigel looked around to see if anyone in the empty room or corridor were listening, ". . . it's all taxable. You know? There's no cash . . . At least, now, you can put a little . . . You know what I mean."

"But with your background and connections, you're a cinch," Marc said lightly. "I mean with Harry Seigel behind you."

"Sure, connections and pull, I got the best," Seigel conceded. "But still, I'm not interested, you get me? If the Mayor said tomorrow, here, Seigel, the job is yours, I don't know I'd take it. I mean it. Besides making a lousy living, you're stuck every day. Not like the old days, you could come and go the way you wanted. You didn't have to show up, you didn't want to. Now, they have the newspapers looking over one shoulder, the Judicial Conference over the other. It's a job, you get me? Who needs it?"

"You sure don't," said Marc. "Why would you even consider a judgeship then?" He was enjoying baiting Seigel.

"Prestige, I guess. That's about all the job's got to offer," Seigel said after some thought.

"Prestige is only what other people think about what you're doing," said Marc. "How about what you think about it? If it's a lousy job, who cares what other people think about it. You get me?"

Seigel studied Marc again. He shrugged dismissingly, realizing Marc didn't understand the finer points of life. He picked up his *Wall Street Journal,* peering at Marc over the top of the paper.

The door to the conference room opened. George Emerson followed Del Gato out. Del Gato turned and went out of the building. Emerson continued to walk to the waiting area.

"Mister Conte?" he inquired.

"Yes."

Emerson shook Marc's hand. "I'm George Emerson. The Committee would like to see you now."

Seigel lowered his paper. He nodded, jutting his chin out to Marc

235

in encouragement. Emerson and Marc started back across the corridor.

The conference room was very large, dominated by a long table of highly polished wood. Around the table were seated perhaps twenty men and two women. On the table before each was a yellow pad.

Emerson led Marc toward the head of the table. "Mister Conte, this is Mister Anthony Chapin, our Chairman."

Chapin was a tall man, heavily built, with dark hair. He wore a vest and a chain. Chapin shook Marc's hand and waved him toward a chair directly next to the head of the table.

"Mister Conte, we would like to ask you some questions about your background," said Chapin. "There is nothing personal in any of the questions, nor do we ask any of them to pry into your personal affairs."

"I understand that, sir," replied Marc.

"Very well. Would someone like to start?" asked Chapin, turning to the array.

"Yes, I would," said a woman in a red dress. She had dark hair and glasses. "How much work, Mister Conte, do you actually do in the criminal field?"

"A fair amount," Marc replied. "I actually have a general trial practice, but I do a substantial portion of that work in the criminal field."

"As a result of that," the woman continued, "do you feel that you understand the problems which seem to beset the criminal courts these days?"

"I believe so," replied Marc. "At least some of them."

"How do you feel that you could be a benefit to the courts if appointed to the bench?" asked a man on the left side of the table.

"By knowing and understanding the law and the courts," replied Marc. "And at the same time, by knowing the needs of defendants, understanding some of their problems as a result of having represented so many. I believe I might be able to contribute to a greater respect for the law."

"How could you do that?" the woman in the red dress asked, probing sharply.

"Respect for the law starts in the courtroom," Marc replied. "If defendants respected the law, they might not return to face other charges. And to respect the law, defendants must be respected by the law, treated fairly, impartially, not like filth and human decay, but rather like human beings who have erred, sometimes grievously. There must be firmness and certainty of punishment, but most of all, there must also be fairness and equality of treatment. We cannot possibly expect respect for the law if the system singles out certain individuals—perhaps powerful or wealthy—and gives them special consideration merely because they've got connections. Moreover, I do not see a judge's role as a part-time prosecutor, but as an impartial arbiter of the law."

"Does that mean," asked a man in a dark suit and club tie, "that you would have a tendency to be lenient on defendants?"

"It doesn't mean that at all," replied Marc. "Do you want my frank opinions on these subjects?"

"Surely," replied the Chairman sitting next to Marc.

"Then, I suggest that understanding is not to be confused with lenience; nor fairness with softness," said Marc. "What I said about a judge's role refers to the fact that many judges feel their job is to help the prosecutors get defendants into jail. I don't see it that way. I believe judges are intended to be impartial referees, interpreting the law for the lawyers and jury. I wouldn't be a D.A.'s hatchet man if I were a judge."

"Does that mean that if someone you have represented or a friend of someone you may have represented came before you," asked a small man with a bald head and wire frame glasses, "that you would be, perhaps, I should say, would have a tendency to treat him with a different measure than say someone who was poor and Black?"

"First of all, I represent many defendants by way of assignment by the court. And many of my clients *are poor and Black*. Second, I wouldn't treat anyone differently. I have enough impartiality, guts too, if you will, to treat anyone who would come before me in the same way. And I'd suggest as an example of my capacity to do what I say, is the fact that I sit here before you and tell you my exact feelings. Even if I disqualify myself because of my answers. And, finally," said Marc, "if someone I knew came before me, I would excuse myself from sitting on that case, because that's what a judge should do in such circumstances."

The bald man nodded, and made a note on his yellow pad.

"You have represented many figures who are allegedly connected with organized crime," asked another man, young, with dark hair. He looked like the epitome of a product of the Yale Law School. "What would you do if one of these people came in front of you and you were sitting as a judge?"

"I think I've already answered that," said Marc. "I'd either treat them right down the middle, whoever they were, or I'd disqualify myself from sitting on their particular case because I knew them."

"Do you really think you could do that?" the questioner continued. "That is, be right down the middle, no matter what?"

"There's no question about it in my mind," said Marc.

"What in your opinion is the best method of dealing with organized crime, crime in general," asked another man, gray-haired.

"Those are two separate categories altogether," replied Marc. "Crime in general, I think, as do many others more qualified than myself, is a result of the present socio-economic ills of our society. It will take a great deal of time, effort, and money to eradicate them. But we *are* making slow progress," he added. "As to organized crime, I think that—in a large measure—what we talk about as organized crime is a myth, which has been made bigger than life in order for the governmental authorities to show they know where crime is located and that they're fighting it. It's certainly easier to create the placebo of an organized crime syndicate that's responsible for all our ills, and spend our law enforcement energy fighting it, than it is to fight the vastly more extensive and expensive socio-economic difficulties which I mentioned a moment ago."

"Are you saying that there's no such thing as organized crime?" asked one of the young women.

"Certainly not," replied Marc. "There are certainly gangs engaged in criminal activities. I suggest, however, that there is no monolithic national or international syndicate ruling crime, with a central headquarters, a central treasury, and a common plan of activity. The gangs are more independent, in competition with each other, and we should fight them as such. To create a false myth of a syndicate and then concentrate millions of dollars and hours to go out and fight it, rather than attack the real problem in crime, is to waste time, energy, and to fail in fulfilling governmental responsibility."

The people around the table were silent.

"Any further questions?" asked the Chairman. No one said anything. "Thank you very much, Mister Conte," he said, rising, shaking Marc's hand.

Marc followed Emerson out to the corridor. George Seigel was now pacing the marble floor to the corridor.

"So? How'd it go?" Seigel asked Marc.

Marc shrugged. "Who knows?"

"Well, wish me luck," said Seigel as he followed Emerson into the committee room.

Marc walked out the front entrance. Franco was seated in the car just to the side of the entrance. Marc got in.

"How'd it go?" Franco asked, starting the engine.

"I told them what I really felt on the questions they asked me. I'm not sure that was the wise or political thing to do, but if it isn't, screw it."

Franco smiled. "Where to?"

"We have to go to the Brooklyn Supreme Court," replied Marc. "Pellegrino's being arraigned on that state gun charge."

Franco headed toward the East River Drive.

XXIV

THURSDAY, AUGUST 31, 6:35 P.M.

Two men stood in the shade of a tree across the street from Toni Wainwright's apartment building. They seemed to be studying the façade of the Wainwright building. One of the men was Franco, the other, his old friend Johnny Manno. Johnny was tall and trim, with dark hair. He was an expert burglar, specializing in the burglary of large estates isolated in the midst of sprawling acres. In the grand tradition of times past, when even burglary had its ethic, Johnny Manno never carried a weapon when he worked, nor did he ever come into physical contact with his victims. Johnny was no cheap heist man. He was a specialist in quick, silent, and, sometimes, almost impossible burglaries. It was rumored that Johnny once physically removed a two-hundred-pound safe from the second floor of a great manor house in Virginia while the family was dining quietly on the lower floor.

"What do you think?" Franco said to Johnny, as the two of them continued their observations. The doorman was in the lobby, sitting on a side chair.

Johnny pursed his lips, studying further. "From what I see, Franco, and from the floor plan you drew, the best way to get into the joint without being seen is through that service entrance over there." Johnny looked in the direction of a barred gate at the extreme east end of the building.

"But how would you get to her apartment from there?" asked Franco. "That gate probably only leads to the back elevator. The elevator guy'd see you."

"In this business, Franco, you can't be lazy." Johnny smiled. "There's got to be a fire stairway in there too. So you walk up."

"And get down the same?"

Johnny nodded. "Right."

The two men crossed the street. Johnny, side-glancing as he neared the building, noticed the doorman busy opening the door of a cab for someone. "Keep moving," he whispered.

They walked directly to the gate, swung it open, and closed it behind them. Inside the gate was an arched, whitewashed tunnel, lit by a bare, high-watt bulb. The two of them walked through the tunnel toward the rear of the building. At the end of the tunnel was a large, open air shaft and a double door leading inside. Franco entered; Johnny was right behind him. They were now in a whitewashed brick room which had a large wooden desk against one wall; on the desk was an intercom phone connected with the front entrance and all the apartments above. At the far side of the room there was an interior door. They walked through the doorway. Just inside was a service elevator and, next to that, a steel stairway. The stairway was entirely covered with a heavy steel mesh grating, and at the foot of the steps, there was a locked gate.

Franco looked at the lock on the stairway gate. "This lock only opens from the inside," he said. He looked up as he heard the noise of someone's footsteps. Johnny looked in the direction from which the sound came. But the footsteps faded into a further portion of the basement.

"I could open that faster than most people with the key," said Johnny.

"Yeah, let's do it," Franco said enthusiastically.

Johnny took something from his pocket, pressed it into the side of the lock, and within a moment had opened it.

Franco smiled in admiration.

"Now we're inside," said Johnny. "Easy as that! Go up these stairs, and you'll hit every back door to every apartment in the building. Open those locks, and you're home free to easy pickings."

"That's easy picking for you, Johnny," said Franco. "But what about a guy who is a legitimate guy, and he wants to get in and out secret-like? What do you figure he'd do?"

"Same thing. These stairs are the only way up to the flats without going on the outside fire escape, and without going up on the elevators. He'd have to make it through this gate and the back door. If he could break them, he could do it."

"How about if a guy got a key from somebody?" asked Franco. "Then he wouldn't have to know locks or nothing. This would be a cinch. Only thing, maybe, you might run into the elevator operator."

"With a key, this'd be nothing," replied Johnny. "But what the hell is this all about? You mind telling me?"

"A guy got killed upstairs. We represent the wife."

"Oh, and she croaked him?" Johnny asked.

Franco shrugged. "Who knows! But I got my doubts. That's why I want you to case the setup. I want to see how somebody could come in the apartment and leave without nobody seeing him."

"If he got in and out of these doors, it'd be real easy," said Johnny. "You figure the wife's being framed?"

"Can I help you?" asked a red-faced, short man with an Irish brogue. There was a faint aroma of beer about him. He was dressed in a gray work shirt and pants. The name "James" appeared embroidered on his shirt pocket.

"Hiya, James," said Franco. "We're working with Mrs. Wainwright's lawyer. You know, on the trouble she's got."

James looked at Franco, then Johnny, with dull suspicion.

Franco took out his wallet, which perked up the workman's face. His keenness faded as Franco handed him one of Marc's business cards. The workman looked at the card, then to Franco again, then to Johnny. Franco now took a five-dollar bill out of his wallet, extending it toward the workman.

"We need some information," said Franco. "I thought you might be able to help us out."

The workman's keen eyes lit on the fiver quickly. "I don't know nothing about that trouble that woman has," he said, still looking at the money, "but if I can help you"—he snared the fiver—"I'll tell you whatever I know."

"Who was on duty back here the night Mister Wainwright was killed?" asked Franco.

The workman gazed at the ceiling. "That was a Sunday night, I remember we all talked about it when I got to work the next day."

"Does that mean you didn't work the night Mister Wainwright was killed?" asked Franco.

"Oh, I worked all right, the four to midnight shift," he replied. "I always work four to midnight on Sunday and Monday. The rest of the week, I work the front car, midnight to eight in the morning."

"Who worked midnight to eight the next morning?" Franco pursued. "Who was back here on duty when Wainwright was killed?"

"No one," the workman replied. "There's never a man on the service car—that's this here rear car—for the late shift."

"That'd make it even easier," Johnny said to Franco. "You wouldn't even have to worry about running into the elevator guy."

The buzzer in the service elevator sounded.

"Oh, I have a call. I'll be right back." The man entered the elevator car and slid the doors shut.

"You see, it's a real easy shot," said Johnny. "If you got in here and knew how to open this gate or had a key for it, you could get in and out of any apartment and nobody'd know the difference."

Franco nodded. "But say a guy didn't know from locks. How'd he get a key for the outside door and the stairway gate?"

Johnny shrugged. "Well, if we're talking about a guy who's always around, like you said about her boy friend, who belongs in the building, and who's got plenty of dough, I guess he could work something out with old booze-belly here. I'm sure this creep's got a key."

The elevator descended and the door slid open. A Black woman with laundry cart got off and disappeared into the rear of the basement.

"Do you know Zack Lord?" Franco asked the workman.

"Zack Lord, Zack Lord," he repeated, no look of awareness coming into his face.

"Mrs. Wainwright's boy friend," Franco added.

"Oh, the blond gentleman, you mean?"

"Right, the blond gentleman."

"Sure, I know him. A fine man, a fine man."

"Did you see him the night Wainwright was killed?" asked Franco.

"I told you I wasn't working after midnight," the man emphasized. "Mister Wainwright was killed, as I've been told, after one A.M."

"Before you knocked off work, did you see him?" asked Franco. The man pursed his lips and thought for a moment. "I did."

"When was that? What time?" asked Franco.

"Well, the Mrs. was having a party, a lot of people over for dinner on Sunday night. I remember that, because it was a Sunday and most of the stores were closed, but she had this place humming. When the Mrs. wants to get something done, she gets it done. I don't know if you know her, but she's got some mouth on her. At times, you'd think she was one of the longshore boys on the river."

"What time was it you saw Zack Lord?" Franco asked.

"If it's the blond fellow, who's been seeing the Mrs. since Mister Wainwright moved out, then I saw him in the afternoon. He must have been here, well, I guess it was the early evening. Maybe seven o'clock."

"Where?"

"Right here, of course," said the man, pointing to the basement environs. "The Mrs. has a wine room in the basement here. Stores all her wines in there, she does. It's locked like Fort Knox, too," he bemoaned. "This fella, Mister Lord you say his name is, comes down the back elevator with me. And he goes into that storage room. He's got the keys to all them locks, and he opens the wine

243

room, and I carry a case of wine to the elevator and then into the apartment upstairs."

"You sure this was the night of the party, the night when Mister Wainwright was killed?" asked Franco.

"As sure as I am that we're standing here."

"How come you remember it so good?" asked Franco.

"Because I do, that's all," the workman replied obdurately. "When I get me out of the bed the next morning, I see the papers, and I read about the killing. And I remembered very well, then, that I worked the day before, and that I delivered the case of wine for the party. That's how it is that I remember. Besides, he gave me a bottle of wine," he now whispered confidentially. "That's how I know. It was one hell of a wine, it was, too."

Franco and Johnny looked at each other. "How well *do* you know Mrs. Wainwright's boy friend?" asked Johnny.

"Just from seeing him around, you know? I see him all the time on the front elevator," the workman replied. "You see, like I said, I run the front car on the midnight to eight in the morning shift, three days a week. And I run the service car from four to twelve two days a week. So I'd see the boy friend quite a little when I'm in the front, after he'd take the Mrs. home."

"Was he friendly?"

"Indeed, indeed, he was, indeed he was," replied the workman. "Always right down to earth, if you know what I mean. And yet I'm sure he had the price of a good pair of shoes in his change pocket. Every once in a while, he'd leave a short taste for me in a glass on the foyer table outside the apartment. I'd be doing my nightly cleaning, and what would I see from time to time, but a glass of the spirits sitting there waiting for me as I'm polishing past the Mrs.' floor."

"He'd slip you booze?" said Franco.

"Unless it was the ghosts, it was him all right. He'd leave the glass there on the table for me. The Mrs. sure never left it."

"He ever leave more than one glass for you in one night?" Franco asked.

"You mean, two glasses at a time?" replied the workman.

"No. I mean, after you finished one, did you ever find another one later?"

"I did."

"Do you have a key for these gates and doors?" Johnny asked.

"I do," said the man proudly. He pointed to a ring of keys he wore attached to his belt at his left hip.

"You keep those keys with you?" asked Franco. "Or you leave them back here when you work the front car or go home?"

"Oh no. They stay with me. This is my own key ring, and the keys for the gates and doors is on it. I always have them."

The bell for the elevator sounded again.

"You'll have to excuse me," the man said. "I have to get upstairs now."

"One more question before you go," said Franco.

"What'd that be?" asked the man as he entered the car and was ready to let the doors slide shut.

"Who was on the front elevator that morning, the early morning when Mister Wainwright went up and was killed?"

"It was George McCormick," said the man.

"You sure?" pressed Franco.

"I am. George and me, we spoke about it the next day. I told him about the wine, and he told me about bringing Mister Wainwright himself, Lord have mercy on him, up to the apartment just before he was killed."

"Where's McCormick now?" asked Franco.

"He's on the front elevator this very minute. He's working this shift." The bell sounded again. "Got to go," the man said, letting the door slide shut.

"What now?" asked Johnny.

"I guess we go to see this guy McCormick," replied Franco.

The two men made their way out of the basement, through the tunnel, and into the street again. They walked to the front entrance. The doorman recognized Franco.

"Are you expected?" the doorman asked, moving toward the lobby phone.

"No," said Franco. "I just want to talk to George McCormick for a minute anyway."

"He's up on a run right now," said the doorman. "He should be down in a moment."

Franco and Johnny stood to the side of the lobby. The elevator doors opened a few minutes later. A woman in a pants suit, walking a small Yorkshire terrier, got off and went out to the street. The elevator operator stayed inside the car.

"Are you George McCormick?" asked Franco, walking to the elevator.

"Yes, sir. Did the doorman ring Mrs. Wainwright's apartment for you?"

"I don't want to go up," Franco said. "I just want to talk to you for a moment."

The elevator man looked at Franco, then at Johnny. "What about?"

"About the night Mister Wainwright was killed," replied Franco. "I'm with the attorney for Mrs. Wainwright. You know that. And we have to get an idea of what happened that night." Franco showed McCormick a five-dollar bill, making sure the doorman couldn't see it.

"I don't know what happened," McCormick replied. He glanced at the doorman and deftly took the money. "I was working the elevator. I took Mister Wainwright up, and then the next thing I know, I hear noise. I didn't pay it no mind. But then the police came like it was the St. Patrick's Day parade right through the lobby."

"What time did you go up with Mister Wainwright?" asked Franco.

"I must have taken him up, about, let's say, one o'clock."

"Was he drunk or sober?"

"That's none of my business, you know," McCormick said. "So I mind my own." He paused. Then he couldn't resist the interest of his audience. "If you asked me, though," he whispered, "I'd say he had a few."

Franco asked, "Anything unusual happen that night before you went up there?"

"Nothing much. When we got there, the door was open a little, so Mister Wainwright could get in. That's all."

"The door was open?"

"Yes. I didn't pay it no mind until the next day when I read the papers that he was killed," said McCormick. "Then I remembered taking Mister Wainwright up to the apartment, and I remembered that the door was open."

"Did you see anyone up there when you took him up?" asked Franco.

"Not a soul, not a soul," replied the elevator man. "The place was dead as Kelsey's nuts."

"You left Wainwright up there and came back down?" asked Franco.

"Sure, they were married and all, right? So I went up with him. The door was open. So, I figured the Mrs. left it open for him. I don't ask people to mind my business, so I don't mind theirs. Especially, about them kinds of comings and goings. You know what I mean? So, I left him there."

"Then what?"

"Like I said. Then nothing. I heard some noise. Figured it was a car in the street backfiring. The next thing I know there was more cops here than I could count."

Franco wasn't quite satisfied. "Anything else you remember about that night?"

McCormick thought for a moment. "No."

"Okay. Thanks," said Franco. He and Johnny walked out toward the street, and began to walk toward the car.

"What do you make of it?" asked Johnny.

"I figure," Franco began, "that if someone had the key to the gates and doors in the back, like you said, he could have gone up the stairs, got into the apartment, left the door open for Wainwright and shot him. Then down the stairs again, and good-by. And listen to this," Franco continued, "Zack Lord gets the old guy in the back drunk enough to take his keys. Gets a copy made and then he's got the keys."

"He'd have to get that guy awful drunk," said Johnny.

"From the looks of him, that guy in the back wouldn't complain too much, do you think?" asked Franco.

"Complain. He'd chew the bar rag if you'd let him."

"I know Marc's going to think this is way out, but I think the thing could be put together."

Johnny shrugged. "Search me."

XXV

Marc walked on Broadway from his office toward Wall Street. It was a fine day; clear, bright sunshine, with just a hint that Fall was coming. As he walked, Marc enjoyed studying the people hurrying to work. He noticed that many girls, even older women, in the crowds of office workers were wearing pants. This was not just fashion, Marc thought; it was intended as a statement of their newly developed independence and freedom. It seemed, however, to indicate just the opposite. Since they all had donned the same basic clothes, almost a uniform of pants, it served at once merely to imitate men, as if pants were the real independence, and underscore the women's sheeplike quality to be herded into a style. The really independent female was now wearing a dress, but the female pants wearers wouldn't know that for about another year. Some of the younger women were wearing grotesque, clunky platform shoes, which made them so awkward they could hardly walk. But then, what was comfort or even appearance in the face of current fads.

As Marc turned into Wall Street at the front foot of Trinity Church, bells began to chime 9 A.M. He entered the 1 Wall Street building, walked through the Irving Trust Company with its vaulted red mosaic ceiling, and then through the lobby to the elevators. He was on his way to the twenty-second floor.

As Marc got off the elevators, large letters set into the opposite wall proclaimed that he was now at WAINWRIGHT AND COMPANY.

"May I help you, sir?" asked a darkly sun-tanned, petite girl in a white sweater and blue slacks. She was seated behind the reception table.

"Yes, I have an appointment with Mister DeWitt Wainwright," replied Marc.

The receptionist picked up her phone and pushed a button on

a small switchboard to her left. She waited. "There's someone who has an appointment with DeWitt Wainwright," the girl said into the phone. She turned to Marc. "What's your name, please?"

"Mister Conte."

"Mister Conte." She listened again. "Okay," she said as she replaced the phone. "Someone will be right with you." Her attention returned to a magazine as she waited for her next visitor.

"You have a nice Labor Day vacation?" Marc asked in friendly fashion as he sat and waited.

"Yeah," the girl nodded, looking up only momentarily as she said it. Her long earrings bobbed for quite a while after she nodded her head.

Marc waited until the earrings were still again.

"Did you go to the beach and get some sun over the holiday?"

"Yeah." She smiled a moment to be pleasant, then looked down at her magazine again; the earrings began bobbing again.

Marc wondered how long the earrings would bob if she shook her head negatively. He was just composing a question that would bring a negative answer when a blond girl, fulsome, in a pair of brown pants with wide cuffs, clunky, dark brown, two-inch-platform shoes, and a beige sweater, appeared in a doorway to the right of the reception desk. "Mister Conte?" the blonde said.

"Yes," said Marc, rising.

"This way, please." She led Marc through a corridor spotted on either side with doors to small offices. Small plastic name plates had been inserted into metal slides outside each door, their impermanence perhaps purposely intended to remind the occupants that just as the name plate could be replaced without much trouble, so could they. Marc noticed as he walked that the girl he was following had a fully muscled, kind of pouty, rear end. She entered a larger corridor, where there were two carved wooden office doors, and two desks, one outside each of the carved doors.

"Right this way," she said, opening one of the carved doors. Marc entered a large room, with beige wallpaper and dark green leather upholstered chairs and matching couches. Behind a wooden desk was a heavy-set man, large in stature and face. His eyes were puffy, somewhat squeezed shut in his face by the extra, wrinkled flesh around them.

"Mister Wainwright, this is Mister Conte," the girl announced.

"Hello, Mister Conte," DeWitt Wainwright said, rising. He studied Marc carefully as they shook hands. "How can I help you? I'm not sure I want to; but tell me what you want anyway."

"As I told you over the phone," said Marc, sitting in a leather chair Wainwright had pointed to, "I represent your sister-in-law, Toni Wainwright."

"Just leave it, you represent Toni Wainwright," he said. "It's bad enough she uses my family's name without being reminded that she's related to me too." He frowned with some distaste he wanted Marc to know was there.

"I take it you two don't get along," said Marc.

"You could say that if you wanted to be charitable," Wainwright countered. He took a pack of Camel cigarettes from the desk, offering one to Marc. Marc declined. As he watched Wainwright light up, Marc thought that the old stand-by regular-size Camels seemed small in comparison to the filter and extra-length cigarettes people smoked today. Yet, the old masculinity mystique was there, and it really didn't matter what size they were; they were a man's cigarette.

"In addition to the fact that she shot and killed my brother . . . that lousy bastard," Wainwright hissed, a spume of smoke issuing from his mouth. "Excuse me. You're not here to hear the family scandal. Just let me suggest that Toni and I didn't get along from before." Wainwright now blew some smoke high overhead, as he leaned back in his chair. "But what can I do for you? I know you're only doing a job as her lawyer."

"I wanted to know a little more about a couple of financial matters," said Marc.

"What the hell do finances have to do with my brother's killing?" he asked, coming forward in his chair, his elbows now resting on his desk.

"I'm not sure it has anything to do with it, yet," Marc admitted. "I'm just following up some ideas right now. I don't know where they'll lead."

"Well, let's get it over with," said Wainwright. He looked at his watch. "I have to get to a board meeting in a few minutes. Do you want to know about Toni's interest in my brother's estate?"

"No. I want to know about your brother and Zack Lord."

DeWitt Wainwright studied Marc carefully. "Zack Lord? I know he's screwing the ass off Toni, but what the hell does that have to do with anything?"

"I told you, I'm not sure. I'm just following up some leads."

"You think Zack Lord . . ." Wainwright hesitated. "I mean, are you thinking that Zack Lord had something to do with my brother's death?"

"I haven't said that."

"And you haven't said that wasn't what you said either," Wainwright retorted. "What the hell does Zack Lord have to do with this?" He thought a moment, his puffy eyes narrowing further. "You think that wise-ass Lord had something to do with this? With my brother's . . ." Wainwright was starting to breathe heavily, his jaw muscles rippling.

"Just don't get off on a wrong tack, Mister Wainwright," Marc cautioned. "I haven't said I thought anybody had to do with your brother's death. I just need some information so I can put things together more intelligently. I'd suggest it'd be best if we all did the same."

Wainwright stared at Marc now, his head cocking to one side. He wasn't used to anyone reprimanding him. "Exactly what do you mean? And what do you want?"

"I understand that Wainwright and Company underwrote Zack Lord's business when he first went public. Your brother gave Zack Lord his initial boost into the financial stratosphere, so to say."

"That's a quaint so to say," said Wainwright.

"I'm sorry if I don't get all the exact Wall Street terminology right. I don't invest in the stock market."

"Why not?"

"I don't like the idea of my money being controlled by some faceless board of directors. I'd rather control it myself, make my own decisions."

Wainwright shrugged. "Glad everyone doesn't feel that way."

"Does Wainwright and Company still retain any interest in Lord's original and present conglomerate, his empire?" Marc asked.

"For what you want to know, yes. That is, as you know, Bob, my brother, was the one who originally was interested in Lord. He saw the guy was going places, moving fast. So he brought him

251

into the house. Introduced him. Bob was convinced we could do well with Lord. So we underwrote Lord's first offering. Bob was always the moving force behind Lord around here. And it was Bob who actually held the main portion of our interest in Lord's various holdings. I think in addition to our taking some stock in the firm name, Bob also went heavily into Lord's stock with his own money."

"And did that interest in Lord's company extend right up to the time your brother was killed?"

"Yes, Bob owned a very substantial portion of Lord's stock at the time of his death," Wainwright said, sliding open a lower drawer of his desk. He took out a folder, opened it, and read something. "Bob owned about forty-eight million dollars of Lord's stock when he died." He closed the folder. "I'd say that was substantial. Toni stands to own most of that now."

"Toni Wainwright stands to own the Lord stock personally?" Marc asked with surprise.

"You're the lawyer. She was my brother's wife, legally at least, at the time of his death, wasn't she?" Wainwright begrudged. "It was his personal stock. He left everything to her in his will. Of course, as you know better than I do, if she's convicted of murdering him she wouldn't inherit his estate, would she? Don't think I'm interested in the inheritance, Mister Conte. I'm not being mercenary. I couldn't care less what's done with the money, as long as that little murdering cunt doesn't get her hands on it."

"Are you angry only because of your brother's death? Or are there other reasons that existed before?" asked Marc.

"She was a ball buster from a long time ago, as far as I'm concerned," replied Wainwright. "She used to toss poor Bob around like he was a soccer ball. She used to wrap him around her little finger. It always pissed me off. And I told him so. And her."

"He pretty much listened to what she had to say, then?" Marc asked.

"You said it. Dumb bastard that he was," Wainwright said lovingly. "I used to tell him. But she had some kind of way with him that I couldn't explain."

"What do you know about Lord? About his present business holding?" Marc asked.

"Lord is a first-class prick," Wainwright replied unhesitatingly.

"He doesn't care about anything in the world, except getting more money, making a bigger splash, making a bigger show. He loves to see his name and picture in the newspapers." This last was said with obvious disdain for public showing.

"How did Lord and your brother get along?"

"Great, for some reason. Bob really liked Lord. Zack does have a way about him. He's charming in the way all con men are charming. If you figure that's charm."

"You see Lord as a con man?"

"Maybe that's too strong," Wainwright admitted. "He's got a gift of gab, a good personality, okay? He's hustled his way to the head of a world-wide conglomerate and mutual fund that gobbles up businesses after Zack talks to the owners, charms them, convinces them he'll give them a huge pie in the sky."

"What about Zack and your brother," Marc asked. "He con your brother?"

"I don't know. Bob was a pretty smart guy," said Wainwright. "He was younger than I am. But he wasn't easy to hustle. He and Lord got along really well, however. Bob liked Lord. At least up to the time that Lord started playing around with Toni."

"When was that?" asked Marc. "Before or after your brother and Toni were separated?"

"We never really knew for sure if Zack and Toni were screwing around before she threw Bob out," Wainwright replied. "I sort of figured afterwards that she must have been, that's why she threw him out. But we never knew for sure, to be honest."

"Who is we?"

"Well, Bob and I talked about it some after she threw him out of the apartment and changed the locks. He figured that'd only last awhile. But then, he was shocked when she was really serious about it. She even started seeing Lord."

"I take it, your brother Bob didn't like that?"

"Bet your ass he didn't." Wainwright lit up another little cigarette.

"How did they get along before the breakup, your brother and Lord and Toni?"

"The best of friends," Wainwright replied. "Lord was always with them, or them with him—on their boats, Lord's plane, traveling. He was like horseshit, Lord was; he was everywhere."

"Your brother and Lord were genuinely friends then?"

"Sure. Lord was always sending gifts from where he traveled, flowers to the wife, birthday presents, you know, always remembering special events. I told you he was a good con man. He was always doing the right thing."

"And after the breakup, things changed?" Marc continued.

"Sure. Then Zack started seeing Toni, and Bob was really pissed off about it. But he never could handle Toni. She just pushed him around some more, gave him a line of bullshit. And he'd believe it, go get himself stinking drunk somewhere, then sleep it off for a few days."

"Does Toni Wainwright now actually control the portion of Bob's estate that includes Zack's stocks?"

"We're fighting her in court," replied Wainwright. "But the only leg we stand on is the case where you're defending her. If she's acquitted, she'll own most of Bob's estate."

"What's your opinion of Lord's present business holdings?" Marc asked. "I don't think you answered me before."

He thought a moment. "Well, let me put it this way," Wainwright replied. "If you were asking me to invest your money now, I wouldn't put you into anything that Lord owned."

"He's in that bad shape?"

"More like he's overextended right now. And with the national economy the way it's been for the last year or so, that's a bad position to be in."

"I don't know much about it," admitted Marc. "From the outside, Lord seems to own half the world. Villas, boats, planes. How could he be in rough shape and own or control so much?"

"Easy. It happened like this. First he owned and controlled a few businesses. Pretty successful businesses. Then we underwrote him, he went public, and he got big money. He takes over a couple of more businesses, larger businesses. Starts his conglomerate and his mutual fund. Then he starts taking over even more businesses, gave each of them a piece of his over-all holdings. You know how the conglomerate thing works, don't you?"

"Basically," Marc replied.

"Well, it's like this," explained Wainwright. "Lord controlled some companies. He wants to take over other companies. So he gives the owners or stockholders of a new company a piece of the combined operation. The owners of the one company now own part of a much larger operation. They own, instead of a hundred per cent of their own single company, a smaller per cent of a much vaster, more valuable company. Everybody's happy, especially Zack, because he's growing larger and larger, taking over other companies, using their own money."

"Their own money?"

"Sure," continued Wainwright. "The new company throws in their business. What does Zack throw in? A piece of their own company, and a piece of a lot of other companies he took over the same way. He doesn't put up a dime. They only get back their part of their own business, and part of other people's businesses."

"Okay," said Marc. "How does that set Zack up in a troubled situation now? It sounds like it would make him stronger if he's been picking up the right companies."

"That part's true, all right," agreed Wainwright. "But then Lord started being an entrepreneur. Went into a lot of new ventures, with the assets of all these companies behind him. Lord got into construction, international hotels, for instance, and wildcatting for oil around the world, stuff that costs money. And he finances the new stuff by taking money out of one of his companies. Business A, for example. Now Business A might have good earnings, and been making a financial surplus. So he uses Business A's money. Then, Business A gets a little tapped out, as happens from time to time in any business, say at production time, or at a slow period, or vacation time. Well, since Zack took Business A's cash reserve to sink into one of his other ventures, he has to come up with money from Business B and sink it into Business A. Then when B needs money, he'd have to tap Business C, then Business D, and so on. After a while, each of the companies is leaning on the next one, and each becomes tapped out, and then what? You see what I mean? Lord's overextended himself, and he's built a pyramid of cards which can collapse at any time."

"I'm with you so far," said Marc, "except for the pyramid."

"Easy. All the businesses are tied together now. The money from A is in B, and the money from B is in C, and so on. After all the businesses are interrelated with all the others, pull one out, let it collapse, and what happens to the rest of the companies? The one that collapses pulls down the one leaning on it. And the second one pulls down the third, and the third pulls down the fourth. Like that."

"Is that the condition of Lord's empire right now?"

"In my opinion it sure is," replied Wainwright.

"Bob thought the same thing?"

"He's the one who told me," answered Wainwright. "Bob saw what Lord was doing, and he started to get a little edgy."

"Did Lord know how Bob felt?"

"I guess he was getting the picture," said Wainwright. "Bob was trying to unload his holdings in Lord's empire, as you call it, a little at a time, so as not to depress the market. In other words," Wainwright explained, seeing Marc's face reflect confusion, "Bob didn't want to dump forty-eight million dollars' worth of Lord stock on the market in one day. It would cause a panic, the stock would go into a nose dive, so would the price, and Bob wouldn't get his money out, Lord would be out of business, and like that. So Bob was easing his way the hell out of this Lord empire, a little at a time."

"And Lord knew this?"

"I'm sure he did. He'd have to. He could easily find out whose stock was being sold. I mean, in everyday terms, Bob was selling fairly large lots."

"And what your brother was doing, would it have enough influence in the financial world to really affect Lord's operation?"

"Sure," replied Wainwright. "I mean, we're a prestigious Wall Street firm, if I say so myself. And these were some company-held stocks, in addition to Bob's personal holdings, that were being sold. Now, if Wainwright and Company show signs that we have no confidence in a stock that we originally underwrote, then people on the Street, other investors, get the idea something's wrong. You start them thinking, then doubting. And on Wall Street, panic spreads like a plague."

"I guess that also means that Toni can affect Lord's fortunes once she has total control of your brother's estate."

"If she gets to inherit Bob's estate, she sure could," Wainwright replied. A look of great surprise dawned on his face. "You figure that that slimy weasel Lord is playing around with Toni to control the stock and keep his ass afloat?"

"I don't know too much about the financial world, Mister Wainwright," said Marc. "I'm just trying to find out about a homicide case."

"You bet your ass," Wainwright exclaimed. "That Zack Lord is doing just that. That sneaky, slimy son of a bitch! First he tries to keep my brother wrapped up with birthday presents, and vacations together, flowers for the wife. And then he tries to take over his widow and the stock to boot."

DeWitt Wainwright was still hissing obscenities when Marc took his leave.

XXVI

SATURDAY, SEPTEMBER 9, 3:20 P.M.

Foul weather had moved in quickly late Friday night, and Marc and Franco had spent a very long night fighting through wind and lashing rain back to port. Saturday morning had thundered angrily and darkly, and the weekend's sailing had been scrubbed. Which was a shame, for there weren't many good sailing days left. In the afternoon, a sudden wind blew the storm to sea and the sun came out, but by that time Marc had arranged an appointment to see Zack Lord.

At three o'clock Saturday afternoon, Marc, Franco, and Maria entered the nearly deserted lobby of the Hotel Louis Quinze. Maria said she wanted to meet Zack Lord so she'd have a firsthand impression of the situation. Marc, although he teased Maria about purposely causing the bad weather and the sailing being scrubbed, consented to her coming along. As he picked up one of the house phones near the front desk and asked for Zack Lord, Marc was envisioning billowing spinnakers and brisk winds. He spoke with someone in Zack's suite and was cleared to go up. The front desk gave the elevator operator permission to stop on Lord's floor.

"He lives on the same floor with his offices?" Franco asked the elevator operator as they ascended rapidly.

"Yes, sir," replied the elevator man without turning. "To the right are the living quarters. To the left are the business offices."

"He's got the whole floor?" Franco asked with an air of admiration.

"Yes, sir. The entire twenty-ninth."

"Is that the top floor of the hotel?" Franco continued.

"No, sir. But that's the last occupied floor. The rest of the floors are just for machinery or hotel maintenance."

The elevator stopped and the three of them stepped into the paneled reception area. A young man in a suit and tie was seated behind the desk.

"Marc Conte to see Mister Lord," said Marc.

"Yes, sir, this way." The young man rose and crossed the reception room, toward the right. He held open a door for Maria, then Marc and Franco. Once inside a corridor of blue, softly lit with small spotlights from the ceiling, the young man walked ahead of them and brought them to a closed door. He pressed the door buzzer.

"Is this Zack Lord's private apartment?" Maria asked the young man.

"Yes, ma'am."

A man with a large on-the-rocks cocktail glass in his hand answered the door. There was much noise and laughter swelling out around him from the rooms inside. The man was dressed in white slacks, white patent leather shoes, no socks, and a blue sports shirt open down the middle of a hairless chest.

"This is Mister Conte and his friends," said the young man. "Mister Lord said it was okay for them to come up."

"There's always room for a groovy chick," the man said, as he shrugged and waved them into the noise. He was a little drunk.

Marc's face quickly grew stern. Maria put a quieting hand on Marc's arm. "Take it easy, Marc. He didn't mean anything."

The drunk had turned and walked ahead toward the noise and laughter. He stopped, sipped at his glass, and turned to see where they were. "Come on in," he said. "The audition's in the living room," he said to Maria. "You can change inside." He turned into another corridor.

Maria looked at Marc, then Franco. Franco shrugged. The young man, remaining outside, closed the front door behind them.

Piano music could be heard more distinctly now. Marc, Maria, and Franco followed the drunk into a large living room. There was a fireplace surrounded by massive bookshelves against one wall. Another wall was all glass, leading onto a sunny balcony overlooking Central Park. The other two walls were hung with pictures. Beneath the pictures there were two couches in a large right angle.

Zack Lord, in slacks and an open-necked sports shirt, was seated in the middle of one of the couches. There were two other men on the other couch. They were all eagerly watching a girl with large, bare breasts, dressed only in a small bikini bottom. Her breasts were solid and erect and white, contrasting softly against the deep tan of the rest of her chest. She was in the middle of the large room dancing to the piano music.

Franco's mouth fell open.

"What in the world have we walked in on?" Maria asked in a whisper.

"I don't know. But it looks okay to me," Marc kidded in a return whisper.

Maria gave his leg a healthy pinch.

"Oww . . . take it easy."

"Behave, then."

"Let's get out of here. This ain't no place for you," Franco said to Maria.

"It's okay, Franco. I've seen naked ladies before," she assured him.

As the girl in the center of the room cavorted, her legs kicking to the music, her arms swinging with the rhythm, her bare breasts were grotesquely shifting and lugging against the movement of her body. Marc watched, thinking as he did that when the female breast is unhaltered, stripped of its covering and molding garments, it is also stripped of its mystique, becoming merely a fatty, loose part of the body. There are "tit men" whose fascination stems from fantasies, not reality, but the female breast is far better suited to cheesecake, fondling, and sexual arousal than to bouncy dancing.

Franco stole a glance at Maria. He was embarrassed.

The dancing girl was in dead earnest, concentrating seriously on the music and her improvised dance routine. She paid no attention to her audience, except to look up and flash a strained, show-business smile occasionally.

While the dancing was in progress, many people could be seen through the glass wall, congregated around a bar set up on the balcony overlooking the park. Many of those on the balcony were young women; all wearing bikinis—both parts of the bikini.

"Good thing I came along," Maria replied.

Marc shrugged with feigned uncertainty. "You should have brought your bikini."

Maria gave him another pinch.

"Will you be careful," Marc whispered. "I'll be black and blue and that'll spoil my audition dance."

The girl performing the dance was now going through a series of high kicks. She was really working hard. The piano was pounding out the music. The piano player had a cigarette curling smoke dangling from his mouth. Marc thought for a moment of that piano player and all the lessons he had to take in order to learn to play, all the visions of artistic betterment his mother must have had as she paid for those lessons. And here he was, playing burlesque music for a girl with flying tits.

Zack saw Marc and the others. He studied Maria and nodded approvingly as he waved them to join him and his friends on the couch. Marc moved forward and sat on the nearest couch. Maria hesitated.

"Sit down a minute," Marc urged. Franco stood next to the couch, watching the dancer raptly.

"What the hell is this?" Franco whispered, leaning over to Marc, watching the girl all the while.

"Don't know."

"You see the load of good-looking dames they got on the balcony?" Franco added. "There must be twenty of them."

"I saw them," said Marc.

Maria watched the girl silently. "All these men are middle-aged creeps," she said. "Look at them. Their eyeballs are falling out."

The dancing girl was whirling now. Her breasts were lifting away from her chest with the centrifugal force of her twirling.

A couple of the men from the balcony came to the doorway and, standing there, watched the dancing.

A man in green slacks, green suede shoes, no socks, and a yellow

260

shirt came into the large room from another door leading to the interior of the apartment. Another girl in a bikini was with him. She had her arms behind her back as she entered the room. She was fastening her bra. The man in the green slacks chivalrously let her pass ahead of him as they walked behind the dancing girl toward the balcony. He glanced at Zack and lifted his eyebrows a couple of times, lasciviously approving something. Zack pursed his lips and nodded, his eyes off the dancer momentarily only.

The music ended. The dancer took another couple of steps without the music, and then, suddenly, her dance seemed, like a wound-out music box, to slow, then stop. She looked to Zack, then the others.

"That was really fine, honey," said Zack, applauding a bit. "Really, fine. Go ahead inside," he said. "You can find a bathroom in there. Take a shower; freshen up." Zack pointed to the doorway from which the man with the green slacks had just emerged into the large room.

"Was it all right?" she said anxiously, picking up her bra from a chair and holding it against her breasts. Her chest was slick with perspiration. Zack was standing next to her now. So were two of his guests.

Marc, Maria, and Franco remained where they were.

The girl was young, perhaps in her early twenties. She was dark-haired, with a midwestern accent. Her body was very taut and trim, her legs strong. She had a vague look about her eyes.

"It was fine, really good," said Zack. "One of the best today, don't you think, Harry?"

"Definitely," said Harry. He was semi-bald, with glasses, and was staring at the girl's half-exposed breasts. "What's your name, honey?" asked Harry.

"Sloan Mason," she gushed breathlessly.

"You'd better go ahead and get freshened up, cool off," said Zack. "Harry, show Sloan where to shower."

"Sure," said Harry, lifting his arm to point the way. Sloan smiled, then walked ahead of him, still holding her bra against her.

Zack and the other man watched her rear end as she walked ahead of Harry.

"She's got some pair, that one," said Zack.

"Nice ass, too," said one of the others.

"Marc," Zack said jovially, noticing Marc's disapproval of the language. "You came just at the right moment." He shook hands with Marc, then with Franco, although less cordially. "And with a real doll."

"This is my wife, Maria," Marc said.

"Your wife?"

"It's okay, I won't bite," Maria said, seeing a wariness color the faces of Zack and the others.

Zack managed a smile. "Just a party for a few friends. This is Charlie Ross. This is Marc Conte, Toni Wainwright's lawyer. And this is his wife and his assistant. This is Marty, Stan."

The men shook hands, then smiled at Maria.

"Percy, Percy, get a drink over here," Zack called to a young Black man in a white jacket who was walking through the room, carrying a silver tray.

Maria asked for ginger ale. Franco and Marc took vodkas with tonic.

"There's plenty to eat in the other room," Zack said to Maria pointedly. "Percy, show them where the food is."

"I think I'd like to have something," Maria said tactfully. "You stay here, Marc, and finish your business so we can get going."

"I'll go with you," said Franco.

"Fine, fine," said Zack Lord, relieved.

Maria and Franco followed Percy into another room.

"Wow, your wife!" said Zack.

"She's okay," Marc assured Lord. "She's cool."

"I know, but a wife's a wife."

"Who do you want now?" Charlie Ross asked Zack.

Lord nodded. "You know which one we haven't seen yet," he said, now looking through the glass wall to the balcony. "That little one with the pink bathing suit. With the dark hair."

"The one with the twenty-pound tits?"

"Yeah, yeah," said Zack, smiling toward Marc. "Bring her in. Wait till you see this one, Marc. Too bad your wife is here. Otherwise, I'd give her to you."

Charlie Ross went out to the balcony.

"What's going on, Zack?" asked Marc.

"Oh, we're having our monthly try-outs," Zack replied.

"What are they trying out for?"

Zack laughed. "It's really a put-on, but the girls don't know that. I bring in some of my people from out of town once a month, and some execs from companies I'm looking to take over, and a few guys from around town that I know, and I throw a party with a lot of broads for them. Let them see a little New York action."

"There's more than a little action here today, Zack," said Marc. "But what's the dancing and try-out stuff all about?"

"I bought a couple of meatball screen plays that were hanging around town, with no one to produce them. I gave the writer a couple of bucks for them. I still don't know what the hell they're about." Zack laughed.

Percy returned from the other room without Maria or Franco.

"One of them is called *The Starlet*," Zack continued. "Now I had Cahill, my lawyer, put together a production company for me. It's just a corporation called Lugar Studios, Limited. I even have a card," said Zack, pulling out a business card from the pocket of his shirt.

"Are you really going to produce a picture?" asked Marc, looking at the card.

"Don't be silly," said Zack. "I just have the corporation and a couple of scripts, and I have some ads put in the trade papers, you know, *Variety, Show Business*, stuff like that. They advertise things like, *looking for a young unknown actress to play the lead in a new motion picture production, must be able to dance.* Stuff like that. Every month I throw one of these audition things. And you should see all the broads I get up here. And score with. Unbelievable. They all want to be stars."

"Don't some of the girls get wise to this?" asked Marc.

"The ones who do, walk out," Lord shrugged. "There are still enough would-be stars left to make up a great black book for parties. You want to have a party, I'll get you some of the best broads in town."

"Here she is, Zack," said Charlie Ross, enthusiastically, returning with a petite, dark-haired girl with large breasts that jellied over the top of her bikini. "I told her we had our eyes on her right along, we were saving her for near the end." Charlie was behind the girl, mugging for Zack to go along with the story.

"That's right, honey," said Zack. "We wanted to get through some of the others who weren't really in competition with you.

You know, they came up, we had to let them try out. This is Mister Conte, one of our lawyers."

Marc said hello to the girl.

"Now, why don't we get started," Lord said. "This is a movie entitled *The Starlet*. It's about a young starlet making good in New York, you know, the usual hard times, and then a big break."

"I've lived it," she said with a big smile. "What kind of background does she have? Unhappy? Happy?"

"Unhappy. Very unhappy," said Zack.

"I can do it," she said with a determination born of acting school.

"Now this girl is going to all kinds of lessons, you know. Acting, dancing, everything," continued Zack. "She's really determined to make it. To make money to pay for her lessons herself, because she's not just a lazy slob or a hooker who's going to lie on her back and let some guy pay for her, she gets a job as an exotic dancer. A stripper. You think you can do that?"

"I can do it. It's real. It's believable," said the girl.

"Okay, well, that's what we have to see," said Zack. "We have to know if you can dance, if you have rhythm. If you'll be shocked in front of a camera crew to be dancing naked."

"Not when we're all professionals," she said gamely. "I've been getting myself ready for a long time for a big break. Maybe this could be it?"

"Might be," said Zack. "We've had our eyes on you since you came in."

Marc looked at Zack. He couldn't believe this ugly scenario.

"Okay, let's get going," said Zack. "You think you can manage it with some of your clothes off? You'll have to in front of the camera, you know."

The girl reached behind her back without hesitation and unhooked her bra. As it came away from her chest, her huge breasts sagged flat and long, with large pale nipples. They were not firm breasts, but rather very soft and fleshy. Zack and Charlie Ross stared at her. A couple of the men from the terrace had come into the room. One of them was eating from a plate, forking up macaroni salad when he wasn't staring at the girl's breasts. She too had a deep tan, and the area under the bra was quite light compared to the rest of her.

"More?" she asked, looking at Zack.

"Whatever you can be comfortable with," he said, trying to be nonchalant.

She hooked her thumbs into her bikini bottom and slid it down. She kicked the bottom off to the side. Her pubic hair was pressed down from the bathing suit. A few more men from the balcony, seeing what was happening, entered the room.

"Let's go, Jimmy," Zack said to the piano player. "Some finale strip music."

The pianist started into the usual syncopated strip kind of bounce. The girl started moving around the room as if she were doing a strip number for a camera. She was smiling at the men as if they were the unseen audience in the make-believe theater where The Starlet worked. Zack sat back on the couch. He looked at Charlie and smiled. He looked at Marc and raised his eyebrows a couple of times.

"I don't have time for this kind of shit," Marc said impatiently to Lord. "I'd like to talk to you for a couple of minutes."

Zack pointed to the girl, as if he couldn't leave now. Marc pointed at his watch. Zack's attention was caught by the dancer.

The girl was giving high kicks now, doing what she thought strippers do. The men started to clap, urging her on. More men from outside came into the room. The girl seemed to respond to their enthusiasm. She started kicking harder. The men began to clap harder. Now the girl tried deep-knee bends, her legs spreading open as she did.

Marc signaled Zack again. Zack could hardly take his eyes from the girl. He signaled Marc he'd be right there. Marc turned and walked into the other room where the buffet table and another bar were set up. Maria and Franco were standing looking out a window overlooking Sixty-first Street.

"Some bunch of bastards," said Marc, walking up behind them.

"What happened?" asked Maria.

"Nothing happened," he replied. "Just some bunch of bastards, including Lord." Marc explained The Starlet scheme to Maria and Franco, about the phony production company, the phony scripts, the phony ads, the phony auditions.

"You're right," said Maria. "A real bunch of bastards."

"This is what rich guys do?" asked Franco.

Sloan Mason, the previous dancer, entered the room and stood at the table, surveying the various foods. She was back in both parts of her bikini now. Harry was still with her, helping her select a plate of food.

"Hello," Maria said to Sloan Mason.

The girl smiled.

"I'm Maria Conte, this is my husband Marc, and this is Franco Poveromo," said Maria, moving closer to Sloan.

They all nodded and smiled. Marc looked at Maria, wondering what she was up to. The music and noise was still heard from the other room.

"I'm Sloan Mason," said the girl. "This is, I'm sorry I don't know your name," she giggled to the man.

"Harry. Harry Arnold." He looked at Marc, then Maria, Franco.

"Did you come for an audition?" Maria asked the girl.

"Right. You too?"

Maria shook her head. "The auditions are phony. So is the picture they said they were making."

Harry Arnold seemed offended. He stared at Maria.

"What do you mean phony?" the girl asked.

"It's a phony," Maria repeated. "Nobody here's going to make a picture."

Harry looked angrily at Marc now. Marc shrugged. Harry walked off quickly toward the living room.

"You mean these guys are just putting us on?" asked the girl.

"Exactly," said Maria.

"There's no movie or anything?"

"Right. They fake it just to get girls up here for their parties."

"What a real bunch of deadbeats," she said, putting down the plate of food. Then she thought. "The hell with it, I'm not going to miss the meal, anyway. I'll leave after I eat," she said, picking up her plate again. "I went through the trouble of getting here and doing a number. I might as well get something out of it."

Zack Lord came into the room. "What's the matter, Marc?" he asked.

"Nothing at all," replied Marc.

Harry Arnold was just behind Zack's shoulder.

"Can I see you for a minute?" Zack said to Marc, motioning to the side.

266

"Sure," said Marc. "We have to be going soon, anyway. We don't want to interfere with your party."

"What the hell is your wife pulling off?" Zack demanded of Marc when he thought he was out of earshot.

Maria walked over to them. "If it's about me, I'll tell you what it's about. I think what you're doing stinks."

Zack said nothing to Maria. He looked back to Marc.

"She thinks it stinks," Marc confirmed.

"What are you trying to do, mess up the whole afternoon?" said Zack.

"I'm just telling this girl the real story about the movie, that's all," said Maria.

"You came here to talk to me," Zack said to Marc curtly. "Let's all of us go into my office."

Marc nodded. Lord walked through the apartment to the entrance door and opened it. He waited for the three of them to enter the blue corridor leading back to the reception area and the offices. As they entered the reception area, the receptionist stood.

"Sit down, sit down," Zack said impatiently.

"Yes, Mister Lord." He watched them go into Zack's office.

"I didn't realize you were bringing your wife," Zack said, turning around to face Marc. "And I don't think what I do in my own apartment is anyone else's business. Besides, what the hell? People have a little fun? Who's it hurting?"

"We didn't come here to interfere with your party," said Marc. "None of us did. We're investigating the Wainwright case and I just wanted to ask you some questions."

"Okay, fine. But for Christ's sake, don't go throwing stones at someone's glass house if you live in one yourself."

"What's that mean?" asked Marc.

"Oh, come now. None of us are so pure as to be able to put down the next guy trying to make a score. If you get me? I mean you've been talking to Toni Wainwright, took her out a couple of times," Lord continued, plunging ahead blindly now. "Have I said anything to you?" He paused. "She had to apologize to you for making a pass at you, naked. Did I say anything to you?"

Maria stared at Marc now, a little unsure.

"I'm not responsible for what other people do," said Marc. "Only for what I myself do. And I've done nothing."

"So what the hell are you breaking . . . giving me a hard time here for?" said Zack. He knew he had struck home with Maria. "Some business guys from out of town, some friends come over for a little entertainment. If you don't dig it, fine, just leave it alone."

"Fair enough," said Marc. He felt rotten for Maria now; even though he knew he would easily be able to explain the situation later.

Maria was withdrawn, pensive. She seemed bemused by her fingernails. Franco stood back silently.

"What kind of questions you want to ask me?" Lord said, calming himself. He smiled a slight smile, feeling back in control now. He figured he had Marc where he wanted him: cowed and subservient.

"We've been checking out various things about the night Wainwright was killed," said Marc. "And there are some items which have made me very curious." Marc was abstracted, his mind on other things as he spoke.

"For instance?" said Lord.

"For instance, your plane didn't leave La Guardia until two-thirty on the morning Wainwright was killed. You left the party about twelve midnight to go to the airport. Wainwright was killed a little after one."

Zack stared at Marc. "Do you suspect that I might have had something to do with Wainwright's death?"

"I'm just chasing down all leads," said Marc. "It's an old habit of mine."

Maria remained silent. She seemed to have lost interest and was just waiting for this to be over.

Zack nodded his head slowly, a smile starting to crease his face. "I was told you were good. But I didn't realize that you were so good that you'd take this much trouble to investigate a case. You really suspect me?"

"Just chasing down the leads," Marc repeated.

"That's fascinating. Absolutely fascinating. And I'm absolutely delighted," said Lord.

"How come?" asked Marc.

Franco's eyes were angry. They never left Lord.

"Well, if you're doing that thorough a job, you'll give Toni the

268

best kind of representation. And that's exactly what I want for her." He sat behind his desk now. "But if I did have something to do with it, why would I have hired the best for her? Wouldn't I want her to take the blame?"

"Not necessarily," replied Marc. "This could all be part of a very carefully laid out plan. Commit a crime in such a way that another person is charged. Then have that other person beat the case, and in so doing, beat the case yourself. And in Toni Wainwright's case, earn the gratitude of one of your biggest stockholders."

"Fascinating," said Lord. "You can't imagine how delighted I am that Toni has all this going for her. I really mean that. I can explain about the plane, if you want."

"Certainly."

"Of course, your function is just to defend Toni Wainwright, not be finding the real killer, if there be one," added Lord. "Nor to go investigating a horrible accident into a murder."

"Sometimes it's one and the same," said Marc. "I just want to be careful and thorough."

"Great," said Lord, smiling broadly now. "That's what I want too."

A buzzer sounded. Lord picked up his phone. The receptionist said something to him.

"Will you excuse me for a moment," said Lord. "I have a call from Chicago coming in. It's rather urgent."

"Go ahead," said Marc.

Lord pushed a button on his phone and began to speak about some oil tankers still at sea and how much profit could be made if the entire cargo was sold to a different buyer and the ship rerouted before it even got to port.

Maria leaned very close to Marc. "What's he saying about Mrs. Wainwright? Tell me before I fall over and die right here," she whispered. She was close to tears.

"I saw the woman twice—strictly on business. Once Franco was there. Once he wasn't, but it was in a public bar."

"What about the naked scene. Is it true?"

"The woman is a drunk," Marc parried. "Ask Franco. She got so drunk both times, it was hardly possible to get her to make any sense."

Lord was still talking on the phone.

"You didn't answer me," Maria said.

"I dropped her home the second time. She insisted I drop her at her door."

"And, of course, you, being Sir Galahad, did it."

"Yes. She caused such a shrieking scene in the street, it was easier," said Marc.

"Go on."

"And while I'm questioning the maid—I'll show you my notes if you want—she gets undressed and lies down on the couch."

"Naked?" Maria asked.

"Yes."

"And? What then?"

"I told her I was old, married, and spoken for."

"I'm sure that made a hell of a lot of difference to her," Maria said sarcastically.

Lord sounded as if he were ending his conversation.

"No," said Marc. "So I dragged her to the bathroom and threw her bodily into a cold shower. She screamed so loud, I thought the dead would wake. Then I ran like hell, paid the elevator man ten bucks to get me out of there quick, and here I am. That's the truth, the whole truth, and nothing but the truth."

Lord hung up the phone and swiveled to face them again.

Maria reached for Marc's hand and held it tightly, warmly.

"Now, is there anything else that makes you think I had something to do with Wainwright's death?" Lord said smiling.

"Well, the plane is the main thing," said Marc. "The other things are relatively minor." Marc felt Maria's hand in his jiggle; she wanted his attention. Marc put his other hand over their intertwined hands, patting her hand assuringly. His attention was on Lord.

"You do quite a job." Lord nodded his head in admiration. "And I'm quite pleased. Now about the plane that night. I came home to change and was tired, I put my head down for a minute and I fell asleep. My pilot called me about, oh, about one-twenty, one-thirty. I got up, went downstairs, took a car to the airport, and we left at two-thirty. You can check with the pilot, with the doorman downstairs, whoever was on that night. I'm sure you'll find I'm telling the truth."

"I'll check," Marc assured him.

"Is there anything else?"

"Not right now," said Marc. "I don't want to keep you from the festivities inside."

"That's okay. Anything to help Toni out. I'm sorry for getting a little steamed before. It's just that . . . well, the boys are having a little harmless fun. I mean, who the hell gets hurt?" he said to Maria.

She said nothing, her face was serious and uncompromising.

"Tell me, Mister Lord," said Marc. "Do you keep tapes on all your telephone calls?"

Everyone looked at Marc with surprise, especially Lord.

"What makes you think I have calls taped?" said Lord.

"I know how carefully you operate. I'm sure of it," said Marc.

Zack smiled. "You really do fine work," he admired. "Really fine work. Perhaps my corporation could use an attorney as thorough as yourself."

"That sounds interesting. How about the tapes?"

"The job pays fifty thousand and expenses," said Lord.

"The tapes."

Zack smiled. "Let's just say I occasionally tape a conversation of my key executives on matters of vital business importance. There's nothing wrong with taping my own conversations, is there?"

"No, it's legal," replied Marc. "How about other people's conversations with other people. For instance, Toni Wainwright's phone calls with other people?"

Zack Lord studied Marc. The smile dimmed. "That would be illegal, wouldn't it, Marc?"

"It would."

"Well, I never get involved in illegal things. No, I don't bug anyone else's phone."

Marc nodded. "I guess that about covers it, then," he said.

"Fine," said Lord. "If you'll excuse me, I'll get back to my guests."

"Certainly," said Marc.

Lord rose and led the three of them from his office and rang for the elevator. He turned to the receptionist. "Would you be sure Mister and Mrs. Conte and their friend get on the elevator safely."

"Yes, Mister Lord." The young man rose and walked over to the elevator.

"See you," said Lord. "If you need anything else, please be sure to call me."

"Okay," said Marc.

Lord disappeared through the door leading to his living quarters. The elevator arrived.

"How come you didn't go into any of the other things?" asked Franco as they descended.

Marc nodded toward the elevator operator, and shook his head.

"Did you tell me the truth about this Wainwright woman?" Maria asked as they walked through the lobby.

Marc stopped. "Absolutely. And I love you," he said, kissing her boldly.

"Stop!" she said playfully, pulling away from his kiss. "You'll make everyone in the lobby jealous."

The three of them walked out and stood on the Fifth Avenue sidewalk in front of the hotel. There wasn't much traffic, and the avenue was quiet. The doorman stood silently near the door, reading a paper on his wall desk. Central Park looked limp.

"What was that about tapes all about?" asked Franco. "Where did you get that?"

"I just figured it out as we were talking," Marc replied. "I don't know if either of you agree, but I thought Lord's reaction to our conversation was somewhat strange."

"Strange?" asked Franco.

"Well, in the midst of it, for whatever reason, he mentions that he thinks I've been playing around with Toni Wainwright, his fiancée. What do you think about that?" Marc looked at the others. "Was there anything strange about it?"

Maria thought. Franco rubbed his chin.

"Strange about it," said Maria, "is that he never mentioned it before."

"That's right," said Franco. "He thought you were messing around with his girl, but never says nothing until he gets sore when we interrupt his fun and games over here. If it wasn't for that, he'd maybe never have mentioned the thing at all. Is that strange? Or do rich guys always act like that?"

"It's very strange," said Maria. "Except, of course, if he's just interested in her stock, and couldn't care less what she does."

"Which'd fall right in line with our theory," said Franco. He looked up the façade of the hotel.

"What's even more fascinating about that," said Marc, "is the fact that he knew about it at all. How did he find out?"

"She told him?" said Franco.

"Hardly likely," said Maria.

"One of the servants told him then," suggested Franco. "He could afford to have them all on his payroll spying for him."

"He was talking about a phone conversation. She called me at my office and apologized over the phone for being so drunk and all. He even said so. The servants might be able to tell him something they saw. But this was just a phone conversation he was talking about."

Franco's eyes narrowed as he thought.

"Another thing," said Maria. "Lord didn't even become offended when you mentioned that you might be suspecting him of killing Wainwright. He took it in stride and said it was fascinating. Is that the ordinary reaction to being accused of murder?"

Franco shook his head. "No. That isn't much reacting. If someone said that to me, I'd probably tell them they were out of their ever loving mind or something not so nice as that."

"Me too," said Marc.

"What do you make of it?" Maria asked, looking at Marc.

"I think Lord's got Toni Wainwright's phone bugged. That's how he found out about her apologizing. Now, couple that with the fact that he never said anything about it, and the fact that he took an accusation of murder so calmly, and to me it means that he's a little more involved in this investigation than just a mere outsider."

"That's what we've been telling you right along," said Maria triumphantly.

"I know, I know." Marc smiled.

"But how come you didn't go into the other stuff then?" asked Franco. "About the pistol, and the maid hearing the crying out. All that stuff."

"Because if he's involved, I don't want him to cover the tracks we haven't come across yet," said Marc. "Right now, he thinks the only thing we know is about the plane leaving late. He figures we're just dopes, and he can tolerate the information we have about the plane. I don't want to worry him with the other stuff."

Maria smiled and took Marc's arm. "I love you too," she said.

XXVII

TUESDAY, SEPTEMBER 12, 2:45 P.M.

Marc sat in the second row of seats in a courtroom this day designated Part 51. Mrs. Maricyk sat next to him. Judge Kahn was on the bench, in the process of sentencing a defendant who was standing with his lawyer before the Court.

Part 51 is a special, floating, sentencing part, the location of which varies each day according to which courtroom of 100 Centre Street is not being used in the afternoon of that day. To understand the reason for this, it must first be known that the judge before whom a defendant pleads guilty or who presides at a trial where the defendant is convicted, is the judge who passes sentence on that defendant. If that sentencing judge is no longer sitting in criminal term, having returned to the civil division, or is in some fashion engaged elsewhere than at 100 Centre Street, all the sentences the judge must impose are set down for one afternoon in Part 51.

"What's going to happen today?" asked Mrs. Maricyk.

"The Judge is going to sentence your husband," Marc replied.

"Is he going to put Joey away?"

"I don't know," Marc replied. "The Judge has the Probation Department's investigation and evaluation report . . ."

"Yeah, they came over the house asking questions and everything, the Probation people," she said.

". . . And, he relies on that a great deal," Marc finished.

"What's it say? You see it?"

"No, the Court doesn't let us see the report. It's just for the Judge to use as a guide," Marc explained.

Mrs. Maricyk looked questioningly at Marc. "Suppose they don't put the right thing down. How do you know what they say about my husband?"

"Unless the Judge shows it to me, I don't."

She began shaking her head. "I never seen any other place that works as screwed up as this one," she said. "You sure it's not just you?"

Marc felt a rush of anger. All this work on a not very interesting case and a not very high fee, if any, and now sarcasm, too. Marc looked at Mrs. Maricyk, about to tell her the plain facts of life. But there was that look, that helpless frustration. She was just frightened, he assured himself. "No, it's not me."

"Is this Judge going to give Joey time?" she asked again.

"I don't know. I've already explained that. I don't think he should, but that doesn't mean he won't."

Tears welled up in her confused eyes.

"Don't get upset now," said Marc, trying to console her. "You don't even know what's going to happen."

"I'm upset already. I don't want Joey in jail for no year. Don't let him go to jail, Mister Conte," she pleaded. "Oh, God, please don't let him go to jail, Mister Conte."

Marc wished there was some way to ease the hurt Mrs. Maricyk felt. He always wished he could ease the emotional torture attendant to a sentence. But there really wasn't much he could do except try to provide the best legal representation he could muster for the occasion.

"I'll do my best," Marc assured her. "I don't think there's any point for Joey to go to jail. His record is fairly good, his family situation is good. Let's see what the Judge has to say about it."

"Can't we appeal or something?"

"Yes, if you want, we can appeal the decision the Judge made at the hearing," said Marc. "We can even appeal the sentence if it's harsh. Let's see what happens here first."

Presently, the Maricyk case was called. Maricyk was brought out from the bull pen and stood to Marc's left as the clerk arraigned him for sentence.

"Mister Maricyk, is there any legal reason why sentence should not now be imposed upon you?" the clerk said.

Maricyk looked at Marc.

"No," Marc whispered.

"No."

"Do you wish to speak or do you want your lawyer to speak for you?"

"My lawyer can speak."

"Let me tell you this to save time," said the Judge. "The Probation Report shows the defendant to associate with undesirable people. His work record is spotty. They've suggested a year in jail. He was indicted on a class E felony where he could have gotten four years, but he was permitted to plead to a misdemeanor with the maximum sentence of a year. So he's way ahead of the game already, Counselor. I'm inclined, however, toward nine months. Now, knowing that, go ahead," the Judge nodded.

Marc knew now that Maricyk was headed to a jail sentence. So did Maricyk. He muttered a curse under his breath.

"Your Honor, I know you have a Probation Report before you," said Marc. "But I suggest that the information it contains is apparently incorrect. My client has informed me that his work record is not spotty, but rather he is employed in a seasonal line of work—swimming pool construction—and business presently— even during the summer—is somewhat slow because of general economic conditions. The defendant has been working for the same company for two years now—since he resigned from the Police Department."

"That's another thing," said the Judge. "We can't say your client didn't realize what he was doing. He's a former policeman. He knew fully what he was doing, and did it anyway. That doesn't speak well for him. Go ahead, anything else?"

"Yes, Your Honor," said Marc. "You have indicated an inclination to jail the defendant . . ."

"That's right."

"I do not, nor have I ever been able to comprehend the point or purpose of a jail sentence for a person in the defendant's position. In the first place, if jail is for the purpose of rehabilitating a defendant, to groom him for taking a useful place in society, which our penologists all say is the purpose of jail, then it should first be ascertained that the defendant is in need of rehabilitation. According to further penological studies, it has been found as an actual fact that more than sixty-five per cent of those who commit their first crime will never commit another crime in their life, regardless of sentence, whether you sentence them to one day or one year or even ten years in jail. In other words, there's a self-rehabilitation factor, an awakening, that occurs in almost two thirds of people accused of committing a crime.

"The other thirty-five per cent," Marc continued, "no matter what sentence the courts impose, will commit a crime—regardless of how much time they spend in jail—the moment they're released they'll stick up the taxi driver on the way home. These last are the incorrigibles."

The Judge was listening patiently.

"Now to put the defendant in the least complimentary light, let me say that we don't know what this defendant will do in the future, Your Honor. Yet, if, in fact, he is one of those sixty-five per cent who will never commit another crime, then he's already rehabilitated and jail will serve no useful purpose. There's no need for vindication or denunciation by the People. That's been done. The man has a record now, he's branded for life. Since he has no background of violence; since this is not a crime of violence, he'll be no danger to the community if he's in the street. Therefore, I respectfully suggest he should be put on probation and permitted to continue his role in society.

"We shouldn't assume that this defendant belongs in the other category, in the incorrigible category. For, indeed, he does not. He has never committed one crime before, much less two. I imagine one could speculate about a defendant in this position and say he'll probably become an incorrigible. But that's just guess work, speculation. I can't say accurately, and most respectfully, Judge, neither can you. No one can. He's never been in this kind of trouble before. He has no track record to look at.

"If you *do* give him a chance on probation, however, Your Honor, no matter which category he fits in, there's no danger to the community. First of all, as I've said, the defendant's not charged with a crime of violence. Second, if he's on probation, the minute he steps across the line, even a fraction of an inch, you can always revoke his probation and send him to jail both for this

crime and whatever else he might have done. You will—so to say
—still have your hooks in the defendant if he doesn't live up to
the confidence that you would display by putting him on probation. Thus, it seems pointless, Your Honor, to send this defendant
to jail when he may have already learned his lesson completely,
when he may now, as a result of this experience, be ready to assume a useful, gainful role in society. If we do not know the true
answer, Your Honor, if we are to make a decision, let us lean to
the side of mercy, on the side of lenience. You can always correct
any mistakes by revoking probation. You can't give him the time
back."

"Every lawyer comes up here and says don't send my client to
jail, Mister Conte. We might as well not send anybody to jail
then," said the Judge.

"Perhaps we should not indeed, Your Honor," said Marc. "Except for the most hardened criminals, whose propensities for violence and criminality are already manifest. We should overcome
those archaic concepts that jails are absolutely necessary in dealing with all criminal matters. A man who fails to file income tax
is a cheat. He can be branded with a record, officially, declared a
cheat, but is jail necessary? A man in the position of my defendant—an alleged bribe on a traffic ticket—where is jail required?
He has injured no one physically. The community is not endangered by his presence. Yes, there was a crime. Is society not sufficiently interested in one of its citizens to see if perhaps the man
has learned his lesson without jail?

"I pose this question," Marc continued strongly, his voice full,
"why jail? To what end? For what purpose? If in fact the defendant falls within that category of people who will never commit
another crime, then what purpose is or shall be served by jail?"

"If what you say is so about those studies," said the Judge,
"perhaps your client is in the thirty-five per cent category."

"Does Your Honor suggest we needlessly send two men to jail
who shouldn't be there along with every one man who should be
there? Is that just, reasonable, or fair?"

The Judge shook his head. "He's got to do some time. He's got
a break on his plea already. You want me to give him a medal?"

"That's not necessary, Your Honor," said Marc. "I just want
you to treat the defendant with fairness, with reason . . ."

"You've used that word twice. Are you saying that I'm unreasonable?" the Judge asked with annoyance.

"No, sir. Our system of sentencing, however, is unfair and unrealistic. We are not dealing with children, Your Honor," said Marc. "When a parent reprimands a child, the purpose is to teach him the mores and morals of life. And so it is with the Court. Your purpose, is first to protect society, if such seems necessary, and second to help rehabilitate the defendant. In this case, society is not endangered by this defendant. So then the obligation of this Court is to aid the defendant in becoming again a law-abiding, useful part of society. But when a defendant does not need further rehabilitation than the stigma and humiliation of being a known criminal, then what is the proper function of the Court? Should the defendant be sent to jail, merely because we have jails? Because we have to maintain a prison system? Is there some personal benefit that you get as a judge when the defendant goes to jail? Your Honor?"

"Are you seriously posing that question? Do you think I am personally benefiting from the defendant going to jail?" The Judge was outraged.

"No, I wasn't asking the question seriously, Judge. Not as far as your personal benefit is concerned. But, if you're not getting a benefit, and I'm not getting a benefit, and the clerk here isn't either, nor is anyone else individually, if the individuals in society aren't gaining a benefit from the defendant being sent to jail, then society collectively isn't gaining a benefit either.

"Judge, I ask you this," Marc continued. "If this man will never commit another crime in his life, although he is branded for the rest of his life with a criminal record, if he is ready to toe the mark in life, be a useful, gainfully employed citizen, will you still send him to jail?"

"I've already said he had to do some time, Mister Conte."

"Is there something that I don't see that is compelling a jail sentence, Judge?"

"We have professionals working in our Probation Department, Mister Conte," said the Judge. "And they know as much—maybe more—as your scientists and penologists sitting in their laboratories. The Probation Department is getting paid to work on these reports in aid of the Court. They've recommended one year in this case. Now I'm sure they're not out trying to hurt this defendant. They're doing their job, they're trained, they know the penal system too, you know. And now I have to do my job. Do you have anything else to say?"

"Would anything I say cause you to change your mind, Judge?" asked Marc.

"No. I have to do a job and I'll do it."

"I have nothing further to say except that a system that blindly sends people to jail whether there is a reason for it or not, whether there is a benefit to be gained, a purpose to achieve, or not, is a system that is ludicrous and archaic. It must be updated and made to function in some useful, beneficial fashion, or it will cause its own destruction and do grave harm to both society and many helpless victims caught in its web."

"You've made your record, Mister Conte. Nine months in the custody of the Department of Correction," said the Judge. "Have you advised your client of his right to appeal, Counselor?"

"I have."

The stenographer was recording all that was said on his stenotype machine.

"Very well," said the Judge. "Next case."

"Your Honor, before we do that," said Marc, "I'd like to make an application to have bail set for the defendant Maricyk pending appeal."

The Judge looked at Marc, his brow furrowed, then he looked at the clerk. "Come up, come up," said the Judge, waving the clerk, Marc, and the assistant D.A. to the bench. They all huddled at the edge of the bench. "What's the point of setting bail?" the Judge asked. "Your man's been in jail all this time. He didn't make bail on the case."

"I just want to have it set in the event that his wife may be able to raise bail for him, Your Honor," replied Marc.

"Can I do that?" the Judge asked the clerk.

"The People aren't going to consent to bail, Your Honor," said the D.A.

"That D.A.'s consent isn't really necessary," said Marc. "The Court has inherent power to set bail with or without consent. However, I ask the Court to inquire of the District Attorney if there is some significant reason that he refuses to consent to the setting of a reasonable bail for this defendant?"

"The People are just not consenting to bail, that's all," said the D.A. He was young and had a thin, unsmiling face. "Your man was sentenced and we feel he should start his sentence."

"You don't know anything about this case," said Marc, still facing the Judge. "In due deference to you, you're just covering the Part for the day in case there are any problems. Supposing we appeal, and the defendant is victorious. Are you going to make up the time he has to spend in jail because of your whim about bail?"

The D.A. gave Marc an impatient look. "We don't have to justify ourselves to defense counsel."

"How about to the court and on the record?" Marc asked.

The clerk had taken a law book from the judge's bench and was thumbing through the pages.

"Gentlemen, there's no need for this," said the Judge. "I don't know if I can do it, but since bail has been set all along and the defendant hasn't been able to make it anyway, I'm inclined to set a bail." He looked at the D.A., moving his head in a "what-the-hell" motion.

"Here it is, Judge. Section 480.60," said the clerk, putting the law book in front of the Judge.

The Judge read the section silently, his finger coursing and recoursing under the words, his eye following carefully. "This indicates that the application for bail must be made after a Notice of Appeal is served," he said. "Have you already served your Notice of Appeal?"

"How could I have done that, Judge? You just sentenced the defendant a minute ago," said Marc.

"I don't think I can set bail without the notice being filed," said the Judge, reading the statute again.

"You can set the bail contingent upon the service of a Notice of Appeal this afternoon," said Marc.

The Judge looked doubtful. "No, the statute says it must be served first."

"I'll make it up by hand right here, Judge," said Marc. "It won't be fancy, but it'll be correct."

"I think that the motion has to be made in Part 31, Your Honor," said the clerk.

"And it has to be on paper," said the D.A. "We won't go along with an oral application."

"Judge, the section neither requires an application to be made in Part 31 or that it be written," said Marc. "The section says merely that a Supreme Court—any Supreme Court Judge—or an Appellate Division Judge can set the bail pending appeal. I can make up a Notice of Appeal right here and now, and then I'd like you to set bail. Why should I make another trip, type up formal papers, waste another court's time on a matter you can resolve in the next thirty seconds?"

"What about this Part 31?" the Judge asked the clerk.

"These applications are usually sent there, Judge," said the clerk. "That's the way we do it in this county."

The Judge looked at Marc, shrugging. "That's the procedure then. You'll have to go to Part 31."

"And make the application on paper," said the D.A.

"And I guess you should make it on paper while you're at it," added the Judge.

"You know, Judge," Marc said quietly. The other three men listened as they were still huddled at the bench. "An application like this may be just procedure to us. And a delay while the motion papers are drawn, or sent to this Part or another Part or processed, may just be a convenience, an attempt at keeping things neat and orderly. But the lives of defendants are being wasted in rotten jails while we split hairs. That's why we have riots on our hands."

The D.A. frowned and turned away, walking to his table.

"You must be making quite a fee on this one, Counselor," said the clerk.

"Why do you say that?" asked Marc.

"Why else would you bother breaking your balls so much for a client except you're getting a good fee?"

"A little jail won't hurt any of them, Mister Conte," said the Judge, smiling indulgently. "So, it'll take a couple of days and then you get the bail set. Come on, let's go. I have some other sentences."

"Let me just say this in answer to the clerk's question, Judge," said Marc. "As long as there's something I can do for my clients, I'll do it, paid or not, because their lives are in my hands and I take that responsibility seriously. You, Mister Clerk, you call cases on the calendar. Judge, you dispose of cases, sentence people. The D.A. whether he wins or loses, he represents a book, a statute, a piece of paper. I'm the only one here who personally deals with human beings, and they deal with me personally, and cry on my shoulder, and get angry with me, and hope that I can help them. And by God, I'm ready to go right into the dragon's mouth and pull out his tonsils by hand if I have to. Otherwise, I shouldn't be representing people."

"How can you make a living that way?" said the Judge.

Marc just looked at the Judge, then the clerk. "It's a lot of honest-to-God work, Judge. I'll have the papers in this case filed this afternoon," he said. As Marc walked back to the counsel table, he saw Mrs. Maricyk sitting on the edge of her bench in the audience.

"Don't worry about it, Counselor," said Maricyk. "I know you're fighting for me. Talk to the wife, will you."

A court officer accompanied Maricyk back to the bull pen.

Mrs. Maricyk was shaking her head. She looked stunned as they walked to the elevator.

"Don't get too upset," said Marc. "With time off for good behavior, he'll only have to do six months. He's already served a month, so he'll be out in five months."

"Yeah, well I guess you can look at it that way," said Mrs. Maricyk. "But five months is five months, no matter how you look at it." Tears were rolling down her cheeks. Marc felt rotten that there was no way he could console her.

As they waited for the elevators, Liam O'Connor was walking through the corridor toward the courtrooms.

"Hey, Marc," called O'Connor with an unusual warmth.

"Hello," replied Marc.

"Can I talk to you for a minute?"

"Excuse me," Marc said to Mrs. Maricyk. He walked a short distance away with O'Connor.

"I understand you're up for a judgeship," said O'Connor. He was smiling pleasantly. O'Connor knew enough to become friendly with a prospective judge, even if the prospect was Marc.

"I've just been to the first committee," replied Marc. "I don't know what's going to happen with it. How do you know about it, anyway?"

"News like that travels around here," said O'Connor. "You'll have to take a fantastic cut in income on the bench. And it's a lot of headaches these days. Why would you want a job like that, Marc?"

"I just went for the interview," Marc replied. "I don't think I'll even come close. So I won't have to worry about it."

"Who knows. Good luck, anyway," O'Connor said.

"Thanks. How are your Tombs riot cases coming along?" Marc asked, to be friendly.

"Just finishing up the preliminary motions. We should be on trial in a few days. Probably start the suppression hearing by this Friday."

"You trying them yourself?"

"The first one, anyway." O'Connor nodded.

"Take it easy and thanks again," said Marc, as the down elevator arrived. It was empty.

"You bet, your honor," said O'Connor, grinning.

Marc walked with Mrs. Maricyk through the marble lobby. He was headed back to his office. Outside the building, a long line of people were demonstrating on the sidewalk in front of the building.

"Free all political prisoners. Free all political prisoners," chanted the demonstrators on the sidewalk. They were carrying signs protesting The Tombs trials.

"You know," said Mrs. Maricyk, "maybe these hippies know what the hell they're talking about after all."

Marc didn't think it was the time to get into a philosophical discussion with Mrs. Maricyk. He said nothing.

"Hello, Counselor," said Philly, The Crusher's portly sidekick. He was standing at the edge of the three steps leading down to the sidewalk.

"Hello," said Marc. "You waiting for me?"

"Nah, I just waiting for a friend of mine and Patsy's. He's got a case on today over here."

Marc nodded.

"Mister Conte, I'm going to go," said Mrs. Maricyk. "I can't stand it here another minute."

Marc knew there was nothing more he could do. "Okay. Call me if you need me."

"God forbid," she said. "I mean about needing you. I know you did everything you could." She turned and left hurriedly.

Marc stood at the edge of the steps, watching Mrs. Maricyk disappear into the faceless crowd of demonstrators and pedestrians.

"Look at these punks," said Philly, nodding his square head toward the demonstrators.

Marc became aware of Philly again.

"They're only exercising freedom of speech," he said.

"Is this Freedom of Speech written the same place as the Fifth Amendment?"

"Yes, the Bill of Rights," replied Marc.

"How come it's got more respect than when someone takes the Fifth and doesn't want to be incriminated? Nobody says these punks are committing a crime and they're real punks, aren't they? Anti-American, and all? How come it's a crime to take the Fifth?"

"It's not," replied Marc. "It just seems that way."

They continued to watch the demonstrators move in their slow circle.

Marc thought how small he felt sometimes when he ran headlong into a situation which could not be turned completely to his client's favor. But then he, as the cancer surgeon, had to do the best he could with the situation before him. And that, Marc assured himself, he always did.

"Hi," said Andy Roberts, the pretty young girl who Marc usually saw with The Tombs riot demonstrators. She was carrying a sign which bore the legend: POWER CAN NOT BE DENIED THE PEOPLE: FREE AL-KOBAR. "Remember me? Andy Roberts?"

"Yes, sure," said Marc, his thoughts coming back to the present. "How've you been?"

"Fine." She flashed that bright smile of hers. "I see you're still fighting the good fight," she said. "I saw you in court the other day."

Philly watched them speak, his hands stuffed in his pockets. His eyes were narrowed as he watched Andy carefully.

"I see you're still fighting too," said Marc.

She smiled again and nodded. "I don't want to keep you. Stay

285

cool," she said as she gave Marc a salute with a raised clenched fist. Marc waved as Andy took her place back in the line.

"You got all kinds of friends," Philly said flatly.

"Let's say I talk to all kinds of people," said Marc. "See you, Philly. Say hello to Patsy."

Philly nodded as Marc made his way toward the office.

XXVIII

WEDNESDAY, SEPTEMBER 13, 3:30 P.M.

The phone on George Tishler's desk rang. Without turning from the report he was reading, George reached for the phone and put it to his ear.

"Tishler," he said.

"Mister Tishler, this is Janie," said one of the Mayor's secretaries. "The Mayor asked if you could take a call from Eric Portlac of the *Daily News*. The Mayor said he'd get on the wire in a couple of minutes."

"Portlac?" said George, putting his report down on the desk. "What line is he on?"

Eric Portlac was a political columnist for the New York *Daily News*, as well as the elder statesman of the New York City political scene. He carried a lot of clout in his typewriter.

"Six-eight," Janie answered.

George pushed a button on the phone. "Hello, Eric."

"Hello, Georgie. How's everything?"

George hated being called Georgie; but if it kept Eric Portlac happy, it was a worthwhile sacrifice.

"Fine. Everything's great," George said enthusiastically.

"I'll tell you why I'm calling, George. It's in reference to some judicial appointments the Mayor is considering making before the end of the present term. I really wanted to check it out with the Mayor personally."

"He'll be on in a couple of minutes, Eric," said George. "He's got something very hot he was right in the middle of."

"That sounds dirty, George. I hope she's got big tits." Portlac laughed.

George laughed tolerantly. "Maybe I can help meanwhile," he said as cheerily as possible.

"I don't think so, George. I'll wait to talk to the Mayor. Perhaps you can fill me in on some details while I wait though."

"I'll try."

"You have a fellow going through the mill now, a fellow by the name of Marc Conte," said Portlac. "Are you really serious about his being a judge?"

"Yes, of course. What's the trouble?" George wondered to himself why Portlac would be interested in, even know about, Marc.

"Do you know the kind of background he has in the law, the kind of people he's been representing?"

"To our knowledge," said George, playing it very straight, "he's represented a great variety of people on a great variety of criminal charges. His broad base of actual experience might be a fairly good addition to the Criminal Court bench."

"Did you know that included in the great variety of people are plenty of hoods. He's representing big Mafia boys."

"Isn't everybody entitled to a good defense lawyer?" asked George.

"If you really want my opinion, I'd say no. Not the way some of these bums get away with murder. And I mean that literally. And here you have one of their mouthpieces being considered for a spot on the bench. Don't you think that's just playing right into the hands of organized crime?"

"You saying this man is corrupt, Eric?"

"I'm saying he'd be a perfect target for their fixes and everything."

"Let me just ask you this," said George. "Why the particular interest in Marc Conte? There are so many candidates going through the interviews at the moment."

"I just got wind of what was going on down there, and I wanted to check out if you were serious. I'll have to run some articles on this sort of thing if you are. I mean, I find it a little incredible, in today's world, to be proposing someone like this Conte guy for a judgeship."

"Do you have some hard facts, some particular information that he's venal, corrupt, or that he'll fall easy prey to the syndicate? Do you have some facts to show he lacks integrity?"

"No, nothing like that, George. It's just the people he represents. I mean, how could he transcend the element on which he's apparently cut his eyeteeth?"

"Our information and knowledge has it that he's apparently cut his eyeteeth, as you say, learning everything a lawyer's supposed to know to protect someone's rights in a criminal law proceeding. That's just the kind of knowledge a good Criminal Court Judge should know."

"There's another thing a Criminal Court Judge should know, George, and that's discretion. You know what I mean, when to pull the plug, when to go to his left. For Christ's sake, suppose this guy is sitting on the bench and he gets some big racket guy in front of him. What's he going to do? And whatever he does," Portlac said, answering his own question, "the newspaper people—including myself—I have to be honest with you—will have a field day on the Mayor's head."

"Have you ever met this guy Conte?" George asked. "I mean, do you know him personally? Do you have a good source of information on this and not just some scuttlebutt?"

"I've never met the guy, no. But I have my sources of information. You know I can't tell you who they are. But they're reliable, very reliable. I've heard he's a good lawyer. I'll admit that part's true. But, let's face it, he's too close to the fire to come away without being singed, if you know what I mean?"

"The difficulty with picking judicial candidates according to what you're saying, Eric, is that we'd never be able to tap the vast source of raw material in the private sector of criminal law. After all, there are only two sides to a criminal case, prosecution and defense. The only people from the private sector of criminal law are the lawyers who've defended criminals."

"Nobody said anything about not being able to use defense counsel talent, George. You're not reading me right."

"That's what I thought you were saying," said George. "That this Conte fellow is too practiced in defending criminals to be fair and impartial on the bench. Doesn't a former D.A. have the same problem in reverse?"

"Is the Mayor going to be much longer?" Portlac asked impatiently.

"Let me just check," said George. He buzzed the Mayor's office.

"Yes?" asked Janie.

"Portlac wants to talk to the Mayor. Is he free yet?"

"Yes, he's just come back from the powder room. Is Portlac still on six-eight?"

"Yes," said George.

"I'll get the Mayor on the wire."

George pressed the button on his phone again. "Hello, Eric. The Mayor's going to get on in a second."

"Fine, George. I just think . . ."

"Hello, Eric," the Mayor cut in with a jovial air.

"Hi, Scottie," said Portlac. "Just wanted a rundown on some of your judicial candidates."

"Sure, Eric. How the hell have you been? I'll take it now, George," the Mayor said.

George took the phone from his ear and set the receiver on its cradle. He swiveled his chair and looked out the window. Dark rain clouds were hovering over the Tweed Courthouse behind City Hall. A long time ago, the building had been used as the New York County Supreme Court Building, but was now just office space for the Mayor's administrative assistants. It was called the Tweed Courthouse because it was built during the time Boss Tweed was head of Tammany Hall, and several big politicos of the day went to jail because of the graft that was squeezed out of the building contractors.

As George studied the cloud formations, he thought how difficult, how frustrating it was to get any damn thing done in political life. Every point of view had a variant, an opposite, a reaction, a proponent, an opponent, a thesis, an antithesis. There wasn't anything you could propose that wouldn't almost instantly give rise to an entire new faction of opposition. Just because everyone's entitled to have an opinion doesn't mean they actually have one, he thought. But propose anything, anything, and people will start making noise just to have something to do, something to say. Now, someone was apparently putting a bug in Portlac's ear about judicial candidates, and from what side of the prosecutor's table a good judge ought to come. And the someone particularly didn't want Marc Conte on the bench. George was angry.

The buzzer on George Tishler's desk interrupted his thoughts. He picked up his phone. "Yes, Janie."

"How did you know it was me?"

"Oh, I don't know," replied George. "Just guessed."

"The Mayor wants you to come in."

"Okay." George grabbed for his jacket and made his way through a narrow back passageway, directly to the Mayor's office. The Mayor was seated at his desk, signing some letters.

"You wanted to see me, Mayor," said George, knowing full well why the Mayor had called.

"Yes, George," said Mayor Davies, looking up. He appeared rather tired, his face was drawn around the eyes. The campaign was starting to move a bit more quickly now, and that meant breakfast meetings, lunch meetings, cocktail meetings, before- and after-dinner meetings; and sandwiched in was the work of running New York City; and somewhere around those tasks and duties, were public showings and speeches and smiles and eating pizza and knishes and strudel. The Mayor's patience was usually a bit thin around campaign time. George figured maybe it was all the lousy things he had to eat.

"What the hell is Portlac talking about?" asked the Mayor curtly. "We have a judicial candidate who's connected with the syndicate, with the racket boys?"

"No, Mayor. We have a fine lawyer, a fellow named Conte. You remember, you wanted to get an Italian through the committees so we could satisfy Tucci in Brooklyn; you said you needed Tucci to carry Brooklyn."

"We still need Tucci—that fat little bastard! He has Brooklyn in his pocket, and we have to go catering to his little whims and fancies. Sometimes, George, this political life is a pain. Everybody's in your ear, looking over your shoulder, up your ass. Sometimes, I don't think it's worth it." The Mayor stopped, meditating silently. He shook his head. "But, what the hell would this city be like if they got a bastard like Dworkin as Mayor? This place'd be so filled with goddamn clubhouse loafers, they'd be coming out the windows." The Mayor frowned. "But, what's this Portlac was saying about this lawyer, Cantor . . ." the Mayor tried to think of the name. He snapped his fingers. "Hell, that's Jewish. What's his name, this racket guy?"

"Portlac was talking about Marc Conte, Mayor. He's an excellent criminal lawyer and a man of the highest integrity. I know him very well, and can personally vouch for him. In fact, he's the one we had looking undercover into the Criminal Court problem. Remember?"

"Undercover agents in the Criminal Court?" the Mayor wondered vaguely.

"Yes, after the riots, remember, you wanted someone to check into what was happening in the courts that was causing the problems."

"Right, right. This is the same fellow?"

"That's right, Mayor," replied George. "We've been getting some valuable information from him."

"Mmm." The Mayor thought. "Maybe it'd be better if you told this fellow to forget about working undercover for us," he said. "He may be an excellent man and all that, George, but we don't need any bad press right now. We have enough of it, goddamn it, without going out and waving a red flag."

"Mayor, can I say something?"

"Sure, George."

"I think this call from Portlac is a crock of shit, to use the vernacular. This fellow Conte is a top-notch guy. You know Portlac is Mister Conservative. If it were up to him he'd have all prosecutors on the bench and at counsel table and in the jury box. Someone is juicing him up about Conte for some reason."

"George, you and I both know that sometimes Portlac is a perfect horse's ass. And maybe somebody is putting a bug in his ear. And maybe it's not true about this lawyer. But Portlac writes a pretty effective column. Let me ask you a question, George?"

"Sure, Mayor."

"Do we need any more rocks thrown at us than we already have coming through the windows now?"

"No, Mayor."

"Well, that's where it's at with this lawyer, George. You know as well as I do, in this political whore's game, you not only have to *be* honest, you have to give the *appearance* of being honest. If you ask me which is the more important quality, I'd probably have to go along with the appearance of being honest as more important. Same thing with this lawyer, this . . . whatever the hell this candidate for a judge's name is . . ." The Mayor began absently to snap his fingers again.

"Conte," George supplied.

"Same thing with this Conte. He not only has to actually be straight, honest, without blemish, but he has to appear that way. And in his case, with a guy like Portlac throwing rocks at him, I'll tell you definitely, it's appearances that are more important."

"It'd be a shame to lose such a good man, Mayor."

"Hey, George," said the Mayor, smiling wryly now. "It'd be even more of a shame to lose such a good job." He glanced around his office.

"I guess you're right, Mayor." George smiled. "But one judicial appointment surely isn't going to make or break your campaign."

"Probably not, George," agreed the Mayor. "But who knows? We have to measure everything by the formula that we eliminate every sore point we can. There are enough sore points we can't do anything about. I'm sure there are plenty of lawyers we can put on the bench who won't have *any* problems attached to them, George."

"Not with this man's experience, Mayor. A lawyer can't get experience as a criminal lawyer without representing criminals."

"Then we have to look for someone whose experience won't overqualify him, if you know what I mean, George."

"Okay, Mayor," George said reluctantly.

"Look, George, put it this way. This guy may be a nice guy, a terrific lawyer, wrote all the law books. But, if we have two candidates, both qualified, one who'll get us some bad publicity— even if it ultimately amounts to nothing—and one who's going to give us no bad publicity at all, which one do we pick?"

"The one with no bad publicity at all," said George.

"Of course. We don't need false rumors, true rumors, bad rumors, any kind of rumors, George. Politically it's not worth taking a kicking around because a guy has some problems. We don't need his problems. We have enough of our own."

"Why don't we just let this candidate go through the rest of the committees anyway, Mayor. The committees may say this fellow is so qualified that it'll overcome Portlac's opposition."

"Let him go through if you want," said the Mayor. "It can't hurt to have him going through the committees . . . I don't think," he said pensively now.

"How could going through committees hurt, Mayor?"

"I don't know. I can't imagine why we're getting flack on this lawyer to begin with. Just think what'd happen if we appointed him."

"Shall I let him go through the committees anyway, Mayor?"

The Mayor thought for a moment. "Well, if we don't get any more grief on him, it's all right, George. But any more bad press on him at this stage, and that's the end of it."

XXIX

THURSDAY, SEPTEMBER 14, 9:40 A.M.

A long line of people, three deep, queued up outside Part 37. The corridor was hot and stuffy, despite all the windows being open. It was hot Indian summer weather again. Police-type wooden barriers had been erected in the corridor to keep the spectators waiting to see The Tombs riot trial in line. A squad of regular city police had been stationed there for crowd control and security. People of all races and sexes made up the crowd, but mostly they were young and dressed in jeans and workshirts. While waiting, the spectators were idly chatting about racial issues and the unfairness of the trial. The word "Pig" was muttered often, particularly when one of the policemen came near. The policemen, as they had been ordered to do, ignored the insults, just staring past the mutterers.

"When are we getting into the courtroom?" shouted one of the young people defiantly.

"Court opens at ten o'clock," announced the police sergeant in charge. He was standing near the entrance to the courtroom.

"They don't want us to go in there," goaded someone in the crowd.

"Let them try to keep us out," shouted another defiantly, stirring the crowd.

"Yeah," shouted many of them in reply. There were murmurs and general discontent.

"Right on," shouted others.

The murmurs grew louder.

"Keep it down," advised the sergeant. "There are other courts in this building, other people working."

"Fascist pigs, enslaving the people in this building, that's what they're doing."

"Right on, brother."

The policemen kept patrolling the length of the line on the outside of the wooden barrier.

Many in the waiting crowd were seated on the floor, propping themselves against the wall. There was continuous excited conversation.

"Keep it quiet," said the sergeant, looking down the long line of waiting spectators.

"Open the doors then!"

"What are they trying to do, railroad our brothers?"

"Yeah, how come you're not opening the doors?" shouted a few almost simultaneously.

"Open the doors. Open the doors. Open the doors," a chant began. The crowd was becoming restive.

The police prepared for trouble.

"Stand easy, men," the sergeant cautioned.

The police stood their ground, their night sticks at the ready if a commotion broke out. The crowd was stirring and making more noise.

"All right, keep it down," called the sergeant, now using the bull horn which he had kept in the telephone booth he commandeered as a temporary headquarters. "Keep it down, or nobody's getting in," said the sergeant flatly.

"Trying to railroad our brothers," repeated one of the protesters. "They're trying to stifle our voices."

"Never again."

There was cheering and shouts of encouragement.

"We'll let you in when you calm down," said the sergeant. "Not a minute before. So if you want to get inside you better knock it off."

"Come on, let's keep it down, so we can get in there and help our brothers," a woman pleaded.

"They're trying to keep us out," shouted a disbeliever.

"Let's see what happens. Let's cool it."

"We no fools."

Loud cheers of agreement.

"Nobody gets in until everybody is orderly," the sergeant announced over the crowd. His men still stood at the ready, facing the crowds, their bodies tense with the possibility of action.

The faces of those in the crowd were angry, defiant. There was still much muttering and cursing, and an occasional shout, but the crowd started to quiet.

"That's it," the sergeant encouraged the crowd. He didn't have to use the bull horn now. "That's fine. It's almost time for court. You'll get in shortly. I just want to advise you of one other thing," he added. "Anyone who carries on inside the courtroom is going to be removed."

"Fascist pig."

A supportive roar from the crowd.

"No outbursts like that," the sergeant said, not even ruffled by the insults. He had been hand-picked to head the police detail on his ability to remain calm in the face of provocation. "Any outbursts in the court and we're going to take you right out of there. Remember that. I won't take anyone out unless he disrupts the proceedings. If you want your friends to have a fair trial, then you better keep quiet while you're in there so the jury, the judge, and everybody else can hear."

"Fair trial. How can pigs give someone a fair trial?"

"Yeah. Yeah."

"Okay, let's knock it off," said the sergeant tolerantly. "Another thing. Not everybody on line is going to be able to get a seat. There's only so much room in there."

The crowd started to shift and move toward the door. There was pushing and complaining.

"Take it easy. Nobody's going to get in any faster," said the sergeant. "Just stay in place. We're going to open the door in a couple of minutes. So let's just keep it calm."

"Come on, you pig, open the door."

"Okay, knock it off, or nobody gets in."

A side door near the courtroom entrance opened. There were some excited shouts at the opening of the door, which faded to a hiss of disgust as a policeman came out, closing the door behind him.

"Sergeant, the Judge wants to see you," said the emerging policeman.

"Okay, Murphy," the sergeant called to another policeman. "Take over and keep them calm. And you be sure to keep calm too," he added softly.

"Right, Sarge."

The sergeant walked to the side door and opened it. Inside, a cop was leaning against the wall, looking down at the floor, smoking. He was standing on one foot, the other braced against the wall. When he saw it was the sergeant, the cop stood straight, dropping the cigarette.

"Just stand easy, but keep alert," said the sergeant. "If one of those little creeps comes running in here, you're going to have to move fast."

"Right, Sarge." The cop retrieved the cigarette from the floor.

The sergeant moved toward the back. The corridor bent to the left, then right, ending at another door. A second policeman was posted there. He was gazing out the window at the demonstrators bathed in sunlight in the street below. He turned when he heard the sergeant, then stood to the side sharply.

The sergeant knocked on the door of the judge's robing room.

The robing room was a small, light green office just to the side of the courtroom. Inside was a scarred desk, a chair, a telephone, and two other doors, one to a washroom, the other to the courtroom. Judge Crawford, in his robes, was standing at the window, looking down into the street. His law assistant was standing with him.

"You wanted to see me, Your Honor?" said the sergeant.

The Judge turned. "Oh yes, Sergeant. I just wanted to be sure we were going to have enough men for security and order here today. Looks and sounds like a large crowd."

"Yes, sir. I have twenty men up here. There are many more stationed in the stairwell, and more behind the building. We didn't want to be too visible."

"That's fine. That's fine," said the Judge. "Now, if there's a disturbance, I'm going to order the court cleared. Your men can wade in and help out the court officers."

"Yes, sir. I'll have two of my men posted at the rear of the courtroom. If there's any problem, one of them will come right out to me, and I'll come right in with my men."

"Very well. I have ten court officers in addition, so there should be no difficulties. Shall we get going then?" Judge Crawford turned to his law assistant and to the clerk of the court who had just entered the robing room from the court.

The sergeant nodded and returned to the door leading to the corridors and the crowd. As the sergeant opened the door to the main corridor, he could hear the voice of the crowd rise and murmur. When he emerged, the crowd moaned and cursed their displeasure.

"What's the excuse now, Sergeant Pig?"

One of the officers inside the courtroom unlocked the courtroom entrance doors. There was a loud cheer and general movement toward the door as the crowd jockeyed for position.

"Just stay in line," called the sergeant. "Keep it quiet and stay in line."

A policeman stood on either side of the door just inside the courtroom, watching silently as the crowd filed in. Once inside, there was a rapid scurrying for seats, and within a minute or two at the most, the courtroom was filled with a capacity audience. The air was alive with a holiday-like enthusiasm, the spectators socialized and chatted with each other.

Shortly, a court officer slapped his hand against the door leading from the judge's robing room. "All rise," he called.

The Judge entered, moving quickly up to his bench. He ignored those who refused to rise, as well as the boos that greeted him. He remained standing next to his chair.

"Hear ye, hear ye," announced a court officer, "all people having business with Part 37 of the Supreme Court, New York County, draw near, give your attention, and you shall be heard. The Honorable James J. Crawford presiding."

"Power to the People."

The Judge, now seated, pounded lightly on the top of the bench. "There will be no outbursts from the audience during these proceedings," he said, looking at the spectators. "If we have any disturbances, I'll have no choice but to clear the courtroom."

The crowd murmured and grumbled.

The Judge rapped on the bench again. The crowd became relatively silent.

There were two long tables with many chairs set against the outside of the rail separating the audience from the well of the courtroom. These were marked RESERVED FOR THE PRESS. Some reporters were already seated at these tables. Others now entered the courtroom and took seats. Some of the news media people were well known from appearances on television. Some were staff reporters for newspapers or wire services. Others were bearded, casually dressed reporters, apparently from underground publications.

"Bring out the prisoners," said the Judge.

Three court officers went into the bull pen through a doorway leading from the side of the courtroom. In a few minutes, they emerged with Oscar Johnson, a/k/a Ali Al-Kobar. His head was cleanly shaved and shining. As he entered the courtroom, he lifted a clenched fist in salute to the audience. The audience cheered. Behind Al-Kobar was James Phelan, the white man with the thin lips and the missing tooth. Behind Phelan was Ralph "Fee" Santiago, his mustache and beard trimmed perfectly for the appearance.

O'Connor had picked a politically, racially balanced trio of defendants for the first riots trial.

"Power to the People," shouted Al-Kobar defiantly as he stood at the counsel table.

The crowd loved it. They screamed approval and joyful defiance.

The Judge pounded his bench again. "Mister Johnson or Al-Kobar, however you want to be known, I have already warned the audience that outbursts would not be tolerated in this courtroom." The Judge's lips curled down in the corners. "I told them I would have them ejected from the courtroom. I can do that to you and your co-defendants too. You can watch the trial on closed circuit TV from the jail. Or, I can have you quieted with a gag." He pointed a finger at Al-Kobar. "I do have effective means of stopping even you from disturbing these proceedings. I do not want to do that, however. But, I shall do it, if you make it necessary. Please do not make such a measure necessary."

The crowd booed and hissed.

Standing at the counsel table with the three prisoners were their attorneys. Al-Kobar had Richard Katzenberg, a middle-aged activist lawyer with thinning hair, which he wore very long in back, and glasses. Katzenberg, despite his age, had picked up the beat and was with the new movement. The other two attorneys were younger. One was a Black man with an Afro hair style. He represented Santiago. The third lawyer was a woman in a pants suit.

"Let's proceed," said the Judge, looking to the clerk.

The clerk nodded, then asked each of the defendants, so that the record would be complete, if they were the named defendants, and if the attorneys standing next to them were their attorneys. Each of the defendants acknowledged their identity and their attorneys.

A young, petite blond girl in a pants suit was the stenotypist. She sat at her machine recording every word.

"Today, we are going to have hearings concerned with the suppression of certain physical evidence and the suppression of certain statements allegedly made by the defendants, all of which the prosecution intends to offer into evidence against each of the defendants. Is that correct?" asked the Judge.

"That's correct, Your Honor," said O'Connor, as he rose from the prosecutor's table.

"Very well, can we move this matter to trial, Mister District Attorney?"

"I would like to make a statement," said Al-Kobar, who had now donned a red, green, and black wool cap.

"In the first place, Mister Al-Kobar," said the Judge, "remove your hat in this courtroom."

"This hat is part of my religious beliefs," retorted Al-Kobar.

"Your religious beliefs require you to wear that hat?"

"That's right."

"What religion is that?" the Judge asked.

"I don't have to be answering to you," said Al-Kobar.

The crowd cheered approvingly.

"Oh, but you do," said the Judge coldly. "I run this courtroom, not you and not your friends in the audience. Now unless I know what religion you say requires you to wear that hat, I'm going to have to require that you remove it."

"I am a Muslim."

"Right on."

"That man, that one," said the Judge, looking out to the audience, pointing a finger at a Black man in a flowing dashiki. The guards looked. "Remove him from the audience."

The crowd began to hoot.

"I'll clear the entire audience in a minute," said the Judge.

The court officers walked over to the man in the dashiki and spoke to him. He was reluctant, arguing with them, motioning, resisting.

"I said remove him, not have a conversation," said the Judge firmly. "Now remove him."

The guards spoke to the man, and he began to walk slowly toward the back of the courtroom. He glared at the Judge. Then he raised a fist in salute to Al-Kobar. Al-Kobar returned the salute, then, after the man had left the courtroom, turned back to the Judge.

"I still want to make a statement," said Al-Kobar.

"Not now," said the Judge. "I'll give you full opportunity to be heard, but right now I want to get the hearing started."

"Why can't I make a statement now?" asked Al-Kobar.

"Because I run this courtroom, and I say so," said the Judge, pounding the bench.

"Fascist," shouted many in the crowd.

"Quiet," shouted the Captain in charge of the court officers. It took many minutes for the crowd to quiet down. The Judge waited, glaring at the crowd.

"Is that the way it's going to be in this fascist trial?" demanded Al-Kobar.

"That's right, that's the way it is," replied the Judge. "I run the court and I'll tell you when you can make a speech. Are you ready to proceed, Mister Katzenberg?"

"My client wishes to make a statement," said Katzenberg.

"And I said your client can make his statement later," said the Judge harshly now, leaning forward. "He can speak as long as he wants right after the lunch break. Right now I want you to proceed and I want you to proceed without further delay. I am directing you to do that."

"I want to note for the record that this proceeding is unconstitutional," said Katzenberg. "It violates every right my client has under the Constitution. This is not a duly qualified court of law, and is certainly not the place where these defendants can get a fair trial, I ask the Court to disqualify itself."

"Your motion is denied," said the Judge. "Proceed, Mister O'Connor."

"Yes, Your Honor," said O'Connor. "The People move to trial, the case of People of the State of New York against Oscar Johnson . . . also known as Al-Kobar," O'Connor added this last facetiously. "James Phelan, and Ralph Santiago, under indictment numbers 3250, 3251, and 3252."

"Very well. Are the defendants ready for trial?" asked the Judge.

"I want to make a statement," said Al-Kobar, rising again.

"I'm telling you for the last time, Mister Defendant, and I mean the last time, that you will be given an opportunity to say whatever you wish, but not now. When we come back from lunch break, you will have an opportunity to say whatever you wish. Now, I want to proceed with the hearing."

"Your Honor isn't saying that he is going to complete these hearings before lunch, is he?" asked Katzenberg.

"I haven't said anything of the sort," replied the Judge. "And if you think that the record says that, then I want to clear up that discrepancy without another moment's delay. These trials are going to be fair . . ."

There was a low hiss somewhere in the courtroom. The Judge looked over the audience sternly.

"If that coward wishes to identify himself or herself, I might deal with he or she directly," said the Judge to the audience. No one spoke. The Judge continued to glare, then turned to the lawyers. "Now, these trials are going to be fair and can take as long as is necessary to complete a full and just hearing according to law."

"Thank you, Your Honor," said Katzenberg.

"That doesn't mean I'm going to let you take until next May, Mister Katzenberg," cautioned the Judge. "Full and fair means full and fair to both the defendants *and* the People. Let's proceed."

"The People call as their first witness Department of Correction officer Lewis Adler," said O'Connor.

Adler, in full uniform, took the stand and was sworn by the clerk. He proceeded to tell, under the guidance of O'Connor's questions, exactly what had occurred on the eighth floor on the day of the riots. He told about waiting outside the gate while Captain Casey spoke to inmate Raul DeJesus. He described how Casey was knocked into the cells by Al-Kobar; how the other officers were overcome by the inmates, about being held prisoner himself, and about the actions, threats, and warnings of the defendants as they stood in charge of the rebel group.

Under Katzenberg's heated cross-examination, Adler calmly repeated the details of his story of the day of the riot. The best defense to a searing cross-examination is the truth. For then, no matter how many times the question is posed, no matter how many different ways a question is couched, the witness cannot be flustered or drawn into inconsistencies.

Adler did testify that he was not sure if anyone, including the defendants, actually started out intending to have a riot. He admitted that it might not have been planned, it might have been spontaneous.

Each of the lawyers for the other two defendants cross-examined Adler. By the time they finished with their questions, and by the time O'Connor asked more questions on re-direct examination, Judge Crawford decided to call a luncheon recess rather than start a new witness. The audience filed out under the careful scrutiny of the police and court officers.

"Your Honor," said Katzenberg, just as the Judge rose to leave the bench.

"Yes?" The Judge sank back in his seat.

"Can the attorneys for the defendants return to court early after lunch and spend some time with their clients, going over some matters for the hearing?" Katzenberg asked. "We could stay in the bull pen with the defendants."

The Judge thought for a moment, then nodded. "Yes, if it's all right with the officers and with the Department of Correction."

"It's all right with us, Judge," said the Captain of the court officers. "We'll be here anyway, we're going to eat in the back room. It's too hot to go out today."

"Very well," said the Judge. He rose and left the bench, exiting through the door to the robing room.

As the afternoon session began, the audience filed back into the courtroom. After all the seats were filled, the doors were shut. Still there were crowds outside in the corridor, and there were masses of chanting demonstrators in the streets below.

The defendants and their lawyers came into the courtroom from the bull pen. Al-Kobar was now dressed in a dashiki, red and gold, which hung down below his hips. A roar of approval came from the crowd.

"Have you had an opportunity to confer with your clients, gentlemen?" the Judge asked the defense attorneys, so that the pretty stenotypist could make a proper record. Judge Crawford was determined the record be absolutely clear and complete so that there would be no grounds for appeal.

"Yes, Your Honor," replied Katzenberg, who seemed to be the spokesman for the defense attorneys.

"Your Honor," said Al-Kobar, rising to his feet, "you said that I would be permitted to make a statement before the afternoon session began."

"That I did," said the Judge. "And that you may. Go ahead. Say what you wish."

Al-Kobar remained standing at the defense table. "I want to say that there's just no way that this here trial is going to be fair to the people," he began. "I don't mean the People that this here man talks about." He pointed at O'Connor who was seated at his counsel table. O'Connor remained stolid, facing forward. "I don't mean that empty word. I mean the real people, the Black people, the minority people." Al-Kobar's voice began to rise. "This court is just a play on the part of a corrupt, fascist system."

The crowd buzzed with approval.

Al-Kobar moved away slightly from the counsel table to the

303

area between the two counsel tables, directly in front of the judge's bench. The court officers looked to the Judge. The Judge shook his head slightly.

"And the fascist society is not interested in providing a fair trial for Black men, for oppressed men."

The crowd cheered.

"It is interested only in oppressing those poverty men further. Men like myself, my brothers here, all my brothers out there."

"Right on," shouted someone in the crowd.

The Judge tapped his bench. "Let's not have outbursts or we'll have to stop."

"Yes, brothers, no outbursts," said Al-Kobar. "I want this all on the record."

The Judge nodded, both in approval and for Al-Kobar to continue.

"This society is intent on annihilation, on destroying the Black man, and all minorities," Al-Kobar continued. "The entire drug scene is just whitey's attempt at genocide, at killing off all Black peoples. The white man is supplying the Black man with drugs, to destroy the Black man. But we will overcome."

"Yeah," called someone.

"Yeah," chimed in the others.

The Judge said nothing. He was watching Al-Kobar, listening intently.

"But we are not going to be destroyed," Al-Kobar shouted. "And we are not going to let this society of elite white men, as they want to think they are, destroy the people, the real people."

The crowd cheered. Al-Kobar was still between the defense counsel table and the prosecution table. Just ahead of him directly next to the judge's bench, the blond stenotypist sat at her small desk, her fingers quickly recording each word.

"This system, when it says it speaks for the people, is only speaking for the white man, the rich, the capitalist." Al-Kobar rocked in place as he spoke. "And that system is now saying it wants to give us a fair trial. But that's not in the cards. For their very purpose is to destroy freedom, to destroy the people. You do not have the power to put us on trial here, Your Honor. You do not have the power to subject my fellow defendants, my people, to trials. This system is rotten and decayed."

O'Connor was leaning back in his chair, watching the spectacle with an expression of distaste.

"And this system must have its power stripped from it. Ripped off. The power must be given to the people." This last was shouted.

The spectators shouted lustily in response. The Judge pounded the bench.

In one leap, a sudden burst of movement, amidst the noise, Al-Kobar jumped onto the stenotypist's desk. His foot was on top of her desk before she even knew he had moved. She gave a startled, little scream, and drew backward in alarm. But Al-Kobar only used that desk as a stepping stone. He was now over the side of the judge's platform, next to the Judge.

As the Judge started to rise to his feet, Al-Kobar moved behind him and shoved the Judge back down into his chair. From beneath his dashiki, Al-Kobar pulled out a sawed-off shotgun. He shoved it around the front of the Judge's body, jamming both barrels into the Judge's throat.

"Nobody move," shouted Al-Kobar. "I'll blow his head right off. Tell them, Judge."

"I can't move," the Judge gurgled over the steel barrels under his jaw. "Don't do anything. He's got me."

"That's it. That's it, fools," cried Al-Kobar. "You fascist bastard fools. You two, come up here," he called to the other two defendants.

The D.A., all the court officers, and the cops were down on the floor, their guns drawn, aimed at Al-Kobar. But Al-Kobar was standing directly behind the Judge, only his arm holding the shotgun to the Judge's throat showing.

"Anyone try to stop my brothers from coming over to me," Al-Kobar hissed, "and I'll blow this man's head off. And don't try to shoot me, because as I fall, this shotgun'll still go off. It's got a hair trigger. This thing is going to take his head off unless I get out of here in one piece. Tell them, Judge."

"I can't breathe, it's in my throat, so hard," the Judge gurgled.

"That's good enough. Tell them to stay where they are," Al-Kobar directed.

"Stay where you are."

By this time most of the spectators had fled the courtroom. So had the press except for one reporter who was curled up on the floor in the corner of the room, behind the barrier separating the audience from the well of the court. He had his pencil going, writing a story as he lay there. Occasionally he peered up, then pulled his head back down quickly.

"Come on up here," Al-Kobar shouted impatiently at the other defendants.

Phelan leaped across the defense table, a maniacal grin splitting his face. He ran up to where Al-Kobar was. Santiago stayed where he was, on the floor with the attorneys and the guards.

"There's a gun under my belt," Al-Kobar said to Phelan.

Phelan's eyes were wild as he reached under Al-Kobar's dashiki and came out with a long-barreled pistol. His missing tooth was very evident as he smiled and fondled the pistol. Phelan ducked down behind the judge's bench.

"Fee. Come on up here," Al-Kobar shouted at Santiago.

"No, man," replied Santiago from the floor, "I can beat my case, man. I don't like The Tombs condition. But I ain't bustin' out, man."

"Then stay, traitor pig, and die. I want all you pigs to listen to this, because we're getting out of here," announced Al-Kobar. "I want to get a car over here. Get a car, Captain. Where's the Captain?"

"Here," called the Captain of the court officers, who was lying on the floor.

"We're going to take the Judge with us, and we'll get out of here, and when we're away, we'll release the Judge. Got it, Captain?"

There was no answer.

"You got it, motherfucker Captain?" Al-Kobar demanded.

"I heard you and you can go to hell," shouted the Captain.

Al-Kobar laughed. "I can go to hell? Go to hell, hanh?" He jammed the shotgun fiercely into the Judge's throat. "Tell them, Judgey."

The Judge could only make gurgling sounds. Al-Kobar eased the shotgun out slightly.

"Do what he asks you. He's going to kill me."

"You, stenographer," Al-Kobar shouted over the judge's bench.

The girl was crouching beneath her desk. "Come on up here, stenographer."

The stenographer's face was chalky. She was visibly trembling.

"I said come up here," demanded Al-Kobar. He had another pistol under his dashiki. He held it in his other hand and stretched that hand over the judge's bench and fired a blind shot into the floor near the stenographer's table. "Come up here or I'll kill you where you are."

The girl rose, shaking and pale, moving like a zombie around the judge's bench to the stairway. She walked up the steps to where the Judge was seated. Phelan grabbed her around the throat, putting his pistol to her throat just as Al-Kobar had the shotgun to the Judge's throat.

"Now get that car, Captain, and get it to the side entrance where the judges' elevator comes out. Get it," he demanded.

"I have to get to a phone," said the Captain. "I have to call for a car."

"Do it, then. I don't care if you call for help. If the car that takes us out of here isn't here in two minutes, and I mean two—I'm going to time you with the Judge's own watch—in two minutes, I either start moving out that door, or the Judge's head starts moving out that door."

The Captain crawled across the floor to the door leading to the judge's robing room. Al-Kobar watched him. The Captain opened the door and scooted inside.

"Now the rest of you pigs, start moving over to the far side of the courtroom, away from the doors. Start moving," Al-Kobar commanded sharply.

There was a general movement of guards and officers along the floor on hands and knees, away from the side of the courtroom where the doors were.

"That's it, you officers up here, start moving out into the audience," said Al-Kobar. "I don't want anyone this side of the barrier."

The court officers near Santiago started to comply. So did O'Connor.

"Where's that turncoat bastard?" said Al-Kobar, chancing a quick look toward Santiago. He realized how dangerous it was to emerge from cover and decided not to chance another look. "I'll get you later, you pig. Where's that pig Captain?" shouted Al-Kobar. "Captain, Captain."

The courtroom was silent as Al-Kobar waited for a reply. There was none. He fired a pistol shot into the wall above the door leading to the robing room. The shot echoed thunderously throughout the court.

The door opened slightly.

"Is that you, Captain?" Al-Kobar demanded.

"Yes. I just made the call, it took time to get through."

"There's only a minute fifteen seconds left," said Al-Kobar. "We're starting through the door right where you are in seventy seconds. If there's no car, there ain't going to be no Judge or stenographer either."

"It'll be waiting," said the Captain.

"It better be. Now get someone to get that judges' private elevator up here and hold it up here," directed Al-Kobar.

There was some movement in the courtroom as one of the policemen tried to crawl out the back door. Al-Kobar winged a shot in the direction of that movement.

"I didn't tell anybody to move," Al-Kobar spit out. "And unless I say move, don't move."

"We have the courtroom surrounded, Johnson," announced the sergeant on his bull horn from the outside corridor. "You can't get out of there."

Al-Kobar pegged another shot, this one shattering and hurtling through the glass panel of one of the doors leading to the outside corridor.

"I'm going out with the Judge, and if anybody tries to stop us, this here Judge and this here stenographer are dead," shouted Al-Kobar. "You, cop in the back. You wanted to get out. Go ahead out and tell that to the other pigs out there. Tell them I mean it."

The cop crawled near the entrance, then bolted out, the door swinging behind him.

"Now just in case you other pigs figure that you're going to get out of here one by one, all of you get up and sit in the seats there, them benches."

There was a general shuffling as people, court officers, and the remaining reporter sat up in the spectators' benches.

"Forty-five seconds, Captain," Al-Kobar announced. "You still there, Captain?"

"Yes."

"Did you send someone to get that elevator?"

"Yes."

"Well, send someone else to tell them police pigs in the hall that when I come through, if there's any movement, any trouble, these two people are dead. You got that?"

"Yes."

"Then move it, move it," said Al-Kobar, firing another shot into the wall above the door. "I got all you bastards where I want you now. You have to listen to whatever I tell you now, you miserable bastards," he shouted to the court officers in the spectators' section. "Drop all your guns on the floor in the aisle. Come on," he shouted. "You, brother Phelan. Go out there and get all the bullets out of those guns. Hurry."

"What about the girl?"

"Take her with you," said Al-Kobar. "She looks like she could use a little walk."

Phelan moved down toward the aisle, dragging the girl with him, the gun at her throat. She moved just ahead of him, his body staying directly behind hers.

"Thirty seconds. You hear, Captain?"

"Yes."

"You do what I told you?"

"Yes, it's all done. The car's down there already."

"Remember, no tricks, or I'll kill these two."

"I told them that, Johnson," said the Captain.

"It's Ali Al-Kobar. I ain't no slave," he hurled angrily. He pegged another shot into the wall above the door. "And don't none of you worry about me running out of bullets," said Al-Kobar. "I got plenty. I'm reloading right now. Come on, brother Phelan, come on, get the bullets. Just empty those other guns and put all the bullets in your pocket."

"I'm going as fast as I can," said Phelan.

"Twenty seconds," said Al-Kobar. "I'm coming through that door in eighteen seconds now, Captain. Come on, brother Phelan, you got that done, man?"

"There are too many guns to empty in ten seconds," he said.

309

He let go of the girl as he bent to pick up the pistols. She stood as if in a trance, looking at all the court officers she had known so well, with whom she had joked and drunk coffee. One of them signaled to her with his eyes. He signaled her to move away from Phelan as he was bending.

The stenotypist stared in disbelief. She was too frightened. Her eyes grew wide with terror. She couldn't do it. She couldn't move.

"Ten seconds. You got those bullets, man?"

"Some of them, some of them, for Christ's sake."

"Hurry."

Suddenly, the stenotypist bolted, diving into one of the audience benches.

Phelan rose from his bent position, now exposed in the open. His pistol whirled in the girl's direction. The court officer who had signaled the girl suddenly leveled a hidden revolver and fired point-blank at Phelan. The explosion was violent, rocking the room. It was a .38 magnum shot. There was an intense howl from Phelan as he spun in a circle, landing on his back in the benches on the other side of the courtroom.

"You motherfuckers!" shouted Al-Kobar wildly. "You motherfuckers! You think that's going to stop me?" He sprayed two more shots into the benches where the officers had been sitting. They were all on the floor again.

"Come on, you pigs, sit up, come on you pigs, sit up," Al-Kobar goaded. "I said sit up," he demanded impatiently.

"It's time," the Captain shouted from behind the door, to distract Al-Kobar.

Al-Kobar looked at the door, then out to the audience once again. He decided he was more interested in getting out. "Open the door, you pig bastard," he shouted as he shoved the Judge sideways, staying behind him, the barrel of the shotgun ever in the Judge's throat. He moved sideways down the steps.

"You lead the way, Captain, and no funny business, or I'll blow your head off too," said Al-Kobar.

"No, no funny business," said the Captain.

Al-Kobar moved through the robing room to the other door which led to the interior corridor. The Captain was walking ahead, Al-Kobar following, keeping the Judge in front of him. He shifted the Judge a bit to his side so that he could twist him either front or back, depending on from where the attack might come. The three men moved slowly through the corridor. The door to the main corridor was about twenty feet ahead. The elevator was at the end of the corridor just before the door.

Suddenly, there was a noise ahead, as the door to the main corridor was banged or punched or slammed. Al-Kobar's head twirled, and he shifted the Judge in front of him quickly. From behind him, at that very moment, the policeman who had been posted in the interior hallway stepped from the robing room. He had hidden in the judges' washroom just before Al-Kobar walked through. On this prearranged noise from outside, the policeman emerged and fired a shot at the exposed back of Al-Kobar, to the side away from the Judge's head. Al-Kobar howled. There was a shotgun blast now, and blood flew and splattered the wall. The Captain leaped on Al-Kobar. So did the cop from behind. There were more cops coming in the front way. More from behind. There was screaming and cursing, and people slipping in blood on the terrazzo floor.

XXX

THURSDAY, SEPTEMBER 14, 2:15 P.M.

Marc sat next to Nick Stuart's work bench as Stuart peered through the eyepiece of a microscope with two separate magnifying lenses. This was a comparison microscope which caused two images to appear side by side, thus permitting the study of two bullets, one under each lens, at the same time. By rotating each bullet 360 degrees, every line or mark on one bullet, could simultaneously be compared to every line or mark on the other.

Stuart was studying two bullets he had fired from two separate pistols into a recovery box stuffed with cotton.

"And you want to know if bullets can be studied and positively identified using a microscope like this?" asked Stuart, still peering into the microscope.

"That's right," replied Marc.

"Well, let me tell you this," said Stuart, looking up now. He was thickly built with a bald head and a wide, smiling face. He was employed as a laboratory research technician at Winchester Firearms Company, and part of his duties involved microscopic examination of bullets and shell casings for the purposes of finding better manufacturing methods or eliminating manufacturing defects. "When I was on the police force, in Ballistics, I thought you could. But after working in the lab where I am now, I say there's no way in the world to compare bullets precisely or accurately with a microscope like this."

"Are you kidding?" asked Marc.

"Not at all," said Stuart.

"How come?" asked Franco. "What about the lansing grooves and all?"

"There's no such thing. That's the trouble with all this stuff on TV. It's really fiction."

"Can you explain that a little?" asked Marc.

"Here's a quick lesson," said Stuart. "A bullet is smooth, made of soft metal. And it fits almost exactly into the barrel of the weapon it was made for. But inside the barrel of every weapon—except shotguns—sticks down what's called rifling—grooves. Now when the bullet is fired, it's forced over these grooves that are protruding down into the barrel. And the grooves cut into the soft metal of the bullet as it moves forward. It can't go through otherwise. The bullet then gets caught on these grooves like a trolley on tracks. And since the grooves are spiraled inside the barrel, the bullet gets a spiral spin. It gets to be like a football being thrown with a spiral pass. That lets the bullet go straighter, faster. You got that so far?"

"If the metal wasn't soft, the bullet wouldn't get past the grooves, is that it?" asked Marc.

"Right," said Stuart.

"How about the lansing grooves you always hear about?" said Franco.

"That's land and grooves," said Stuart. "After the bullet is fired, the flat part of the side of the bullet is called lands, and the lines or marks cut into the bullet by the rifling in the barrel are called grooves. So a fired bullet has lands and grooves. I guess that came to sound like lansing grooves. With me so far?"

Franco nodded.

"You say, even with these lands and grooves, you can't compare bullets from the same pistol with this microscope?" asked Marc.

"Right," replied Stuart. "For example. Every Smith and Wesson Chief Special revolver made—that's the pistol detectives use —is made on the same dies or machine and has the same size barrel and the same size and number of grooves as every other similar-model Smith and Wesson Chief Special. The same goes for every other weapon manufactured. Every weapon of a certain model made on the same machines will be practically the same as every other model of the same weapon. That figures, doesn't it?"

"Yes," Marc replied.

"Okay. Now the only way to tell if a bullet you know was fired from one revolver compared with some other bullet found some place else, is to study each bullet fired to see if the particular pistol has left any identifying characteristics in the lands or the grooves on the bullets. Right?"

"So far, so good," said Marc.

"The problem is, you can't look through a microscope like this and make the precise findings or readings necessary to compare bullets. It's just not powerful enough," said Stuart. "I mean maybe it was okay fifty years ago, when there wasn't anything more powerful. But what we do now is actually measure the width and the depth of the grooves, the width and the height of the lands. And we do this with electronic microscopes that enlarge to the millionth of an inch. We have them at the lab." Stuart lit a stubby cigar.

"Go on," Marc said. He was listening carefully.

"The only way to tell if one bullet matches another, is to measure them exactly—and I mean exactly—to match them. No one can tell if the grooves on this bullet," he said, holding up one bullet, "are the same as the grooves on this other bullet, except by measuring them to the millionth or at least ten thousandth of an inch. Of course they look alike. They were fired from the same kind of revolvers, manufactured on the same machines. They were designed to come off the machine exactly the same. Let me ask

313

another thing before I go on. Do you know what the humidity factor is in the laboratory where the police test these bullets?"

"Humidity factor? I don't know," said Marc.

"I do. I worked there fifteen years. It's the same as outdoors. Maybe they got air conditioning now. But that won't help. You see, these bullets are lead. If I just breathe hard from my mouth on them, and you're looking at them with the big microscopes at the lab, you'll see the needle measuring them fluctuate. These bullets react very much to atmosphere. If you don't control a constant humidity at their lab, which the cops don't, you can't compare a damn thing. From second to second, a wind could change a measurement reading."

"Are you telling me," said Marc, "that the police can't accurately compare bullets because they don't precisely measure the lands and the grooves, and therefore, can't really tell anything except a general description of the model of the weapon the bullet was fired from?"

"That's right. They can tell if the bullet has right or left twist, five or six grooves. In other words, they can tell if the bullet was fired from the same *type* of weapon. But to say this bullet came from this particular Chief Special as opposed to that Chief Special, that's not possible unless they measure the markings on the bullets precisely. After all, we're dealing with something that to the gross eye, or even with the naked eye aided by a seven-power microscope is very small; the variations are only, say, a thousandth of an inch. And a thousandth of an inch is a significant factor in bullet tolerance."

"Then all this stuff about ballistics in court isn't in the least bit scientific or accurate."

"Do they measure the width, or depth, or height of the marks and grooves?" Stuart asked.

"No. They just say I studied the bullet and the bullets compare positively—without giving any basis except it's their opinion."

"How can they give a precise answer when they're not dealing with precise information? I told you these weapons are manufactured by precision machine—not by hand. If they're off—one slightly different from another—they're off a hair. I mean that literally, a hair. You put two similar hairs together under one of these seven-power microscopes and tell me if you can see which is thicker. If they're as close together in size as two manufactured revolvers, you're going to have one hell of a time telling me precisely, scientifically, which is thicker just by looking through one of these old-fashioned microscopes."

"Go on, I'm fascinated," said Marc.

"Another thing," said Stuart. "The police don't measure the angle or pitch of the grooves when they compare."

"What does that mean?" asked Franco.

"Well, you see, this is the kind of work we do at the lab. The tool dies used to manufacture the weapons sometimes create—despite expensive precautions—slight variation in the angle of the grooves. It's very slight, but it's there. Anyway, that variation can be to the right or the left. Now suppose one revolver has a variation or deflection of a half of one degree or more to the right, and another has a variation of a half of one degree or more to the left. That means that the angle of the grooves on the bullets will be one or two degrees different. You get what I mean?"

"Not really."

"Okay, I'll try it again. The grooves in one revolver are off a little, one degree to the left. Another revolver of the same manufacturer, is off one degree to the right. That variation is actually tolerable. They'll both fire accurately. There's no problem with that. But there is a two-degree difference in the line the grooves will cut into a bullet. Now, unless the police measure the angle or pitch of the grooves, how can they tell that a bullet came from a particular weapon? It may look the same; one degree doesn't look like much, but it's sure as hell different."

"I can hardly believe what you're telling me," said Marc.

"You give a set of bullets to people who have access to the equipment I use, and you'll probably end up with as many opinions about the bullets as there are people who examine them. Even when you measure the way I'm saying is necessary, it's very difficult to say with any certainty that a bullet came out of a particular weapon."

"Will you come to court to testify for me if I need you?"

"Why not? I just won't be able to bring any testing equipment. These microscopes are gigantic," Stuart replied.

Marc rose. "I'll be in touch with you shortly if I need you. And I really appreciate your help."

"Glad to be able to help you." Stuart shook hands with Marc. "I've been really re-educated about ballistics since I work in the lab. It'd be a pleasure to set the record straight."

Franco stopped the car at a red light. Marc, in the passenger seat, was idly whistling the music being broadcast over the car radio. Suddenly, the sound of a clacking teletype machine loudly cut out the music, signifying a special news announcement was to be made.

WE INTERRUPT THE REGULAR PROGRAMING AT THIS TIME TO BRING YOU A SPECIAL NEWS BULLETIN [the radio announcer said gravely]. A DARING, ARMED COURTROOM ESCAPE BY TWO MEN ON TRIAL FOR INCITING THE TOMBS RIOTS LAST AUGUST HAS JUST BEEN FOILED BY HEROIC POLICE WORK AT THE CRIMINAL COURTS BUILDING, 100 CENTRE STREET, MANHATTAN. IN THE MELEE, WHERE SEVERAL GUNSHOTS WERE EXCHANGED—INCLUDING A SHOTGUN BLAST—JUDGE JAMES J. CRAWFORD, PRESIDING AT THE TRIAL, RECEIVED FACIAL WOUNDS WHEN ONE OF THE DEFENDANTS FIRED A SHOTGUN AT HIM FROM POINT-BLANK RANGE. THE JUDGE IS IN SATISFACTORY CONDITION AT BEEKMAN DOWNTOWN HOSPITAL.

"Holy Christ," exclaimed Franco, turning the radio louder.

ALSO IN BEEKMAN DOWNTOWN HOSPITAL IN CRITICAL CONDITION IS OSCAR JOHNSON, ONE OF THE DEFENDANTS WHO WAS ATTEMPTING TO ESCAPE. JOHNSON, ALSO KNOWN AS ALI AL-KOBAR, IS CONSIDERED BY AUTHORITIES TO BE THE RINGLEADER OF THE ESCAPE GROUP. IT WAS JOHNSON WHO ALLEGEDLY SHOT JUDGE CRAWFORD.

ALSO IN BEEKMAN DOWNTOWN HOSPITAL WITH SERIOUS WOUNDS RECEIVED AS HE TRIED TO ESCAPE IS DEFENDANT JAMES PHELAN. RALPH SANTIAGO, A THIRD DEFENDANT ON TRIAL, DID NOT TAKE PART IN THE ATTEMPTED ESCAPE.

IT IS NOT KNOWN AT THIS TIME HOW THE DEFENDANTS OBTAINED THE WEAPONS WITH WHICH THEY ATTEMPTED TO ESCAPE, ALTHOUGH IT IS SUSPECTED THAT AN ATTORNEY FOR ONE OF THE PRISONERS MAY HAVE SLIPPED THE WEAPONS TO THE PRISONERS DURING A LUNCHEON RECESS. TWO OF THE ATTORNEYS ARE BEING HELD FOR INVESTIGATION AT THIS TIME.

IT HAS BEEN ASCERTAINED THAT THE SAWED-OFF SHOTGUN USED BY JOHNSON OR AL-KOBAR TO WOUND JUDGE CRAWFORD WAS FABRICATED FROM A SHOTGUN OWNED AND REGISTERED TO SPENCER ROBERTS OF OLD LYME, CONNECTICUT. AFTER INVESTIGATION, THE POLICE HAVE ASCERTAINED THAT THE SHOTGUN HAD LAST BEEN IN THE POSSESSION OF MISTER ROBERTS' DAUGHTER, ANDREA ROBERTS, A RESIDENT OF THE EAST VILLAGE IN MANHATTAN. MISS ROBERTS IS AN ALLEGED MEMBER OF THE PEOPLE'S REVOLUTIONARY ARMY AND A DEMONSTRATION LEADER WHO IS A FAMILIAR SIGHT ON MANY LEFT-WING PICKET LINES . . .

Marc and Franco were transfixed by the broadcast. Franco had brought the car to a stop, the motor still running as they listened.

AN ALL-POINTS BULLETIN HAS BEEN ISSUED FOR THE ARREST OF ANDREA ROBERTS IN CONNECTION WITH CONSPIRACY TO ATTEMPT MURDER, ESCAPE, ASSAULT, POSSESSION OF UNREGISTERED WEAPONS, AND OTHER CRIMES. WE NOW RETURN YOU TO THE REGULAR BROADCAST.

"Did you hear that?" asked Marc.

"I sure did."

"I've seen that girl around, even spoken to her a couple of times," said Marc.

"I know," said Franco. "I've seen you. She seemed like just a nice little kid from the country. It's hard to understand why she'd get involved in this."

"It's hard to understand why anyone gets involved in crime," said Marc. "Let's go back to my office. Maybe she'll call. She took my card once and told me she'd call if she needed a lawyer."

Marc was silent as Franco pulled away from the traffic light. He wondered if Andrea Roberts would call. He wondered whether, if she did, he could help her.

XXXI

On the twenty-ninth floor of the Hotel Louis Quinze, Johnny Manno eased silently through the darkness, expertly dodging the shadowed furniture, eluding pools of light which drifted through the windows from the world outside. He stopped behind Zack Lord's large desk. He slid open the top center drawer of the desk and, mostly by deft touch, studied the contents. There were the usual papers, pencils, paper clips, small books. Nothing unusual. Johnny bent to his left, and pulled open a side drawer. There were some books, a tissue box, a shoe-shine brush. There was another drawer on the left side of the desk, lower than the first. Johnny opened it. There was some sort of machine in the lower drawer. Johnny felt the machine. It was a tape recorder. Suddenly, Zack Lord's desk phone rang, tearing the silence of the room, resounding from the dark walls. As the phone rang, a light on one of the phone buttons lit up intermittently, casting a feeble glow through the room. Johnny stood back and watched the flashing light silently. Abruptly, the ringing stopped, but the phone light remained on steadily, as if someone, perhaps an answering service, had answered the phone. At the moment that the phone was answered, the recorder in Lord's desk started to turn, a small indicator light went on. Johnny watched the machine recording. When the light on the phone went out, so did the indicator light, and the machine stopped recording.

Johnny slid the drawer with the recorder shut and went through the rest of Lord's desk. There were the usual office items, but no sign of the automatic pistol Franco had mentioned.

Johnny turned to a long, low cabinet against the wall behind Lord's desk. The cabinet had four separate doors. Johnny knelt and opened the first door. There were many corporate seals, checkbooks, papers, and other documents. He moved to another of the compartments. There were more papers and books and documents. The third door contained the same. The fourth door was locked. There was no key in the key hole. Johnny looked about for a key. There were none in any of the other compartment doors. He rose and turned back to Lord's desk. He felt inside the top center drawer; it was too risky to put on a light. He felt for a key but found none. Johnny let his hand feel the underside of the center drawer. Still no key. He felt the bottom of the top drawer on the left side. His fingers touched a key attached with Scotch tape to the underside of the drawer. Johnny removed the key and tried it in the lock on the fourth compartment in the cabinet. It fit.

Inside, Johnny found another tape recorder similar to the one in Lord's desk. Also inside the cabinet, above the recorder, were several stacks of recording tape reels. Johnny took several reels to one of the pools of light entering the office through the windows. He made sure his body remained in the shadows as he studied the reels. They were each dated with several days of recordings on each reel. There seemed to be two separate divisions of the tapes. One set of tapes was for Lord's office phone number. The phone number was written and Scotch-taped to the reels along with the dates. The other tapes were marked with a phone number Johnny didn't recognize. Johnny made a mental note of the second phone number, then returned the tapes to the cabinet in which he found them. He locked the cabinet again and returned the key to its hiding place. Still he found no pistol. Perhaps Lord had a safe nearby. Johnny began to search for the safe.

Occasionally Johnny stopped working, as he heard the noises of elevators, or of doors on the floor below, being shut. He knew Lord was not in the apartment; he had looked. When the sounds subsided, Johnny continued to search. The safe was not in any of the walls of the office. Johnny began to tap the floor lightly, listening carefully to the sound. In a few minutes, he found Zack Lord's safe under the rug, near the desk.

Marc stood in the darkness at the railing of his apartment balcony. The late evening air had cooled to a clear, exhilarating crispness. He gazed across the empty river, absently studying the shimmering lights of New Jersey, thinking about the strategy of the trial he was going to begin in the morning. He wore a light sweater; the chill of fall had begun.

Maria walked slowly, sleepily, through the dark, carrying a small glass of *Cuarenta Tres*. She had fallen asleep watching TV, and had now awakened to join Marc.

"Don't you think you ought to go to bed now?" Maria said. "You have a trial in the morning." She put her arm through his and snuggled against him.

"In a few minutes," Marc replied. "I have a few more pages of pre-trial testimony to read first."

The phone rang. Maria turned. She saw Franco in the living room move quickly to answer it. Through the windows he could be seen looking at his watch as he spoke into the phone. Both Marc and Maria watched him. A look of concern came over Franco's face. He spoke again into the phone. Then he put the phone down on a table and walked out to the balcony.

"It's Johnny Manno."

"What's the matter?" asked Marc.

"Nothing's the matter," replied Franco. "It's just that he was out doing something for me." Franco looked away from Marc's gaze. "He just told me something a little peculiar."

"What's it all about, Franco?" Marc asked, seeing the sheepish look on Franco's face.

"I had him go into Zack Lord's office," Franco admitted.

"You had him what?" Marc was open-mouthed. He looked at Maria, annoyed, as he did, to find she was not as surprised as he was.

"I figured he could find the pistol that belonged to Lord—the one that's the same as Toni Wainwright's—and we could take a couple of test shots with it and then we'd have what we wanted." Franco talked nervously fast.

"Have you lost your sense of proportion?" asked Marc. "The both of you?"

"Don't get sore at anyone but me, boss," Franco implored. "It's all my fault. I was the one who wanted to find out for sure if Lord killed Wainwright. I mean, we can't let that dame, even if she's a creep, take a bad fall, can we?"

"We expect the D.A. and the police to do things the right way, don't we?" said Marc. "I think we're required to do the same. And here you get someone involved in burglary and larceny, committing a crime to protect our clients from being convicted of other crimes. It's as bad as the Special State Prosecutor Belacian getting people to perjure themselves so he can discover other people perjuring themselves."

"When the police start playing fair, so can we," said Maria.

Marc looked at her reprovingly. "Did he find Lord's pistol, at least?" Marc asked Franco.

"Yeah, he got that," Franco replied. "It was in the safe. But that's not the problem."

"He doesn't know how to test-fire it without making too much noise?"

"No, he did that too," replied Franco. "He fired it into a pillow with a phone book behind the pillow to stop the bullet. We worked that out before he went up."

"You weren't involved in that?" Marc asked Maria.

"No. I done it all on my own, boss, honest," said Franco.

"Then what's Johnny's problem?" Marc asked.

"He found the tape recorder Lord uses to tape phone conversations in his office," said Franco.

"He did?" Maria asked excitedly.

"That's not too surprising," replied Marc. "We already figured that out."

"Yeah, but he found two tape machines," Franco said emphatically, "recording two differing numbers. And a lot of tapes."

"Franco, please spare us your piece-by-piece narrative, and tell me what the hell is on your burglar friend's mind," said Marc.

"The other tape machine is recording Toni Wainwright's phone," Franco revealed. "He saw the tapes."

"You were right," said Maria, turning to Marc.

Marc was silent.

"And there are a lot of them, with dates and all," Franco added hastily. "They go back quite a while." He saw his reprieve in Marc's eyes.

"You were right about Lord knowing too much about Toni Wainwright's phone conversations," said Maria.

"He's probably worried she's fooling around with some other guys," said Franco.

"And with a woman like that, he's got something to worry about," said Maria.

"I doubt he's worried about her amorous affairs at all," said Marc. "I'm sure he's more interested in knowing that she's not selling him down the river when it comes to the stocks she controls. Where is Johnny now?"

"He's still there. He knew we were on a case and figured maybe it was important, so he took a shot and called," Franco replied.

"Is he still on the phone?"

Franco nodded.

Marc walked over and picked up the phone. "Johnny."

"Yeah. Hiya, Marc."

"How far back do the tapes go?" Marc asked.

"You mean in dates?"

"Yes."

"A month or so in one cabinet," said Johnny. "But I found another compartment in a safe place, you know what I mean. There were tapes there too. Those go back about four or five months."

"Can you take a tape out of there for me?" asked Marc.

"If you want, Marc. What ones do you want?"

"I want the tapes from both machines for August 13."

"I don't know if they're there," replied Johnny. "But if they are, and you want them, I'll get them."

"Get the tapes for the twelfth and the fourteenth too," Marc added.

"Tell me everything you want now," said Johnny. "I want to make a move right away."

"Johnny. Are there spare tape reels there, with tape that hasn't been used yet?" asked Marc.

"Yeah, sure," Johnny answered. "He's got like a closet with a pile of extra tapes."

"Good. Take some of those extra tapes and put the same dates on them as are on the reels that you take. Put the blank reels with the dates back in the safe."

"You want me to put the blank tapes with the dates in the safe so this guy don't know the real ones are gone. Is that it?" Johnny asked, to be sure he understood.

"Yes."

"Okay, Marc," said Johnny. "Let me get going."

Marc put down the phone but remained standing, looking at it as if it contained the answer to a perplexing puzzle. Maria walked over and locked her arms around his chest.

Four hours later Marc, Maria, and Franco were huddled around the tape player in their apartment. "Well, there's nothing we can use on Lord's office phone tapes," said Marc. "Let's hear the others."

"You want me to play the tapes of Toni Wainwright's phone *now?*" asked Franco. He looked at his watch. It was 4 A.M.

"Not now, Marc," said Maria. "You have to start the trial in a couple of hours. You'll be exhausted."

"I'm okay," said Marc. "I'm invigorated by new evidence. Don't you two want to hear if your theory holds together?"

"As long as you're okay, yes," said Maria.

"Play the tapes of the twelfth of August, the day of the party," said Marc. "Then play the early morning of the thirteenth, when Wainwright was killed."

"That's all on one tape," said Franco as he put the reel on the tape recorder and started the machine.

It was a voice activated recording of every telephone call made to or from Toni Wainwright's apartment on the twelfth of August. If no one was speaking, the recorder stopped automatically. When there was another conversation, the recorder began again. The tape contained phone calls made by Toni Wainwright and some made to her by friends, about lunch, about people they knew, about who was divorcing whom, about the servant problem, about stocks and bonds, about how there were millions being lost as the stocks tumbled. There were calls to a beauty parlor; there were calls from the servants to their friends; there were calls to various suppliers and grocers concerning the dinner party that Toni Wainwright was having that evening. There were panic calls when too few lobsters were sent. The fish man said he would deliver them personally in his car.

"Sounds like we're getting into the late afternoon now," said Maria.

Marc nodded, listening carefully to each conversation. "Now this must be a call Zack Lord made on Toni Wainwright's phone," said Marc as he listened to Lord's voice. "He must have arrived at the apartment by then."

On the tape, Zack called his pilot to tell him to have the plane ready to leave for Chicago about twelve-thirty that night.

"Maybe he was telling the truth all the time," said Franco somewhat unhappily. "Maybe he did fall asleep by mistake."

"Don't lose faith so quickly," Maria cautioned.

There were other recorded conversations between people who must have been guests at the party and other people they called from the Wainwright apartment. Then there were calls which the servants answered, advising the callers to phone back since Madam was having dinner and could not be disturbed.

"Now we're right in the midst of the dinner party," said Marc, turning the volume up louder.

There were a couple of additional calls to Toni Wainwright from friends.

"Hello, Toni," said a heavy male voice from the tape. The man's words were thick and slurred. "This is Bob, your husband."

They all perked up.

"He sounds quite drunk," said Maria.

Marc put the volume up a bit louder.

"What do *you* want?" Toni asked angrily on the tape. Her words too were thick and slurred.

"They were *both* really stinking drunk when they had this conversation," said Franco. Marc raised a silencing finger to his lips.

"I just wanted to talk to you," said Wainwright's voice.

"About what? About the fact that you fucked up my dinner party, made all the guests feel uncomfortable?"

"Come on, honey," they heard Wainwright plead again. "Don't be such a bitch."

"Come on, what? Come on, what?" Toni demanded drunkenly. "You come over here, uninvited, mess up my party, make everyone uncomfortable, and then you call and say, come on, honey. Go fuck yourself." She hung up.

"Charming," said Maria.

"As usual," added Franco.

Marc smiled slightly as the tape continued.

"Hello?" asked a now sleepier, as well as drunker, Toni Wainwright on the tape.

"Hello, Toni," said her husband's voice, he too more slurred and drunk.

324

"Why are you waking me up now?" Toni Wainwright asked with impatience. "What time is it, anyway?"

"Now? It's a quarter to one."

"Now?" Toni Wainwright slashed. "Now, you ask? What do you think I want to know, yesterday's time? You drunken ass! What do you want?"

"I told you a little while ago, I just wanted to explain."

"Look, it's a quarter to one, ten to one, whatever the hell time it is." The three listeners could hear movement as Toni Wainwright must have twisted to see the clock.

"There's the time reference," Marc whispered, listening carefully.

Maria nodded.

"My dinner party was a bomb because of you," Toni Wainwright's recorded voice continued. "My guests are all gone. The evening was shit. And now will you leave me alone so I can at least enjoy a little peace."

"What the hell kind of a lousy remark is that to make to me?" Wainwright demanded indignantly.

"What lousy remark?" asked Toni Wainwright.

"You want a little piece. Is Zack Lord there? Is that what you're doing, fucking him? And telling me about it just because you want to make me jealous? Is that it, you lousy bitch?"

"What the hell are you talking about?" asked Toni Wainwright.

"You know what I'm talking about. For Christ's sake, Toni. I still love you. And you tell me about having a little piece. Don't you have any consideration?"

"Could Zack Lord have been there at a quarter to one?" Maria whispered to Marc. "Maybe that's where he fell asleep. Not in his own apartment, but at Toni Wainwright's."

Marc stopped the tape momentarily. "That might explain a lot of things," he said. "How Lord got in; how he knew what was going on; everything." He looked at Franco, then Maria. She nodded the possibility. Marc let the tape play again.

Toni Wainwright laughed viciously on the phone. "Isn't that too bad," she said to Wainwright. "First you mess up my party, then you wake me up, twice now, and then I'm not supposed to tell you what I'm doing because it'll make you angry and jealous. Poor little fella," she mimicked. "Well, you bum, that's what I'm doing. I'm fucking Zack Lord, and I'm going to go back and give him an extra fuck just for you. Now leave me alone." She hung up again.

"What a rotten bitch," said Franco. "I'd tell her a couple of things if she ever said that to me. I'm sorry," he said to Maria to excuse his language.

Maria smiled. "But you aren't in love with her, Franco. Wainwright was. Marc," she said, turning. "If Zack was there, that would explain everything."

Marc stopped the tape again. "I *don't* think he was."

"What makes you say that?" asked Franco.

Marc re-wound a portion of the tape. "Listen to this again." Marc started the tape forward again.

"Look, it's a quarter to one, ten to one, whatever the hell time it is," Toni Wainwright's voice repeated. "My dinner party was a bomb because of you, my guests are all gone. The evening was shit. And now will you leave me alone so I can at least enjoy a little peace."

"What the hell kind of lousy remark is that to make to me?" Wainwright demanded again.

"What are you getting at?" Franco whispered quickly to Marc.

Maria listened raptly, watching the rotating reels of the machine.

Marc put a finger to his lips.

"What lousy remark?" asked Toni Wainwright's voice.

"You want a little piece. Is Zack Lord there?" the voice continued. "Is that what you're doing, fucking him? And telling me about it just because you want to make me jealous? Is that it, you lousy bitch?"

"What the hell are you talking about?" asked Toni Wainwright.

Marc stopped the tape again. "Did you hear that?" he asked.

"Yeah, I heard it," said Franco, unimpressed.

Maria was pensive.

"I don't think Zack was there," Marc explained. "Toni Wainwright was very slow on the uptake. She was drunk, and didn't get what Wainwright said to her at first. Then when she realized she had a good opportunity to really stick a barb in him because he was jealous, she did it just because she wanted to get back at him for ruining her party."

"Could be that way, I guess," said Maria. "Sounds like a woman's logic. But Lord could have been right there with her anyway."

"She's already told us personally that he wasn't. That he had gone home," said Marc.

"Maybe she didn't want to admit to us that Zack was sleeping over," Franco suggested.

"You think that she's too demure to admit an affair with Zack? Think she'd be embarrassed?"

"That creep?" laughed Maria. "I doubt it. She obviously has the modesty of a water buffalo."

"But then where are we now?" asked Franco. "I mean, what the heck do these tapes do for us, except, if you're right that Zack wasn't there, leave us right back where we were?"

"On the contrary," said Marc. "If Zack *was* sleeping over, that would explain how he got all the information he got, and how he would have been there in the apartment to kill Wainwright. *If* your theory is correct. If he wasn't there, the tapes still explain how he got his information. The only difference would be his location at the time he got the information."

"I don't get you," said Franco, nodding.

"Let's say Zack was in his own apartment," Marc continued. "He was going to Chicago on business. Maybe he walked into his office. We know it's right on the same floor with his apartment. He finds the machine that's bugging Toni's phone moving. He waits till the machine stops and listens to the replay. He finds out that Wainwright is calling his wife. They're both drunk as skunks. He decides to wait and listen to any further conversation, see if there are any further developments."

"Let's listen ourselves," said Maria anxiously.

Marc turned the tape to forward play again.

"Hello?" asked Toni Wainwright's recording.

"Listen, you fresh bitch, I'm not going to take that kind of shit lying down," slurred Wainwright angrily.

"Why not? I am," said Toni Wainwright, laughing cruelly.

"Why you rotten bastard, I'm coming over. You hear? I'm coming over, and I'm going to knock the shit out of you and that son of a bitch Zack Lord."

"Don't you dare. I'll call the police, you bum," warned Toni Wainwright.

"I'm on my way. And when I get there, we'll see just how smart you two bastards are." Wainwright hung up this time.

Maria and Franco looked to Marc.

"Well?" Maria asked.

"Well, if Lord was there, he had it made," said Marc. "Wainwright was coming over and if he had a plan to kill Wainwright, it all fell right into his lap. Lord might have figured it'd be easier to deal with Toni Wainwright than with her husband. She seemed to have some emotional reaction to him, limited as it was. And here she was, so drunk she didn't know what she was doing. He could have figured, if Wainwright did break into the apartment . . ."

"Or got in because the door was left open," Maria suggested.

"Right. Still Wainwright'd be called an intruder according to the law. It wasn't his apartment. Toni Wainwright could kill him and not be guilty of murder. And she wouldn't know she didn't really kill him, she was so drunk. She'd be acquitted, inherit the estate, and save Lord's empire by not dumping the stock."

"That sounds fine," said Franco. "But what if he wasn't there?"

"No difference," said Marc. "If your theory holds water about his having a key and all the ways he could get into the apartment without anyone seeing him, then he could have heard the tape in his office, gone to Toni's apartment, let himself in, waited for Wainwright, and everything else would be the same."

"I guess that's possible," agreed Franco.

"The only difference then would be that he'd have to get from his apartment to the Wainwright apartment before the husband," Maria suggested tentatively.

"It only takes five minutes for him to get to her apartment," said Franco. "There's no problem there. What now?"

"When Toni Wainwright gets back into town, I think I ought to ask her a few questions," said Marc.

"Where is she?" asked Franco.

"Just out to East Hampton for the weekend. Marguerite put in a call to her for me today, and the servants told her," Marc explained, seeing Maria watching him carefully. "When she gets back the beginning of next week I think it'd be a good idea to talk to her again."

"Not without me, it won't," said Maria.

XXXII

MONDAY, SEPTEMBER 18, 1:30 P.M.

The detective at the front door of City Hall nodded to Marc as he entered and walked across the marble rotunda toward George Tishler's office. Two more detectives stood at the railing and gate across an interior corridor.

"George Tishler," Marc said to one of the detectives who stopped him.

"He's okay," said the other detective, recognizing Marc. "Go ahead in." He pressed a button which released the locked gate.

Marc walked through a doorway on the right, past several secretaries, to Tishler's cubicle, which was still awash in papers, folders, reports, graphs, and books. George, in his shirt sleeves, was seated at his desk, talking on the phone. He saw Marc, smiled, and waved him in.

Marc cleared the morning papers and Tishler's jacket from a chair at the side of the desk and sat.

"All right, then, Sam," George was saying, "see if you have an eighty-five-hundred-dollar line in your department meanwhile." He put his hand over the mouthpiece of the phone and looked at Marc, smiling again. "I'll be right with you, buddy. How the hell are you?"

"Good, good." Marc smiled.

George removed his hand from the mouthpiece. "No, she's now on a sixty-five-hundred-dollar line with Marine and Aviation. I want to get her an eighty-five-hundred-dollar line somewhere, anywhere, for the time being. I looked at my sheets and I know you have a couple of open lines at the right salary."

A *line*, thought Marc. What a ridiculous term for a sinecure.

City government has its own jargon, and a line meant a job slot written into the budget of a particular city department or commission. Each job with each department is a line, with its own salary and duties prescribed. It didn't mean, necessarily, that the person on the line had to show up for work, or perform that work, merely that he was supposed to and was compensated accordingly. "No show" jobs were usually only held by people involved closely with the Mayor's political team—a person working campaign liaison or public relations—and they were paid a salary on a line from a city department they'd never been to or seen.

"All right," George went on, "so we can put her with you on one of your eighty-five-hundred-dollar lines meanwhile. This is a gal that's done a great deal of advance work for the Mayor, and the Mayor wants to continue her on a line somewhere." George listened. "No, of course she's not going to show up for work at your Parks Department office. What the hell does she know about parks?" George paused again. "Okay, you can have the sixty-five-hundred-dollar line she comes off in Marine and Aviation. And I'll trade you another eighty-five-hundred-dollar line as soon as one comes available in another department. Okay?"

Marc smiled to himself as he thought about the absurdity of job lines. Trading these lines is a common practice in New York City government, even when people actually worked on City business. When an agency or department wanted to hire someone, but didn't have an available line in their budget, or the only available lines provided too little pay, the person could be officially employed on another line, in another department. Thus, they worked in one office but got their pay from another department totally disconnected with their actual work. What a mass of confusion, thought Marc; just like the rest of the city. Some people say that New York is ungovernable. Not so. After all, there are many governmental jurisdictions far larger than New York City that are managed comfortably. No, it's always the same story. The people who *run* the City are confused, not the City.

George was still talking. "Great," he said. "I'll have this gal come over and fill out the necessary information and whatever the hell else she has to do. I'll have her call you. Okay? Remember her name, Rhoda Green."

George hung up and turned to Marc. "Hi, Marc. How the hell are you?"

"Good."

"What's new?"

"Just came from the New York County Lawyers Judiciary Committee," he replied.

"Oh, yeah. Your second interview," said George. "Did you have any problems?"

"No, it went all right."

"I'm glad. I didn't think you'd have any difficulty with the interviews. You got past the Mayor's Committee. Don't tell anyone I told you that."

"Can't figure out how I did that," said Marc. "I figured they'd bomb me."

"Not at all. They seem to like your approach once they meet you and see you in person. A little different, maybe a little unnerving for them at first, but they like it. Why shouldn't they? You're the kind of guy we need on the bench. If I didn't think so, I wouldn't have recommended you." George sat back in his chair. "I'll tell you something else though, Marc. And this I tell you because you're my friend and because I got you involved in these committees to begin with. You apparently have a lot of enemies out there."

"Enemies?"

George nodded. He leaned forward. "We've been getting more flack about you probably than anyone else we've ever sent before the committees."

"Flack about what?"

"All kinds of bullshit," George replied softly. "You wouldn't believe it. I guess mostly it's people who don't know you, haven't met you. They don't like the idea that you represent criminals, really important criminals sometimes, and perhaps you do it too well, with too much gusto."

"Is this a joke?" Marc asked.

"No joke," replied George. "That's the bad part about it. We've gotten several calls asking if we're really serious about putting Conte on the bench. And I answer them, sure, why not? And then they come back with all kinds of reasons, starting with your connections with organized crime to your lack of experience. I think someone's doing a number on you. They've even got a couple of newspaper people interested."

"Who the hell are *they* anyway?" Marc asked annoyedly.

"I can't go into names, Marc. Just suffice it to say they are people in the judge-making world; that little world of a hundred or so people I told you about. Apparently they think it wouldn't be a good idea to have a guy like you on the bench. I happen to disagree with them vehemently, but they're there, and they're making their presence known and heard."

"George, I wasn't too thrilled about this idea in the first place, but I'm not ashamed of representing the people I represent," said Marc. "Defendants need the finest damn lawyers they can get to outweigh the cards stacked against them every time they turn around in the criminal courts. I'll be damned if I'm going to apologize to anyone for representing people accused of crimes."

"You don't have to. Don't get steamed, Marc."

"I don't like this crap, George. The problem seems to be that I'm not a company man, one of the guys who's been sucking the government tit all along. Apparently, they don't want anyone else horning in or upsetting their cozy little arrangement. Why don't they tell me this stuff to my face, or at least bring it out into the open?"

"How the hell can anyone do that?" asked George. "There isn't anything to bring out into the open, except that you're not one of the old-line establishment."

"The yellow bastards," Marc said angrily. "The hell with it, George. I'm not interested in following this thing up any more. It's a waste of time, and I don't have the patience to listen to a lot of narrow-minded, sanctimonious baloney."

"Take it easy, Marc. If every lawyer who had quality and intelligence felt that way, we'd end up with all old hacks on the bench."

"I know, you gave me that story already."

"Still goes," said George. "Come on, buddy, don't get teed off. The bench, the Mayor, the law need new blood like yours."

"Does the Mayor have enough balls to appoint someone over the complaints of the snipers and back-stabbers?"

"I hope so."

"Christ, George, what the hell are you wasting my time for, if he doesn't have the balls to appoint me."

"Let's put it this way," said George. "If we take a shot, it's against the odds, that's true. But if we don't take a shot at all—well, what chance do we have then?"

"Okay," Marc agreed. "There's only one more committee interview, day after tomorrow, anyway."

"Don't let this stuff bother you. You're right, they're yellow bastards, so why be upset by yellow bastards?"

"Why indeed? What's new, George, beside the shooting over at the courthouse? Your telephone must have been burning since that happened."

"Wasn't that a son of a bitch," said George. "Right in the courtroom, the crazy bastard. With a shotgun, yet. The cops are still looking for the girl. And Johnson's lawyer, Katzenberg, has disappeared now. They got the other two lawyers, but Katzenberg must have slipped the guns to Johnson during lunch."

"He's lucky he didn't kill anyone," said Marc.

"*He's lucky?* We're lucky. I'm afraid if Al-Kobar had killed Crawford, it would have started anti-Black riots all over the city. It's been bad enough as it is."

"I know the girl," said Marc.

"The girl with the shotgun?"

Marc nodded.

"I should have known. You don't happen to be hiding her by any chance, do you, buddy?"

"You know I wouldn't do that. But if I knew where she was, until she decided to turn herself in, I couldn't tell you anything anyway."

"Of course, you're absolutely right," said George. "Just kidding."

Marc rose. "I've got to get back to the office, George."

"Give me a ring if you get finished early. We'll have a drink."

"Okay." Marc made his way back to the main lobby and out to City Hall Plaza. He walked along the edge of the park surrounding City Hall toward his building. Franco was supposed to be waiting in front with the car.

"Hiya, Marc," said the news dealer on the corner. He was bouncing over a bundle of newspapers.

"Hi, Champ. You okay?"

333

"Good shape, good shape," the news dealer said as he folded an early edition and handed it to Marc.

As he was ready to cross the street, Marc saw Philly, The Crusher's friend, standing at curbside in front of his office. He was talking to Franco. The car was parked next to them. Marc crossed.

"You waiting for me, Philly?" Marc saw anxiety on Franco's face. "Anything wrong?" he asked, turning to Franco.

"It'll wait," Franco replied.

"Hello, Counselor," said Philly, nodding, shaking Marc's hand feebly.

Marc noted the limp handshake, wondering why men who are strong and gruff often seem to be embarrassed, or at least uncomfortable, with handshakes.

Philly looked over his shoulder cautiously. He motioned with his head that they should walk—a moving voice is harder to hit. Marc started walking slowly next to Philly. "You never know who's bugged these days, or who's following you," Philly warned. "They been following me for days now. If I don't come out of the house by a certain hour in the morning, the rats come and knock on the door and bother my wife. Can you imagine! They want to make sure I don't give them the slip over the back fence. They think who the fuck they are that I'm going to run from them, the slimy rats!" Philly looked over his shoulder again.

Marc was convinced that the love of adventure, the excitement of the challenge and intrigue of criminal life were as important to Philly and The Crusher as any ill-gotten profits. If they weren't followed, they'd want to think they were; they'd want their peers to think they were. After all, if somebody wasn't following you, looking to serve you with a subpoena, well, you probably weren't too important.

"It's about The Crusher," said Philly.

"What's the matter now?"

"He told me to tell you he's being followed; and his phone is bugged. He figures there'll be more trouble. He didn't want to come over himself because they're following him." Philly looked at Marc for direction.

"I can't do anything about it until it happens," said Marc. "But you tell Patsy to call, day or night, if there's trouble."

"That's what he wanted to know, Counselor. Thanks." Philly stuck out his limp hand again.

"Okay," said Marc, watching Philly walk across the street. He wished he was able to calm all his clients as easily.

Marc walked back to the car. "Now what's the matter?" he asked Franco.

"Nothing the matter. You got a call in the office from Andy Roberts," Franco replied excitedly. "That's the girl wanted for giving the shotguns to the prisoners who tried to escape from the courtroom the other day."

"Yes, I know. What did she say?" Marc asked quickly. "Did you talk to her?"

"No. Marguerite told me. She said this Andy Roberts said she wants to talk to you and she'll call you again tomorrow or the next day for sure. She said she was moving around so you couldn't call her."

"Did she say anything else?"

"Just that she needed some protection; she didn't do what they're accusing her of. Then she started in about fair trials and fascist systems. So Marguerite told her to talk to you."

"Okay. We'll be back shortly," said Marc. "First, I want to go to Mrs. Wainwright's apartment for a few minutes. While we're there, you call Marguerite and tell her to call me at Mrs. Wainwright's."

"Okay."

Marc got into the passenger seat of the car.

"Wainwright's?"

"Yes," said Marc. "Let's ask her about those phone calls with her husband."

"Didn't your wife say she wanted to come along on this one to meet Mrs. Wainwright?" Franco was smiling. "Shouldn't we call her?"

"Are you kidding? That's exactly why I'm doing this now while she's busy in school. This case is complicated enough without getting involved with jealous women."

Franco laughed as he headed the car uptown.

"Of course Zack didn't stay over the night Bob was killed,"

Toni Wainwright insisted. She was dressed in slacks and a sweater, sitting on the couch in her library.

"Are you sure of that?" asked Marc. He and Franco were sitting in chairs opposite her. Franco had already called Marguerite with the message about Andy Roberts.

"Yes, I'm sure. Why are you asking that?"

"Did you have any phone calls from your husband before he came over that night?" Marc pressed.

"No." She looked at Marc, puzzled.

"Are you sure?"

"Of course, I'm sure. Why are you asking these questions?"

"Because we know that your husband did, in fact, call here three times before he came over."

"He called? Here? That's ridiculous," said Toni Wainwright. "Why wouldn't I have told you that if it had, in fact, happened?"

"It did happen," Marc said flatly.

"Don't be ridiculous."

"Franco, get the tape recorder," Marc said.

Franco rose and walked out to the vestibule where he had left the portable tape recorder.

"What is this?" Toni asked. She looked from Marc to Franco who came back into the library carrying the recorder.

"I'm going to let you listen to the tapes of three conversations you had the night your husband was killed," said Marc. "All of them were before he came over here."

"You're kidding."

Marc motioned for Franco to begin.

Franco fitted a copy tape on the machine—the original was in Marc's office safe—then pressed a button, starting the tape. Marc watched Toni Wainwright as she listened to herself and her late husband. She was absolutely stunned, listening, her eyes fixed on the tape as it turned.

"Incredible," she said. "Where did you get those?"

"That is you and your husband speaking, isn't it?" Marc asked.

"Of course it is. Where did you get them?"

"I'll explain all of that in a little while," said Marc.

"No, tell me now," she insisted. "It's incredible."

"I don't want to say anything until I'm absolutely sure about everything," said Marc.

336

"Sure about what?"

"It won't be more than one day before I'm able to tell you everything," said Marc. "Please trust me and have patience."

"I do. I do trust you, that is. I haven't much patience. I want to know everything. That's just wild," Toni exclaimed. "I don't even remember having those conversations. My God!"

"May I suggest, most respectfully," Marc said lightly, "that the reason you don't remember is that you were a little in your cups at the time?"

"Boy, you better believe I must have been," she laughed. "So was Bob. We sound ridiculous. Where did you get those tapes?"

"Let me just keep that to myself for a little while longer. I'll tell you tomorrow."

"You're fantastic," she said to Marc. She smiled warmly.

"It was really Franco and my wife who brought all of this about," Marc said.

Toni Wainwright turned to Franco, looking into his face. "You fooled me," she said. "I'm sorry I was so rotten."

"That's okay," said Franco, smiling, now embarrassed.

"You sure you don't remember having those conversations?" asked Marc.

"Absolutely not."

"I want you to realize, however, that these conversations could indicate quite a different situation as to your culpability, your guilt, in the death of your husband," said Marc.

"What do you mean?" She was puzzled. "You mean . . . what do you mean?"

"It might be said that you knew he was coming over. It wasn't a surprise, and you set up an ambush for him."

"I don't even remember those conversations," she protested.

"Being intoxicated does not necessarily excuse homicide."

"I swear to you, I didn't know I had those conversations with Bob. I didn't know he was coming here until he kicked in the door. You saw the door shattered. If I was going to ambush him, would I make him break down the door first?"

"I don't think you ambushed him," smiled Marc. "I think I know the answer. Let me ask you again. Are you sure now that

Zack Lord didn't stay over with you the night your husband was killed, leaving right after the shooting?"

"Right now, I'm not sure about anything."

XXXIII

WEDNESDAY, SEPTEMBER 20, 2:40 P.M.

"How can you just sit there so calm?" asked Franco as he drove toward the Association of the Bar building.

Maria was seated quietly in the back seat.

"I mean with this whole Wainwright case coming to a head, and expecting a call from this Andy Roberts girl," Franco continued, "how can you just sit there and have me drive you to this interview with the judges' Committee?"

"You don't even want to be a judge," Maria chimed in from the rear.

"First of all, I told George Tishler I'd go to the meeting of the committee. It's the last one," replied Marc. "And in the second place, Zack Lord doesn't know that we really suspect him, so he feels reasonably safe. He's not going to run away at this point and create suspicion about himself. And, in the third place, we don't even know if Andy Roberts will call. This Committee interview is only going to take half an hour anyway."

"Then can we go to see that creep Zack Lord?" Maria asked anxiously.

"Right after this interview, okay?"

"Okay," Maria agreed reluctantly. "But don't talk too much in there. Make it a fast one."

Franco nodded in agreement.

Marc laughed. "Okay."

The Joint Judiciary and Criminal Courts Committees of the Association of the Bar of the City of New York were now in session. It was the usual committee setup—the large oval table with

338

perhaps twenty-five people seated about it. All of them were looking toward Marc, who was seated next to the Committee Chairman at the head of the table.

"Mister Conte, we understand that you represent several clients
who are connected with organized crime?" asked one young man
with dark hair and gold wire-framed glasses seated near the far end
of the table.

"Is that a question?" Marc asked. Suddenly his mind resolved to
lay it right on the line, to hammer the questions and questioners
as hard as they hoped to hammer him.

The young man glanced across the table at others on the Committee. "Yes. I'd like to know about your practice."

"Without getting into a debate on the subject of organized
crime," said Marc, "I have and still do represent many people accused of crime. Most of them are not in any fashion connected
with what is popularly categorized as organized crime. Many of
the people I represent are indigent. I am assigned by the court
to represent them, and paid by the court. Of all my clients, and I
handle literally hundreds each year, I would say less than five per
cent could in any fashion be said to be involved with what you
refer to as organized crime."

"Let me put it another way," the man with the wire glasses said.
"Have you represented people who are members of the Italian-
American Freedom Council?"

Marc wondered why he had let George Tishler convince him
to go through this sandbagging interview. They didn't want answers, they already were briefed on his practice and his clients.
They were just going through the motions to get this all on the
table. It was a setup.

"Yes," Marc answered.

"Are you a member of the Italian-American Council yourself?"
asked another voice from the table.

"No," Marc replied in the direction of the voice.

"Have you ever picketed with the Italian-American Council?"
asked the same voice.

"No."

"I hope you don't think that there's anything wrong with the
Italian-American Freedom Council picketing," said the questioner hurriedly. "I didn't intend to imply that."

"No," assured the Chairman. "I don't think, Mister Gorin, that your question in any fashion suggested that there was any impropriety in that organization—or any organization—picketing and expressing its opinions pursuant to the First Amendment."

"Do you think that there's anything wrong with the Italian-American Freedom Council picketing?" asked the same inquisitor.

"I think it's perfectly proper, pursuant to the Constitution of the United States, for any person or organization to exercise his, or her or its, absolute right to freedom of expression. *Even a lawyer.*"

The Committee was silent momentarily.

"You mentioned before that you didn't want to get into a discussion about organized crime. Why not?" asked a woman two seats away from Marc.

"Not that I don't wish to discuss it, ma'am," replied Marc. "I'd be pleased to, if you wish. Just that my view of organized crime, and the view often and popularly expressed in newspapers and other news media seems to be somewhat at odds."

"How's that?" asked the woman.

"It's merely that I do not accept the very dramatic concept of a nationwide, monolithic, criminal semi-government engaged in a single, nationwide criminal enterprise. I suggest rather that there are gangs, perhaps, loosely known to each other, but almost invariably independent of, even in competition with, each other. I should add that many gangs are Italian, so you don't think I'm trying to bend over backward to defend my position, because I'm Italian. There are also Jewish gangs, Irish gangs, Black gangs. Gangs of every nationality, just as there are criminals of every nationality."

"How do you know all of this about organized crime?" asked an elderly man.

"Studying the findings and treatises of penologists and criminologists, professional intellectual investigators, professors in universities and the like," replied Marc. "I do this to keep up with newer and more proper treatment of accused and convicted individuals. I have also seen and experienced many things through people I have represented. I might add that every penologist I have read agrees with my concept of organized crime. That the

340

newspapers, which are also aware of the actual facts, print dramatic but unfounded pap is almost a crime in itself."

"You say you draw your knowledge in part from your own personal experience?" asked another voice down the table. Marc couldn't see who asked the question.

"My experience as a defense counsel only," said Marc carefully. "I have no other knowledge or experience on the subject."

"You think, therefore, that this problem of organized crime is magnified out of proportion by the press?" asked another woman's voice.

"Not only the press," replied Marc. "The press is fed its information, in part, by the public relations departments of law enforcement agencies. And the real tragedy is that this misrepresentation detracts funds and attention from the real problems, the real causes of crime, the archaic penal system, the ineptitude of judges, the medieval approach to criminal justice, the apathy of the public. I'd say the proportion of attention given organized crime via newspapers and the like is wasteful. Do you want to know what I believe the real problems are?" Marc inquired.

"I'd like to ask something before we change the subject," asked the man called Gorin.

"Oh, I wasn't changing the subject," said Marc. "I thought you might be interested in what I know about the real problem of crime and criminals."

"Supposing any of the people who you represent came before you as a judge," asked Gorin. "Could you handle the case objectively?"

"I probably wouldn't handle the case at all."

"What does that mean?" Gorin pursued.

"I would disqualify myself, as I think any judge should in a case of a defendant known to the judge."

"Supposing the newspapers started writing stories about the Mayor, especially during this time of such bad publicity about the courts and corruption. Supposing the newspapers said that the Mayor had appointed a man to the bench who had connections— no that's not the right word—a man who had represented organized crime figures. Suppose such stories appeared, would you be able to withstand that kind of pressure and still function properly as a judge?"

"In the first instance, I don't know what kind of pressure you refer to, sir. The fact that I have represented people in criminal proceedings doesn't cause me any difficulty, pressure, or feelings of discomfort whatever. I am not ashamed of defending people charged with crime. I think of it as equally sacred a duty in the context of a democracy as the prosecution of criminals." Marc thought he was getting a little hammy now. But why not? He believed in what he was saying.

"No one said you should be. Ashamed, that is," said the Chairman.

"I'm not, Mister Chairman," Marc replied forcefully. "I have represented all sorts of people, murderers, white-collar criminals, madmen, all sorts, and I have not become a criminal thereby, nor have I become a member of organized crime as a result of representing people who may or may not be so involved. The fact that the newspapers might mention that I am a defense counsel in private practice wouldn't create pressure for me in the least."

"That wouldn't bother you?" asked a man.

"Not in the least," repeated Marc. "I have no idea why it should. Can you, sir, tell me why it should?"

The man didn't answer Marc. He was silent, gazing now at some notes on the table. The people around the table were silent.

"Anyone have any other questions?" asked the Chairman.

No one spoke.

"Well, thank you, Mister Conte," said the Chairman, smiling.

Marc rose, shook hands with the Chairman, and made his way out to the marble corridor.

There were several more people sitting and waiting to be interviewed. They all turned and watched Marc come out of the committee room. He walked to the exit and made his way to the street.

"Well, Your Honor, how'd it go?" Franco asked. He was standing on the sidewalk near the car. Maria was seated in the rear of the car, reading.

Marc didn't answer. He got into the car next to Maria and waited for Franco to get behind the driver's wheel.

"Anything the matter?" asked Maria.

"Just a little annoying, that's all," replied Marc. "To hell with annoyance. Let's go do something important. Let's go see Zack Lord."

"Now you're talking," said Franco, smiling. He started the motor.

"They give you a rough time?" Maria asked.

"No, not rough. Annoying," repeated Marc.

Franco began driving toward the Hotel Louis Quinze. He glanced occasionally at Marc through the rear-view mirror.

"Just one or two of them ever set foot in a criminal court or were even within throwing distance of a criminal," said Marc. "And they're deciding who should or shouldn't be a criminal judge. They don't know what the courts are all about, or even what's going on in court. And that's one very real and one very big reason why the problems exist. They just go through the motions, while they pick out judicial candidates who fit the same old, stale, playball patterns. The D.A. might as well pick the judges out for them."

"You think that's maybe what they do?" asked Maria.

Franco turned off Park Avenue, heading toward Fifth Avenue.

"I don't know. But I do know I've been thinking about being a judge, and I've decided I'm needed more in the street than I am on the bench. People in the street, the little people accused of crime, even big people accused of crime, need help to save them from being steamrollered by all the people who want to be on the right side, and who think that the only right side is the government side. When you're indicted, you stand all alone out there, and nobody wants to know you. Only truth is important," Marc said emphatically. "Sides don't mean a damn. Lying and cheating to help the government win is still lying and cheating—and isn't justice."

"Justice? That's just ice, and it's all melted," said Franco.

"Did you make that up?"

"Yeah, what do you think?"

Marc put his tongue between his lips and blew a raspberry.

Maria and Franco laughed.

"You want me to go up with you, don't you?" Franco asked hopefully as he parked the car in the forward end of the NO PARKING zone in front of the Hotel Louis Quinze.

"Of course I do," replied Marc. "You two started this whole thing, didn't you?" Marc was feeling better. "So you better be in on the finish of it."

"That's what I want to see," said Maria with delight. "I want to

343

see this heel, Lord, take a dive as they say in the street. Right, Franco?"

"Right," he smiled.

Marc handed a dollar bill to the doorman who was on his way to say Franco couldn't park where he had. Marc mentioned they were going to see Zack Lord. The doorman nodded, then stuffed the dollar in his pocket as he walked to the house phone to announce them.

"What can I do for you today?" Zack Lord asked Marc, smiling easily. He saw Maria and his smile dimmed slightly.

"Just wanted to discuss the Wainwright case a little more," said Marc.

"Certainly, certainly," said Zack. He sat back in the big chair behind his desk. "Can I offer you a drink?"

Maria sat in a chair in front of Lord's desk. She shook her head as she put her leather handbag on the side of the desk. Marc sat in another chair.

"Not for me," said Marc.

"Me either." Franco was impatient.

"All right. Now what do you want to discuss?" asked Zack Lord. "Anything to help Toni."

"I know this might sound foolish to you at this late date," Marc began, "but we're still investigating the case. And it seems to us that certain aspects of the case—including your involvement—just don't make sense."

"My involvement? You're still not investigating the time I left the airport?" Zack laughed with that tight, toothy smile of his. He looked from Marc to Maria to Franco.

"Among other things, yes," said Marc.

"I thought we went all through that the last time," Zack said, idly swiveling his chair to the left, then to the right again.

"We did. But some other things have come up."

Maria was watching Lord's every move.

"What other things?" Lord's smile was slightly more strained now.

"There's your pistol, the exact same as Toni's," said Marc. "And there's the fact that you were down in the basement of Toni Wainwright's building the night Bob Wainwright was killed."

Lord had stopped swiveling now.

"That was quite early. I went down to get some wine," Lord explained.

"We know," replied Marc. "And there's the fact that you had been so friendly with the elevator operator. That you used to feed him liquor. That's curious, especially since he carries keys to the back entrance and stairway, which could give somebody access to the rear of all the apartments in the building."

Marc glanced at Maria. Her hand was at the side of her chair, counting the items on her fingers. "The cook," she suggested.

"Yes, and the fact that the cook in Toni Wainwright's house heard Bob Wainwright calling out Zack, your name, as he lay dying. Then she heard a moving noise as if someone were walking out of the apartment."

Zack listened silently, his eyes narrowed. "None of this seems to mean anything much," he said finally. "You're not accusing me of this crime, are you?"

"No," answered Marc. "That's not my job. We were just wondering about some things we didn't clear up with you the last time. Oh, there's one more thing. The tapes you recorded when you bugged Toni Wainwright's phone contained conversations Bob Wainwright had with his wife the night he was killed."

Zack's eyes opened a bit, then returned to even narrower slits.

"Tapes? What tapes?" asked Lord.

"Not the ones recorded in your lower left-hand desk drawer," said Marc. "The ones that you record with the tape machine in the credenza behind you. The tapes you keep in your safe."

Maria wasn't missing the slightest reaction on Lord's part.

Lord was staring at Marc now. "You never stop working, do you?"

"Hardly ever," said Marc.

"How could you possibly know about the tape machines?" he mused aloud. "Of course! The day you were all up here at the party," he answered himself.

"No," said Marc. "We're just guessing."

"Don't try to kid a kidder," Lord said flatly. "You mentioned tapes in the safe too." He thought. "Did you have some burglar go through the safe and the rest of the place?"

"That wouldn't be proper," replied Marc. "I'd never ask anyone to do that."

Lord looked at Marc, studying his face. Then he studied Maria; then Franco. Finally, he smiled, but it was strained, and the lines at the sides of his eyes were pulled and taut. "You're fantastic, really fantastic! I want you to seriously consider my previous offer. That position as my personal counsel is still open," said Lord. "Name your own price."

"I already have a client," said Marc. "When I finish with this Wainwright case, I'll be happy to consider your offer more seriously. If it's still open."

"Of course it will be, of course, it will." Zack's smile disappeared now. "You realize these are very serious accusations you're making."

"I'm not making any accusations, Mister Lord," said Marc. "Just asking questions."

"They wouldn't stand up in court, and you know it," Zack added. "And if they wouldn't stand up in court, you're running a very serious risk of lawsuit for defamation if you even mention them to anyone." Lord was angry now. His eyes were harsh and vicious.

"I haven't mentioned them to anyone but you . . . so far," said Marc.

"What does that mean, so far?"

"That means that I've come to tell you about what I have first."

Lord nodded. "I get it. I get it," he smiled harshly. "You're trying to sell me some information? Is that it? A little fast money?"

"No, Mister Lord, I don't go in for blackmail," said Marc. "I'm just informing you of the progress of our investigation. I was sure you'd be interested."

"Look, I've never been one to waste time," said Lord. "So let's get it over with. Just how much money do you want for this information? How much to turn it over to me and forget it?"

"You've got it wrong, Mister Lord," said Marc. "I'm just trying to defend my client as best I can."

"Okay, okay," Lord said dismissingly. "Now tell me how much you're looking for for your information? How much? Tell me."

Maria was trying hard not to let her surprise show.

"Nothing like that, Mister Lord," said Marc calmly, purposely goading Lord. "Really. I just wanted to explore some of the facts with you. Get some answers."

"For what? To shake me down, to get a bigger fee? Stop horse-shitting and get to the point. How much?"

"First of all, don't talk like that in front of my wife," Marc said. "And, second, I told you, I'm merely defending my client."

"You must be joking about me," said Lord, attempting a big smile. It soured before it got to the corners of his mouth.

"No, I'm quite serious . . . and you know it."

"I have a very busy schedule," Lord said abruptly. "If you have nothing further for me, I'll appreciate if you'll excuse me."

"Sure, we'll be going now," said Marc.

"This stuff you came up with is just a lot of little nonsense that means nothing," said Lord. "It's coincidental."

"Including the tapes?" said Marc.

"What tapes? I don't know what you're talking about." Lord walked with them to the elevator to make sure he saw them out of his premises. He even pressed the elevator button for them.

"You mean there aren't any tapes?" Marc asked Lord.

"I don't know what you're talking about is what I mean," Lord replied flatly. There was no smile now.

The elevator arrived. Maria entered first, then Marc. Lord remained outside, watching them.

"I'll send you a copy of the tapes, so you'll know what I'm talking about," Marc said.

The elevator man stood ready to close the door.

Lord stared at Marc.

"And by the way . . . I'll also send you a copy of today's tape," Marc said, taking Maria's handbag from her. He removed a small tape recorder from the bag. "That bit about buying evidence will be very interesting to the D.A. I'm sure."

Zack Lord's jaw muscles twitched as he stared at the tape machine. His eyes closed slowly.

"Good-by, Mister Lord," Maria said with great pleasure.

XXXIV

"Did you see Zack Lord's face just now?" crowed Maria as they reached the street in front of the hotel.

"I did, I did indeed," said Marc.

"What do you figure he'll do now?" asked Franco.

"I'm not sure," replied Marc. "I'm sure he's not going to skip town. Where could he go that he wouldn't be recognized?"

"We've got him cold," exulted Maria.

"Not so," said Marc. "We've got a lot of material that casts great suspicion and doubt on Toni Wainwright's having killed her husband. But we don't have Zack Lord cold at all."

Franco looked confused. "What are we going to do now?"

"We've done our job to defend our client," said Marc. "Now I think we ought to give this information, including the tape we just recorded, to our good assistant D.A., Mister O'Connor."

They got into the car and Franco began driving downtown.

"You think he'll do anything about it?"

"He'll be absolutely overjoyed to prosecute Zack Lord," replied Marc. "Mrs. Wainwright might have been a socialite, but prosecuting Zack Lord is world news. It's the best thing O'Connor could ever have dreamed of. Headlines all over the place."

"You really don't think we've put together a good case against Lord?" asked Maria.

"Well, let's say it's at least as good as they had against Mrs. Wainwright. Maybe better," Marc assured them. "And to think it's all because of you two."

Franco smiled. "Our ideas are pretty good, hanh?"

Marc smiled. "They were great." He saw a phone booth on a street corner they were approaching. "Stop here at the curb," he said. "Let me call the office."

Marc got out of the car and entered the phone booth, closing the door. He quickly opened it again. Even on Fifth Avenue the phone booths were used almost as often for urinals as for phone calls.

"Mister Conte's office," answered Marguerite.

"This is Mister Conte. Any messages?"

"Yes, sir," she said excitedly. "Andy Roberts has been calling."

"What did she say?" Marc asked. "Did she leave any message?"

"Yes, sir. She said she wanted to talk to you, and she wanted to know where she could meet you. She should be calling back any minute. What should I tell her?"

Marc thought for a moment. "Tell her to meet me at the boat at the marina."

"*Pescadorito?* Is that the name?"

"Yes."

"Just a minute," said Marguerite, "the other phone is ringing. Maybe it's she. I'll put you on hold, okay?"

"Okay."

"It is Andy Roberts," said Marguerite, coming back on the phone. "I told her about the boat. She said she isn't far from there. She'd meet you in a few minutes."

"Okay," said Marc. "I'll talk to you later." He moved out of the phone booth and into the car hurriedly. "Come on, let's move," he said to Franco.

"What's the matter?" Franco asked, looking around the street.

"Nothing here. Andy Roberts is going to meet me at the boat."

"Oh," exclaimed Franco, moving the car out into the Avenue quickly. They entered a side street and headed toward the East River.

Marc began moving rapidly toward the boat the moment Franco stopped the car at the marina. Maria and Franco reluctantly agreed it would be better for them to wait in the car.

When he reached *Pescadorito*'s berth, Marc looked around. There was no one paying attention to him. He tugged at one of the hausers securing the boat and, as the boat moved closer to him, stepped aboard. He could see that someone had opened the doors to the aft cabin. They were still slightly open. He walked toward the stern.

"Andy. Andy, that you?"

He heard nothing. He opened the cabin door. As light fell into the cabin, there, sitting on the bunk, propped up against one wall was Andy Roberts, pale, her hair stringy, her face frightened and drawn.

"Hi," Marc said, moving down the stairs. He closed the door behind him and turned on a cabin light.

"Hi," Andy said. She tried a smile, but it immediately turned into tears. She put her hands to her face, then gamely lifted her head, drying her tears with the back of one hand.

Marc sat on a small corner chair and opened his tie. "Take it easy. It's all right now," he said soothingly. "I'll help you with the rest of it."

"Oh, Mister Conte, it's really a mess," she moaned, her head dropping down again. "It really is."

"It's not so bad," Marc assured her.

"Oh, Christ, Mister Conte. How could it be worse?" she said, looking up now. "They're looking all over for me. I'm a wanted criminal."

"Well, you've made the first step in the right direction by calling me. At least we can stop things from getting worse," said Marc. "I can start straightening it out."

"How can you straighten it out, Mister Conte?" she said angrily now. "You think they'll listen to you? You think those rotten creeps in charge of this police state are going to give me a chance? You think this elitist court system can be fair, can give one of the people a fair chance?"

"I'll get you the chance," Marc said firmly. "You know I can fight well, I'll make them listen. But first I want to listen. Let me hear the answer to the first question. Were you involved in this thing, Andy?"

"I didn't have anything to do with it."

"Well, let me give you set speech number sixteen."

"What's that?"

"Simply this," said Marc. "I don't have the time or inclination to check out your story. I'll believe whatever you tell me. It's not that I don't care, mind you. But, I'm your lawyer. And if you don't care enough about yourself to tell me the truth, why should I care? I'll fashion your defense on whatever you tell me. If it's a phony story, that blows up in my face . . . well, I'll look foolish but you'll look convicted. So let me ask again. Did you have anything to do with it?"

She lifted her head proudly. "I swear, I didn't have anything to do with it," she said firmly.

"That's good enough for me," said Marc smiling.

Andy smiled too.

"This is a little confusing, though. How did your father's shotgun get into the hands of Ali Al-Kobar?"

"I was living with this guy, one of the People's Army. We had a falling out a little while ago. But he still had a key to the pad. You see my old man, my father, that is, is a lawyer too, in Connecticut. And he's a trapshooting nut. When I moved to my own apartment, he gave me an old shotgun for protection. It was in the apartment. I think my old man—the one I was living with—came in one night and took the shotgun."

"But why would he give a shotgun with your father's name on it to someone who was going to use it the way this shotgun was used? It was an invitation to trouble."

"He's a mean son of a bitch, Mister Conte. He'd do it just to get back at me, because it'd throw suspicion on me and embarrass my father. You see, my father didn't approve of him. He thought he was a deadbeat."

"Do you know where this nice guy is now?" Marc asked.

"No. I've been trying to get in touch with him myself," Andy said. "That's why I've been moving around. But I haven't been able to find him. He's taken off. Why?"

"If this guy is punk enough to get you involved in this, he could use a little heat from the police who are looking for you," said Marc.

"What good is heat on Billie—that's his name—going to do me?" Andy asked. "When the cops get their hands on me, they're going to deliver me over to a fat D.A. who's going to run me through the court machine like I was a sausage going into a casing."

"That won't happen," Marc assured her.

"How can you stop it?"

"First, I'll surrender you. And that'll weigh greatly in your favor, that you faced up to the charges voluntarily rather than having to be ferreted out like a mole."

"And then what? They'll railroad me. You know that. This is a system that caters to the rich, the known, the people with connections." Andy was afraid. The fear was plain in her eyes.

"I'm a specialist in defending knowns *and* unknowns," said Marc, trying to be light. "Let me take care of it."

"Those bastards just want to hang me," Andy said, almost without hearing Marc. "You think anyone involved in a political case like mine can get a fair trial? The whole system stinks. It has to be torn down, wrecked, burned, destroyed."

"Andy, you're getting hysterical underneath that pretty calm of yours," said Marc. "You're talking nonsense."

"Oh no I'm not, and I'm not turning myself in."

"Let's say for the sake of argument that what you say about the present system is so, Andy. After you destroy the system, tear it apart, wreck it, what will you and the one hundred, or one hundred thousand or one million people you think are worthwhile, what will you do with the world then?"

"Build a better world, that's what."

"And how are these worthwhile people going to handle the problems of the millions, billions of other people in the world? Who's going to distribute the food? Who's going to run the electric generators, the railroads? Someone's got to be in charge of things. Who's it going to be?"

"Of course someone has to be in charge," Andy answered. She was wary now, knowing Marc was leading her somewhere.

"And that person who's in charge of the whole thing will have to have help, won't he or she? Assistants to be in charge of New York, California, Utah?"

"This is childish," she balked.

"Humor me then. Answer the question."

"I guess," she answered hesitantly.

"Well, then, aren't you on your way to building another system, another hierarchy? Just like the one we have now, only with different people in charge?"

"Yes, but the people who'll be in charge will be a different kind of people," insisted Andy, "people not interested just in profit, in greed, but in helping, in having understanding, in tolerance, in peace."

"Don't you realize what you're saying?" Marc asked. The wake of a passing boat out in the river made *Pescadorito* heave gently in its berth.

"What *am* I saying?" she asked, stalling for time, realizing she was becoming enmeshed in the web that Marc was spinning.

"You're saying that you're going to tear down the system that exists and eliminate the corrupt people who run it, and immediately replace it with another system, with other people in charge. Except for some variations in personnel, you're going to end up exactly where you started out. Why not just modify what there is now?"

"No, the present system is too corrupt, and rotten."

"Will you stop with that old rebellion boiler plate and listen to what you're actually saying," Marc insisted in turn. "In the first place, a world filled with people requires some people to work in one area, some in another, some to farm, some to manufacture, some to co-ordinate, some to determine policy. It's absolutely essential to existence. And in the second place, it's not the system that's wrong; it's us, it's people. We're not perfect. Not the farmers, not the drill press operators, not the police, and not the judges. And you can't expect total perfection from any place, including the courts, because people make mistakes. They have. They do. And they'll continue to. So, after all this bloody revolution of yours, unless you slaughter millions of people, you're still going to have to bear with the frailties and imperfections of humanity. Seems like a waste of time and effort to mount a revolution to destroy inanimate institutions. Why not try and educate people instead? Make them better."

"It's not a waste of time," Andy said softly, less belligerently.

"Your main hope is that the new people who are put in charge of the system do not become corrupt, do not become avaricious, do not make the same mistakes. Isn't that right?" Marc continued.

"Yes."

"And what if they do?" Marc asked. "What if they aren't perfect?"

"They'll have to be replaced with better people," she answered.

"By another revolution?"

"No. Just replace them."

"Then why can't the present people who you say are corrupt be replaced?—just as easily as you've suggested the replacement of the new people?" asked Marc. "Without revolution?"

Andy studied Marc quietly, pensively, biting her bottom lip. "Because the whole system is too corrupt. You can't build on it," she replied, regaining her strength.

"Nonsense. A system is merely a method of handling or co-ordinating things. If there is a need for changing the method because of different needs, different desires, what's the big problem in modifying the present system? Or even making entirely new ones without having a revolution?"

Andy said nothing.

"The system is only a set of rules in a book somewhere, an in-animate entity," said Marc. "It's nothing. It doesn't go unless people move it. If those people are useless, corrupt, dumb, replace them now. Who's stopping you?"

"That's not the point," said Andy. "It's this fascistic gov-ernment."

"It *is* the point," Marc insisted. "Government is merely the method of governing, running things. There's one now. You want a different one, run by different people. Okay," said Marc. "That doesn't seem like a big problem. Elect them, change them now."

"They won't let you."

"Forgive me, but that's bullshit," said Marc. "Who's stopping anybody from voting? Unless you don't believe in voting and rule by a majority of the people."

"Of course I do. Everybody should have a say."

"Well, you have the majority of the people voting for what there is now. Are you of the opinion that the voice of the lesser numbers should drown out the voice of the greater numbers?"

"No."

"Then what the hell are you talking about?"

"What does all of this have to do with me and the police looking for me?" asked Andy.

"It has to do with the fact that I'm here to protect you. Do you think I'm avaricious . . ."

"No."

". . . corrupt . . ."

"No."

"Dumb?"

354

"No."

"You think I'll sell you out?"

"No."

"Then let me defend you," said Marc. "Let's work at changing the system now, together. Running away is a cop out. If you really believe in what you say then you have to stand and fight for what you believe."

"In other words, you want me to turn myself in?"

"Not in other words, in those words exactly," replied Marc. "And if we lose?"

"You can't win unless you stand and fight. Besides, we won't lose," said Marc. "They have a lousy case against you. And you'll be free to go out and tell others to join up, to change what you call a stinking, rotten system."

"I'm afraid, Mister Conte."

"Don't let that stop you, Andy. No one ever did anything brave without being afraid. If you're not afraid of something, there's no bravery in doing it, is there?"

"I guess not," Andy replied.

"Be brave. I'll be right beside you every step of the way."

"What if it goes wrong?" asked Andy.

"Don't be concerned about things going wrong," replied Marc. "They can't go right unless we do something about them."

"You won't sell me out, will you, Mister Conte?"

"I'd be selling myself out then, Andy."

"You won't let anything happen to me, will you?"

"I can only guarantee this, Andy. If you don't face it, I guarantee you won't win; if you don't fight out in the open, I guarantee nothing will change. Let's get the fight out where everybody can see it, not in alleys and back streets."

"You sure you'll get me a fair trial?"

"I'll go down with my bloody fists swinging," said Marc. "I can't do more than that."

Perhaps there ought to be more, Marc thought. Perhaps he should do more. But that's all that can be done, all there is; to do the best one can. One can't do more than his best. None of us made the world, Marc thought. We have to accept it and live in it the way it was, the way it is. And in the midst of that, try one's best to make the world work a little better in the future. That's all.

355

Andy shook her head in disbelief of her own decision. "Okay, Mister Conte. Let's go, before I change my mind again."

Marc smiled, and took her arm. He helped her off the *Pescadorito* and guided her toward the car where Franco and Maria were waiting.